Road Trip

to

Miracles

Road Trip to Miracles

Sueann Pugh

GREEN PLACE BOOKS
Brattleboro, Vermont

Printed in the United States by Kase Printing Hudson, NH

10 9 8 7 6 5 4 3 2 1

Green Writers Press is a Vermont-based publisher whose mission is to spread a message of hope and renewal through the words and images we publish. Throughout we will adhere to our commitment to preserving and protecting the natural resources of the earth. To that end, a percentage of our proceeds will be donated to environmental and social-activist groups. Green Writers Press gratefully acknowledges support from individual donors, friends, and readers to help support the environment and our publishing initiative. Green Place Books curates books that tell literary and compelling stories with a focus on writing about place—these books are more personal stories/memoir and biographies.

Giving Voice to Writers & Artists Who Will Make the World a Better Place
Green Writers Press | Brattleboro, Vermont
www.greenwriterspress.com

ISBN: 979-8-9870707-6-5

Cover art by Stephen Morath

www.stephenmorathart.com

PRINTED ON PAPER WITH PULP THAT COMES FROM FSC®-CERTIFIED FORESTS, MANAGED FORESTS THAT GUARANTEE RESPONSIBLE ENVIRONMENTAL, SOCIAL, AND ECONOMIC PRACTICES.

For   Hilda and Burrell

Claudia and Jim

Fran and Del

Linda and Dan

whose love endured, strong and whole,
when everything else in life changed.

And for Mark, who sees a miracle in
every sunset.

Book One

Miracles surround us at every turn
if we but sharpen our perception of them.

—WILLA CATHER

CHAPTER 1

☼

SEPTEMBER 2005

Beth

I don't want to die with half a slice of Key Lime pie left on my plate. The thought got me to the hospital—that and the unrelenting concern of my best friend Clarice.

Having a heart attack is an incredibly embarrassing event. For one thing, it's so noisy. My dear friend blurted out ridiculous statements like "We need to call 911." She talked so loudly the waitress heard her and told the restaurant manager. I heard the siren from the ambulance I told them not to call. All the other diners heard it too and the room roared with whispers. "It's her, that old woman over there. Something's wrong with her." I was an Emergency, surrounded by strangers who were talking about me, touching me, making decisions for me. I was the center of attention, and I didn't have one speck of control. When my heart attacked me, everything changed.

I'd just wanted to treat myself to a quiet dinner with Clarice, my reward for finishing my do-it-yourself condo redecorating. I'd been climbing up and down ladders for a month, taupe-covered paintbrush in hand. Looking back, painting seems a poor way to celebrate retirement from forty-two years of teaching fourth grade. I'd never been so exhausted. Even my toenails were tired. It took my last bit of energy to call Clarice, shower, and drive over to the Cajun Inn, Centerburg's only attempt at a good restaurant. As I stared at the whipped cream melting over the partially eaten wedge of dessert, I began to wonder if my fatigue was coming from something other than just overdoing.

"Is it hot in here? I asked Clarice.

Humidity enveloped me like my own personal cloud. I tried to focus on Clarice, to stop the waves of nausea traveling from my stomach to my throat. The only bright spot in the restaurant was the red hat perched on her head. Clarice is one of those Red Hat women, and she'd come out that night in uniform. Under the hat I could see her mouth was moving so I tried to concentrate on what she was saying. "It's always hot in here," she said. "I don't know why you wouldn't come over and eat on our patio. Jim would have grilled us steaks before he left for the lodge. Beth, honey, you look terrible."

"Thank you," I told her. "I feel terrible. I guess I'm just tired. Maybe I've picked up a summer flu bug. Or it could be the paint fumes. I've been living in paint fumes for weeks. I think I'll get a to-go box for this pie."

"So, did you decide to go with some color on your walls instead of beige?" she said.

"It's not beige, it's taupe," I said. "Desert khaki, to be exact."

"That's still not a color," she said. "After twenty years of white walls, I'd think you'd want a real change. The Home and Garden Network always starts a redo by painting the walls some yellow color."

"Yellow annoys me," I said. As I sat trying to picture some bright, inviting accent color for my new beige—excuse me— taupe living room, trickles of perspiration ran down my forehead and neck, soaking my favorite Koret knit top, the one I purchased for fifty percent off at Toppers last August. "Besides, I want a neutral shade that will blend with my furniture."

"Beth, your couch is beige too."

She was right.

The Cajun Inn was rapidly running out of fresh air, and as I turned my concentration to breathing, I realized fainting might be a real possibility. I had fainted once during a summer vacation tour to Cancun when I had food poisoning from eating at a street vendor's stall instead of with my group at our designated luncheon spot. I'd fainted again on a Christmas Eve some thirty odd years ago, when my then-husband Pete poured me a last glass of champagne and told me he intended spending New Years Eve, and the rest of his life for that matter, with his new girlfriend instead of with me and our eight-year-old daughter. So, fainting has never been one of my favorite activities, and I hoped I could avoid it this time.

"I think I better go home. I'm not feeling too well."

One glance at Clarice made me realize how sick I really was. Her eyes were fixed on my face, and she looked scared. And determined.

"You sit right there," she ordered, loudly enough for the couple at the next table to hear. "I'm going to get us some help."

From the sound of her voice, I knew I had no choice but to sit back and sink into the commotion I was causing. The noises of my condition started swimming around me— Clarice issuing demands, cell phones slapping from hand to hand, chairs creaking against wood floors as diners squirmed to get a better view. The tiny whine of an ambulance turned into a scream as it raced closer. Every sound grew larger as my eyesight started to narrow. I tried to focus on Clarice as my vision turned the room into a tunnel. At its end I could see her, eyes still glaring, mouth still moving, and on top of her head, that silly red hat.

Thankfully, in addition to watching the Home and Garden Network, Clarice also watches CNN. Her favorite segment is Dr. Sanjay Gupta's *House Call*, which she memorizes and then quotes to anyone she sees making health errors. So, of course, Clarice recognized the classic symptoms of my Women's Heart Attack, never to be confused with the more blatant, run-of-the-mill Men's Heart Attack symptoms. She forgot to make me suck on an aspirin before my paramedic whisked me off to the emergency room, but I survived anyway.

Which brings me here, Mile 0.2 of my one-mile treadmill hike. After two cardiac stents and four weeks of home health care, I'm out in the world again. This is the first September I haven't been in school since I was six years old, save for the year Kathy was a baby. Oh my, I was looking forward to this September. I thought maybe I'd take a bus trip to New England to see the fall colors or drive down to visit Cousin Cheryl at Panama City Beach now that the tourists have left after Labor Day. But instead, with the assistance of my new travel agent/cardiologist Doctor Sam, I'm vacationing here at Mary of Mercy Hospital, Cardiac Rehab Services, First Floor, Suite 107.

Mile 0.3

Everybody I run into wants to know how it feels to be retired. I always say, "Oh, it's just great, except for the heart attack and the exercise classes and the diet." Then I try to smile like I'm having the time of my life, my Golden Years, my reward for working hard and saving wisely for the past forty-two years. But bottom line, I still feel just like me and I wonder, "Is this it?"

Not that my chosen vocation was so horrible. Teaching was easier than having a baby and raising her. Motherhood is a tough job, and it doesn't pay very well either. There are no lesson plans for motherhood. How do you program for your heart to stop hurting when your daughter screams "I hate you" and slams her bedroom door in the apartment you've just rented, so you can survive on one salary instead of two? How do you teach her that it's not her fault, or her mother's either, that life has turned upside down, and she'll just have to get used to it? What do you do when she spends her entire teenage life in her bedroom, only coming out to grab a can of Coke from the refrigerator or to sneer at you when you ask her if she's done her homework? I couldn't send her to the principal or schedule a parent conference. But somehow, we made it through—me saying all the things I supposed a good mother should be saying, when she gave me a few spare moments to be face-to-face with her, and her, spending her time drawing in her room and writing dark poetry. I assume it was dark. She never let me read any of it.

And yet, three days after my heart attack, my daughter flew to me. London to Centerburg. Kathy burst into my hospital room the day before my release, clad for business in a camel cashmere blazer, ivory linen pants, and soft brown boots. Kathy is tall and slender. She has hazel eyes and wavy auburn hair cut to a precise length for efficient care. People look at her when she enters a room. She doesn't seem to notice. I've never told her I see her father every time I look at her. I can never detect a speck of my DNA in this creature who is my daughter, except for, perhaps, the neutrality of her color choices.

Kathy kissed me, pulled the vinyl chair to the side of the bed, and extracted a laptop from a leather case that matched her boots. "You look a bit tired. Are you sure you are healthy enough to return home?" She gazed at me long enough to make an assessment, adjusted her tortoise shell reading glasses, and started her research into Mother's Heart Attack and Regime for Recovery.

Kathy was here for a week, arguing with Doctor Sam over better procedures and prescriptions. She and Clarice and Jim moved my furniture back to where I had it before I painted. Kathy stocked my kitchen with all the food I'm now required to eat: healthy frozen dinners, brown rice, and six cans of Italian style tuna packed in olive oil, at $3.99 a can. Kathy found recipes on her laptop for me to labor over, using ingredients I have no intention of ever buying, such as lentils and pine nuts and arugula.

"What's arugula?" I'd asked her.

"Really, Mum," she'd said. "How can anyone who's sixty-five years old be so uninformed?"

Kathy's been calling me Mum for several years now. She's acquired an English accent. I still cringe every time she says it. What I want to say to Kathy is, "How can anyone who's forty years old still be trying to figure out who she is?"

I'm not supposed to call my daughter Kathy anymore. When she was thirteen, she told me she was to be called "my proper name, Katherine." And now that she's English, she's Kate. Kathy/Katherine/Kate has also revealed she's a lesbian. Kathy and her (how am I supposed to say this) partner Zoe informed me of their lifestyle on my last visit to London three years ago. Zoe patted my hand as Kathy looked at me stone-eyed and said, "Mum, there's something you need to know."

I can understand why Kathy loves Zoe. Zoe is sweet and wise. I'm just bewildered my Kathy is a lesbian. Why didn't I realize this when she was a little girl? Has she always known? Did she mistrust me so much she could never talk about it? Does she mistrust me still? I don't ask my daughter the questions because I fear the answers, so I only talk to Clarice.

"Kathy's fine. Why are you afraid?" Clarice asked me.

"I'm not afraid," I told her. "I just don't want her to be hurt. You know how judgmental people can be. In twenty-four hours, everybody in town would be talking about her."

"Honey, she doesn't even live here," said Clarice. "And besides, in another twenty-four hours, they'd be talking about someone else. So who cares?"

Mile 0.4

The perky rehab therapist tells us that as we do the tread-mill, we need to imagine walking down a lovely path in the woods or down a beach at sunrise. "Look straight ahead, have a nice sunny hike," she chirps. I like her part-time assistant better. She's thirty pounds too heavy, like me, and she only gets perky when she talks about what she had for lunch or what she is going to have for supper. We like to discuss the weekly specials at the Dairy Queen. She says wise things like "Sometimes talking about food is as good as eating it."

Mile 0.6

The treadmill creaks to incline so my body thinks it's walking uphill. The first week of rehab I only walked half a mile on level ground, but now I've graduated to hills. The controls are set for us before we start each machine. "You need to get healthy slowly," Miss Perky says. "Every little step you take makes your heart happier." She has the practiced voice of someone who spends too much time in rooms full of old, weak, fat people. She knows it's all about motivating the disbelievers. I know that voice, it's a teacher's voice. Try to convince a nine-year-old multiplication is fun. I wonder if I ever sounded perky.

Mile 0.8

I'm heading downhill now. I just want to go home. I'm hot and tired and I want a hot-fudge-brownie delight. There's a coupon for one in my purse. I have no idea if I'll have the willpower to drive past the Dairy Queen to go home and eat my microwave-in-minutes lemon-pepper chicken breast and broccoli.

Mile 1, Almost

Some old guy is meandering around the room, nodding his head to every exercise biker and treadmill walker he passes. I don't recognize him but my visual memory for my fellow rehab class members isn't that sharp. He doesn't fit the pattern for most of the other males in the class. He has a little more hair and a little less stomach, and instead of sweats he's wearing a pleasant plaid shirt and corduroy slacks. He's the only person in the room who can tuck his shirt into his pants. Just as I reach Mile 1, he wanders up to me.

"So, have you been to Green Bay?"

"I beg your pardon?" I say.

"Green Bay. I was wondering if you'd been there. I'm sorry. I didn't mean to startle you. You were really concentrating on the workout, weren't you?"

"I'm concentrating on it being over," I say. I can't imagine what he's talking about and I really don't feel like chatting while I'm standing here sweating with my feet straddling this machine. This is the most dangerous part of my exercise regime, trying to sidestep the moving belt as it slows down. I'd feel really embarrassed if I fell off the treadmill and broke my leg as I was trying to rehabilitate my heart. There are only three treadmills so exercise time on them comes at a premium. There's a sign-up sheet policy so people don't snatch up the machines in an uncivilized manner. Obviously this old guy doesn't understand the treadmill-usage rules.

"You'll need to sign in before you use this machine. I'll be finished in a minute," I tell him.

"Oh, no. I'm not waiting for it. The machine. I'm supposed to do the bikes," he says. "I was just wondering . . ."

"I think you have to sign up for those too," I tell him.

"No, I've finished," he says.

"We'll see you Wednesday, Michael," Miss Perky yells from across the room. "Tell Ramona hello for me."

I send her a thank you smile. She's good. Poor man doesn't seem to know exactly where he is, but she's managed to redirect him just fine, reminded him of time and place and wife, all with one sentence. Saved his dignity. I guess you need to be smart as well as perky to deal with some of these old folks.

Old Folks. Is that who I am now?

•

I compromise. I go to the drive-thru for my sundae so I can take it home and put it in my freezer. Then I can eat Healthy Choice and have half a hot fudge brownie delight for dessert. I think I'll be able to diet if I can just sneak up on it, not face it head-on.

The owner of the Dairy Queen is working the drive-thru window this afternoon.

"Hello, Mrs. St. Clair," he says. "How're you feeling?"

"Great," I tell him. "Thank you for asking."

He was in my class the year I started teaching. It's hard to merge the memory of that cute little blonde boy with the gray-haired man who hands me my ice cream. That first year of teaching seems like eons ago. After I graduated from Illinois State, I interviewed for a teaching job in St. Louis and one right here in Centerburg, where my parents knew the Superintendent of Schools. The idea of me in big, bad St. Louis scared my folks so I took the hometown job option. That first classroom smelled like fifty years of chalk dust.

When I get home, I slide my sundae in the freezer and grab the top box from my Healthy Choice pile. Kathy instructed me to purchase seven of these cardboard dinners every week. I suppose it would be cheaper if I actually pre-pared meals, now that I have all this free time, but cooking and I have never been best friends.

I put my dinner in the microwave without reading the directions. It doesn't matter much if you pierce the correct section or turn after four minutes or let stand before eating, the food's going to taste the same, bland and rubbery. I think about brownies as I peel off my clothes and put on my favor-ite robe. I guess I should buy some leisurewear outfits, now that I'm a woman of leisure. Wearing a bathrobe all evening smacks of sloth.

I'll call Clarice tomorrow and see if she wants to go to Walmart. Or maybe we could drive over to the Penney's at

East River Plaza by St. Louis. She's been nagging me for weeks to buy new living room curtains and throw pillows to match the purple vase she bought me as a get well present. She's decided my accent colors are to be plums and greens. I could use some more clothes for exercise class too. Not those clingy, stripy outfits that the kids wear, but a few pairs of lightweight sweatpants and shirts. The sweatshirt I had on today was way too hot for exercising.

I wonder how old this sweatshirt is. I bet I bought it the summer I went on the bus tour to Branson, and we stopped at an outlet center. The only bargain I found there was a table full of two-dollar sweatshirts. I must have bought five or six of them and then I had to lug them around for the rest of the trip.

I pick up the old green sweatshirt from the top of my dirty laundry pile and check out the label. Men's X-Large. I seem to have grown into it over the last few years. It has yellow letters across the front. GREEN BAY. I usually don't care for words on my clothing or pictures of kittens or Teddy bears, but I guess I figured a bargain was a bargain.

Where have I heard GREEN BAY mentioned today?

That old guy was asking me something about Green Bay. Oh, for heaven's sake, he was reading my sweatshirt. What did I say back to him? I thought he was completely disoriented. I bet he thinks I'm really rude, or really stupid.

A flush of embarrassment crawls up my chest. He was just being friendly. He probably isn't even senile. I try to remember how he looked. I guess his eyes didn't look dull. They were sparkly and blue, as I recall.

Come to think of it, he had the bluest eyes I've ever seen.

CHAPTER 2

※

Michael

It can take a lifetime to learn out how to live a life, I suppose. Up until now, I didn't have to spend much time thinking about it, I just lived. Now I'm bogged down in figuring out what to do about my life and I'm getting real tired of it. All this thinking only leads to bellyaching or boasting. I've been Michael Bartoli for sixty-nine years, but I don't know how to be me anymore.

My dog Sunny and I have been at my daughter Ramona's house since my birthday in May. "Just come for a few days," Ramona begged. "We'll have a little party, anything you want." She didn't mention it, but I know she was thinking about her mother. My wife Evelyn died a year ago, a few days before my birthday. Ramona didn't want me to be sad, and I didn't want Ramona to be sad, so Sunny and I drove down to Centerburg from my house in Des Plaines. The truth is, I've been sad for the last ten years as I watched my pretty, smart, hard-working wife turn into a person I didn't know, a person who didn't know me. Evelyn left us long before she died.

Two days after my birthday, I had a heart attack. The next day I had bypass surgery. For the last four months, as Ramona has worried over me and taken care of me, I've been sitting here in a house that's not mine, trying to figure out how to get back into my life. *Bellyaching!*

In another hour the first morning light will pop through the kitchen window, and I'll watch Ramona and her husband Ravi and my grandson Lucas drift past me as they head into the day. I'll just sit here at the kitchen table, drinking coffee. Ramona's one of those midwife doula nurses, my son-in-law Ravi is an anesthesiologist, and Lucas is a teenage boy, so none of them spend much time at home. The least I can do is have a pot of coffee ready for the family when they get up. I'd make breakfast or a coffee cake, but no one stays around long enough to eat it.

I hope today's sunrise is as pretty as it was yesterday, when half the sky turned pink. A pretty sunrise is full of promises for the day. Maybe I'll make a lasagna for supper. I'll make a grocery list and go shopping. And I need to call my son Mike before he goes to work. When Evelyn got sick, we all decided I'd stay home with her full-time, so I retired and turned over the family business to Mike. Mike's Hot Dogs has passed from my dad to me to Mike. Cooking and running a hot dog joint are the only things I know how to do. I'm good at both. *Boasting!*

Mike is taking care of his family and working full time, and now he's checking in on my house and taking care of my bills. He'd never complain, but it will be easier for everyone when I get back home. Maybe I should sell my house in Des Plaines and get me a little place back in my hometown, in Green Bay. When I saw that woman in Rehab wearing a Green Bay sweatshirt, it put me in a homesick mood. She looked so unhappy, trudging along on a treadmill. Her face was pink and sweaty from walking to nowhere. My melancholy Green Bay lady. I've been thinking about her since the minute I saw her.

"Good morning, Daddy!"

My daughter bounces into the kitchen, looking more like a sixteen-year-old than the mother of a sixteen-year-old. She kisses me on the top of my head, then rushes to the coffee pot. Brown curly hair and big brown eyes. Tiny and determined. She's so like her mother, back when Evelyn was the center of our lives.

I watch her scurry around the kitchen, filling her travel mug with coffee, collecting what she'll need for her day, shuffling papers. She grabs her cell phone, punches it a few times, frowns. *I'm running late*, she announces. Her back is toward me as she peers into the refrigerator, in search of some healthy snacks to stuff in her bag.

I miss working. Seven days a week, ten hours a day, I was at Mike's Hot Dogs. Running a restaurant is hard work and I loved every minute. Evelyn did all the bookkeeping for the restaurant on top of doing everything at our home. She took care of our house, raised our kids, looked after our granddaughter Emma when her folks were working. We were a team. But I never asked her if she loved her job.

"Do you think your mother was happy? I mean before…" The question slips out of my mouth.

Ramona slowly closes the refrigerator door and turns to look at me. "Oh, Daddy," she says, then picks up her travel mug and sets it on the table across from me. She takes off her coat, hangs it on the back of her chair and sits down. Her huge brown eyes search my face. "Yes, I think she was happy, before."

Her eyes fill with tears. It breaks my heart I've made my daughter cry.

She wipes her eyes and the sad smile returns. She reaches across the table and takes my hand. "I know you miss her so," she says. "We all do."

"Yes, I miss her," I say, lying to my daughter.

My son-in-law walks into the kitchen, dressed in work-out clothes, carrying a suitcoat on a hanger. "Good morning, Michael," he says. "How did you sleep?" We both chuckle.

When I first got here, Ravi would ask me this every

morning. "At least you don't make my dad get up and shake your hand," Ramona had teased him. Ravi was a little hurt.

"I'm sorry, Michael. I didn't mean to sound so formal," he'd told me. "I ask because I care."

Ravi's parents still live in India. They sent him to medical school in Chicago and now he's a US citizen. He acts very self-assured, but I think he's constantly worried about doing the correct thing.

"And you, Mrs. Patel, how did you sleep?" He walks toward Ramona, his hand outstretched. She giggles. When she gets up to shake his hand, he pulls her toward him and wraps his arm around her. She snuggles for a few seconds before she pushes him away, laughing.

My daughter is happy.

Ravi grabs his car keys from a hook by the door to the garage and yells, "Lucas, I'm leaving now. Hurry up."

Sunny sits up and his tail pounds the floor with excitement when my grandson walks into the kitchen. He loves Lucas.

"Hi Buddy," Lucas says as he pats Sunny on the head. "Morning, Grandpa." He kisses his mom on the cheek.

"Are you leaving now, too?" Ravi asks Ramona, opening the door for Lucas.

"No, I was supposed to pick up donuts for our staff meeting, but Daddy and I got to talking.

I'll leave in a bit. The meeting will go a lot faster if we don't have any treats."

"OK, see you tonight," Ravi says. "The game is at eight, right? Michael, are you coming?"

My grandson plays high school basketball. After watching his game last week, I'd say he's their best player. "Sure, I'll be there," I say. I make a mental note to forget about the lasagna.

After Ravi and Lucas leave, Ramona sits down with me again. "Honey," I say, "why don't you let me bake something for your meetings? I'd like that."

Ramona shakes her head. "No, you don't need to go to all that trouble."

I feel my smile fade. Ramona sees it.

"OK," she says. "That does sound great. I'll sign you up for next Friday. Everybody will be ecstatic when I walk in with goodies baked by my Precious Pop."

Doctor Sam's waiting room is packed, as usual. I take the only available chair, nod to the man sitting to my left, and settle in to spend the afternoon at my cardiologist's office. One would think everyone in Centerburg has heart problems, but Ramona told me the reason Doctor Sam's office is so crowded is because he spends too much time with each patient. His nurses are always trying to get him to speed up, but he won't move onto his next patient until he's sure the one in front of him is feeling good and has all their questions answered.

I sit for about an hour, flipping through a year-old *Prevention* magazine. Finally, a frazzled nurse calls my name, puts me in a room and takes my blood pressure. I wait another twenty minutes before Doctor Sam walks through the door.

"Michael! Great to see you."

He asks me about Ramona and Ravi and tells me he's heard I have a basketball superstar for a grandson. "Your blood pressure is a little high," he says. "It's nothing to worry over. Just ask Ramona to check it later." I feel myself relax, like I'm talking to an old friend instead of my new doctor. Then he puts his hand on my knee, looks me in the eye and says, "How are you?"

And this is what I do not say: I'm scared. I'm trapped. I'm lonesome. I want to go home but home has nothing left for me. I loved my job, but it's gone. My wife is dead—I couldn't take care of her any longer. She ended her life hating me. Sometimes I hated her too, when I got so tired I forgot I loved her.

"I'm just fine, Doc," I say, lying to Doctor Sam.

By the time I get to Rehab, it's four-thirty and all five exercise bikes are available. I pick a bike that gives me a view of the whole room, pull myself onto it and set the timer for twenty minutes. There are only half a dozen folks here. It's probably slack time of the day for exercising, now that it's almost suppertime. My Green Bay lady isn't working out on the treadmills. I'm disappointed. I'd got myself hoping I'd see her again today. Last time I saw her she looked every bit as miserable as I feel most all the time. Maybe if we talked about it, we would both get to feeling better.

My mind wanders as I pedal. Maybe I'll make a blueberry buckle coffee cake for Ramona's staff meeting. No, cinnamon rolls. That's the ticket. They're a crowd pleaser and making them will keep me busy for a whole day. I'll need yeast and flour and pecans, and Sunny needs more dog food. As soon as I get home, I'll make a list. I glance up and see a woman walk through the door, carrying a coat and a pocketbook. It's her. Instead of her Green Bay sweatshirt, she's wearing a purple color outfit and it suits her a lot better. The material is soft and velvety. She looks real pretty.

Instead of walking to a treadmill, she pulls on her coat and walks over to talk to the Rehab nurse. She's leaving instead of coming. My heart starts pounding. My timer still says fifteen minutes. By the time I get done, she'll be gone. *Michael, get a grip.* I don't know what's wrong with me. She's probably married and here I am, looking at the way that purple material fits around her body.

Maybe my wishing it makes it happen. Instead of walking out the door, she walks straight over to me and says, "I believe I owe you an apology."

"I'm sorry?" I ask. The only word I get is apology. I try to get off the bicycle while I figure out what to say to her. I can't seem to get myself together enough to do either. To top it off, she puts out her hand for me to shake, so I grab ahold of the bike with my left hand and manage to shake her right hand without falling off.

"I'm Beth St. Clair," she says. "I think I was rude to you a few days ago, and I'm sorry. No, please, don't stop your exercise. I just wanted to apologize."

She looks like she's going to walk away and leave me barely hanging on to the bike, not getting to say a single word. I decide to give up trying to get off the bike so I can concentrate on saying something back to her.

"Pleased to meet you," I manage to say. "I'm Michael Bartoli."

That stops her from walking away.

"And I'm sorry. I didn't quite get what you said. Something about an apology?"

"Yes, the other day. You said something to me, and I thought you were, well, anyway, I didn't understand why you said 'Green Bay' because I didn't remember what I had on, but later, well, then I noticed. So, bottom line, I was rude to you and I'm sorry." She looks nervous.

"Now, Beth St. Clair, I don't recall you being rude to me, so don't worry about it."

"Well, OK," she says. "I guess I better be going. It was nice to meet you."

"My pleasure," I say. "I guess it is about suppertime. You probably have to get home to your husband."

"Oh, no," she says. "I'm not married. The only thing I'm going home to is a TV dinner."

Looking back over my life, there have been moments when events tumble into place, times when gravity has pulled me in just the right direction. I've learned not to question these moments with *If I hadn't* or *Thank God I didn't.* I've learned to believe in *What Is, Is* and grab onto these moments with both hands.

I turn the timer on my bike handle to zero, still the

pedals, slide off the bike without a falter or a stumble, and place myself square in front of my Green Bay lady. She's only about two inches shorter than me. I can look her right in the eye.

"In that case, let me buy you a cup of coffee. I think we need to delay that TV dinner as long as possible."

"Oh, no, that's not what I meant. No, you don't have to do that," she says. I'm standing close enough to see twitches of worry and fear sprout around her eyes. She won't look at me for more than a second.

"Well, I understand. Some other time maybe," I say. "I don't even know where to get a cup of coffee around here. I'm just visiting my daughter. Maybe you don't even drink coffee."

Slowly she looks at me. "Well, they do have coffee right here in the cafeteria. And pretty good cherry pie."

Mary of Mercy Hospital cafeteria smells a little more like a restaurant than I'd expected it would. Green beans must be on the menu tonight, probably cooked without a speck of bacon or onion. All the other diners look like they work here at the hospital. They're mostly women wearing bright colored hospital blouses, some with flowers or balloons, a few with teddy bears. I expect those are the nurses from pediatrics. I can't stand to think of a sick child. There's a whole table of ladies wearing gold-colored blouses. Ramona told me they are all volunteers, like candy stripers, except they're fifty years older than that, so they call themselves Golden Girls.

The dining room is starting to fill up as we walk in, but we find an empty table in the back by a window. I pull a chair out for Beth.

"Let me go with you to help," she says. "I'll pay for mine."

"No, you sit here and relax," I tell her. "Let me buy us some pie. If it's not as good as you say, I'll let you pay me back."

My stomach tightens up on me as I walk over to the cafeteria line and glance back to our table. Beth is sitting straight and proper, her hands in her lap. Her eyes survey the cafeteria, then glance in my direction. Her face is tight with worry. My pie and coffee invitation may be a real bad idea. I get a tray and two forks, walk around the line of women gathering in front of the steam table, and go straight to the dessert counter. I hope passing them by isn't breaking some kind of rule, but I want to get back to our table before Beth decides to bolt for the door.

Beth was right. The cherry pie is the best offering here. It looks flaky and fresh, sitting on the shelf next to little bowls of tapioca and chocolate pudding topped with day-old Cool Whip. I put two pieces on my tray and fill up two coffee cups. I throw a few creams and sugars and some packages of Sweet'n Low on the tray, pay for it, and head back to Beth.

Beth gives me a weak smile as I set our food out on the table. "This pie looks real good," I say as I sit down. "I don't know if I could have baked a prettier one myself."

"Oh, do you bake?" Beth perks up.

"Yes, Ma'am," I say. "I love to cook."

My stomach doesn't feel like it can hold a piece of pie right now, so I sip my coffee and watch Beth. She is giving the pie her total attention. I watch the first bite travel from her plate to her fork to her lips. She's not wearing lipstick—maybe ladies don't wear makeup to exercise class. She doesn't have her fingernails painted either, but they look pretty anyway. Short and tidy and pink. Each time she takes a bite of pie she closes her eyes as she chews. I can almost hear her sigh. Then she drinks a sip of coffee and carefully cuts another little forkful, making sure to get all the cherry filling off the plate. With every bite, her face relaxes a little more.

After half her pie is eaten, she looks up at me. "What brings you to our Cardiac Rehab adventure?"

I can't remember the last time I talked to a woman who wasn't a nurse or a doctor or a relative. My words tumble out. I tell her about visiting Ramona for my birthday and having a heart attack. I tell her about growing up in Green Bay, the reason I'd asked her about her sweatshirt. I tell her about Des Plaines and Evelyn and our kids and grandkids. I tell her about running Mike's Hot Dog stand and how I loved it.

"Evelyn's been dead for over a year now," I say. I stop short before I say anything more.

"Do you still live in Des Plaines?" Beth asks. Her plate is empty. My pie hasn't been touched.

"I guess I do, but I don't feel like it," I say. "How's the pie?"

"It's wonderful," she says. "I guess I won't have to pay you back."

I take a bite. I might have given the crust an egg white wash and sprinkled it with sugar, but the pie tastes OK for a hospital cafeteria.

There are so many things I want to ask her. Why aren't you going home to a husband who loves you? Why are you in Rehab? Is your heart badly damaged? I want to tell her my cherry pie tastes better than the one she's eaten. I want to tell her more about Green Bay and Des Plaines and Evelyn. I want to tell her how lonesome and homesick I am here in this sleepy little town and that I'm afraid I'll never be happy and healthy again.

Instead, I take another bite of pie. Beth sips her coffee. Maybe I'll have a chance to say it all, maybe not. But right now, these few moments are the happiest I've spent in quite a while.

Beth sets her coffee cup down, wipes her mouth with a corner of her napkin and looks around the room. She starts to look nervous again.

"How long have you lived in Centerburg?" I ask to fill in the quiet.

"Oh, all my life, except for the four years I was in college," she says.

The thought of this woman spending her whole life in this town fills me with sadness. I put down my fork and pat the back of her hand. Her hand is soft and warm but before I let my hand curl over it, I let go.

"Oh, my darling, I'm so sorry," I say.

The second I say it, I regret it. I'm criticizing her town. I'm calling a woman I don't know Darling. It sounds awful. I hope she doesn't hear how awful it sounds. I look at her to try to explain.

Her eyes open wide as her face explodes into a smile. A laugh bubbles up from her throat.

"To be truthful, Michael, quite often I'm sorry about my living arrangements too." She reaches across the table and as she laughs again, her soft warm hand folds over mine.

CHAPTER 3

❋

Beth

"Beth, I'm at the Target here at East River and there's a duvet cover on sale that would carry your plums and greens into your bedroom. Do you want me to get it for you?"

I'm still not used to the idea of cell phones, but Clarice has embraced them totally. She loves to be in constant communication with her entire world. Once she called me from a drive-thru car wash. I guess she was bored for the three minutes it was taking for the rinse cycle.

"Good morning. What are you talking about?" I ask her.

"A duvet cover," she says. "This pattern would be perfect in your bedroom. It's on sale for eighty bucks, but it's Seniors' Day so I can save you another 10 per cent."

Clarice is probably on a shopping trip with her daughter-in-law. Clarice and Jim have three married children, but her daughter-in-law Jennifer is the only family member who has time for outings with Clarice. Even Clarice's grandkids are getting too old to play with her. As a reward for her attentive attitude, Clarice will probably treat her to lunch.

"What's a duvet?" I ask her. "Is that like a décolletage? I always try to keep my décolletage covered, but I didn't know I had to worry about my duvet too. Do I even have a duvet?"

"I'm serious, Beth. You could slide your comforter in it. It's a queen, right?

"Oh, Clarice, I don't know. No one's ever going to look in

my bedroom. And besides, then you'll want me to get new drapes. You know I'm on a fixed income."

"You need to let go of a little of that fixed income," she tells me. "If you like this duvet cover, they've got the same colors for your kitchen and bathroom linens. And there's the cutest set of plates in a grape pattern that would pull it all together."

"I am not buying new dishes!"

"Well, I'll just get you this cover then. By the way," Clarice says, "I had the strangest phone call last night from Shirley Eubanks. She said she saw you sitting in the hospital cafeteria holding hands with some man. Do you suppose she's finally lost her mind?"

"It wouldn't be a big loss," I tell her. "Listen, I've got to go. Give me a call when you get back in town."

My hands are trembling as I put down the phone. Rage mixed with humiliation. Count on Shirley Eubanks, or someone just like her, to turn an innocent snack into a tawdry escapade. I figured it would happen as soon as I saw her at the Golden Girls cafeteria table. I should have just gone over, said hello, and explained myself. "Hello, Shirley," I could have said. "Do you suppose it would be alright if I let this strange man buy me a cup of coffee? Can I possibly do that without you calling everyone in town to tell them you've spotted a potential news alert about Beth?" I'm sure the only reason she volunteers at the hospital is so she'll be the first in town to know who's sick and dying.

For a couple of minutes, I fantasize I'll just call her up and tell her to mind her own business. I'll listen to her sputter and choke, and then she'll apologize for being a small-minded, evil-tongued harpy. But, like always, I decide to do nothing.

Friday morning, I wake up late, unfurl myself from my new plum and green duvet cover, and ooze out of bed. When Clarice and her daughter-in-law stormed into my house yesterday, they were so excited about unwrapping the duvet, stuffing my comforter in it, and *oohing* and *aahing* over the results of their purchase that Clarice forgot to interrogate me about Shirley Eubanks' phone call. I wrote out a check as fast as I could and told them I was on my way to the grocery store. Maybe the whole embarrassing mess will blow over so Clarice will never have cause to question me further.

A donut is what I need for a little morning energy. Somehow a dozen donuts fell into my shopping cart yesterday. I slide into my bathrobe and go to my kitchen to brew myself a pot of coffee. Instead of a new bedspread, I wish Clarice had decided I needed one of those coffee pots with a timer. It would be a real luxury to wake up to a pot of freshly brewed coffee. As I'm waiting for my coffee, I open the box of donuts, eat one, and put two more on a paper plate. Fifteen seconds in the microwave freshens up two donuts perfectly. It's not exactly baking, like a cherry pie, but it's fine for me. I carry my breakfast pick-me-up into the living room so I can watch TV as I eat. It's so late I've missed *Good Morning America*, so I turn on CNN.

Should I switch to morning exercise classes? I'd thought afternoons would be less crowded, but I think I read somewhere that one should exercise early, for the best caloric-burning benefits. It's not that I'm trying to avoid Michael. He seemed very nice. I just need a good reason to get up a bit earlier. If I plan on morning exercises, I could spring right up, put on my exercise clothes, and leave for class by seven-thirty or eight o'clock. Maybe I could even get a cup of coffee at the McDonalds drive-thru to sip on the way. My new plan gives me the energy I thought I'd get from the donuts. I'm out of my door in thirty minutes.

At the McDonalds drive-thru, I order a bacon, egg, and cheese biscuit to go with my coffee. Donuts aren't the most nutritious breakfast. I should have a little protein. By the time I pull into Mary of Mercy Visitors Parking, my biscuit and coffee are finished. I park and walk around to the side entrance. It's a longer walk than going through the lobby past the information station where the Golden Girls sit. I'm not trying to avoid Shirley Eubanks. She probably never works the morning shift anyway. One just needs to take advantage of exercise opportunities whenever one can. Next week I'll park at the far side of the lot, so I can walk even further.

The exercise room is crowded. A gentleman is walking on my treadmill, but by the time I hang up my jacket and purse, he's finished. *This is a much better schedule* I tell myself as I settle in for the twenty-minute stroll on my treadmill. Next week, I'll get here an hour or two earlier. Then I can just enjoy myself for the rest of the day.

What am I going to do for the rest of the day?

I'd always planned to read more "once I retire," and what else? Travel, but my heart's temporary setback has put a hold on that. I could plan a few day trips, weekend trips, even real vacations, come spring. I might just stop by the library this afternoon, after lunch, and see if they have any travel books. I haven't been to the library for years. Who knows what wonders I might find there. Maybe I'll even try "surfing the internet" on one of the library computers.

My twenty minutes on the treadmill just fly by, and I only look over at Michael's exercise bike once or twice. The lady using it this morning looks familiar. She might be the mother of some former student. As I'm looking at her, she looks up at me and smiles. I smile back, just enough to let her think I remember her. All those parental faces blend together in my memory. I'm always running into people who seem to know me, and I have no idea who they are.

I hope this woman doesn't know Shirley Eubanks.

I treat myself to a nice lunch at Kentucky Fried Chicken, but, keeping my health in mind, I order the two-piece regular meal instead of the three-piece Extra Crispy. Then I drive to the library. I've always loved this old building. It was built with Carnegie money around the turn of the century, and it sets on one of the prettiest pieces of land in downtown Centerburg. The cement slab in front of the entrance is indented from all the foot traffic it's supported over the last hundred years. I wonder how many times I've stepped in the indentation. I used to come to the library at least once a week as I was growing up. When I was eight or nine my mother would let me walk here, all by myself, since my two older brothers refused to escort me. I always felt so grown-up as I selected my three books and checked them out with my very own library card.

The stuffy basement smell of old books surrounds me as soon as I walk into the lobby. I close my eyes and breathe in a lungful of the cold, damp air. The Children's Books area is to the left and Young Adult to the right. It's called YA now at all the teacher conferences. Both rooms are deserted. A few years back, there was a big controversy over whether to build a new library or revamp this one. As with most issues in Centerburg, it split the town in two. Eventually, instead of building a new state of the art library, it was decided to put an elevator in this building, along with a few more stalls in both restrooms.

I take the old wooden stairs to Adult Reading instead of the elevator. My exercise regime is in full swing. I hear footsteps echoing around the second floor. Hopefully it's no one I know. I'm really not in the mood to stop my research to chat.

Before I search for my travel books, I peek into the little study room where I used to meet my boyfriend, back when we were teenagers. Six computers sitting in six metal cubicles have replaced the wooden tables and chairs of my youth. The room smells like electronics instead of old books.

Between the two windows on the east wall, I find shelves of travel guides from all over the world. Amazingly, my little library has a wonderful travel section: *Exploring the Midwest*, *Wandering with the Mississippi River*, *Sun-Drenched Beaches of the*

Gulf of Mexico. My eyes travel from the Caribbean, to Europe, to Kenya and Thailand and China. New Zealand appeals to me, all those green hills. Or Hawaii? I close my eyes and smell pineapples and orchids. As my eyes drift back to the US, I spot *A Seniors Guide to Healthy Travel* and pull it from its shelf. The cover promises tips for those traveling with heart concerns, so I carry the book over to a wooden chair for a quick perusal. The Index lists heart disease right between diarrhea and hepatitis. On page 78, I learn that I should:

1.   Check insurance coverage before traveling.
2.   Never travel to high altitude destinations.
3.   Stay inside at midday.
4.   Always, always, obtain a doctor's permission before traveling.

My world starts to narrow a bit as I return the book to its shelf. Maybe I'll just stay within US borders for a while. Perhaps a bus trip, where everything is arranged and pre-paid? My travel guide could tell me what to eat and where to sleep and which direction to look for the best views from my bus window. I'd meet forty strangers and we could all act like we were interested in each other's lives. "Beth," they'd say, "what do you do?" I can't imagine what I'd answer.

I'm starting to feel small and Centerburg-bound. The memory of Michael's sympathetic words floods me with unexpected sadness. Maybe I'm just tired and hungry. A little hypoglycemic. I quickly select two books, *Frommer's USA* and *Great American Rail Journeys*, as thoughts of supper start to creep into my mind.

Before I carry my books to the downstairs checkout desk, I peek into my old study room/new computer room. I had planned to try out these computers too.

A frazzled woman I take to be the librarian is leaning over one computer, her left hand propping herself on the table and her right hand frantically punching the keyboard.

"We're having server problems today," she tells me when I take a few steps into the room. "You can try to log-on, but I don't think you'll get on-line. If we're not up by the time school's out this afternoon, I'll probably have a riot in here."

The only words I fully understand are "school" and "riot" but those two are enough to make me reconsider today's plan for computer exploration.

"Oh, I'm sorry," I tell her. "I don't know anything about computers. I just thought I'd try one out, but today doesn't seem the best time."

"Stay away from them. They'll ruin your life," she tells me. "Do you want to check those books out?"

"Yes, but do you need to use the computers to do that?"

"No, that function is an internal program. It doesn't interface with the internet server," she says as she leads me downstairs to the checkout area.

I nod my head like I've found meaning in what she's just told me as I hand her my library card.

"I've never seen one like this," she says as she turns my library card back and forth as if it were a scapula from a saber-toothed tiger she's just unearthed. She informs me she'll need to input updated information on me into her database, which amounts to me answering all types of questions seemingly irrelevant to my taking home a copy of *Frommer's USA*. She tells me I'll receive a brand-new library card in two days, my books are due in three weeks, and, if I care to, I can renew on-line at the web address printed on my new card. I guess she's too concerned about the upcoming riot to remember I don't know anything about computers.

I can't believe I'd considered traveling to foreign lands no more than twenty minutes ago. I can't even navigate through my library. As I walk back to my car I hear a *whoosh* as the world passes me by.

Thankfully, it's a short drive from the library to the Dairy Queen. My day of exercise and exploration has left me exhausted and starving. Instead of the drive-thru, I park, go inside, and take my place at the back of a line. In front of me are all the school kids who aren't rioting at the library. Half of them look familiar but I'm too tired to remember any names, so I just give the whole group my recognition smile and direct my attention to the menu that covers the entire back wall. It would be nice to dine at a little café where a waiter would take my order, bring it to me, and then chat for a few minutes after my meal. A daydream flickers across my brain. I'm sitting in a booth in a dark restaurant, listening to piano music. I smell the roses sitting in a bud vase on the table. Someone touches my hand and I look across the table at Michael.

"May I help you, Mrs. St. Clair?" The voice pulls me back to Place your Order Here.

"Oh, yes. You're busy this afternoon, aren't you?" I try to give myself a few seconds to read the sprawling menu. "I'll have the special, I guess."

The special is a chili cheese dog, fries, and a small shake. I could choose something a bit more nutritious if I had time to read every food selection listed on the wall, but I hear another line of students gathering behind me. What I really want is dessert, followed by a Dilly Bar, and I want to eat it in the cozy café of my daydream, instead of here, sharing my dining experience with two dozen teenagers.

"And make it to-go, please."

At 7 a.m., my bedside clock radio wakes me from a dream of Pete St. Clair. I lie in bed and remember. I dreamed Pete came back home to me, carrying a red paper bag. He smiled and handed it to me, and I peered inside. The bag was filled with a soft pile of white material. I pulled it out and held it up. I couldn't tell if it was a lacy nightgown or a wedding dress, so I looked at the label. Girl's Size 12. I knew it was the wrong size, but when I slid it over my naked body, it fit perfectly. Pete smiled at me, pulled me into his arms, and whispered in my ear, "Oh my darling, I'm so sorry."

I dream about Pete once or twice a year, but I usually don't wake from these dreams feeling as good as I do right now. I try not to think about him when I'm fully conscious. Kathy last heard from him around the time she graduated from college. Then he was living in Miami, but she didn't tell me if he was married or divorced again or jailed, and I didn't ask her. But I did wonder.

Clarice tells me I'm repressed. She especially likes to tell me I'm sexually repressed. I guess it's true I've tamped down all those feelings, over the years. Pete was a cad, my parent's word, but for a while it was wonderful. I met him the summer after my first year of teaching. My best friends at the time, Linda and Claudia and I went to Panama City Beach to visit my cousin Cheryl, who was pregnant with her second child. We met Pete at a local beach bar, of course. The amazing thing about Pete was he chose to talk to me instead of Linda or Claudia. I never asked him why, and now I know he wouldn't have answered truthfully anyway. At the end of our two-week vacation, Linda and Claudia returned to Centerburg and I stayed on. I told my folks it was to help Cheryl.

Pete and I saw each other every night of that hot, steamy summer. He was working most days, selling construction material all around the Panhandle. At night we'd eat raw oysters and drink cold beers and make love for hours. I relished every moment of it. I would have done anything for Pete St. Clair. When I found out I was pregnant, I was amazed, not panicky or guilt-ridden. Right away Pete said, "Well, I guess we better tie the knot." It wasn't the most romantic proposal, but it still made me feel loved.

My poor mother helped me plan a rushed wedding, and Pete and I were married and living in my apartment in Centerburg, all before school started in September. Kathy came a few weeks early, so my mom could say "premature" to all her friends who were counting backwards from birth to wedding day.,

I loved my new life. I was a wife and a mother and a teacher. Pete was on the road a lot, selling whatever it was he was currently selling, but every weekend he'd come home bringing a box of Whitman's Samplers for Kathy and me. I liked to read the lid to find out what kind of candy I was getting before I bit into it, but as she got older, my silly Kathy would switch around all the pieces, just to tease me. And night times, after Kathy was in her room asleep, Pete and I would look at each other and Pete would get that serious set to his mouth and say, "Woman, why don't you go get naked and get in bed."

I didn't feel guilty or ashamed of a thing—until he left me.

"Beth, you've gained five pounds since your last check-up."

I don't like Doctor Sam's tone. It's incredulous and accusatory. Very unprofessional for someone who's supposedly guiding me back to full recovery.

"That's impossible," I tell him. "You must have transposed a number."

"Should we check it again?" he says, lifting his right eyebrow in a manner I don't appreciate.

"No, I suppose I may have gained a few pounds, but I've started a new rehab routine, in the mornings. I guess all the exercising is improving my appetite. Or maybe I'm replacing fat with muscle. Muscle weighs more than fat, you know."

Instead of responding, Doctor Sam looks me in the eye and drops his gaze downward over my body. Then he has the nerve to write something in my chart. He definitely needs a refresher course in bedside manner.

On my way home, I drive past the McDonald's, past the Dairy Queen, past the Kentucky Fried Chicken. I aim my car toward the IGA, turn into the lot, park, and go inside, walking past the bakery and past the deli-counter, which is featuring a fried chicken and mashed potato meal for $4.99. I place myself squarely in front of the frozen-foods shelves and stare at all the healthy choices, as if an omnipotent dietitian has grabbed me by the arm, pulled me here and said, "Now you stand right here, look at these dinners, and think about what you should be eating."

The pictures on the boxes make the meals look almost edible. I select two boxes, beef and portabella with mashed red skin potatoes, and spaghetti with four meatballs perched on top. I still have three or four frozen dinners at home. I don't know why I thought I'd find something more appealing here.

"If you put those back right now, I'll make you dinner."

I turn around and see Michael, standing beside a cart full of food. It takes me one second to decide to put those frozen dinners back on the shelf.

CHAPTER 4

❋

Michael

Beth bursts through the front doors of the IGA grocery store just as I push my cart to the end of the checkout line. She grabs an empty cart, throws her purse in it, and steers it toward the back of the store. As quickly as she appears, she's gone. After watching for her at Rehab all week, I got up the courage to ask our nurse if anything had happened to Mrs. St. Claire. She told me Beth had switched to mornings. Maybe she didn't want to see me anymore. If that's the case, she won't want to see me now. But maybe she had to rearrange her schedule for a reason other than a pestering old coot. Well *Michael*, I tell myself, *there's only one way to find out*. I pull my cart out of the checkout line and set out to find her.

The IGA grocery store is a short drive from Ramona's house and the staff is real friendly, so I do all my shopping here. Ramona told me the same family has owned it for seventy years. It's passed father to son, Italian style, just like in our family. I sure hope Mike will be able to keep Mike's Chicago Dogs afloat. He's clever at marketing and he's got a better feel for finance than I ever did. I'd never have made it without Evelyn keeping her eagle eye on our money. Right now, the parking lot is worth more than the business, I imagine, being that downtown Des Plaines is sprucing up, trying to get the Chicago commuter trade. But it's Mike's call. I promised him, and myself when I gave it to him, that I wouldn't interfere with anything he wanted to do. This IGA store has gone through some changes too, I imagine. I'd like to chat with the family who owns this place, tell them I know how it is, working and then letting go.

Ramona's been harping about low fat, and she's right, I suppose, so I have my cart filled with healthy options— Italian turkey sausage and a family pack of chicken breasts, bell peppers and mushrooms and Roma tomatoes. I was thinking of making a stir-fry, maybe chicken cacciatore.

The wine aisle here is always a disappointment. After searching for a nice, dry chianti, I had to settle for a red blend. There were some nice-looking pork roasts on special, but I'd get the evil eye from Ramona if I brought one home. Roasted pork used to be one of my specialties. I haven't made one in years.

I was cooking a pork roast the first time Evelyn wandered away from home. She'd been out of eyesight for a few minutes, but back then I had no reason to suspect anything was wrong. I'd just mixed up the flour and water for my gravy and the pan was ready for it. I remember being happy for the first time in days. The roast was perfect and there were plenty of pan drippings.

A car honked and when I went to the front door, it was wide open. I found Evelyn just before she got to the Main Street stop light. I shouldn't have, I know now, but I grabbed her by the arm and yelled, "Where do you think you're going?"

She whirled toward me. "Get your hands off me, you bastard!" she yelled. Her eyes glared with rage. The look she gave me cut my heart in two.

I didn't let go. I pulled her along with me for half a block before my brain started working again. Finally, I said, "Let's go home, Evelyn. You're missing *The Price Is Right*," and she walked back with me, just as easy as pie. By the time I got her settled in front of the TV, that gravy was ruined.

I told my son Mike about it all. He called Ramona and she ordered one of those ID bracelets, in case Evelyn left again. Evelyn threw a fit when I tried to put it on her, so I told her it was a Christmas present from Ramona and she settled down. Seeing that damn dog tag bracelet around my wife's wrist always reminded me everything in our lives had changed.

By the time I spot Beth in the frozen food aisle my heart is pounding. I have no idea what to say to her. Maybe just, "Hello Beth, nice to see you again," but that sounds too casual for what I've been feeling. She's holding two of those diet TV dinners, one in each hand like she's trying to decide between arsenic and rat poison. I take a few deep breaths, hoping more oxygen will stop my heart from pumping so fast, push my cart right up to hers, and say the first thing that pops into my brain. "If you put those back right now, I'll make you supper."

Beth turns around, looks at me, and her face explodes into a smile. "That sounds wonderful," she says.

I want to memorize her, the way her eyes look full and happy, the way her lips are just about to say something teasing, the way a smile bounced from me to her and back to me.

"Are you sure you want to go to all the trouble? As you can see, I have the palate of a gourmet."

"My spaghetti and meatballs can beat out that frozen stuff," I say. "I love to cook but my family is usually too busy to eat." I look at all the food in my cart. "This is way too much food just for me."

Beth's smile fades. "I wouldn't want to barge in without warning." Her eyes flicker from me to the mass of groceries in my cart. The smile creeps back. "But if you'd like to come over to my house, we could try to whip up a little supper." She laughs. "By *we* I mean *you*."

My mouth drops open. A laugh escapes. I got myself a date.

Thank heavens no one's home to see me when I get back to Ramona's. By the time I get the groceries unloaded and put away, I'm in a panic. I sit at the kitchen table and try to calm myself down. Beth's phone number and directions to her house are on a piece of paper in my wallet. The smart thing to do would be to call her up and tell her I'm sorry for inviting myself over. Back out of this whole ordeal. I don't know this woman. I don't even know how to get to know this woman. What will I talk about while I'm cooking dinner in her kitchen? Is she just too shy to tell me to stop bothering her?

I take Beth's note out of my wallet and stare at the directions. She's got pretty handwriting. "I'm in the middle condo," she told me. "Number thirty-one." She's probably in her own panic, realizing she's given her address to some stranger. I guess the best way to prove I'm OK would be to fix her a nice meal, something simple. She probably eats healthy. She was picking out those good-for-you frozen dinners. Salad, with the leftover vinegar and oil dressing I mixed up last night, some greens out of the refrigerator, a cuke, a tomato. I start piling food on the kitchen table. Chicken breasts, mushrooms, zucchini. A little pepperoni and olives for spice. Some wine, for cooking and drinking. I wonder if she has a big pot for cooking the spaghetti. A sauté pan? Olive oil? I'd better take everything. And I need to write a note to Ramona, to tell her . . . what? Your father is a lonely old man who is about to make a fool of himself? This whole situation is out-of-control.

By the time I finish, the kitchen table is covered with food and cooking supplies. The back door bursts open. Ramona is home early. "What's going on here? Are you moving back home?" she laughs.

I look at her and take a deep breath. "Well, honey, I'm not exactly sure what I'm doing," I say.

After I explain why her kitchen is now stacked on her

table, Ramona simply walks over to me and puts her hand on my arm. "Have a wonderful evening, Daddy," she says, and kisses me on the cheek.

Beth's house is easy to find. I park in a spot for guests, just like she told me. All the food and cooking gear is packed in a grocery bag and a big cardboard box that's set in the back seat. The hard part is going to be carrying everything up to her door in one trip. I wrap both arms around the box and grip the handle of the grocery bag. I have to push the door shut with my hip and then kick it shut when it doesn't close all the way. Hopefully, Beth's not watching me from her window. She'll think I'm moving in with her.

I wonder if I should have bought her some flowers. It doesn't look real romantic, calling on a lady with a grocery bag and a cardboard box full of pots and pans.

Did I turn off my headlights?

As I swing around to check, my bag hits a stubby little evergreen bush and rips right down the side. The wine flies free and explodes in the middle of the sidewalk. The second it hits the cement, Beth flings open the front door. She looks terrified!

No, no, no, my pretty, sad lady, I never want to scare you. Beth's dressed up—a white silky blouse, lipstick. Ready for the date I'm already ruining.

"Quick, get me some towels and a broom." I try not to yell as she steps toward me.

"Stop! You'll get wine all over your shoes!"

Beth whirls around and disappears into her house. In an instant she's back. Under a halo of brown and silver curls, her face is shining with amusement. "Does this mean we won't be having wine with supper?"

I want to hug her, but I'm still holding my box of pots and pans and there's a lake of Carlo Rossi between us.

"Aren't you glad I came over?" I ask.

"You do make quite an entrance." She walks around my

disaster area, hands me a broom, and begins to unroll paper towels.

"No, I'll get it," I tell her. A picnic of tomatoes and cucumbers and cheese is scattered over Beth's lawn and her sidewalk smells like a vineyard. "If you just go back in your house for a while and act like this isn't happening, I'll appreciate it for the rest of my life."

That's just what she does.

I gather up the wayward vegetables, pile my dinner fixings in the box, towel up the puddles of wine, and sweep up all the glass and oozing towels. Then I stuff it into what's left of the grocery bag, throw the miserable mess into my car trunk, and slam it shut, a little too hard. I heft up the box and carry it to her condo. The second my finger touches the bell, Beth swings open the door, smiling at me like we share a secret joke. "Michael, good evening," she says. "How nice to see you. Please come in."

Beth's house smells like lemon cleaner. Through the tiny galley kitchen, a table set for two sits in a dark dining room.

I set my box on the spotless counter and start to unpack. "You got a nice place here."

Beth takes a head of lettuce from the top of the box, looks around for a place to set it and puts it back in the box. "Thank you," she says, reaching toward me. "Let me take your coat?"

"I better keep it on," I say. "I need to go buy us another bottle of wine, unless you have some you can spare."

"No, but let me go get it." She sounds happy I gave her a reason to leave. "It's the least I can do."

I start to argue, but she rushes out of the room and comes back carrying her coat and a pocketbook. "I'll be back in a jiffy," she says.

I try to help her with her coat and knock the French bread to the floor. "I should be the one buying more wine," I tell her, grabbing for my wallet in my back pocket. It's not there.

"I don't know much about wine," she says as I fumble. "What do you need?"

"Anything," I say. "Something red. Not too sweet." I stuff my hands in my coat pockets. My wallet's not there either. "Just buy whatever you like." I must have left it at Ramona's. "White wine is fine too. I hate to have you go out in the dark." I don't mention my wallet. I don't want to sound like a dead beat.

Beth smiles and pats me on the arm. "I'll be back in a bit," she says.

I'm on a date with a woman that's not Evelyn. And I'm alone in her kitchen, about to cook her dinner. Is it OK to feel happy? I'll think about it later. Now I got to get the pasta water boiling and my chicken started. The wine can be added later, so I'll sauté everything right up to the point where I need it.

As my pans heat up, I chop the pepperoni and the vegetables, using my good knife and Ramona's cutting board. I forgot a salad bowl and wine glasses, but I did bring that pretty oil lamp Ramona had sitting on her porch. I put it on the table between the two plates and light it with the matches I found in Ramona's kitchen drawer. Does Beth sit at her table when she eats one of those TV dinners? Which chair will Beth have me sit in?

I walk into her living room to see if I can turn on some music. Mike's family got me and Evelyn a CD player and radio—one of those fancy Bose ones—a couple of years back. I love listening to Tony Bennett and Frank Sinatra, all the good old music. The dancing kind. I wonder if Beth likes to dance.

Beth's townhouse is a tunnel with a kitchen window in the front and a floor-to-ceiling drape at the rear. Does it cover a sliding glass door? Is there a little patio out back? Besides me, the only thing in Beth's living room looking out of place is a big purple vase on the end table by the telephone. Evelyn would have called it a dust collector. Evelyn had hundreds of little figurines and plates and whatnots sitting all over the house. I think she enjoyed dusting them. In those last few years, when I was doing the dusting, I had to be careful not to set them out of place. If she spotted something that was put back wrong, she'd scream, "What's that doing way over there?" It always amazed me she had the whole house memorized like that.

Don't be thinking about Evelyn all evening, I remind myself.

There's no radio, so I grab the remote and turn the TV to the local channel. Events and advertisements scroll down the screen while background music plays. I listen for a minute—it's that sax player from a few years back. I turn off the living room lamps so the light from the TV makes the room soft blue.

I hope Beth doesn't think I've got motives. Do I have motives? I barely remember what a motive is!

The doorbell chimes. I open the door to a chuckling Beth hanging on to a lumpy paper bag with both hands, a key ring dangling from her index finger. She bustles in and eases the bag down on the counter. "For a minute I thought we might have a replay of the sidewalk wine incident," she says as I help her take off her coat. Her eyes flicker around the room and come to rest on the sizzling skillet of chicken. Her body stills. Her shoulders drop. "My kitchen has never smelled so wonderful," she sighs, then starts pulling bottles of wine from the bag. "I wasn't sure what to buy so I got a few choices."

I pick up a bottle of chianti. "I've been looking for something like this for weeks."

"I went to the Liquor Store." Beth sets three more bottles of wine on the counter. "I heard you mention red, then white, so I bought both. I asked the owner for help in picking them out. Two reds and two whites. I can save what's left for Thanksgiving. Michael, you can tell me to be quiet and start helping you at any point." Beth's face is flushed. She's talking loud and fast. We both need to calm down.

"Let's sip a glass of wine while I finish up." I open the chianti as Beth puts her coat away and fetches the water glasses from the dining room table. "After running a restaurant for forty years, you learn to eyeball when you pour. This is four ounces of wine, the perfect medicine for our hearts." I raise my glass to her, she raises hers to me. "To our health," I say as the rims touch, "and to our happiness."

Ramona's oil lamp barely lights the space between Beth and me as we eat. Since I turned off the fluorescent light in the kitchen, the only other light source is the blue flickering from the TV. Instead of romantic dinner, my mood lighting says power outage.

Beth uses her garlic bread to guide an olive over to a piece of chicken. She spears them with her fork and looks at them a second before she slides the food between her lips. Her eyes close as she chews. I try so hard to focus on something other than Beth's face, in case she looks up, that I barely taste the food. I thought we could talk during our meal, but Beth is having too much fun eating. Instead of trying to think up something to say, I stare at a beige wall. Who lives on the other side? Are they noisy? Do they have a dining room window to bring in some sunshine?

When she puts down her fork, I ask her if she'd like more chicken, another glass of wine.

"No, I better not." She dabs her lips with her napkin. "Doctor Sam suggested I should watch my weight." She pushes her chair away from the table. "Actually, he put it more indelicately than that."

I mumble I think she looks just fine. As I'm thinking *You look beautiful,* I drop my gaze to my plate. Only half of my meal is gone, and I forgot to eat my salad. "You sit still," I tell her. "Cleaning is my job." If I get the table cleared, maybe she won't notice I didn't eat. Beth settles back in her chair and refolds her napkin so the lipstick stain is hidden.

"I brought a loaf of zucchini bread," I say over my shoulder, as I scrape the last of my meal into the trash can. I flick on the fluorescent light and walk back to the table to blow out the oil lamp. Citronella replaces the scent of my chicken and garlic bread. In the dark room, Beth looks small and soft and alone. I walk to her but instead of touching her, my hands reach for her chair. "Let's have some dessert," I say pulling her chair to me as she rises, "if you think Doctor Sam wouldn't mind."

"You know how to make zucchini bread?" Beth follows me back to the kitchen. Her face glows in the brightness.

"Well, sure. It's not hard. I can write down the recipe for you."

"In my wildest imaginings I can't envision baking." Beth opens a cabinet and pulls out two plates. "But I'll make us a pot of coffee. I do know how to cook that."

I cut the zucchini bread and Beth holds the plates for me. She smells like fresh sheets pulled from the dryer. When our hips bump together as she fills the coffee pot with tap water, she giggles. "This kitchen wasn't made for two cooks," she says. The coffee pot gurgles. I'm on a date and the lady is enjoying being with me. At least she enjoys my cooking. She'll like this bread. I used a touch of cocoa and a lot of cinnamon. Maybe next time I'll bake us a pie.

The idea of next time stops me cold. I guess it's up to me to figure it out. I'll need to talk to her about where and when and how before I drive home tonight. "Just play it by ear, Michael," I whisper to myself.

"I beg your pardon?" Beth says.

"Oh, nothing," I say. "I was just wondering if I could bake you a pie some time?"

"That would be grand," she says.

As we carry our dessert to the living room, my nerves creep back. In the center of the room is a brown tweedy couch and chair—should I sit on the couch or should I sit in the chair? Neither look comfortable. On the coffee table is a stack of magazines and travel books, a crossword book with a pen sticking out of it. Maybe Beth was doing the puzzle this afternoon before she got dressed up for our date? Was she feeling nervous too?

Beth sits in the chair, legs together, feet flat on the carpet. One hand pushes her curls into a straight line across her forehead, the other hand reaches for her coffee. I sit on the couch, at the end close to her. Our seating arrangement is finalized. "I thought the music on the Centerburg channel was pretty," I say, "but we can turn it off. Or maybe watch something else."

"I don't watch television much in the evenings," she says.

"How do you like to spend your time?" I hope I'm not being too nosy.

She shrugs her shoulders and looks into the coffee cup. "I don't know," she says. "I have no idea what I do now that I'm retired." She looks at the zucchini bread like she forgot it was there, cuts a corner off with her fork, takes a bite of bread, then another.

"I been wondering the same thing," I say. "When I quit running the restaurant to take care of Evelyn, every minute was busy, but now, I don't know . . . I'm kind of on hold, waiting until Doc Sam says I can go back to Des Plaines."

Beth glances up, startled. "When do you think that will be?"

"If my daughter gets her way, never." I slide my coffee cup away from the stack of travel books to avoid a sip. "I feel like I'm floating here, with no anchor. I need to set my feet back down in my house."

"I can imagine how you feel," she says. "But still, it's nice your daughter wants you with her."

"Ramona is great. My son Mike, he's top notch too." The couch is hard and scratchy. I lean against the armrest. "I can't take credit though," I say. "Evelyn raised them right." I make a note not to say Evelyn's name again for the rest of the evening.

The Centerburg channel is scrolling through the dates for a musical performed by the local theatre group, an announcement for a chili supper at the Lutheran Church. The music is some generic theme from *Mash*. I ask Beth about teaching and the travel books on her table. She asks me about my heart attack, and I ask her about hers. Our medical war stories. She says she likes my zucchini bread. "Chocolate is a wonderful condiment for vegetables," she says. I tell her she makes a good pot of coffee. She laughs.

When the phone screams from the end table, Beth jumps, grabs the receiver, puts her hand over the mouthpiece. "Michael, I'm sorry. I imagine this is my friend Clarice and she'll call the police if I don't answer."

"Hello?" Beth eyes widen. "Oh, Kathy, I didn't think this would be you. Isn't it late there? Is anything wrong?"

Beth lowers her voice, bows her head. I pick up our coffee cups and dessert plates and carry them back to her kitchen. By the time she hangs up, I've got our dishes rinsed, the counters cleared, and all my pots and pans stacked in my cardboard box. Should I just come right out and ask her about a second date? I march back to the living room.

She's sitting in her chair, her hands in her lap, eyes staring toward something only she can see. She looks at me and smiles a weak little smile, making me want to hold her in my arms. Instead, I sit back down on the stiff couch.

"Anything wrong?"

"Not really," she says. "That was my daughter. She's fine." Her hands hug her shoulders, her body curls inward.

"I didn't know you had kids," I tell her. "I'm sorry I didn't ask. How many children do you have?"

"Only Kathy," she says. "She lives in London." Beth looks past me, then down to her lap. "I usually talk to her every Sunday, but she's going to Edinburgh for a lecture, so she called tonight instead. She wanted to discuss Christmas plans." Beth looks at the silent phone. "I don't know what to tell her."

"It must be hard, not having her closer," I say.

"She wouldn't be closer if she lived next door," Beth says. She lifts her head and forces a smile to her face. "So, when are you going to bake us a pie?"

CHAPTER 5

✴

Beth

I need to avoid drinking coffee before I go to bed. Or if I do drink coffee, I need to avoid life upheavals before bed. The combination makes me churn all night, twisting my flannel gown and punching my pillow. I time my sleeplessness on my bedside clock—12:15, 1:34, 2:22, 3:08. My brain grinds with irritations, amazements, resentments. A perfectly lovely evening with a perfectly lovely gentleman sandwiched between a four-minute confrontation with Shirley Eubanks in the wine aisle of a liquor store and a five-minute telephone conversation with my distant daughter.

My parents were teetotalers, probably because both my grandfathers enjoyed alcohol a bit too much. Nothing was ever said, just a parental raised eyebrow or pursed lips whenever alcohol was seen or discussed. So, an aura of sin had me feeling at risk even before I walked into the neon glare of G and F Liquor in search of wine for Michael's dinner. The owner was restocking the whiskey shelves, and I asked, as discreetly as I could, for advice on wine for an upcoming meal prepared by an unspecified person. Due to my vagueness, I ended up with four bottles of wine.

I am not opposed to drinking. I am opposed to how expensive wine is. I was mentally doing the math when someone tapped me on the shoulder. I spun around to see Shirley

Eubank. In her hand was a tiny bottle of Crème de menthe.

Shirley looked in my cart. "Are you having a party?" she asked, raising her right eyebrow and pursing her lips.

"No, I'm planning on drinking all of this myself," I told her.

In my brief moments of sleep, I dream in fits and spurts. Budweiser in neon, my dining room in candlelight. Michael emerging from dark corners, concerned and nervous. Zucchini morphing into moist cinnamon cakes. Wine bottles crashing, telephones screaming, my house an old-fashioned pizzeria, with too many customers and only myself, as waitress and chef.

I jolt awake, remembering Kathy's call. She'd sounded tense when she'd told me about her upcoming business trip to Edinburg. She'd asked me about my diet, instead of inquiring about my health. As I listened, pots were clanking, water running, my refrigerator door opening and closing as Michael cleaned up all traces of our evening.

"Is everything alright there?" I asked Kathy, hoping to sound concerned instead of confrontational.

"We have some news," she said. "We're going to be married in December." Her voice sounded more triumphant than joyous.

Why didn't I say, *How wonderful. I'm thrilled for you. I know you two will be so happy together?* Why did I say, *Married? You and Zoe?*

"Yes, Mother, *married*." Kathy's tone had turned to ice.

There was a slight hesitation before she said, "The atmosphere here for same-sex marriage is much more progressive than in the States, as you can imagine."

My mind was swimming with scenes from CNN. Mass same sex marriage ceremonies, two brides in white gowns, being interviewed, as couples of two grooms kissed in the background. Michael carried his cardboard box to my front door, set it down, returned to the kitchen.

"Will it be a big ceremony?" I asked.

"Just Zoe and me, and possibly a few friends, and you are invited, of course."

"Oh, thank you, honey."

My ear ached from the phone clamped against it. I switched it to my other ear, closed my eyes. Zoe murmured something. "Well then, you speak with her," I heard Kathy say. More muffled whispers, a cell phone slapping from hand to hand.

"Beth, I know this is all a bit of a shock." Zoe's soothing voice replaced Kathy's. "I'm so sorry we've sprung this on you this way, but we both would so love for you to attend. Perhaps you could stay over for the Christmas holidays as well?" She paused. I said nothing. "It's been years since we were able to entertain you in our home. Just think about it and Kate will ring you next week after you have a chance to digest all this."

Before I'd said one word, Kathy was speaking again. "We'll be in touch. It's horribly late and I've yet to pack."

"Have a nice trip," I whispered. "I love you."

"I love you too, Mum."

I looked up to see Michael walking to me, coat on. On his face I saw all the bewilderment I was feeling.

In between replaying last night's conversations, watching the clock, and battling my bedclothes, I agonize over future decisions. Should I consider going? Is it called a wedding? Will it be in a church? Can I book a flight over the holidays? Will Doctor Sam say I'm healthy enough to fly, and if so, will a ticket cost a thousand dollars? And Michael! At my age . . . dating? The word conjures up impossible, embarrassing scenarios. Michael and me at the Illinois Theater with the entire audience watching us instead of the movie, or worse, at a high school basketball game, like he mentioned last night. Good grief, the only thing worse would be attending a church service together. What am I looking for? Companionship, a romantic encounter, sex? None of the above, that's exactly what I need. Michael is in mourn-ing. He's homesick and lonely. The moment I decide I enjoy his company, he'll be moving back to Des Plaines. Then Shirley Eubank can make her town report. "He's left her. She's heartbroken, but what could she expect, acting like a teenager, at her age? And it's not like this has never hap-pened to her before. By the way, did you hear her daughter's a lesbian?"

I wake with a jolt at 7:15. I must have fallen asleep for a few hours, but I'm not exactly refreshed. I should get up, get ready for my exercise class. Maybe a warm shower will ease me into the morning. My head flops back onto my pillow. I close my eyes and picture Michael standing in my doorway, after he'd hauled his boxful of cooking supplies back to his car. "You have Ramona's number," he said. "Call me and let me know when I should bake us that pie."

It was an awkward parting. We both wanted to say more. Michael took my hand between his and said, "I had a nice evening, Beth."

"Thank you, Michael, so did I," was the only thing I had the energy to say.

My morning shower just gets me wet, not energized. And it certainly doesn't defog my mind or lift my spir-its. I'm not one for dwelling on problems. Usually I solve them quickly or push them aside and get on with my life. One can't be mopey when there's a classroom full of nine-year-olds anxiously awaiting a spelling test. And I don't discuss my troubles. All these therapies and soul-searchings and support groups are tedious. Depression and serotonin uptake inhibitors and seasonal mood swings are not for me. Doctor Sam told me, "It's very common to feel depressed after a heart attack. Let me know and I can prescribe a mild anti-depressant."

"Sure, and how much will those cost?" I wanted to say. "It's life. I'll deal with it."

So it surprises me some when, instead of pulling on my exercise clothes and walking out my door to drive to Rehab, I walk over to my phone and call Clarice.

My doorbell rings fifteen minutes after I call her. I put a last slice of zucchini bread on a platter, turn on my coffee pot, and open the door to a fashionable female Sherlock Holmes—black and white herringbone cape, matching cap, black wool pants tucked into the new, overpriced leather boots she bought on our last shopping trip to St. Louis. Over her shoulder, a huge red bag, in her right hand, as usual, her cell phone.

"OK, what's up?" Clarice bustles in, plants a quick kiss on my cheek and steps back to give me a worried look.

"Good morning," I say.

She swoops into my kitchen, amidst a cloud of *L'air du Temps*, her daughter-in-law's standard Christmas gift. The perfume erases every last scent of Michael's cooking.

"What is this, banana bread?" Clarice zeros in on the platter. "It looks homemade."

I hand her the platter. "Let's have some."

The coffee pot begins to spurt and splatter, and Clarice helps me carry our snack to the living room. Avoiding eye contact, I place a napkin and fork to the left of each plate, as she drapes her cape on my couch and drops her bag on top.

"A mystery phone call and homemade bakery items, what's going on here?" She sits on the edge of the couch, ready to spring. "You're not feeling sick again, are you? Your eyes are puffy."

"I didn't sleep well last night." I begin with a tiny truth.

Her cell phone chirps. She frowns, pushes a button, then abandons it to the top of my pile of library books. She pinches a corner off the top slice on the platter and pops it in her mouth. "My, this is wonderful. Where'd you get it?"

"Well, that's one of the reasons I need to talk to you." I take a deep breath. "Michael baked it. He's a man I met at Rehab. We had supper here last night."

From the look on Clarice's face, you'd think I just handed her a thousand dollars.

"You've met a fella!" She raises her hands to the heavens, then points a red fingernail at me. "Oh, my gosh, you *were* holding hands in the hospital cafeteria like Shirley Eubank said." She grabs the rest of the slice of bread and drops it on her plate. "And he can bake!"

"We were not holding hands! Shirley Eubank needs a permanent gag order."

In the kitchen the coffee pot gasps with a final pop of steam. I jump up and flee toward the sound.

The aroma of Folgers seeps through my kitchen. I pour French vanilla creamer into my cup. Clarice takes her coffee black.

"OK, now tell me more," she says as I set cups by our plates and return to my chair.

I watch Clarice take a sip of coffee, her eyes never leaving my face. "There's really nothing to tell." I try for a casual tone. "He's staying with his daughter while he recovers. He seems nice."

"Who's his daughter?" Clarice question jabs into my controlled narrative.

"She's a nurse. Her husband is that new anesthesiologist who moved here a few years ago. Dr. Patel."

"Ramona Patel? She's wonderful! She gave a talk at one of our Red Hat luncheons." Clarice pops another piece of bread in her mouth. I should have just left the fork in my silverware drawer. "Honey, if you'd get out more, you'd know people. So . . ." Clarice settles back against the couch and tucks one leg under her, "you're dating her father. Beth, this is amazing."

"I am not dating her father!" Clarice's listening skills are deplorable. I calm myself by sliding a bite of banana bread between my lips. "That's not why I called you."

"Well, let's have it." Clarice's booted leg swings back and forth, bumping the coffee table. "You aren't pregnant, are you?"

"Stop it, Clarice. You aren't funny," I say. "I'd hate to have to find another best friend."

Clarice flicks her fingers through her salt and pepper hair, fluffing it back to a precise shag. Out back a leaf blower's purr turns to growl as it nears my patio. Mid-morning and the curtains are still closed, my normal routines abandoned.

"Kathy called last night." I stare into the space above my coffee table, trying to find the next sentence. "She's marrying Zoe."

I glance at my friend's face. Her eyes widen the faintest bit. She uncrosses her legs, straightens her back and says, "You like Zoe, don't you?"

I remember Zoe's warm words softening the edginess of Kathy's news. "She's very kind," I say.

The leaf blower roars. I walk to the glass door and pull open the draperies. Full autumn sunshine floods in. The lawn serviceman is whipping fallen leaves into a whirlpool against my patio fence. He waves at me, then swings the blower back and forth until the leaves are herded into a line marching ahead of him. He waves again before he disappears around the fence. I peek into the corner of my patio where a pile of leaves resided all last winter. At the moment, it's clean and tidy.

Clarice joins me and puts an arm around my shoulder as we gaze into the sunny morning. She's a hugger, the only one in my life. Her other hand smooths a fold in the drapes she made me buy. All the sweet touches in my house are hers.

"I'm OK now. I just needed to tell someone," I say. "I'll just think this through and decide what to do."

"Oh no you won't," Clarice drops her arm and faces me. "After I leave, you'll decide to do nothing."

Two steaming cups later, Clarice is dragging it all out of me.

"How do you feel about the wedding?"

"It scares me. It seems like such a difficult life," I say. "I know the situation is different in London, but I can't stand the thought of anyone being mean to her or belittling her."

Clarice nods. The Christmas red ring on her hand matches her red earrings, which match her reading glasses, dangling from a beaded chain around her neck. I have a pair of tiny ruby earrings in a box in my underwear drawer, a gift from Zoe. "I'm so sorry. I'll return them," she'd said when she noticed I didn't have pierced ears. I told her no, I'd always intended to get my ears pierced, her earrings would give me a lovely excuse to have it done. But I never did.

"And this Michael," Clarice asks, "how do you feel about him?"

"It scares me," I say again.

"That's because you're a control freak." Clarice reaches over and puts her hand on mine. "Bless your heart, honey. You've turned two lovely life events into tragedies."

"I know this isn't tragic," I say, "but still, it's a lot to take in, especially if one is a control freak."

From the top of the pile of books, Clarice's cell phone chirps again. "When things got out of hand, my daddy used to say, 'I'm feeling half a bubble off plumb.'" Clarice's father has been dead for about twelve years, but she still gets tears when she talks about him.

"Off plumb, yes, that's how I feel." Off plumb sounds better than completely distraught.

"I think it's fun to be a little off center," says Clarice. "Who wants to be level all the time?" She picks up her cell phone, looks at it, then explains, "I'm supposed to meet the Red Hat group for lunch so we can plan our Christmas party." She taps at her cell with both thumbs. Now that she has my life rearranged, she can text others into submission. "Say, why don't you come along? You should think about joining, now that you have all this free time."

"I still think the Red Hats may be a cult," I say.

"OK, I know how you hate to have fun." Clarice gathers all her personal effects.

"Thanks," I say as we walk to the front door. "I feel better in spite of you calling me a control freak. But you have to promise you won't mention any of this to anyone."

"I promise, but next session we're going to discuss your obsession about What-will-people-think." Clarice hugs me goodbye.

"Oh, by the way," I yell as she walks to her car, "Shirley Eubank may call you to report she spotted me at a liquor store."

"She called last night," Clarice yells back. "I suggested she mind her own business." She blows me a kiss and gets in her car.

As I close my door, I feel the smile sprawl across my face.

Having spent the morning in Clarice Therapy, I decide to skip lunch and haul myself to an early afternoon Rehab class. I may see Michael there, I may not, but I'm feeling I can handle either alternative in a wise and confident manner. Maybe. I'm not quite confident enough to take the Shirley Eubank's Main Lobby entrance to the hospital, but thinking of her phone call to Clarice cheers me as I walk through the side door.

"We were a little worried when we didn't see you this morning," Miss Perky says as I put my name on the treadmill sign-up sheet. "Have you decided to change back to afternoon classes?"

"I think I might," I say. "Would that be all right?"

"Absolutely, just as long as we still get to see you." She gives me her professional smile.

I set the timer for my treadmill, longing for an iPod in my ears. I dread listening to myself think for the next twenty minutes. If I had the ability to clear my mind, I could meditate myself to inner peace, but that's not likely to happen.

Control freak. Clarice is one to talk. Besides, what's wrong with being in control? I certainly prefer self-control to aimlessly buffeting from whim to whim, never knowing where some errant breeze will blow me. Planning and self-discipline make life a lot more manageable. More plumb.

In the eighteen minutes I have left to exercise, I think about Kathy. I should just go. Make the necessary phone calls—Doctor Sam, my insurance company, the airlines. I hate to ask Clarice to drive me to the airport in December. The weather will be so unpredictable. I'll need to arrange transportation on the London side, too. Maybe take that train to Victoria Station, like last time. London subways? Will I be killed in a terrorist attack? That would be annoying, after I'd made all my plans.

Completely lost in a fog of unattainable, swirling To Do's, I'm shocked when my treadmill timer screams, sending me asunder again. To make it worse, just as I step off the treadmill Michael walks into the exercise room, looks straight at me and waves, pushing my bubble completely off plumb.

CHAPTER 6

✳

Michael

This morning we drive south, toward an old-timey restaurant close to a national forest. My car smells of McDonald's coffee and the Jergens lotion Beth has just smoothed on her hands. Beth has researched the restaurant's menu and location and has handwritten directions paper-clipped to the Illinois page of the Atlas wedged beside her seat. In her purse is a crossword puzzle book. On the way home, she'll pull it out and do a puzzle as I drive.

We lose the frequency of the local radio station about thirty miles south of Centerburg. "You want to find us some more music?" I ask.

She takes a sip of her McDonalds coffee, sets it back in the cup holder. "No, let's just listen to the wheels on the highway." She looks out her window at an ancient oil field, pumps still grinding up and down.

I love driving. Beth loves exploring. I can't imagine any-place I'd rather be than here, with Beth, traveling south.

When I'm not with Beth, I worry. Am I taking things too slow or too fast? What do I even mean by *things*? We hold hands, I kiss her on the cheek. I don't have any guidelines for this, except thinking back to when I was eighteen, or when my kids were eighteen. Then Evelyn was the one to put the guidelines on me and later, our kids. Not that they paid much attention to her. On the topic of my kids, Ramona has hinted that she'd love to meet Beth. I'd like that a lot more than Beth would, I think. Dating shouldn't be so complicated, it should be as easy as breathing, as easy as steering a car down a long, welcoming highway.

Leaves crunch under our feet as we walk up the path to a farmhouse turned restaurant. We cozy in at one of the wooden tables in the room that used to be a parlor. A log crackles in a huge brick fireplace, the smell of fresh baked bread and fried chicken is in every room.

The meal is the best we've had since we've been going out. When Beth finishes her last bite of blackberry cobbler, she looks happier than I've ever seen her. Maybe this would be a good time to move forward a little bit. "Too bad this place isn't closer to Centerburg. Then we could eat here every day," I say. "And if it were closer, we could invite Ramona to have lunch with us sometime."

"That would be great for our diets, wouldn't it?" She sips her iced tea. "It's a good thing we have to drive an hour and a half to get here."

On the way home we take the back roads. Autumn colored forests give way to harvested cornfields. I slow down for a red pickup truck turning into a farm driveway. Its driver waves as we pass by. When Beth looks up from her crossword puzzle, I decide to give it another try. "Honey, maybe we could stick a little closer to Centerburg next week." I've been experimenting with calling her *honey*. She doesn't seem to mind. "Lucas has a home game on Friday. You could come over to Ramona's first and I'll fix us all supper."

Beth closes her puzzle book, sighs, and looks at me. "Oh, Michael, I really don't want to impose on a family event. And Ramona will have enough to do, getting everyone to the game." She reaches over and pats my hand. "Thank you anyway, darling. It's sweet of you to ask."

Darling! I forget to be disappointed about her No. *One step at a time, Michael,* I tell myself.

•

The house is Sunday-morning quiet. I arrange my breakfast stuff on the table—Honey Oat Cheerios, a banana, bowl, milk, spoon. Ramona and Ravi are off jogging somewhere, Lucas is probably in bed. To keep me from being by myself, my dog Sunny pads into the kitchen and plops down by my feet. He knows he'll get the milk when I'm finished.

Mike and his wife Libby decided I needed a dog after Evelyn died so they brought me Sunny. He was about a year old and living at some golden retriever adoption agency for unmanageable dogs. The young couple who owned him worked all the time, I guess, and left him alone, so he'd chew all their furniture. He wanted some company, and so did I, even though I didn't think so at the time. He's never chewed anything of mine, not since I got him. He doesn't have to panic when I'm gone. He trusts me. He knows I'll be back.

Just as I pour the milk on my cereal, the phone rings. I reach across the table to grab it. My son calls most Sunday mornings, right before he leaves to open the restaurant. Neither of my kids go to church anymore. I don't blame them. I haven't set a good example.

"Morning, Pop. What's going on there?"

"Oh, not much," I say with a chuckle. He tells me about work, a busy week since the weather's cool, he thinks.

"Pop," he says. "Are you ever coming home?"

"I know I should be heading back," I tell him.

I'm starting to dread the thought of moving back. Still, it's home. I can't stay here with Ramona for the rest of my life, sleeping in the guest room. Mike's got to be tired of caring for two houses. It took him three days to rake my leaves and get them bagged up. He's getting my mail and paying my bills and making sure the furnace is running, so my pipes don't freeze. My whole living situation is a mess, so why do I feel so blasted happy? Beth St. Clair, that's why.

When Lucas walks into the kitchen, Sunny jumps up,

tail wagging. Lucas wrestles with him for a few minutes, grabs some orange juice, and heads to the basement to play computer games. Sunny looks at me, asking if it's okay to follow.

"Go on with your buddy," I tell him and turn my attention back to Mike.

"Let me talk to your sister," I say. "She may be about ready to throw me out of here."

"I doubt that," Mike says. "She'll be mad at me for asking you to come home."

Purple sweet gum leaves fall outside the kitchen window. The tree's almost bare. To keep everything tidy, Ramona has a yard service come once a week. I haven't raked one leaf this fall.

"I sure do appreciate all you kids are doing for me," I say.

"No problem," Mike says. "The thing is, it's Emma's birthday on the twenty-third and with Thanksgiving and all, well, we were hoping you'd be here with us. Emma's never had a birthday party without her grandpa, and this is an important one. Thirteen. Can you believe she's going to be a teenager?"

Emma is my darling. Evelyn practically raised her. Libby was putting in fifty or sixty hours a week at United Airlines, back when Emma was a toddler. The hours were just about the same for Mike, working with me at the restaurant. As she was growing up, Emma was at our house more than she was at hers. If anybody could get me back to Des Plaines, it would be her.

"You tell Emma I'll be there," I say. "Put me down for a birthday cake and a lasagna." I glance at the oak cabinets lining the kitchen wall. No chance Ramona would own a quarter sheet baking pan. To make Emma's favorite meal, I'll need to be back in my own kitchen.

"I suppose my oven still works?"

"I'll check it, next time I'm over there. But why don't you plan on staying here with us for a while?"

"Oh, I don't know about that." Staying with Mike wouldn't feel like home any more than being here with Ramona does.

"And I was thinking, I could come down and get you, so you don't have to drive by yourself." Mike's next words sound like he's practiced saying them. "We could plan for a Monday. Business is slow and my new guy could run the place for the day, I'm pretty sure. What is it from here to Centerburg? Five hours?"

"About that." My cereal has turned soggy. I lay my spoon down. "But driving down here's too much trouble. And I'd want to have my car."

"Do you think you're up to driving for five hours?"

Now doesn't this beat all. I can't even get back to my own house without everybody thinking they need to help. "Hell, yes, I can drive for five hours by myself. I'm not an invalid." The words fly out before I can halt them.

"I'm sorry, Pop."

I'm more hurt than angry. Do my kids really think I can't take care of myself anymore? Has my life changed even more than I thought? One thing I do know, I never plan to take my anger out on my kids.

"Don't you pay any attention to me, Son. I'm sorry!" I say. "I know you're worried about your old man. Let me think it over. I promise I'll be there for Emma's birthday."

"Just let me know how I can help." Mike sounds like my son again. "And tell Ramona not to be mad at me for trying to steal you away for a while."

"I can handle Ramona," I say, knowing I can't. "Give my love to Libby and Emma. Thank you, Son."

Sunny wanders back in the kitchen as I'm finishing the last of my soggy cereal, so I set the bowl of leftover milk on the floor for him. There have been plenty of times, over the last few years, when Cheerios got me through some rough spots.

Evelyn practically lived on cereal until she started thinking I was poisoning her.

"Well Sunny," I say. "Do you think we should be heading back home?"

Sunny looks at me before he starts slurping his milk. He's already home, just as long as he's with me.

I picture myself, all alone, driving north to Des Plaines, then walking into the big empty space that used to be my home. A hard sadness settles in my stomach. Maybe Mike is right, maybe I can't make this trip alone.

As I clear off the table a tiny spark of a plan comes to me—Beth. Is there any chance?

I spend the next hour trying to wind through a maze of problems. Would Beth even consider going to Mike's house for Thanksgiving when she won't drive across town for a bowl of chili here at Ramona's? Has Ramona told Mike about Beth? Do they both think I'm acting like a lovesick old fool? Is that why Mike wants to get me back home? *She called you Darling, Michael.* The knot in my gut eases a little when I remember driving south, into a crisp, brilliant fall day, Beth sitting at my side. If there's any chance she'll drive north, into the heart of my family, I'll need to ask. Even if she says No, she might call me *Darling* again.

I'm all ready to make the phone call when it occurs to me Ramona will be broken-hearted if I ask Beth for Thanksgiving in Des Plaines before she and Beth have met. And I put myself right back in the middle of my maze.

Sunny needs to go out, so I slip on my jacket. As I watch him race around the back yard, I put my hands in my pockets, lean against the trunk of the sweet gum tree, and slide back into my worries.

"Are you OK, Daddy?"

Ramona and Ravi are standing behind me, sweaty and vibrating with energy from their jog. "I'm fine," I tell her. "I didn't hear you. Sorry. I just got caught up in my thoughts."

My wise daughter stares at me for five seconds, then says, "Let's take Sunny for a walk."

As we walk, Ramona listens. She says *Aw, how nice* when I tell her Beth called me *Darling*. She chuckles when I tell her Mike is afraid that he'll make her mad. As we turn the corner on the way back home, Ramona says, "Whatever you decide to do will be perfect."

As Beth and I are talking on the phone a few days later, I give it one last try. "I know you think it will be too much bother," I say, "but I'd really like you to meet my family. Chili is easy, or we could just have hot dogs. You can come over early and help me cook." I hear her laugh a little—a good sign. "And if you'd like to see my grandson's game, we don't have to go with Ravi and Ramona. We can drive separately and leave any time. It won't be any trouble for anybody, but I'll understand if you don't want to come."

Perfect. I've said everything I wanted to say. Whatever Beth says next will be perfect, too. It takes her a few seconds to respond. I hear a soft sign, I picture her shoulders falling, then straighten as she takes a deep breath.

"Darling, that all sounds lovely," she says. "Everything except the part about helping you cook."

Driving three hundred miles to Des Plaines would be easier than herding Ramona's family together for a meal with Beth. This morning Ramona reminded Lucas to come home right after school. "Do not slip away to McD's with your friends and forget about it!" Ravi heard her and said, "Is that tonight?" She groaned and announced to the room, "I better see both of you in this kitchen tonight at six o'clock."

While I cook, Ramona sets the kitchen table. A meal in the dining room is too formal, we decided, and besides, Ramona said it would take her hours to clear the papers and mail and sports equipment off the table.

Her cell rings at 4:15. "OK, no, that's fine," she says. "You don't have to put him on the phone, I believe you. See you at the game." She punches a button and puts the cell on the counter. Ramona turns to me, laughing. "Lucas has to be at a Pep Rally after school and his coach wants all the players to stay there until the game." She walks to the table and removes one place setting. "He wanted his coach to ask me if it was OK for him to miss our supper. Isn't that cute?" She laughs again. "I like it that my son is a little afraid of me."

My chili is on simmer and the cherry pie is cooling on the counter. When Beth sees it, she'll know it is my special thank you to her for coming over. I'm putting on my coat to leave for Beth's house when Ramona's cell rings again. "Oh, no!" She listens for a few more seconds. "Thank you. I understand. Tell him to come when he can." She turns to me. "Ravi has to assist with an emergency surgery, an appendectomy. He remembered he was supposed to be home early and asked a volunteer to call me right before he started to scrub up." She smiles and shakes her head. "Well, we almost had a little dinner party!" She's rearranging the table for three as I leave to get Beth.

I eat my chili and marvel at the women in my life. Beth walked into our kitchen, hugged Ramona, then burst out laughing when she spied the pie on the counter. "Your father has been promising me a cherry pie since the day I met him," she said. I serve as Ramona and Beth settle at the table, as easy as two friends meeting for a meal to catch up on each other's lives. Ramona tells Beth she thinks teaching must be the hardest job in the world, and the most important. "Just think of all the lives you've helped to shape."

Ramona explains her doula job to Beth. Beth says she wished she had someone like Ramona with her when Kathy was born. "I felt so alone, so isolated, at a time that should have been so special," Beth says. "And men had control of it all."

"They still do," says Ramona.

Beth and I huddle in the center of the Centerburg basketball fans. I was glad for my coat as we crossed the parking lot and lumbered up the sidewalk to the doors of the gymnasium, but now I'm pinned in its bulky heat as we stand shoulder to shoulder waiting to file into the gym. Sweat trickles down my forehead. I'd take off my coat if I could move my arms. I can smell the popcorn from the prom fundraiser booth tucked against a sidewall and hear the shrieks of teenagers greeting other teenagers. Beside me Beth is clutching her purse. She looks up at me and smiles a brave smile. She's doing this all for me.

Following some prearranged schedule, the doors to the gym open and our herd begins a slow migration. I try to match my steps to the crowd so I don't get trampled. Every few paces, someone shouts "Mrs. Patel, Hi!" or "Hello Ramona!" A young woman in a puffy pink ski jacket inches over, trying to talk to Ramona over the din. "Call me any-time," Ramona yells, before the woman fades back into the crowd.

The gymnasium smells like a week's worth of boys' Physical Education classes and a quick Friday afternoon pine-scented floor mopping. Both teams are shooting prac-tice baskets as Ramona leads us to our seats in the middle of the home section and Ravi veers off to get us popcorn. On the floor, Lucas takes a shot, makes the basket, looks up at us, and waves.

As Ravi, Beth, and I munch popcorn, Ramona chats with a constant flow of people on the way to their seats. A woman thanks her *for making all those phone calls*. "She's the high school principal," Beth tells me. A man thanks her for helping with a fundraiser. "He's the mayor," Beth whispers.

The band plays the National Anthem. I feel so bad for Ravi and Beth. Ravi's new here, but Beth's lived here her entire life. No one seems to know either one of them. When we sit back down, I whisper to Beth, "Honey, I'm sorry Ramona is getting all the attention."

"I know," Beth gleams. "Isn't it wonderful!"

CHAPTER 7

※

Beth

It takes Clarice five weeks to wheedle and coerce me. "When will you let us meet him?" she asks daily, sometimes twice daily, if I'm home to answer her newly instituted evening phone calls. Michael's tactic for introducing me to his family was thoughtful and subtle. I try the direct approach.

"Michael," I say, "my best friend Clarice needs to inspect you, and I can't hold her off any longer. Do you want to have dinner at their house?"

I know Michael would be happy to meet my friends. I'm the one struggling. I don't even know how to name what we're doing. *Dating* or *seeing someone* sounds so purposeful, so results-oriented. Michael and I just *occupy the same space* occasionally, at a movie or in a restaurant. And not at a Centerburg movie or restaurant either, although spending the evening with Ramona and her family was pleasant. We didn't run into Shirley Eubank or her ilk, and all eyes were on Lucas or his mother. Still, I feel so much happier sitting in Michael's car, driving away from Centerburg.

We arrive at Clarice and Jim's house with a bottle of wine and an apple pie, warm from Michael's oven.

"I had to bake a pie for Ramona too," Michael says as

we take our hostess gifts out of his car trunk. "She's jealous. She says I'm taking all the good stuff to my lady friend's house, and she doesn't get to eat her poppa's cooking anymore."

I'm not sure I like the sound of *lady friend*. It makes me feel old and plump.

"Do you want me to carry that?" I ask Michael. "I know you have difficulty with wine and sidewalks."

He chuckles, hands me the bottle, and plants a quick kiss on my cheek. He's just being friendly. He's Italian. They do that. But I hope Clarice isn't looking out the window.

Clarice and Jim's home is circa 1950s, like all the ranch style houses on this street. I've been here hundreds of times, but quivers race through my stomach as we walk up the sidewalk. Clarice flings open her door the instant Michael's finger touches the doorbell and, ignoring me, screams, "Michael, I'm so happy to meet you!" She gasps over the pie, grabs his arm, and practically carries him into her living room while I close her door and shift the wine from hand to hand as I peel off my coat. Apparently, Clarice is nervous too.

"Pleased to meet you, Clarice. Thanks for asking us over." Michael hands her the pie, turns to me. "Let me get that for you," he says, taking the wine and helping me with my coat. "You have a nice place here," he says over his shoulder.

"Oh, thank you. It's a work in progress." Clarice's voice is decibels higher than normal.

"We just put in new carpet but now I hate this wallpaper," she says flinging her arm Vanna White style, toward the burgundy and mint stripes behind her forest green couch. "We aren't in this room that much, luckily."

Clarice has been tearing down and sprucing up since she and Jim bought this house thirty-odd years ago. Clarice is the type of person who repaints bedrooms to relax.

"Jim, we have company," Clarice yells toward the kitchen. Even with my limited decorating enthusiasm, I love walking into Clarice and Jim's kitchen. Autumn afternoon sunshine floods through a wall of windows behind the dining room table.

Silver-veined granite, open shelves displaying stacks of white plates and bowls, stainless steel everywhere—I can see why that living room wallpaper has to go. Jim is standing at the island, a beer in one hand, sprinkling something over a huge platter of steaks. When he sees us, he wipes his hands on his corduroys, and bounds to Michael.

"Welcome, welcome," Jim is taller and stockier but both men have the same ready, wide-open smile. "Glad you could come over." He gives me a hug and shakes Michael's hand. "I hear you're a chef. I may need your expertise with these steaks."

"I'm just a short order cook, but I'd be glad to help."

Clarice is spinning around the room, side-swiping Jim as she races from refrigerator to island with a pitcher of iced tea and a bowl of lemon slices. She plucks four wine glasses from a shelf of stemware, opens one drawer, slams it shut, opens another. "Where's the wine opener?" she says to the silverware drawer. Jim ignores her.

"Let's get a drink and we'll throw these steaks on the grill," Jim claps Michael on the shoulder. "Wine, beer, something stronger? I think we have the fixings for a martini."

"A beer would be great," Michael says. Clarice sets the wine glasses back on her shelf.

As soon as the men leave for the patio, Clarice slides into a stool at the island and pours two glasses of tea. "I'm a wreck," she says, resting her forearms on the cool granite. "Jim is so angry with me for meddling. I told him you expected me to meddle." She rakes her fingers through her hair. Every strand falls back into place. "You aren't mad at me too, are you?" She grabs my wrist. Her fingers are cold and wet. "I just wanted to meet Michael so much."

"Of course I'm not mad." I pat her hand.

Clarice looks over her shoulder to the patio. "He's very

nice looking. Did I see him kiss you? Never mind, it's none of my business. Are steaks OK?"

"I'm sure he'll eat anything you put on his plate." I squeeze a lemon slice into my glass.

Clarice picks up the pitcher and her glass. "Let's sit at the kitchen table so we can spy on them."

The sun lowers, the shadows lengthen. We watch them talking and laughing, drinking beers, flipping steaks. Jim waves at us, points to his watch, and takes the steaks off the grill. Michael carries in the sizzling platter. A bowl of salad is pulled from the refrigerator, a baked potato is placed on each plate. Clarice waves us toward the table. Michael pulls out the chair for me, then does the same for Clarice.

"Oh, no," Jim tells him. "Just when I was starting to like you, you go and spoil all the women in my life."

"Steaks are great," we say as we eat. "Can't wait for dessert." "Another beer?" Clarice teases Jim and he winks at her. All is forgiven.

A thud jars the glass behind us. I jump. All four of us look to the window, where a confused female cardinal has hit the glass and lies motionless on the patio cement. Clarice points at Jim with her fork. "I keep telling you we have to hang something there, so those birds can tell it's glass."

Michael pushes back his chair, gets up and walks through the kitchen. I hear the back door open, then shut. And there is Michael, standing by Jim's grill, then kneeling by the bird, his lips moving with soothing words I can't hear. Michael is motionless as he and the injured bird assess each other. *Please let her be OK, for Michael's sake.* We watch the cardinal totter up on her little bird legs. Her eyes are wide open, her throat is quivering, she will survive. The cardinal flutter-walks down the length of the brick wall and when she comes to the three steps leading into the yard, she flies down into the safety of the evergreen hedge.

In two minutes, Michael is back at the table. "She can fly. I think she'll be all right."

"Was the male in the yard?" Clarice asks.

"He was probably afraid to come out," says Jim. "The whole thing was probably his fault."

"Right," Clarice says, "and besides, now she has a headache, so he won't have any fun tonight."

We laugh. Clarice and Jim's steaks are almost gone. Michael's is only half eaten, but now he picks up his knife and fork, and turns his concentration to his meal. My steak is barely touched. Clarice will have a fit later, as we clear the table, but I know she'll let me take it home to finish tomorrow. Jim starts talking about golf. Instead of eating, I dig around the inside of my baked potato as a warmth settles in my stomach, more filling than a steak dinner.

It occurs to me, in years to come, I just might remember this as the moment I fell in love with Michael Bartoli.

In the backseat of Michael's car is my carry-on suitcase and my birthday present to Emma—a set of colored pencils and drawing pad. In the trunk is everything else Michael deems necessary for a thirteen-year-old's birthday party and a family Thanksgiving dinner. After an evening with Ramona's family and a dinner party with Clarice and Jim, we are making the final stop of our Integrate with Family and Friends Tour. Surprisingly, I've enjoyed every moment. Not surprisingly, so has Michael.

My stomach starts to rumble, as the smell of lasagna drifts through the car. I try to quell it with a large sip of coffee. Michael turns to me, his face gentle and relaxed. I think he's happiest when he's driving.

"It was sure nice of Clarice to loan me her lasagna dish and sheet pans," Michael says. "Was she upset when you told her you wouldn't be at her house for Thanksgiving?"

"Heavens no, she was thrilled," I laugh. "I think she's more excited about our Thanksgiving trip than we are."

I didn't say that well. Michael takes my words so seriously.

"I'm teasing, honey," I try to explain. "I'm so looking forward to meeting Mike and Libby. And Emma. You know Clarice is relishing in our . . . friendship." Michael winces just a tiny bit. "Clarice thinks you're wonderful." I pat his gloved hand. "And so do I." Michael beams.

"Clarice is a good friend," he says.

As we passed in Mike and Libby's hallway this morning, Michael whispered, "I'll take you to lunch, just the two of us, before we drive back to Centerburg." Everyone else was either working or Black Friday shopping, and I was relieved that today I didn't have to meet a single new person. Now here he is, bringing me a tray brimming with food. Pride creases the corners of his blue eyes, which are shining brighter than the neon of the Order Here counter.

We dine alone in the back booth of Mike's Chicago Dogs. *Let's Twist Again* plays on the juke box. Black and white tiled floor, Formica-topped tables, a dozen booths filling fast with shoppers and kids on Thanksgiving break. Michael and I work quietly arranging the feast—Cokes to the right, a basket of French fries in the center, and sitting in front of each of us, the main attraction, smelling of mustard and onions, topped with tomatoes and shining with pickle relish. Chicago hotdogs.

Michael puts a napkin in his lap. "Before we eat, there's something I need to ask you." He's serious, a little fearful.

My hand stops midair, as it reaches for my Coke. "I don't have to think up another Thankfulness, do I?" I ask.

Instead of a prayer, we twelve guests at Mike and Libby's Thanksgiving dinner took turns saying something we were thankful for. Libby's mom was thankful for family and health, and Mike and Libby's neighbors said *good food and good friendships*. Libby said she was thankful she'd only burned the rolls instead of the turkey. Michael looked like he was going to cry when Emma said she was thankful her grandpa came to her birthday party. Mike was thankful the Bears game was on at eight p.m. instead of during our midday meal. "I'll drink to that!" Libby's dad said, holding up his bottle of Bud Light.

When it was my turn, I said, "Since Michael and I both decided to have heart attacks, I'm thankful they occurred at the same time, in the same town." Then I reached under the table to hold Michael's hand.

He chuckles and relaxes. "Nothing like that. Mike and Libby are cooking up a plan." I sip my Coke. Soda in a tall glass always tastes colder, fresher, more sparkling. "The kids have been after me to come home for Christmas, stay with them for a while." Michael looks at the basket of fries instead of me. "But after meeting you, Mike told me he understands why I've been dragging my feet on coming back."

His shy little glance at me melts my heart. I sample a French fry.

"So last night Mike asked if we'd both like to spend Christmas in Des Plaines, I told him probably not, since your daughter wants you to go to London."

Behind Michael's words I hear Elvis pleading about his blue suede shoes. The big debate as a teenage girl, Elvis or Ricky Nelson? I always chose Ozzie and Harriet's son over loose-limbed, hip-gyrating Elvis. "Oh Michael, I'm probably not going to London," I confess. "I should have already made arrangements, but it's so expensive. And the weather . . . " My excuses sound as vague as they did last Sunday when I said the same words to Kathy.

"You haven't bought an airline ticket yet?" Michael seems unexpectedly thrilled.

After I tell him I haven't even called the airlines to check availability, a fact I'd neglected to mention to Kathy, Michael launches into The Plan. Since Libby works at United, she can arrange everything—finding flights, booking hotels, two stand-by tickets out of O'Hare, free-free-free. Michael pauses, breathless then troubled. "You might not want me to go to London with you. I'm sorry. I'm assuming too much."

At the next table, an older couple is finishing their lunch. The husband stacks the empty plates and bowls and utensils in the center of the table, then takes a napkin and wipes up every crumb. They ate their meal without conversation, all their needs and desires silently assumed. Watching them, I want to cry with longing.

"What a lovely, generous gift," I say. I'm immediately overwhelmed by all the words I'll have to say—the reason for this trip, my reluctance, my fears and hopes. My next words may bring an ending, or maybe a beginning. "Michael, there's something I need to tell you about this trip to London."

Michael holds my gaze, his hand rests on mine, and I say the words. When I'm finished, he says, "I don't think folks need to be telling other folks who to love and who not to love. This sorry old world needs all the love people can muster up. Let's go help Kathy and Zoe celebrate."

I should feel cozier, stretched out on my couch in my new easy-care, easy-wear workout clothes. Within reach, I have a cup of hot tea and a plate of cheese and crackers, but my living room is still cold and dark and silent. I'm avoiding the call. I've already unpacked and laundered, cleaned a bathroom, made a grocery list. I've located my passport in the bottom drawer of my desk, in case Kathy OK's this new plan. I get up and open the curtains, flooding the room with more grey.

Michael has succeeded in integrating me into his family. The task of merging my family and Michael won't be as effortless or rewarding. Michael called an hour ago. "Do you want to go out for breakfast?" he'd asked, anticipating I'd say no. He knows my Sunday morning ritual of awkward mother-daughter telephone conversations. This morning, I'll say sentences brimming with new names, places, emotions. Like me—maybe because of me—Kathy has little experience with the overwhelming love and generosity of family.

•

Please don't answer. Please let your voice mail record my speech.

"Hello Mum," my daughter says after five rings. "You're calling fifteen minutes late."

Kathy's mocking carries no affection. Her barb gives me a little rush of courage. *Your Mum isn't quite as inflexible and boring as you think, Young Lady.*

Kathy fills the first few moments with safe trivia. She and Zoe walked through fog to get a coffee, made some phone calls, watched a splendid documentary about . . . .

"Honey, I have a little news." I say into the first lull of dialogue. "If I'm still invited, we've made plans to come to your wedding, and if it's all right, to stay over until Christmas morning."

"We?" Kathy picks out the important word.

Beside my phone is a blue index card with a list of facts and questions I've prepared for this call. I take a deep breath and forge ahead. "I've found a friend who can accompany me. His name is Michael Bartoli. You don't know him."

Instead of rapid-fire questions, Kathy fills my phone with silence. I'd allow her a few moments to adjust to my news, but this is an overseas rate.

"I can't give you an exact flight or arrival time, we'll be flying stand-by, so don't worry about meeting us at the airport. I think I remember how to take the subway to your flat. Is your wedding still planned for the twenty-third?"

"Did you say a 'Michael' is coming with you?" Kathy asks her boring, pathologically predictable mother.

"I'm sure you'll like him. He's very nice." I'm delighted. I'm energized. All the rest will be so easy.

"Mother, are you bringing a date to my wedding?"

"No, just a friend. We met at Cardiac Rehab exercise classes." I like that touch, as I say it. There's nothing romantic about Cardiac Rehab. "One more thing. Michael will stay at a hotel close to the Gloucester Road station. Will it be all right if I stay with you and Zoe in your sunroom like I did last time, or do you have other guests staying with you?"

"Mother, is this really you? The voice sounds like you, but all the words are wrong. Is this really Beth St. Clair? And if not, what have you done with my mother?" I hear Kathy's laugh springing from her throat, lifting skyward to a communications satellite and beaming back to earth. It's been a while since I've heard my daughter laugh.

"Yes, this is your mother." I laugh too. "I know this is a jumble of plans to throw at you, just as you're planning a wedding. But I so want to be there." I realize this is true as soon as I say it. "And after we get settled in, we'll have a chance to talk. I'll see you in a few weeks. I love you."

Another quiet second, another lovely laugh, then, "I love you too, Mum."

CHAPTER 8

☼

Michael

After an hour and twelve minutes in the waiting room, sitting in a clump with two dozen fellow patients, I make it to Doctor Sam's exam room. Ramona got me into this mess. "Don't you think you should get a quick exam, Pop, just to make sure your heart is fit for your flight to London?" I said *No*, but here I am.

Beth talked to Doctor Sam last week and came out bustling with news about special airplane socks and hydration warnings and airplane heart defibrillators. She took notes during her exam and read them to me as we ate supper at the Dairy Queen.

Once my pants and shirt are in a pile on a chair, and my rear end is resting on a stainless-steel exam table, I hear a little knock and Doctor Sam walks into the room.

"Michael, good to see you. What brings you to my neck of the woods?"

Doctor Sam grew up in India, like Ravi, but he and his family have lived in Centerburg for more than twenty years. Folks that don't know him still call him *that new doctor.* I like him better than any doctor I've ever had. He can make a fella feel better just talking to him though it would be nice to not wait an hour and twelve minutes.

He leafs through my chart, frowns. "You've gained seven pounds since your last appointment."

"I figured I might be putting on a little weight," I say. "I've been eating out a lot lately, and I'm back to baking a few times a week. I'd bring you a pie if you'd cut an hour off the wait time here."

Doctor Sam looks up and smiles. "Are you still going to Rehab?"

"Three times a week."

He jots something down. "Your blood pressure is good, but you don't want to stress your heart with any extra weight. Let's have a listen."

The stethoscope is cold on my chest, Doctor Sam's hand is warm on my shoulder. I breathe deep, like he tells me. Then comfort words, "It's doesn't seem to be a problem yet, but I think you need to drop a few pounds. Is there any reason for your increased appetite?"

"Well, Doc, there is something I wanted to talk to you about."

I was hoping to slide my questions into the conversation easy, but sitting here half naked, I feel too awkward to be talking about Beth. "Mind if I put my clothes back on first?"

Doctor Sam slides his chair to the computer on his desk in the corner. As soon as I'm dressed, he rolls his chair over to me. I plunge in.

"I've met a real nice lady. We're taking a trip together." I grab hold of my knees to anchor myself. "I'm having some romantic feelings for her. But I'm about seventy, you know, and with this heart trouble—and she's got heart problems too. Besides, I haven't been with anybody other than Evelyn, my wife, for—well, never. And is it even healthy, with our bad hearts and all? I didn't expect to be falling for someone, at my age."

I hold my breath and stare at Doctor Sam's face. He doesn't smirk or look surprised.

"A loving, sexual relationship is the best thing that can happen to a heart," he says. "I don't know of any physical reasons for you to avoid sex. Some medications can decrease libido, but you're not taking any of those. Are you worried that you might not be able to perform sexually?"

I relax and start breathing again. "Hell no, Doc, I'm not worried about that."

A smile breaks out across Doctor Sam's face. "How does your friend feel about a sexual relationship?"

"Now you've got to the heart of the matter," I say. "Sometimes I think she likes me a lot, and sometimes I think she's just being polite. I don't want to say the wrong things and scare her off."

I picture Beth, frowning at some of my words, laughing at others. Sometimes grabbing my hand while we watch a movie. Sometimes kissing me, just when I think I've made her mad.

"I was a married man for forty-six years, and I never fooled around. I don't want her thinking I'm just some horny old guy. I want her to know I'm serious."

Doctor Sam claps me on the knee. "Michael, you've just described the woes of all mankind. If you can figure it all out, let me know.

Being on an airplane is a great way to get rid of all my romantic intentions. Even though Beth's warm body is sitting so close to mine, I can't shake my jitters about flying. I didn't want to tell her I'm not a fan of air travel, but I suspect Ramona did. Those two are getting real close.

Vibrations shake the whole cabin as tiny tires roar down the runway and the plane struggles to free itself from gravity. Beth turns to me, her face glowing. "This is my favorite part," she whispers. "I like to close my eyes so I can feel the plane lift into the sky. I hope dying feels like this."

Her words don't help my nerves. I grab her hand.

We both close our eyes. The battle beneath us intensifies, the hold of the earth, the lure of the sky. Louder, faster, faster. Then silent calm. We're aloft. I open my eyes. Beth is gazing out her window as the earth drops away.

"Are we in heaven now?" I ask.

"Yes, we are," she says.

We're settled in our little nest for the next nine hours. I wonder if I'll be able to sleep. I glance at Beth, gauging how our bodies might align. It would be cozy, drifting to sleep, Beth's head just touching my shoulder, but I'd enjoy it a lot more if we weren't on an airplane. To distract myself I go over my list of worries—how will Beth and I handle being together for a whole week? Will she get tired of me? Will Kathy be mad I've horned in on her wedding day? When I asked Ramona if this trip was a big mistake, she said, "I imagine it will be wonderful, but who knows?" It wasn't the most reassuring answer.

"Do you think Libby will remember to call Kathy and tell her we're on our way?" Beth asks.

"I'm sure she will. She's real efficient," I say. "What time is it in England?" Another worry—this plane is going to plop me down in another time zone.

"Let's set your watch to the time it is in London." Beth is using a sympathetic teacher voice. Now I'm sure she and Ramona have talked. As the flight attendants explain the rules and events of our flight, Beth fiddles with my watch.

"Do you want some chocolate-covered almonds for an appetizer?" she asks as she hands the watch back to me. "I have a couple packages in my bag. It'll probably be a while before supper."

"That's the ticket," I say. "Let's have some candy."

Beth has stowed a huge black bag under the seat in front of her. She says it holds everything we would need in case our luggage doesn't accompany us to London—another worry. She unbuckles her seatbelt, leans over, pulls on the bag's straps. It's thoroughly wedged under the seat. Beth contorts and tugs. The plane lunges and bolts. I try to grab Beth as the plane jerks us both down. Beth's head slams against the seat in front of her. The bag still won't budge.

I grab Beth's shoulder, the only part of her I can reach. I

hold her shoulder as tight as I can. "What's going on?" I yell. "Beth, look!"

In front of us, three oxygen masks are dangling at eye level. I look around the plane. Yellow plastic cups are everywhere. Gasps and cries erupt from the passengers. The flight attendants rush to join us.

"This is your Captain. Oxygen masks have deployed. Please secure yourselves in your seats and activate your masks. Flight attendants, do the same."

A woman from somewhere behind us screams, "Oh My God, Oh My God, Oh My God," each time louder. At the front of our cabin, four flight attendants fit the yellow cups over their faces and scan the scene. One of them breaks out of the pack and charges down the aisle toward the screaming woman.

Beth stares at me, then yells, "Michael, put on your oxygen mask!" I don't understand what she means. I don't know what is happening.

The flight attendant stops by us and grabs one of our three masks. She breathes through it, takes it away from her mouth and says, "Ma'am, put on your oxygen mask, then fasten your seat belt."

The flight attendant breathes through the oxygen mask again, then slides a mask over my mouth and nose. She has huge blue eyes. Her hands are warm and soft as they touch my cheeks. "Are you OK?" she asks Beth. Beth nods. Our flight attendant winks at Beth, scans behind us and works her way toward the screaming woman.

Beth's hand finds mine and we braid our fingers together. Then I drop my hand, push the armrest up, and wrap my arms around her, cradling her head against my shoulder. The whole cabin is still. We're all tucked in for the night as I start praying for another miracle.

It must have been about six years ago when I asked for that first miracle. Pastor Terry was there to respond. "Don't pray for miracles, Michael. Pray for grace. If you have grace, the miracles will come."

I was looking for a safe place, somewhere I could hide for a while, so I'd parked my Buick in the parking lot of St. Peter's, backed under the branches of the big sugar maple tree at the far corner. When we attended church on a regular basis, there was always some discussion about chopping it down to free up more parking space. It always struck me as wrong, so I was happy to see my old tree still standing, offering me shelter in the empty lot.

Through the front windshield, I looked up at the stained-glass windows. Inside the colors would sparkle purple and red and blue, but from my hideout, all the colors looked black. I didn't notice Pastor Terry walking up until I heard him tap-tap on the drivers' side window.

"If you'd like to go in the church, I'll unlock the door," Pastor Terry said, not mentioning he hadn't seen me for years.

"No, no. I was just taking a little breather, you know. I guess I'm praying for a miracle." But it wasn't a miracle I was praying for. I was asking for something too ugly to put in a prayer—an end.

I had to get out of the house, so I called Mike. "Can you watch your Mom for a few hours?"

He always said *Sure Pop.* He'd have done anything to help, a lot more if he'd known how bad it was, but I wasn't about to tell him. After being caught by Pastor Terry, I drove back home. The car radio was set at the soft music station. Sometimes music calmed Evelyn down, sometimes she'd even sing along. Her voice was still pretty but hearing her sing made me ache for the old days. I turned the radio off.

When I walked in the front door Evelyn flew at me, screaming. "Get away from me! Get out of my house!" Her left hand, the hand that wore my wedding ring, struck me full and hard across my face, knocking off my glasses.

Mike saw it all. He called Ramona, and she took off work

to drive up to Des Plaines. A week later the four of us drove to Harvest Manor.

It takes a torn-up airplane to get me praying again. This time I pray for life, for beginnings. And miracles and grace. *Anything You can do, God.* We float gently downward. Losing altitude is soft and simple. Every so often, the plane shudders and moans. How long does it take to fall from heaven? Seconds, minutes, a lifetime?

CHAPTER 9

Beth

*S*o *this is how Beth St. Clair dies,* I think. *Killed in an airplane crash at age sixty-five.*

My calm amazes me. My life isn't flashing before my eyes. Nothing hurts, my heart beats steady, I'm wrapped in loving arms. My Cajun Inn heart attack was humiliating. Here, in our little ailing plane, I'm just one of the crowd. No one is focused on me. No one except my darling Michael. I open my eyes, take off my oxygen mask, and hold his face between my hands. He opens his eyes to stare into mine. He looks so bewildered.

"Michael, everything is fine. I only wish I had the next ten years to spend with you instead of the next ten minutes."

I kiss him on the forehead, right above his yellow oxygen cup, put my mask back on, and rest my head on his shoulder. Michael and I settle back in our nest, our bodies perfectly aligned, our eyes closed, to wait for our second lift-off into heaven.

Our death is interrupted by our Captain.

"Sorry about the rocky road back there, folks. We've had a decompression problem, but we've descended to ten thousand feet so we can breathe cabin air now. If you're experiencing any problems, please ask your flight attendant for assistance. I've contacted JFK in New York and they're going to have a plane waiting for us, so we can all proceed to London more comfortably. We should be in New York in about two hours."

Jubilation fills the cabin. The oxygen-filled air abounds with laughter and prayers as we shuck off our oxygen masks. *Thank God, thank God, thank God,* someone says, each time a little softer. Instead of letting me go, Michael hugs me tighter. When he finally releases me, his old Michael-eyes are back. Blue sparkle has replaced terror.

"I love you, Beth St. Clair," he laughs.

It seems a most natural sentence to hear.

"Michael Bartoli, you old rascal, I'm beginning to think I love you too."

It seems a most natural sentence to say.

After I realize we are to be alive for the rest of the flight, I'm energized. But poor Michael, he's looking so frail. And kind of pecked. As the flight attendants move through the cabin, I finally tug my bag free and rummage down to the bottom. I've not had a chance to get those chocolate-covered almonds, what with the potential plane crash and all.

My black bag contains a brand-new crossword puzzle book, a street guide to London complete with subway diagram, an extra toothbrush, and a pair of underwear. I'd thought about asking Michael if he wanted me to pack a pair of his underwear too, but I decided I don't know him well enough to ask. I pull out two boxes of candy, a pair of black, extra-large pressure socks—maybe I should have invested in two pairs, but I guess we can share—and a blood pressure monitor with a self-inflating cuff. It works great. I'd tried it out at home when I put in the batteries.

"Michael, roll up your sleeve and I'll take your blood pressure," I tell him. "You look pale."

We munch on candy and take each other's blood pressure. Michael's is pretty good, 135 over 85 and mine is perfect. The little beeping sound attracts the attention of the man across the aisle from us, so I let him use it too. His is a little high, 150 over 93, so we share some candy with him to get his mind off it.

"Michael, take off your shoes and socks and wear these pressure socks for a while," I suggest. "Maybe they'll push some color back into your face."

He doesn't argue. By the time our flight attendant comes by to offer us a beverage of our choice, Michael is snoozing, his head on my shoulder.

"You take such good care of your husband," she whispers.

"Oh, he's not . . ." I look at Michael, safe and warm by my side, and it doesn't seem necessary to correct her. "He's not hard to take care of," I say. "It's my pleasure."

Kathy sits between Michael and me at the metal sidewalk table, tapping her cell phone with her manicured nails, twitching her gabardine-panted leg, stirring the coffee in the gold rimmed cup, around and around and around. "Well, the main thing is, we didn't die." I try a touch of humor, then a deflection. "Michael, this rhubarb tart is delicious. I'm so glad our plane didn't crash. I'd have been irritated to have missed this. Do you want to taste it?"

Kathy met us at Heathrow in a state of high alarm. She'd called the airlines from her office and learned about the airplane swap at JFK, so she left work and grabbed the express link from Paddington Station out to the airport. She'd been there for hours, agitating every airline employee she could find until she saw us coming down the corridor from customs. She pleaded with us to take a cab back into London, even offered to pay for it, which I flat out refused. "We're just fine," I had to say at least ten times while she sputtered and whirled around us. "Let's just stop at the Currency Exchange and then take the Express back into town."

When we three emerged from the subway at Gloucester Station, the first thing Michael spotted was a little French pastry shop, so he suggested a snack. If Kathy hadn't been here, I'd have dropped my bag and hugged him.

As soon as we had settled at a table, a waiter took our order and in moments, returned with our snacks which now sit before us. I cut a little section of my rhubarb tart to share with Michael, he does the same for me with his cheesecake. As we munch, Kathy twitches with nerves. I'd be picked bare with questions by now were it not for Michael's presence.

"I believe your tart is tastier than my cheesecake," Michael says, "but this cheesecake isn't bad. Beth, I didn't know you liked rhubarb." He smiles at me like it's just the two of us sitting here, then turns his attention to my daughter. "Are you sure I can't get you something to go with your coffee?"

Kathy explodes. "All right. Enough!" Her palms slam the table, splashing her coffee onto the matching saucer. I grab my dessert to protect it. Her body stills as she focuses on every word. "All I want to have with my coffee is an explanation of what happened on that airplane."

No please, let's not do this, not now. The blood from my body drains to my stomach to reside with the rhubarb tart. My throat constricts, trapping all the words I need to say. My eyes find Michael. He looks at my daughter with compassion and nods his head.

"Yes, Kathy, it's been quite a day for all of us. Thank you for helping us through it. First, please call me Michael." He begins our story, gathering up all the tensions and questions and rage at the table, holding them close to his warm heart, and handing them back, caressed and healed.

As he talks, Kathy's eyes narrow, then open wider to scan for any errors in his speech. She sips her coffee. Her hands rest in her lap. By the time he's finished, a vague smile creeps across her face.

"You'll need to call me Kate, Michael. The only one who calls me Kathy is my mother."

Michael

The lobby of my hotel is small and fancy. Four gold and blue chairs sit in front of a fireplace, leather bound books and brass candlesticks are arranged on the mantle, a uniformed receptionist stands behind a walnut front desk and glares at the three of us as we walk in. I wonder how much it costs to stay here. Ramona and Mike are paying for my room as a Christmas present. Maybe Libby found them a deal through the airlines.

"I'll get checked in. You ladies don't have to wait for me." Beth looks so tired, so troubled. I set my suitcase beside hers, put my hands on her shoulders and pull her toward me. I can feel her melt into me through three layers of clothing. "You're as worn out as I am, aren't you?" I whisper into her ear. "Why don't you go back to Kate's and get settled." I look at Kate. She's watching my every move. "I've got a wad of this English money. I'll just grab a sandwich across the road and turn in early," I say as I release her mother.

Beth looks panicked. "Honey, would you watch my luggage?" she says to Kate. "I'll make sure Michael gets to his room." Kate nods and drops into one of the overstuffed chairs. She's exhausted too.

After I tell him my name, the receptionist looks at his computer and seems disappointed to find my reservation. He hands me a key card and manages a stiff smile as he gives us directions to the room.

The elevators doors open as soon as Beth pushes the button, a nicer welcome. We enter, the doors creak shut. Side by side, silent and alone. Beth leans against my shoulder, I put my arm around her. I'd like to stay in this elevator all evening, riding up and down with Beth.

Too soon, she selects the room button that will move us on. A trembling finger pushes four. Beth's hands are shaking. By the time we get into Room 407, her whole body is shaking.

I don't know what to say, but my body knows what to do. I set my suitcase down, peel off my coat, walk to her and take her into my arms. Her body is shuddering so I hold her as tight as I can to stop the tremors. When she starts sobbing, my hands move slowly up and down her back as her tears soak my shirt. I'll hold her for the rest of my life if it will help her sadness go away.

"It's OK, you're fine, we're safe," I hear myself saying over and over until her sobbing stops.

Beth pulls away from me, tries to wipe her face with the back of her hand. I soothe away the last few tears with my thumb. She takes my hand and kisses it.

"Michael, I'm sorry. I never cry," she says. "All at once everything that's happened today closed in on me, but I feel better now. Thank you, honey." She kisses me quickly on the lips. "I better get back downstairs before Kathy storms your room. Can I just wash my face in your bathroom?" She looks at me and laughs. "And you better take off that soggy shirt. I'll wash it at Kathy's."

"No, I brought plenty. You go wash up," I tell her.

My room is tiny like the lobby. Heavy drapes hide a view of the street below. The only light comes from a brass lamp setting on the desk.

I unpack my suitcase while Beth is in my bathroom. Her sadness becomes mine. In a few moments I'll be alone in this tiny, dark room, an ocean away from everything that is familiar. Everything except Beth.

When she walks out of the bathroom, I go to her, take her freshly washed cheeks between my hands and look into her soft, tired eyes. "Did you mean what you said, back in the airplane?" I ask, "when you thought we were going down? About wishing for ten years together?"

"Yes," she says. "I meant it."

"Stay with me," I say. "It would be so nice if you could stay here with me tonight." I drop my hands and wait for a reply. There is none.

"No, you need to head back to your daughter's place," I say. "I'm just talking silly. I'm sorry."

Now Beth's arms wrap around me, her hands move up and down my back, her head is on my chest. Now the tears are in my eyes. Beth sees them, smiles, wipes them away.

"Michael, I'd love to stay here with you tonight, but I think we better wait."

"I know. I'm sorry I said anything," I say. "I need to ask you proper. We'll wait as long as you want."

The teasing twinkle returns to Beth's eyes. "Michael," she says, "we only have to wait until we get back to Centerburg."

Kate and Zoe's wedding day is gray and damp. From the third story window of their breakfast nook, I can see the top of a brave little hawthorn tree growing on a square of lawn wedged between their apartment building and three others. Half a dozen other families have windows facing the same view. I wonder if any of those folks are as happy as I am this morning, eating breakfast with Beth while two lovely ladies get ready for their special day.

It's too bad the day is dreary. Our last two days were beautiful—sunny and crisp. On Tuesday while the girls were at work, Beth and I spent the entire day sightseeing. We took the open-top bus tour past Big Ben and Westminster Abbey and Buckingham Castle, then walked down the Thames River to see the Tower of London. We walked miles. I can't wait to get back to Rehab to tell everyone how healthy we are. We ended the day at the grandest department store I've ever seen—Harrods.

"How about I buy the girls a wedding present here?" I asked Beth as we walked through the huge green front doors.

"Everything here is way too expensive," she said. "I just

wanted to look around for a bit. Besides, you're cooking for their party. That's enough."

I didn't care for her answer. Kate and Zoe need a special little something. "What are you giving them?" I asked Beth.

"Money. I wouldn't know what to buy them," she said. "They have everything they need."

I didn't like that answer any better. I put my hand on the small of her back and guided Beth into the outrageous luxury of Harrods.

Beth and I are enjoying the morning of her daughter's wedding day in the breakfast nook when Zoe joins us. She has on her robe and slippers; her curly brown hair is still damp from the shower. "Zoe, I was hoping your wedding day would be sunny like the last few days," I tell her.

"Michael, you're a love." She plants a kiss on top of my head. Affection is easy for her. Zoe is everything Kate is not—short, plumpish, gleeful, welcoming. "Are you positive this is enough breakfast?" Zoe asks as she sits down to join us. "We could pop around the corner for a proper meal as soon as Kate gets up."

"I'm fine. How about you, Beth?" I ask.

Beth's mouth is full of scones and clotted cream. "If I gain one more pound, Kathy will send me home early," she says after she swallows. "And aren't we having lunch before the ceremony?"

"Yes, let's do," says Zoe. "I remember a little cafe on High Street. We could do a bit of sightseeing. Windsor's a lovely town." Zoe sets down her coffee cup, crosses her hands over her heart and says, "Beth, Michael, thank you. You being here today means more than you can possibly know."

Yesterday Zoe and I spent the whole day together. It felt like a reunion. Kate had to go to work for a special project and Beth was perfectly happy to drink tea and work crossword puzzles all day, so Zoe took the day off so we could shop for groceries and cook. They'd planned on catered appetizers and a cake for a little party after their wedding but once we got to talking, we four decided we'd make everything. Or as Kate and Beth had restated, *Michael and Zoe will make everything.*

Zoe took me to their neighborhood grocery store, then a bakery for fresh bread, then a butcher shop where the owner gave us free samples of deli sausage and cheeses. I've never had so much fun grocery shopping.

All afternoon Zoe and I stood side by side in their tiny kitchen. I told each of the ladies I'd make their favorite pie, so Zoe measured ingredients as I mixed up a cherry pie for Beth, mincemeat for Zoe, and a pumpkin cheesecake for Kate. Zoe and Beth had complained cheesecake wasn't a pie, but I told Kate I'd be proud to alter the rules for her. Zoe wrote down the recipe so she could make cheesecake for Kate again sometime.

As I got my sauce simmering, Zoe said, "Michael, how about I roast these veggies for our lasagna? It gives them a little extra flavor." I immediately declared her head chef instead of assistant. She got to work on chopping zucchini and mushrooms and peppers. We decided yes for eggplant and no for broccoli—too overpowering. Definitely yes for lots of spinach.

"Michael, may I ask you something?" Zoe had started washing the first batch of dirty pots and pans so we would have counterspace to assemble two lasagnas.

"Sure, honey," I said.

"Does Beth ever talk about Kate's father?"

Behind Zoe's words are layers of questions and concerns, hints of small hurts and huge injustices, hopes for answers and healing. Zoe's questions were my own.

"No," I said. "She never talks about him. I only know they divorced when Kate was young."

Zoe considered my words for a minute, then nodded her

head. "Silence says so much, doesn't it? Kate doesn't speak of her father often, but his leaving was horribly hurtful, I believe." She took my hand. "Let me tell you what Kate's told me. It's helpful to understanding these women we love."

Beth

At three o'clock, Kathy and Zoe are scheduled to be at Guildhall where Prince Charles and Camille were married. "And Elton John," Kathy had added. Since Zoe and Kathy don't own a car, Zoe's boss Inez and her husband are squeezing the six of us into theirs for the short drive. On my last visit to London, Kathy and Zoe took me for a tour of the Victoria and Albert Museum, where they both work. They introduced me to Inez, who is poised and brilliant. Zoe and Kathy adore her. I tried not to be thoroughly intimidated.

"I know Inez and her husband will be at your party. Have I met any of your other guests?" I ask Zoe. Kathy and Zoe have been vague about their guest list. Anxiety creeps into my stomach, and I reach for another scone. I know nothing of my daughter's life. In twelve hours, Michael and I may be in the midst of tattooed artists and poets discussing topics I have no hope of understanding. Michael is so accepting. Will I be able to follow his lead? I picture myself hiding in the bathroom, with a spoon and my cherry pie.

My second scone is half-eaten when my daughter emerges from their bedroom, dressed for her wedding day in a two-piece suit of winter white wool. Soft material folds around her slim body. Under her jacket is a lacy camisole in a chocolate brown color that matches her shoes. She's put a wave in her hair and tucked one side behind her ear to expose an emerald earring. She's lovely.

"Oh, honey, you look so pretty," I gasp. I hope she won't take my astonishment as an insult.

Kathy's face softens as she smiles. There's shyness instead of sarcasm in her voice as she whispers thank-you.

"I suppose I better get ready, too," Zoe says, picking up her breakfast plate. She doesn't comment on Kathy's appearance. She's not surprised by my daughter's beauty.

"How long will the wedding ceremony take?" I ask.

"The proper term is civil partnership, not wedding," my lovely, pink-cheeked daughter informs me as our six-member wedding party meanders down High Street toward Guildhall. Windsor is picture perfect with Christmas trimmings in all the little woolen shops and stationery and toy stores. It could be the inspiration behind those ceramic Christmas villages ladies so love to collect, one expensive piece at a time.

My nervous questions are irritating Kathy. It's not my intention. I'm feeling awkward and wordless at the end of the procession. In the lead, Michael and Inez's husband are man-chatting. I can't hear their conversation, just an occasional chuckle of agreement. The middle couple, Zoe and Inez, are slowing our progress with their window shopping. Kathy and I trudge behind. I hate the silence between us. Surely there are gentle, motherly questions I should be asking. Tender, wise words of advice. I can think of nothing to warm the icy space between me and my self-confident daughter.

Kathy stops to gaze in the window of an antique store as the rest of our party marches ahead.

"Do you want to go in, honey, or should we be worrying about the time?" I ask her.

"I'd rather not worry about anything today," she snipes.

I've irritated my daughter again. Years of not knowing what to do, not knowing what to say have crippled my every word. "Honey, I'm sorry," I say. "I'm so sorry."

Kathy is unaccustomed to her mother's apologies. She sighs, her face softens. "Mum, look at this," she says. She points to a display of delicate china and crystal in the shop's window. "That little dish in the center," she says. "Didn't Grandma have a little dish like that?"

"Maybe, the pattern looks familiar," I say. "I don't really recall."

"Let's step in and take a look," Kathy says. "Hold up a bit," she directs the rest of her procession as we detour into the shop.

Kathy gently plucks the dish from the display and traces its garland of delicate white roses with her finger. "Grandma had a dish just like this on her dining room table," she says. "She'd put candies in it for special occasions."

Kathy gently turns the plate over, searching for information my memory can't supply.

"If she had a dish like this, it would have been a wedding present," I say. My eyes dart to the price tag and I try not to gasp.

"I wonder what became of it?" Such a sad question. Kathy returns the plate to the window display.

I picture the card tables in my parent's yard, piled with the contents of their lives. I'd sold most everything after my father died. There wasn't much.

"Should we press on?" Kathy says.

As our procession resumes the walk to Guildhall, I whisper in Kathy's ear, "I'm glad you saw that little candy dish. Your grandmother would be pleased we thought of her today."

Kathy weaves her arm though mine. I'm filled with wonder. I've just said wise and motherly words to my daughter on the way to her wedding.

Michael has me stationed against the entry wall between pictures of a Scottish coastline and a sunset over an abandoned mill, both painted by my daughter. Kathy never hung any of her paintings on a wall until she met Zoe.

I watch Michael slice his desserts as I keep an eye out to

see if anyone needs more wine or coffee or sliced salami to replenish the antipasto platter. Michael was so concerned he hadn't baked enough dessert, he's cutting the pies into eight wedges instead of his standard six. But there's going to be plenty for everyone. I watch him remove one piece of cherry pie, put it on a dessert plate, cover it with plastic and wink at me. My breakfast.

I needn't have worried over Kathy and Zoe's wedding soiree. The guests are a sedate and tweed-covered group. The living room is warm and candlelit, and, thanks to Michael, a delicious aroma fills the air.

The guests have drifted into three clumps. A work-related cluster stands at the buffet table, laughing over shared gossip from the Museum. The neighbor contingent is led by a strikingly beautiful lady, who's an event caterer. She's the bright spot in the room, a red silk suit bobbing in a sea of muted herringbones. She and her husband live in the flat next door. I imagine his shoes cost more than my living room furniture.

The third group is Zoe's niece, her stone-lipped husband, and their two bored children. After filling their plates with lasagna, the family marched *en masse* to the sunroom to sit in a line on my daybed. As we were setting up the buffet table last night, Zoe told me she's from a large family, but her parents are both deceased. Her brothers and sisters live too far from London, have other holiday plans or just didn't care to attend. Zoe's sad gaze as she told me made my heart quake. She yearns for the comfort of family, I think. Maybe we can help each other, Zoe and I? I glance in the sunroom and imagine their family conversation after the arrival of the wedding invitation. I remember my panic-stricken phone call to Clarice. It seems like a decade ago.

From my observation post I listen to snippets of conversation about deadlines and catering events and minced pie. "Michael, you're brilliant. We've all decided you and Beth need to immigrate to London." The event caterer says

Michael's béchamel is the best she's ever tasted. He says he didn't know he could make béchamel; he thought it was white sauce. He laughed, but I could tell he was pleased and proud. And then everyone said congratulations one last time and headed out for subways and trains.

By ten o'clock, even Michael has kissed us three remaining ladies good night and left for his hotel room. As we check the living room for any stray wine glasses, I wander into the kitchen. Michael has left it spotless. There's a satisfying fullness in my stomach, no need for that last piece of cherry pie. Kathy shuffles past, carrying an empty coffee cup in one hand and her high heels in the other. She sits the cup on the clean counter. "Off to bed," she says. "We can spend tomorrow relaxing." She gives me air kisses on both cheeks, the same farewell she gave her departing guests, and heads to her bedroom. Like Zoe, I realize I yearn for a bit more from my family.

I rinse her cup as Zoe comes into the kitchen. "Beth, we can't ever begin to thank you and Michael for your help and support." She looks tired and soft-eyed. "It means so much."

"You are so welcome, honey," I say. We hug goodnight and Zoe pads away to bed. The words *wedding night* flicker across my exhausted brain. *Don't be encombered by other's expectations, my darling daughter. Don't be like your mother*—my unspoken wedding wish.

Michael and I had decided against formally presenting our little wedding presents. Wrapping them would have been cumbersome, especially the two crystal wine glasses and bottle of chianti Michael selected at Harrods. As the ladies were welcoming their guests, I slipped in and arranged everything on their bedside table. I'm glad now I didn't just give them a card and cash. Michael's suggestion was perfect. They'll have a small surprise from us. Something special to keep.

I turn off all the lights except the table lamp by my daybed, draw the drapes and slip off my dress. As I'm sliding into my flannel gown, I turn to see my daughter standing at the entrance to the sunroom, her face tear-streaked and glowing in the lamplight. In her hands is my wedding gift.

"Is this the little bonbon dish from the antique shop?" she asks. "How did you manage this? We were with you all day."

I laugh. "As you were ordering coffees and arguing over the luncheon bill, I slipped back to the little shop and bought it. It's a shame I didn't save your grandmother's for you since you liked it so much."

Tears fill Kathy's eyes. The only tears I've seen in her eyes before this evening were spurred by rage. Rage at me, her absent father, her unbearable circumstances. It was my rage too, mirrored in her eyes. Our anger immobilized us. The rift it gouged seemed insurmountable. Neither of us had the energy or inclination to span the divide.

I put my arms around her and draw her to me. She doesn't pull away.

"It's been a grand day," I say. "Thank you for including me."

Kathy moves back just enough for me to see her face.

"I love you, Mom," says my daughter.

Mom—a tiny golden nugget.

"And I love you," I say. "I love you, Kate."

CHAPTER 10

✺

Michael

It starts snowing a few hours after we leave Mike's. My old Buick is filled with the only Christmas music I could find on the radio. Most of the stations have gone back to playing the regular songs, but this little central Illinois station is keeping the spirit alive for a few more days. My car is warm and running smooth. The tires have plenty of tread. We'll be safe for this winter drive. I watch the snowflakes swirl across the hood and listen to the familiar words—chestnuts and fireplaces, drums and a newborn King.

Beth is sitting in the passenger's seat, working on her new crossword puzzle book. "Oh, this is perfect. I finished my last book at Kate and Zoe's," she'd said yesterday as we opened presents at Mike and Libby's house. Mike and Libby saved a little Christmas celebration for us. We had a nice supper and opened our presents. Since I wasn't sure what to buy Beth, Libby helped me select a couple of gifts. Now I can think of dozens of presents I'd love to give her—a little camera, a fancy coffee pot like Libby got for Christmas. A gold necklace. A silky blue blouse. I'd like to buy her ruby earrings. I've always liked rubies.

"Beth, when's your birthday?" I ask her.

She glances at me, then out the windshield. "February twentieth. I'll be sixty-six, if I recall correctly."

"We'll have to do something special," I say.

"I've always preferred to ignore the whole event." She puts her pen in the book to mark her page and closes it. "But yes, I'd love to do something special with you on my birthday."

Beth puts her hand on my leg, and I put my hand on top of it. Our fingers weave together. I slow my speed to match the semi in front of me. These drivers are top notch, so I'll just let him guide me down the road. It feels like I'm driving home instead of away from it. Maybe I should put my place in Des Plaines on the market in the spring and start thinking about a new place to hang my hat.

I've been working on a little speech to say to Beth, but I couldn't find any time to say it during the last five days, with the sightseeing and shopping and getting Kate and Zoe married. Now I have time to settle back in my seat and enjoy our closeness, the feeling of her hand in mine. I just about got her hand memorized. My thumb runs across the top of her index finger. There's a little bump at her knuckle. A touch of arthritis? I wonder if this little finger hurts sometimes. I hope not. When I press my fingers into Beth's soft palm, her fingers close over mine. Our hands are so comfortable with each other and now it feels like our hearts have caught up.

As soon as we walk into Beth's condo, I pull a Ziplock bag of vegetable soup out of her freezer, dump it into a pot and get it on the stove. Beth says she's changing from traveling to relaxing clothes and lugs her bags upstairs. I set the soup to simmer, turn off the kitchen lights, flick on the little lamp on Beth's desk. The living room is cool and dark, perfect for getting cozy. Beth's couch is becoming an old friend. I plop down in the center. If I sit at the end, there's a chance Beth might sit at the other side. That's too far away.

Beth comes downstairs wearing her purple exercising clothes, her face is scrubbed and happy. "How long before our soup's ready?" she asks and, sure enough, sits down right beside me.

"Oh, probably hours." A little lie, the soup will probably go from frozen to bubbling in thirty minutes.

"Hours?" Beth snuggles close. "We have hours, just to be alone?"

"That's how I have it planned." I don't care if that soup burns.

Beth rests her head on my shoulder and whispers, "I like your plan."

My arm ends up around her, my hand rubs the velvety softness of her shoulder. The top of her head nestles my neck, a curl of her hair tickles my jaw.

"Beth, I've been thinking about something."

"I've been thinking about something, too," she says.

I take a deep breath. My speech is about how thankful I am to have met her, how happy she makes me. I want to take care of her and love her and make sure every minute of her life is full of joy because that's the way I've felt since I've met her. Trouble is, I can't remember exactly how to put it all together.

"Beth, what do you think about us getting married?" I say.

She pulls out of my arms and faces me, wide-eyed. The room's not dark enough to hide the irritation on her face. Then worse, amusement. "Michael, I thought you were try-ing to seduce me, not propose."

The couch stiffens against my back. The smell of left-over soup drifts to my nostrils, making my stomach turn. *I'm sorry* are the only words I can get out of my mouth.

"Well, it's a shame you weren't trying to seduce me, because it was working." She puts her hand on my leg. "Honey, I don't want to be married again. It didn't work out very well the first time, you know." I stare at her face, all the lipstick and powder are washed off, leaving just her prettiness. Her lips are pink instead of red, her cheeks peachy. She takes my face between her hands and kisses me, soft and quick. Her lips are minty from toothpaste.

Beth said no. My heart gears down to stand-by. In another condo a door slams, in the parking lot a car starts. It's probably still snowing. I should get up, look out the window, turn on the lights, stir the soup. Maybe we can find a funny movie on the TV or order a pizza if the soup is ruined. Maybe I can figure out how to get my heart to start beating again, long enough to get me through one more night.

"I'm sorry," I say again, leaning back, staring at my knees. "I wasn't thinking right. I just got all caught up in, well, loving you, and I didn't even think about how you were feeling."

Beth shifts closer, reaches for me, her fingers touch my cheek. "You're the sweetest man I've ever known. Please don't think I don't care about you. I do." She takes my hand in hers and my heart starts beating again.

"Zoe told me Kate's father wasn't the most responsible man." I press her warm palm to my lips and look in her eyes. "I'd never have left you."

"Oh, Pete was from another lifetime." Beth says his name so easy. I hate hearing his name. "It's just that I'm used to taking care of myself. I'm not good at compromising or sharing." Her lips twist to teasing. "And why would I? I've never had the option of having a romance with the sweetest man in the world." Her hand touches my knee. "Not until now."

A romance! My little talk might work out after all. Maybe Beth does love me? I'll just slow down my marrying feelings and rev up some others.

Beth rests her head against my shoulder and my hands slide to her waist. They're learning her body. Round and warm and yielding. As I pull her closer, her hand circles my back and she lifts her face to me. Her eyes are closed, her lips waiting.

"I wasn't trying to seduce you, you know," I say. Her eyes blink open. "Well, I guess I was, but . . . only if we both . . . you did say my seduction was working, didn't you?" Her brow wrinkles, the lips that were waiting for me to kiss them are frowning. I'm saying everything wrong.

She touches my lips with her finger, hushing me. "Michael, I can think of nothing lovelier than the two of us alone, right here, right now."

Somewhere inside me a small voice whispers *Be quiet, Michael. Stop thinking, stop planning. Love her.* My hands and lips follow the advice. I open my arms and Beth moves to me. She smells like flowers. She's so close, there's no part of her my hands can't touch. My lips move over the softness of her neck.

The telephone rings.

We bolt away from each other and glare at the screaming phone. Beth doesn't pick up the receiver until the fourth ring.

"Hello? Mike? Yes, he is." Her smile is guilty as she hands me the phone. She's been caught kissing Mike's father.

"Anything wrong there?" I try to keep the irritation out of my voice.

Mike says they're fine, just wanted to make sure we got in okay, and since Ramona is out of town, he wasn't sure I'd pick up if he called there. "I'm sure glad we had Beth's number," he says.

"Yes, I'm sure glad you got hold of us." I wink at Beth and she chuckles. I listen to Mike as Beth gets up and unpacks her black airplane bag. He's talked to Ramona, they're fine too, he'll call her back and tell her I'm here with Beth. Beth stacks her new puzzle books on the coffee table, puts the blood pressure machine in her desk and disappears into the kitchen. Mike thanks me for the Christmas presents we brought them from London—teas for Libby, a Paddington Bear for Emma, both Beth's idea. By the time I hang up, Beth has a bowl of chocolate-covered almonds, a bottle of wine and two glasses sitting on the coffee table.

"Look what I found," she says, sliding to me. Our hands are confident as we find each other again. I'm relaxed and excited at the same time. She kisses me, starting with two little pecks at the corners of my mouth. She moves inches away from my face and closes her eyes. Her next kiss is hard against my lips. I close my eyes too.

The telephone rings.

Beth collapses against my chest, groans, crawls over me and grabs the phone. She shouts *Hello!* into the receiver, then a softer *Yes, we just got back.* She mouths *Clarice* to me as she resettles herself against the couch cushions instead of my chest.

My heart is pounding. I need to relax so I don't ruin our evening by passing out on the couch. I concentrate on breathing as Beth talks. While they talk, I get up to check on my soup. It's been simmering for over an hour. I sample the broth, thick with potatoes and onion. It's edible. I turn the burner to low.

Beth is still talking when I return to the couch. "It was wonderful but we're so tired, no, actually he's here right now." Beth gives me a crinkle-eyed smile. She listens for a few minutes and her smile fades. She turns to me and says, "Clarice has turkey for sandwiches and an entire pecan pie she wants to share with us." Beth mouths *I'm sorry,* her eyebrows ask me yes or no.

"Tell Clarice to get on over here," I say. "The soup's ready."

Beth sets her dining room table for four, the first time she's ever done this, she says. "It seems appropriate my first dinner party is all leftovers, none of which I've cooked." As Beth gets a pot of coffee ready, I search for two more wine glasses, then settle for water tumblers. We haven't had one sip of our romancing wine, there's plenty left for Clarice and Jim.

From Beth's kitchen window, I can see the snow has almost stopped with barely an inch of new powder on my car. I'm disappointed. A few feet of new snow might strand me here for a day or two. We need some alone time. In fifteen minutes

Clarice and Jim will be here, tomorrow Ramona's crew will be back. Sandwiching in a night of passion doesn't feel right even if I knew how to go about suggesting it. It should be easier for a man and a woman to love each other.

"Let's go on a vacation, just the two of us," I say to Beth's back. She's searching through the refrigerator, looking for something else to add to the dinner menu. So far she's only found a jar of dill pickles and some mayonnaise for the sandwiches.

She whirls around with a carton of peppermint ice cream in her hand. "You haven't even unpacked from our last vacation," she laughs. "Look! I forgot we bought this. Now we can have two desserts." She throws the ice cream back in the freezer and walks right into my arms. "My place isn't working out very well for us, is it? I'm sorry." She kisses my nose. "Where can we go to hide out for a few days?"

As I hold her, I picture Beth and me driving toward the sun. I've got a hankering to see mountains and deserts and cacti. Eat some Mexican food. I've been looking at Illinois too long. Beth's arms are around my waist, my hands move down her back, pulling her close.

The doorbell rings.

CHAPTER 11

※

Michael

Caribbean Cruise. I liked the sound of the words the minute I heard them. Long and lazy and sexy. Beth and I on a cruise, I can't imagine a better way to spend a winter week.

As we ate our leftover Christmas supper, Beth filled Clarice in on our trip to London. Clarice was getting more jealous with every detail. "We never go anywhere," she said. "The kids wanted to send us on a cruise for our fortieth anniversary, but Jim said No."

"I'm not getting on any boat that's going to be floating around in the middle of an ocean," Jim said. "We wouldn't know anybody, and our cell phones wouldn't work. I'd feel trapped."

Clarice rolled her eyes and groaned but Beth looked at me and winked. A week later she had the whole cruise planned.

I've never noticed a southern Illinois sunrise before, but it's very striking in a snow-packed, sullen kind of way. Ramona is driving us to St. Louis, and she wants to get in some big city shopping after she drops us off at the airport, so we left at five this morning. Beth and Ramona sit up front and chat while I sit in the back seat, all by myself, and try to decide if I should worry or relax or just look at the pretty pink sky over the flat, white fields. This get-away is just what we need to give us the chance to, well, get to know each other better. I'm excited as I can be, scared but excited. We pass a farmer bundled-up in a heavy coat and orange hat, trudging out to get the newspaper from his mailbox. He doesn't know we're flying off to summertime. As I listen to the murmur of my two favorite ladies talking, I close my eyes and picture a huge white ship floating in a harbor, just waiting for Beth and me.

Our huge white ship is waiting for thousands of us, from the look of the lines of folks inching toward it. When we got off our plane, a lady from Sunny Fun Travels met us, put a sticker on our shirts and stuck us on a bus. When the bus got to the dock, another lady directed us to here—the end of a line so long we can't even see where we're heading.

"I wonder how long it'll take us to get on the ship?" I ask Beth.

"Probably an hour or so," she says. "It would have been nice to get here early enough to board before noon, but I couldn't arrange a flight that early. This will be fine."

As we creep ahead, I have plenty of time to start worrying again. Front and center of my concerns—I'm heading off on a romantic vacation, a honeymoon, with a woman who's not my wife. Beth is so calm, standing beside me in the muggy Miami air. She is as fresh and pretty as her peachy-colored clothes. After we'd bought our cruise tickets, we drove to a nice shopping center over by St. Louis to pick out our resort wear, as Beth called it. She tried on bright colored blouses and short pants that showed off her calves and ankles. I told her she had beautiful legs and she giggled like a sixteen-year-old. She bought all the clothes she tried on.

The couple in front of us drag their carry-on suitcases and coats as we all move forward toward a three-story wall of glass separating us from our boat.

"Didn't I see you folks on the plane from St. Louis?" I ask them. They look like I feel: nervous and hot and tired.

"Probably," the lady says. A trickle of sweat runs down her forehead and her husband—I assume it's her husband—chuckles and wipes it away with his thumb.

"You two dressed smarter than we did," the lady says. "This is our first cruise. I can't believe it's so hot."

"This is my—our—first cruise too," I tell her. "But Beth read up on it, so she knew how to dress. Funny isn't it, just a few hours ago we were standing in snow."

"I'm starting to wish I were still standing in snow," the lady says. We all take a few steps.

"My wife is grumpy 'cause she's starving," the man says. "She thought we'd have breakfast on the plane."

"It's a shame the airlines don't feed us anymore, isn't it," Beth says. "Here, let me find you something to munch on." Beth reaches in her black bag and pulls out an unopened package of Fig Newtons. Beth hands the bag to the lady who grabs it like a life-preserver. "Why don't you keep the package?" Beth says. "I'll have all the food I want for the next five days."

It doesn't look like the woman is going to share the cookies with her husband. She's got a death grip on the bag as she slides a second cookie into her mouth. "We're celebrating our fifth anniversary with a cruise," the man says. "How about you folks? How long have you been married?"

I don't have any idea how to answer. I look at Beth.

"Not as long as it would seem, from the looks of us," Beth says. "Say, look at our line. I think we're starting to move."

All at once we're trotting along at a good clip. Our ship's getting bigger and taller the closer we get. Cruise people shout directions. I don't get all the words, but Beth does. A man in white shorts pushes us in front of a big cardboard sign and takes our picture. "Have a great cruise," he says to two thousand people, one by one.

I've never seen anything like the inside of a cruise ship. Pinks and blues and shiny brass. Plants and flowers and sparkling mirrored walls. Everybody's excited. Music's play-ing. Crew people are acting like they've never been happier now that Beth and Michael are on board. We walk past the hungry woman and her husband. She's looking a lot better, and her husband is pointing a video camera at everything he sees. "Hi guys," he says. We wave into his movie.

"I suppose we need to find our cabin," Beth says. "Look right here. This is a map."

Beth is staring at a pretty brass picture on the wall. In no time at all she's decided on a direction to our cabin. It beats me how she can figure everything out. She leads me up curv-ing stairways, into talking elevators, down hallways. Every so often she finds another shiny map.

"Don't leave me behind or I'll be lost," I tell her. "I'll never be able to maneuver around on this boat." I try to say it lightly, but fear is creeping into my stomach.

Beth stops walking and turns around. "Sure you will Michael." She crinkles her eyebrows. "You'll get your bear-ings. As soon as we get to our cabin, I'm going to give you a big hug."

The hallways get narrower and longer. We start counting off numbers . . . 6406, 6410, 6414. I can't wait to get to 6428. Then we'll be safe.

Finally, Beth says, "OK, here we are." She's out of breath.

"Let me find my key card," I say. "Where did I put it?"

"It's in your wallet," she says. "I watched you put it there, but I've got mine right here."

She pulls open our cabin door and we both walk into our little love nest.

Our room smells clean and tropical, like orange-pine-apple sherbet. Somebody's twisted the towels up into fish shapes and put welcome notes on the dresser and ice in the ice bucket. I stare at the beds. There are two of them where I was expecting one. Beth sees me looking.

"I'd asked for a king bed. Well, we'll figure something out. Michael, do you like the room? Is it OK?"

"It's wonderful. I can hardly believe we're here," I tell her. There's barely enough room to walk between the beds and turn around. "Didn't I hear you say something about a hug?"

Her hug folds around me. When I first took her in my arms months ago, I could feel her spine tighten and her shoulders tense like she was ready to spring away from me. Her body's learned to trust me. I move my hands over her back, pulling every part closer. Her hands are on my back, doing the same. I let Beth's body soften away my worries and add some new ones at the same time.

After long minutes, we pull away from each other. I glance at the beds. I count them again. Will I lead her to the bed on the left or right? And after, do I have to leave the warmth of Beth for the coldness of the other bed, two feet away?

"Are you as hungry as I am?" Beth asks.

It takes me a few seconds to realize she's talking about food.

"The elevators have a trickiness to them," Beth says. Not all of them go to every deck, but this one seems to be able to take us in the direction of food. I try to memorize floor numbers. Six down to Two. It would be easier if I was driving my Buick, the sun giving me direction. These hallways shut me in, and all my nerves crawl back into my brain. I can't get clear headed. The elevator doors open, and a blue neon blaze surrounds us. People are rushing in every direction. It feels like we're in a shopping mall instead of a boat floating in an ocean.

"Let's find a deck and look at the water for a few minutes before we eat. Maybe we can find a place to watch the sunset." I have to yell at Beth who's three feet ahead of me, hustling toward the prospect of supper.

She breaks and turns around. "Well sure, Michael."

I put my arm on Beth's shoulder as we get back into the elevator and she snuggles against me. Two past Six to Lido. The doors open to a calmer hubbub. Folks are walking instead of scurrying; couples are sitting at little glass tables sipping fancy drinks piled with tropical fruit. Past the clusters of tables and chairs, a wall of windows hints at a view of a black ocean. We're surrounded by the smells of pizza and Greek gyros, the sounds of burgers sizzling and blenders whirring as they whip up the drink of the day.

"These little food places are open all the time," Beth tells me. "It's all included in the cost. I wonder what's in a Welcome to Paradise Punch?"

"Do you want me to get you a drink?" I ask her but she doesn't hear me. Suddenly the extravagance of the ship panics me—too much color, too much sound. I need to feel real air on my face. My eyes need to rest on a pale moon in a black sky.

"I'm going to ask that waiter how to get outside," I yell.

I leave Beth standing by a six-foot potted palm and race toward the Drink of the Day man who's just turned off his blender.

"I need to find the way outside," I say.

"Yes sir, exactly where are you trying to go?"

"I don't know."

His nametag says Eduardo. I tell him I need to breathe some air, to see the ocean, to find a little bit of quiet for me and Beth. I tell him Beth is my friend. Saying it makes me so sad.

"Ah, a cruise with a special friend. Wonderful," Eduardo says. "Let me show you and Beth the finest spot on this ship."

I wave Beth over to us. "This fella is going to show us a quiet place where we can relax for a few minutes," I tell her. Eduardo shakes Beth's hand.

"Oh, that's nice of you," she says. "It has been a long day."

Eduardo doesn't ask "Where are you folks from?" He doesn't say "How long have you two known each other?" He just quietly leads us around counters stacked high with melons and pineapples, past trays of cakes and cookies, to a bronze framed glass door. He opens it for us and waves us through.

"Welcome to the real paradise," Eduardo says and noiselessly closes the door behind him. A little deck. Two chairs sitting side by side. A stack of lifeboats, just in case. A sturdy rail separating us from the sea. Deep blue quiet.

"Oh, Michael, this is perfect. Thank you."

"I'd never have found this deck without Eduardo," I say.

"No, I mean this vacation, this ship, with you," Beth says. "You make me so happy. Thank you."

We sit and stare at the strip of orange sky until it turns purple, then sapphire blue. The moon decides to sprinkle light on top of every wave.

At last Beth says, "Well, I suppose we need to be finding the dining room."

"I hate to leave this pretty place," I say, getting up from my chair. "We'll be able to find it again, won't we?"

"Oh, sure," Beth says, taking my hand as I help her up. "This will be our private balcony. Maybe Eduardo will push some plants in front of it so no one will notice the door."

When we walk past Eduardo, he's mixing drinks. I catch his eye and wave thank you to him. He salutes me.

I know how to find the elevator and punch the buttons. Lido past Six to Two. I'm starting to get the hang of this boat. The pang in my stomach is hunger, not nerves. We enter the cavern of a dining room, and a waiter leads us toward our assigned table, past hundreds of folks already eating. Halfway across the room the waiter stops in front of a round table where four men and four ladies are busy with seafood appetizers. The men all rise to greet Beth. I'm proud to be escorting this lovely lady into our fancy dining room.

"Oh please, go ahead with your meal," Beth says as she sits down. "We've been a bit lost all day, so we're late."

We all introduce ourselves, then they go back to eating

and talking to each other. From their conversation, I take it the eight are friends on a cruise together. Our waiter zips right over as soon as we get settled and I order two glasses of Chianti before we start to study our menus. In no time at all, a waiter has placed a feast in front of us. Every forkful of food tastes better than the one before. If I'm this happy with my meal, Beth must be in heaven.

As the rest of the table talks about Houston and oil and housing markets, Beth finishes her last bites of lobster, neatly drizzled in butter and lemon. Then she focuses on her twice-baked potato.

We eat until breathing becomes a chore. Our waiter returns with offers of dessert. Or coffee. Or anything we want. I order crème brûlée, thinking it's the lightest option. Beth decides on a chocolate mocha cake. One of the ladies at the table tells Beth she had that cake last night and it's better than sex ever hoped to be. Everyone laughs.

I eat my crème brûlée and rethink the same thoughts I've been thinking for months, ever since I saw Beth on her treadmill at Rehab. I'd wanted to take her in my arms, feel her body against mine. It was a glorious fantasy to think about while I pedaled my exercise bike.

I was all set for a life without sex. Sure, once upon a time, when I was seventeen or eighteen, I didn't spend much time thinking about anything else. In my junior year of high school, I recall a pony-tailed girl who sat in front of me in math class. My eyes would follow the curves from her hairline down her neck. I'd wish I could slip inside her sweater and trace all her curves with my tongue instead of my eyes. I got a D in math that year.

The summer after I graduated, Evelyn walked up to the order window of my Pop's sandwich shop. I was working the window that day instead of peeling potatoes. From that moment on, all my thoughts of sex were mingled with thoughts of Evelyn. She'd ordered the Italian beef, our specialty, and fries and a Coke. We sold those Cokes in icy glass bottles. I snapped off the cap, handed her the food, and gave her back change from the two dollars she'd given me. I overcharged her, I guess. Like I said, I'd almost flunked math. She walked away but in a few minutes she was back. She'd written down the prices of all the items she'd ordered and added them up. She showed me her handful of change and pleasantly but firmly requested another twenty-four cents. My Pop heard it all. He came to the window with the money, asked her if she lived close by, asked her if she had a job. When she said no, he hired her.

My life began that day. In the last few years, I'd been thinking all the sweet parts of my life were over until I ran into a lady who'd had a heart attack and decided to go on living, just like I did.

Beth is totally engaged with her better-than-sex chocolate cake. The friends at the table are talking about tax shelters while they sip after dinner drinks. "As Time Goes By" drifts to us from the grand piano in the corner of the room. I wonder if Beth likes to dance. More wine is poured in Beth's glass, then mine. Beth finishes the last swirls of mocha icing. Her nails are pale pink from a manicure done in preparation for our trip.

"Should we head back to our cabin, Michael?"

My throat is too tight to answer. I nod yes.

This time I lead. We walk without talking, my hand on Beth's back. I know which floor number to press in the elevator. I know to turn left when I see the vase of purple flowers. I count the numbers in a slow steady pace . . . 6406, 6410, 6414. At 6428 we stop. It's my key opening the door this time.

We'd left the little bedside lamp on. I pull Beth into the pool of warm light between our beds and wrap my arms around her. She moves against me so easily.

"Listen, do you hear that?" Beth whispers.

"The hum? It's probably the AC system."

"No. I'm talking about the other sound. The sound of us being all alone. There's no phone ringing. No doorbells. Isn't it the loveliest sound you've ever heard?"

Beth's face is so inviting, without a trace of fear or doubt. Her cheeks are pink and soft. She looks like my blushing bride. Except she isn't.

Slow, molten sadness suffocates me. "Beth, I want you so much, but not like this." I push the words through the gravel in my throat. My voice is pleading, I hate the sound of it. "Let's get married. I want you to be my wife."

Silence.

"Maybe we could get married right on this ship?" My brain is swarming with words I didn't know I'd say. "Can the Captain marry us? I could ask him."

Beth steps back from me. Her blushing cheeks turn to red flame. She's stone quiet.

I step closer, again fold her into my arms. Her shoulders are oak.

What can I do to soften her arms, so they'll fold back around me? I hold her tighter, bury my face against her neck and whisper, "Beth, you know I love you and I'd never do anything to hurt you, I promise." I tip her head back before she has a chance to speak. Her shoulders soften a bit with my kiss, and she places her palms against my chest. When I open my eyes, she's looking into my face. Her palms gently, firmly, push me away. She peels herself out of my arms. Her eyes bore into me. I need to say more, try to explain. I just stare. Her face softens to sadness right before she turns and rushes out of our room.

CHAPTER 12

❋

Beth

Please God, please somebody, help me.

I never pray unless I'm scared. And then it's no churchy, eyes-closed, down-on-my-knees type of prayer. Not that there's anything wrong with that, I used to go to church often. I'm still pro-God, even though He—or She or Whoever—doesn't always seem to be pro-Beth.

Please God, help me. I'm so scared. I'm all alone here, clinging to this steel railing. If I let go, I'll plunge so far into despair I'll never find my way out.

I should be elated. There's a wonderful man two decks down in our cabin, probably the kindest man I've ever met, who's just said to me, "I love you. Let's get married right now." I recall he kissed me, right before my heart started pounding, and my scrumptious supper churned in my stomach. And then I just fled from that sweet little room with the mango-scented soap and the towel folded into the shape of a dolphin.

I've been thinking *romance, fine. I can give romance another try.* This ship is twelve hundred miles from Centerburg. No one needs to know. We have space and time and the freedom of an ocean. We only told the essential people—Ramona and Clarice, who'd stab me if I'd kept it a secret from her. I'd worked up the courage to see Doctor Sam to talk about sex and heart disease and estrogen creams for dreaded vaginal dryness. I reread my old paperback copy of *Sweet Savage Love* looking for inspiration and tips. I even packed the horrible black peignoir Clarice gave me as a bon voyage present. Does anyone say peignoir anymore?

A romantic ocean cruise. Now Michael has ruined it.

Clarice's face slips into my frantic prayer. Clarice would love to see me married more than Michael, more than God. She's been trying to match me up with every available male who drifted through Centerburg for the last three decades, and there weren't many, believe me. Clarice was the instigator behind my dating the new foreman at the fiberboard plant, who wore white leather shoes on every one of our dates. I was so happy when the company he worked for fell into financial distress and moved to Mexico. Fifty people lost their jobs, but I was saved.

I ease my grip on the railing just a bit, to make sure I can stand upright without its support. Music drifts through the sturdy door. The two teak deck chairs behind me are empty. I turn, walk to mine, and sink in. If I had a blanket and pillow, I'd stay right here, alone and safe. Emotional breakdown takes such energy.

My darling Michael, my sweet old coot, who do you think you are, storming into my life, feeding me lasagna and being so darn nice? Making my friends and daughter love you?

I stare through steel rails. I'm sick of plotting my course, anticipating life's every pitfall. Can I allow myself the luxury of unplanned happiness? I look at Michael's empty chair. *No* is such an empty, lonely word. My heart says *Yes*.

Muffled voices gather just beyond my private balcony. The door eases open and Michael's head slides through. "She's here. Thank you," he says to someone over his shoulder. "Oh Beth, I was so scared. I'm sorry. I just wanted to say . . . I just wanted to find you, to see if you were OK. I'll just leave you alone."

Before he slips back through the half open door, I'm on

my feet. "I'm fine. It's still lovely out here. Come and sit down with me. I've saved you a chair."

He sits down, words tumbling out. "I shouldn't have asked again. I'm sorry. Don't be mad. I'll never ask again."

"Michael Bartoli, you mean to tell me you're withdrawing your proposal just when I've decided to marry you?"

I watch Michael register my words. His smile explodes. He gets on his knees in front of me and grabs me. We kiss. It's unplanned, unromantic, awkward. Our noses bump, our mouths are too full of laughter. Michael kisses my eyes, my nose. "I don't believe it. Really? Do you mean it?" he says in gasps between laughter and kisses.

How is it possible, Beth St. Clair, I ask myself, *that you've made another human being so joyful?*

After we leave the quiet darkness of our private balcony, walking back into the lounge feels like a jolt back into daytime. I'm surprised my watch says ten-thirty. Michael leads me to a corner, and we settle into two flamingo-print cushioned chairs facing Eduardo's bar. A band is playing. A few couples are dancing. The frantic pace of embarking has settled into ocean cruising.

"Look at all these folks," Michael says. "Not a one of them is as happy as I am."

A couple dressed in tux and evening gown swirl by us, bodies entwined. They look pretty happy to me.

"You poor man, you just don't know what you're getting into."

"Yes, I do," he says. "I figured we should be together from the minute I saw you in our Rehab class. Do you still have that Green Bay sweatshirt?"

"Of course. I keep it in my seduction clothes drawer." Michael's eyes always cloud a bit when I tease him. "It's been a long, lovely day. Maybe we should head back to our cabin."

"Let me check on something first," Michael says. "Do you want one of Eduardo's drinks?'

He rushes over to Eduardo's Drink of the Day bar. I settle back in my chair and watch my *fiancé*. I chuckle. I like the word much better than *boyfriend*.

Michael and Eduardo delve deep into a conversation. Michael waves his arms and gestures toward me, Eduardo claps him on the shoulder and shakes his hand. Eduardo looks at me, waves, holds his hands over his heart. Even though Michael's back is to me, I know he's telling Eduardo about the events of the last ten minutes. Their excitement calms into a less animated exchange. Michael leans in to say something and Eduardo shakes his head, thinks and points his finger skyward with an idea. After he pours our two drinks, Eduardo takes a beeper from his belt and begins tapping it as Michael returns to our table, looking confident.

"How about a dance?" Michael says.

"I'm not much of a dancer." I look at the couples in each other's arms. The music is slow and soft while the singer's voice is strong and deep. The contrast is appealing. "Do you like to dance?"

"I love to dance. Come dance with me."

Michael's hand is on my back as he leads me to the dance floor. He draws me to him and coaxes my body to drift back and forth with his. Our stomachs touch, his thighs slide against mine, my feet move where he directs them.

"It's easy to dance with you," I say pulling away to look in his eyes.

One song ends, another begins. We just dance.

A red-haired woman in a turquoise blouse taps Michael's shoulder.

"Mr. Bartoli? I'm Lisette. May I speak with you a moment?" She leads us back to our chairs where Eduardo is waiting.

Oh Michael, what have you done? I gather myself into a

protective mode. Will this woman and Eduardo want to pitch an irresistible time-share condo on an exotic island? Maybe a cleaning product sales pyramid. Those folks can be found anywhere. My sweet Michael is a naive traveler, and he trusts everyone. I should have warned him. I feel my face flush with anger as Michael proudly introduces me and Lisette shakes my hand in a very businesslike fashion. We all sit down, and I ready myself for battle.

Lisette leans toward us as she speaks, the sincere salesman's body language.

"Eduardo just told me your good news," she says. "Congratulations. I believe we can help you with your wedding arrangements, if you'd like. We happen to have a Justice of the Peace on board so he can do the ceremony when we dock in the Cayman Islands on Tuesday morning. That will give me a day to make all the arrangements." She flashes an alluring smile and turns toward Michael. "I know you asked Eduardo about getting married at sea, but we have to be docked for Brother Carlos to perform a legal ceremony." She turns back to her two-person audience. "So, what do you think?"

Michael grabs my hand. "Beth, this is wonderful. Can you believe it?"

Will I be able to extricate us from Lisette and Eduardo's dubious venture without hurting Michael's feelings? Has Michael been out of my eyeshot long enough to have signed some type of contract? I don't recall seeing him pen-in-hand at the Drink of the Day bar. Just as I'd decided to freefall into happiness, I'm bombarded with unplanned monetary commitments.

I direct my response to the ring-leader Lisette. "I assume you want us to purchase some type of wedding-cruise package and we do appreciate all your time and effort—I think this is a clever touch since Lisette only has about fifteen minutes invested in her ruse—but I'm sure we can't afford this.

Apparently you have not discussed any fees with Michael?" I hope my eye-contact is as intimidating as hers.

Eduardo is bubbling to get into the conversation. "Your surprise engagement is perfectly timed. A young couple . . ." He looks at me cautiously. "I mean to say, a couple not as sure of their love to each other, younger and not as wise, had planned their wedding for this cruise, but there was a problem and they canceled yesterday. We are all set for wedding, we only need a bride and groom." He holds his palms heavenward, shrugs his shoulders at the logic.

Aaah, so Michael and Beth arrived just in time to cover the cost of a canceled wedding. My anger sends another hot flare to my cheeks. I direct my controlled seething to Lisette. "I'm sorry for your unfortunate situation, but we cannot afford a shipboard wedding."

Lisette understands my glare. "There will be no fee for your ceremony. The couple had a prepaid, non-refundable contract. The wedding is arranged, Brother Carlos is traveling with us, we have flowers and cake. As Eduardo said, the only thing lacking is a bride and groom."

"But aren't there legal protocols? Forms and documents? Advanced planning?" I ask Lisette.

"Lisette IS the wedding planner!" Eduardo looks at her with pride, takes her hand. Her perfectly formed red lips break into a laugh, she leans toward him and rests her hand on his knee.

"Eduardo is a horrible romantic. He's so excited about your upcoming wedding." Now I understand. Eduardo and Lisette aren't con artists. They're lovers.

"Let's do it, Beth, let's get married right now," my very own romantic says to me. "I'm sorry for those young folks, though. I hope they're OK."

"It was good timing for them also." Eduardo laughs. "It seems there was an indiscretion. The discovery was made a few days before the wedding."

"Oh, I'm so sorry," says Michael. "It must have been really sad for everybody."

Of course my sweet Michael is troubled by a tale of unfaithful lovers. My heart isn't as large. Their encounter with indiscretion strikes me as ironic. Marital unfaithfulness is paying off for me at last. What a nice deal. I turn to this man sitting next to me, my soon-to-be-husband. "You astonish me every day. Is this what life is going to be like, being married to you?"

"Yep." Michael's voice is confident and proud.

Eduardo looks over his shoulder to his empty bar, the celebration is winding down. Last dance is announced to the three remaining couples on the dance floor. I turn to our new wedding planner, "What do Michael and I need to do?"

Lisette pulls her chair closer to mine, back to business. Michael and Eduardo talk and laugh and clap each other on the shoulders as I listen to Lisette outline the simple steps needed to rearrange the rest of our lives. Will Eduardo be Michael's best man? A pang of loneliness stabs me . . . I need Clarice beside me, jumping up and down and shrieking. Another ache—I want to call my daughter. I've never experienced the desire to place phone calls, but I usually don't have such joyous news.

"We'll be docked at Grand Cayman on Tuesday morning so Brother Carlos could do the ceremony at seven a.m. I'm sorry it's so early but I have other obligations for the reminder of the day." Lisette turns her brilliant smile to Eduardo. "We thought it would be lovely to have a sunrise wedding on the little balcony you like so much. The location was Eduardo's idea."

"As soon as I have your passports, I can begin," Lisette says, concluding our meeting. "Should I start tonight, or do you want me to wait until tomorrow?"

"Let's start now. I want to get this ball rolling before Beth jumps ship," Michael says.

"No, wait until tomorrow." Eduardo looks at his watch. "This is your first cruise, correct? The Midnight Dessert Buffet begins in fifteen minutes. You must go."

Michael and I join the group of weary cruise-goers, waiting for the last extravaganza of the day. Two uniformed sentinels stand at attention in front of the closed double doors. At midnight the doors open, Cinderella-in-reverse, and hundreds of feet, clad in flip-flops or sensible walking shoes instead of glass slippers, file into our ballroom. Chocolates form stately towers. Multi-layered platters offer cakes and cookies and tiny pies. Mountains of pastel fruits landscape the buffet tables, some familiar, others with flavors I've yet to taste. This room holds every sweet I've ever wanted, more than I could ever eat.

I drop into an empty chair and Michael leaves me to select a few gourmet morsels. I watch him dip a strawberry the size of a hen's egg into a bath of chocolate. He carefully places it on his small plate, then plucks the tastiest torte from a platter holding two dozen options. He returns to me to share the bounty.

"Michael, there's nothing here I need. What I need is for you to take me back to our cabin."

"Yes, Beth, that's exactly what I need too."

Michael leaves the plate of untouched desserts on a side table, takes my hand and leads me away from the room of diversions.

We retrace our steps, I reread the numbers. 6406, 6410, 6414. Could I carry any more emotions down this narrow hallway? Desire, desperation, fear, anticipation, fatigue. I wonder what emotions Michael is carrying, which ones he is setting aside. His left hand is familiar against my back, his right hand grasps our key card. His walk is purposeful as he leads me down this well-traveled hallway.

At 6428, he pauses, steps in front of me, takes my face

in his hands. He doesn't smile, the corners of his eyes don't crinkle with amusement. His look is serious and consuming. I've not seen this face before. He closes his eyes and kisses me. His lips cover mine completely. Then he pulls away to open the door.

Our room is just as we've left it, two beds bathed in lamp light, but now the glow is focused, harsh, revealing. I'm exposed. Words start tumbling out of me, to drown out Michael's silence.

"Should I turn off that light? It seems so bright, but maybe not. I'll just slip into the bathroom for a minute and freshen up after the long day. Wonderful, but long. I'll just be a few minutes. Do you want to use the bathroom first?"

"No, you go ahead," Michael says as he plops his suitcase down on one bed.

I close the door and turn off every light except the night-light above the hair dryer. The dark and the smallness comfort me. In seconds, Michael will see me—every part of me. I feel huge. My stomach, oh, I wish I hadn't eaten all that butter, the baked potato, the chocolate cake. I turn on the shower and the sink, flush the toilet a few times, trying to let the sounds pound out my brain's frayed neural pathways. I shower, brush my teeth, and stuff myself into Clarice's present, the itchy black lace gown.

I feel ridiculous as I walk out of the bathroom. Beth the Vamp, seducing Cary Grant/Michael, who's standing with his back to me, clad in white boxer shorts and a sleeveless undershirt. On the bed beside his suitcase is a ball of crinkled cellophane, in his hands, a rectangle of brown patterned pajamas. He's cursing softly as he picks pins from the folded cloth.

He turns to me, irritated and embarrassed. "There must be a hundred straight pins holding this together." He picks up a stray pin from the bedspread and gently puts it on the bedside table. "Ramona bought these. I don't wear pajamas."

"Clarice bought this gown for me," I confess. "I sleep in cotton nightshirts—I have hot flashes." I walk to him, put my arms around his body, feeling his soft cotton t-shirt against my lace-covered breasts. "Oh, Michael what are we doing? I don't even know who we are right now. I'm just so tired." I lay my head against his chest.

He pulls away and looks at me. "Beth, you're so beautiful. You don't have to get all gussied up for me. Why don't you put on one of those pajama shirts?"

"I didn't pack any of them."

I sink against him as he folds me into his arms, smooths me with his words. "Just relax . . . you're so tired . . . I'm here . . . it's OK." There's no passion in his touch as he rubs his hands up and down my back.

Michael moves his hands to my shoulders. Eyes teasing, he says, "You want to share these pajamas with me? You can wear the top and I'll take the bottoms. Then we can crawl into bed and get some sleep." He hands me the rectangle of cloth. "You can find the rest of the blasted pins while I wash up."

"You wouldn't think new pajamas would be such a dangerous proposition," I say, "but I'd love to share these with you."

Michael grabs a brand-new toiletries case, probably also Ramona's doing, and disappears into the bathroom while I de-pin our nightwear. The comforting sound of shower water drifts through our little cabin as I stare at our side-by-side suitcases resting on a twin bed. I move the pillow to our bed, fold down the covers, slide out of black satin and into permanent press cotton blend.

"How's about I sleep next to the wall," says Michael. He's bare-chested and pajama bottom clad. Silver and brown hairs curl across his chest, making me smile. I love men with hairy chests. "Let's see if this bed will hold both of us."

Michael pulls back the covers, crawls as far as possible to

the cabin wall, and punches his pillow into a tight mound. He holds up the covers up, inviting me to join him, and I turn off the lamp and slid in.

"Do you have enough room? If you get too hot from those flashes, just throw off the covers." Michael moves an inch closer to the wall.

Should I lie on my side facing him or away? If I curl into my old familiar sleeping position, I'll stab Michael in the stomach with my knees, but it seems rude to turn my back to this man who loves me.

I settle on my back, my head snuggled into my pillow. I stretch my right leg and rest it against Michael's. His right hand rubs my arm from shoulder to wrist and up again to curl around my elbow. He doesn't kiss me. He doesn't say good night. I only hear his soft exhale of breath as I shut my eyes.

Nine-year-old Beth was a fitful sleeper. When I couldn't sleep from fear of World Wars or disloyal girlfriends or upcoming tests on long-division, my mother would sit by my bed and stroke my hair and say, "Relax your toes, relax your ankles, relax your legs." By the time my mother said "Relax your head" I was always asleep.

I wonder how my mother knew of this technique. She probably read it in *Good Housekeeping* or *Ladies Home Journal*. Did she also suffer from a life so confusing, so out of control? Did she turn off her fears each night with the same refrain? Did she grieve she'd passed her fears down to her daughter, just as I worry I've passed mine to Kate?

I close my eyes and relax my toes, tucked around Michael's ankles. I breathe in and out, smelling the mango soap we've both used to wash our faces. It's a tight fit in our bed. We calm together, Michael on his side, making room for me to lie flat on my back. We're grounded in our almost-firm mattress adrift in a black, pulsing sea. I relax my ankles, my legs. My breathing slows. My mind shifts from overdrive to idle. Old visions surface as I slide into a black silken sleep. Vacations long past, other sunsets, different seas, humid summer nights. My breathing takes on the ebb and flow of a forgotten ocean. Pete walks into my dream, flooding me with old desires and regrets. I stir myself awake without opening my eyes.

I'm so disappointed in my subconscious. What is Pete St. Clair doing in this bed? Did his memory arise from Eduardo's conversation of love gone awry or my anticipation of the night ahead?

Sometimes I wish I'd had a hundred lovers.

We did have some fine times, Pete and I. He woke up my woman body. Truth be told, it was wide awake already, yawning and stretching and waiting for some attention. Pete made my first time so lovely. He'd had his first years before, and he was proud to show off his skills. There was no part of sex I didn't like. The phone calls before, the planning. The anticipation was welcomed agony. Sometimes Pete would ask me sweetly, gently. Sometimes he'd whisper forbidden words, all the words nice ladies should never hear or utter. Those words would hit me hard and hot. They stirred me more than his sweet murmurings. I could not wait for nightfall, back seats, Pete's shacky apartment, and later, our very own little house, where we made love in every room, even the backyard. I knew just what he was going to do, what I'd do in response. And then, he'd surprise me with a delicious twist or turn. A few times I surprised him. I could see him smiling in the darkness.

If I'd had a hundred lovers, sex would be my own. It wouldn't be something Pete had brought to me, and then taken away.

When I awake minutes—perhaps hours—later, Michael is still on his side facing me, his head propped on one arm. The fingers of his other hand are stroking my cheek, up to my eyelashes and down to the corner of my lips. So gentle is his touch, I can barely feel his skin on mine. I open my eyes to look into his. "Close your eyes and get some rest," he says in a voice as soft as my mother's. One tear flows down my cheek. Michael brushes it away and I fall back to sleep.

CHAPTER 13

✺

Michael

After our frantic, awful, wonderful Sunday on the ship, Beth and I settled into bed together so easily. She was exhausted. I was too, I guess, but every cell in my body was awake. Beth said *YES*. The wonder of it. I knew I wouldn't be able to sleep, just from amazement. Beth, I was thinking, wouldn't be able to sleep from jitters. She was nervous, over-whelmed by the speed of it all. It was a freefall for Beth who likes to plan and plot and handle things. A romantic cruise, an engagement, a wedding all planned—it was a lot for one day. My poor Beth.

Yet, there she was, standing in front of me wearing the top half of my new pajamas, talking a mile a minute, exhausted, and finally lying down beside me, quiet and breathing deep and steady, her leg against mine. My heart surprised me. Instead of beating out of control, it was full and calm in my chest.

A few hours after midnight, I must have fallen asleep. I was so happy lying next to Beth, watching her sleep, I didn't want to sleep myself. Resting next to her, seeing her in the filtered neon from the bathroom's partially opened door, feeling her leg against my thigh, her hip against my stomach, I couldn't imagine sleeping would give me more comfort. But my arm kept falling asleep on its own, as I propped myself up to look at her, to rub my finger across her cheek. When I lay down on my back, to try to get rid of the numbness and prickly tingles in my arm, the rest of my body must have grabbed the opportunity and dozed off.

I wake to Beth's hand on my stomach, her touch pulling me back up from the best sleep I'd had in years. I hear a silent song through my body. Feeling her hand on my stomach in the early hours of a Monday morning, I know without her having to say the words. Beth knows I love her.

Warm sleeping smells surround us as we wake to each other. Beth turns to me. I turn to her. Her hand moves from my stomach to my back, pulling me close. As I unbutton her pajamas and slide my hands under the cotton to her skin, rustles of cloth and murmurs from Beth's throat drift to my ears.

Our bodies welcome each other, new friends excited by the prospect of things to come, old friends who've been apart too many years. Beth's hands are so familiar as they pull me closer. *Oh, my darling, I've missed you.* We float to familiar music. I forget I'm Michael. I forget Beth is Beth. We are each other, as we drift together, apart, together. No pasts, no comparisons. Each sensation a discovery, every movement a new exploration.

We are still in bed when the phone rings, well past breakfast, slightly past lunch. "Brother Carlos is here in my office," Lisette says. "He wants to speak with you and Beth for just a few moments, if you two are available this afternoon."

I was hoping to talk Beth into missing supper also, or maybe ordering room service, but after I relay Lisette's message, she groans and stretches and turns to me for one last kiss before we rise from the warmth of our little twin bed.

Beth giggles. "Do you think he'll still marry us, after our morning of pre-meditated, pre-marital sex?"

"Beth, Michael, you walked swiftly to each other, to this moment. It wasn't a grand procession, yet each step was perfectly timed, as all miracles are. Let our eyes see the miracles surrounding us: this improbable scene, this glorious sunrise, these two souls who are here to declare their love with amazement still on their tongues.

"Glory in the smallness of Divine Order as well as Its overwhelming grace. Witness the vast simplicity of life. Don't doubt. Don't anguish. Immerse yourselves in the love that is life's gift. Be joyous all the rest of your days and beyond. With that joy, I declare you husband and wife."

Beyond the balcony rails, layers of pink spread across the sky. A human being couldn't look at this sky and not think of God. I'm in heaven right now, standing beside Beth and Brother Carlos, Eduardo and Lisette. And Evelyn, my Momma, and Pop. I'd like to think they're here too, beneath this pink and blue sky.

My new wife smells of suntan lotion—brown sugar and coconuts. On our little balcony, floating on a sunlit sea, I kiss her and shake the hand of the man who has just married us.

"Thank you," I say to Brother Carlos. "That was a kind of miracle, the way the sun rose just as you pronounced us husband and wife."

Brother Carlos smiles. "I have a sun chart and an excellent watch, and I'm fairly disciplined with my words. I didn't make the sunrise. That miracle occurs every morning. I just made you notice."

Beth's hand grasps mine and we watch the blazing colors fade into daylight. Blue sky, blue ocean. The sun lifts into Tuesday, our wedding day.

Beth is wearing her fancy outfit for dress-up dinners on the ship—black shiny pants and a sparkly white blouse. She bought it at an after-Christmas sale at her favorite Centerburg ladies' shop. She wouldn't let me go with her since she's so sensitive about gossip. I wonder how she's going to handle the explosion of talk in Centerburg when she comes back from a cruise with a husband. I hope she'll be happy to tell her news.

"How about kissing me one more time. Then we'll go have some breakfast," Beth says.

Eduardo and Lisette clap for us as we have a second married kiss.

"I hope you like wedding cake with your eggs," says Lisette, as our wedding party leaves our balcony for the air conditioning lounge.

Eduardo is beaming with excitement. "Look at what we've arranged for your party!" Next to the Drink of the Day bar is a round table covered with a white cloth. At its center stands a four-tiered wedding cake, swirling with strawberries and topped with a tiny bride and groom. Stacks of plates, piles of napkins, and rows of forks complete the table. They are an invitation for everyone to share in our celebration. Above the bar is a banner—Beth and Michael's Sunrise Toast. We are the drink of the day. Eduardo begins to pour orange and red liquids into champagne glasses. When he has a tray full of Beth and Michael Sunrise Toasts, he steps away from the bar, raises a glass in our direction and addresses the gathering crowd.

"We have a new bride, a new groom, this beautiful morning: Beth and Michael. Please, everyone, join us in celebrating."

A semi-circle of cruise-goers forms around us, cheering and clapping, enticed by an unexpected party and free cake. Lisette pushes Beth to my side and shoves a silver knife in her hand.

"Just cut a little piece right here," Lisette whispers. "We'll save the top for you to take home for your first anniversary."

Beth is flushed. She carves a bit of cake, picks it up, and pops it into my mouth. The crowd cheers. I do the same, being careful not to smear cake across Beth's lips to embarrass her more. Cameras flash at us. Eduardo pushes drinks in our hands.

Strangers, now our wedding guests, crowd closer as Lisette takes the knife. I hold empty plates for her to fill as the knife slides again and again through the tower of cake. Some folks stop to shake our hands before grabbing a plate and scurrying away. A familiar face approaches and I recognize it as the hungry woman we met as we were boarding the ship. She hugs Beth, who's trying to inch away from the cake, Lisette, and me.

"Cookies, now cake. You are my new best friend," I hear her say.

Her husband shakes my hand, then aims his movie camera our way. "This is the couple we met as we were getting on the ship," he says to the camera, documenting. "Their names are Beth and Michael and they just got married."

"Michael, let's go." Beth's voice is quivering.

I look at the cake. It's only half cut. It's our party. Cameras are still flashing. Everyone is so happy for us.

"Beth, I don't think we should leave yet."

With a food server's practiced eye, I scan the crowd, estimating how long it will take to feed them all. No more than twenty minutes, if I can clamp down on my chatting. At the back of the gathering Brother Carlos is tall and bald and serene, holding a cup of coffee instead of a glass of Beth and Michael Sunrise Toast. Our eyes meet, and I wave him toward us.

Brother Carlos, Lisette told us, was a wealthy businessman from Argentina. Lisette is unsure of his religion or current economic situation. She just knows he's Justice of the Peace. He lives here and there—on an island, on a ship, in Miami, in South America. Wherever he feels he can help. I can't guess his age. He looks newly born, but his eyes are ancient.

I watch Brother Carlos weave his way through our crowd. His body moves like it's not quite under his control, as if a force other than his own is carrying him where he needs to be. And this morning, it seems, he is carried to us.

"I was wondering if you and Beth could go get us some coffee?" I say.

Brother Carlos looks at Beth, Lisette, then back at me. "Beth, come with me. Michael will join us later."

"Thank you." Beth exhales. "I'd really like to sit down for a bit." She turns to me for another kiss. Again, there is a barrage of flashes from cameras and fancy cell phones.

"I'll find you in half an hour," I yell to my retreating bride.

Brother Carlos takes Beth's elbow and weaves her through the crowd.

After Lisette and I fill half a dozen more plates with cake and line them across the front of the serving table, I walk around the room and gather plates and forks and quite a few drained Beth and Michael Sunrise Toast glasses, and place everything in the two tubs behind Eduardo's bar.

"Michael, you need to fill out an employment application for us," Lisette laughs. She's enjoying the party so much more than my Beth was.

More cameras flash at Lisette and me. A voice from the back, a newcomer, clicks her fork against her champagne glass. Mistaking our wedding planner for the bride, a new cheer arises. "A kiss! Beth and Michael, a kiss?"

We plan on spending our last morning on the Bartoli Deck, as Lisette has named it. As we dress for breakfast, we hear a knock on our cabin door and open it to find our friend with the video camera and his wife. After seeing them again at the cake-cutting, he has been aiming his camera our way for the rest of the week—at the Captain's Dinner, on our Bartoli Deck, at our port visit to Grand Cayman as we were walking out of the jewelry store Eduardo recommended. Beth had waved at him and flashed her new wedding ring.

"We were afraid we'd miss seeing you today, so I convinced that bar guy to give us your cabin number. We've been right down the hallway from you the whole cruise," he says.

"Here, we want you to have this." His wife hands Beth a purple bag. Inside is a movie made for us, our own DVD. On its cover, a photo of Beth and me sitting in our teak chairs. The title of our movie is printed across the front. *Our Wedding Cruise.*

"I can't believe this." Beth turns the DVD over, looking at the front, the back. "We don't have a single picture. Let us pay you!"

"No, it's our wedding gift. A thank you for saving my life as we were boarding." She turns to her husband. "He loves to tinker with stuff like this."

After breakfast, Beth leans back in her teak chair, her face skyward and her eyes closed. In her lap is the square plastic box with our picture on the front. Too precious to pack in her suitcase, she'd said. Her lips are full and smiling at the thoughts flickering across her mind. Two bands of white are etched across each tanned foot, a pattern formed by sandals and a week of sunshine. Somewhere our packed suitcases are waiting to return to our real life, our new life. Eduardo is in the habit of securing the deck just for us, keeping the door locked if he thinks we'll be heading this way, and locking us out here as we lounge, so no one will disturb us. When I tap on the door three times, our code, he'll open the door to let us back into the ship. This morning I'm dreading the thought of leaving this little space. It holds my whole life.

I'm jealous of Beth. My mind is roaring with questions of where or what or how we will go about living once we fly away from this perfect week. Beth has yet to notice what I've done to her. As she dozes, I stew.

When she finally opens her eyes, I start apologizing. "I'm afraid I've got us into a real mess. How do we go about telling everyone about all this? We don't know where we're going to live. We don't even know where we're going to sleep tonight. I should have planned out our life, before . . . I'm sorry." Beth turns her face to me as I rant, but her head still rests on the back of her chair.

"And there's Sunny," I say. "I don't even know if you like dogs."

Beth laughs and stretches her toes toward the ocean. "Michael, I do believe you've turned into a worrywart. We've only been married five days and already you're starting to sound like me." She reaches across to grasp my hand. "Relax, everything will tumble into place."

Beth's been sounding like this all week. Maybe it's cruise ship talk. *No worries*, as Eduardo always says. I lay my head against the chair and try to relax.

"I hate to think we have to leave here in just a few hours," I say.

"Everything we've found here, we'll take with us," Beth says. Her fingers tighten around mine. "Everything's fine. Although wherever we live, I'd sure like to have a little porch with two chairs just like these."

Beth

We hatch the plan on the flight from Miami to St. Louis. Instead of looking out my window, I hold Michael's hand and listen. His every sentence starts with "Should we . . . ? How can we . . . ? What will we . . . ?" And then the agonized, "I just don't know." My new husband is in need of definite goals and paths to them. Finally, I pull my black carry-on from under the seat in front of me, take out a pen and the notebook I've been using for a trip log. I open to a clean page.

"Michael, let's just plan today and tomorrow and not worry about the rest of our life just now."

With our exchange of vows, I seem to have acquired all of Michael's unwavering optimism. Seeing me pen in hand, he calms some.

"How about this?" Michael says. "We keep our wedding a secret for one more day. We can make a big announcement tomorrow, invite Clarice and Jim over to Ramona's house, call up Mike's family and Kate and Zoe." As his plan bubbles out, I write. "We'll show everybody our movie. We can eat the top of the cake Lisette packed for us. I'll buy champagne."

A party. My Michael is back.

By the time our pilot announces our descent into St. Louis, I have three pages of directives: a guest list—in person and via telephone, a menu and shopping list, and an hour-by-hour guide as to how to accomplish it all. Michael is ecstatic.

The truth is this state of wellbeing didn't arise from our lovely wedding ceremony. Warm, alluring peacefulness settled upon me an hour later, during my breakfast with Carlos.

During breakfast, Carlos sipped strong coffee. "A vice," he said, but he was raised on the taste, the smell. "I'm wiser in my food choices for the rest of the day, but I do love my morning coffee." He ordered yogurt with granola and a bowl of fruit. I thought briefly about making a similar healthy choice, then ordered scrambled eggs and French toast. Carlos didn't ask me about my past. He didn't ask about our plans for the future. He just said, "Beth, tell me, are you happy? Did you have the opportunity to enjoy your wedding?"

"I did," I said, "and then the reception closed in on me. We were in the middle of a festival, we were the Drink of the Day." I dropped my hands to my lap, sighed, confessed. "I don't like to be at the center of things. Michael is such a people-person. Everyone loves him. I should make an attempt to be more out-going."

"You're perfect just the way you are, Beth," Carlos said, making me laugh.

"Oh no. I don't think so. I'm a long way from perfect."

"Beth, listen to me. You are perfect. All you need to be, you already are. You love and you are loved. All you need to do is breathe and enjoy."

"I wish it were that simple," I said. I meant my reply to be sarcastic reality, but as I said it an inkling of desire crept into my heart. Maybe Carlos was right? Maybe I could be happy? Maybe I was already happy? I just wasn't used to the feeling.

I looked at my French toast, crispy and hot and sprinkled with powdered sugar. "I love French toast," I said and started to cry.

My tears didn't bother Carlos one bit. "Don't stop crying," he said, "until all the fear is gone."

The crying started in my nose and moved to my throat, my stomach, my heart. Carlos handed me napkin after napkin. By the time twelve soggy napkins were piled next to my breakfast plate, I was exhausted. And hungry. And happy.

"I feel so much better." I laughed. "Thank you."

"Thank you for letting me into your heart, Beth." Carlos had one last sip of coffee as I cut my first bite of French toast. "And now, should I go see how Michael is doing? I expect your wedding cake has been completely shared by now."

Carlos wiped his lips and held me in his gaze. "This peace you're feeling," Carlos said, "will always be with you. It's Beth. And a secret—unlike wedding cake, the more you share it, the larger it becomes." Carlos set his napkin beside his plate, pushed back his chair. "Now, let me go find your husband."

As Carlos walked away, I wondered if it was possible he was correct. Was I perfect? And might I be happy for the rest of my life? Again, I answered *Yes*. But just in case I forget his words, his cell phone number is tucked in my purse, right under my emergency medical card.

The Italian Wedding soup (Michael's clever touch) is simmering on Ramona's stove as he pulls his homemade pizza from the oven. The *Our Wedding Cruise* DVD is tucked in my purse and the top of our wedding cake is in a nondescript pastry box in Ramona's refrigerator. In the kitchen, Ramona and Clarice have turned the counter into a buffet. In the family room, Ravi and Jim, and Lucas and New Girlfriend are clustered in front of Monday night football on the TV. It's half time. Michael and I have rehashed and rehearsed the steps from dinner party to Big Surprise. So far, our plan is picture-perfect.

"OK, everybody," Michael yells as he places the pizza in the center of the buffet, "Order's Up." He winks at me, then delivers the next line. "While this pie rests for a minute, Beth and I want to show you some pictures from our cruise."

I hear groaning from the family room. Lucas? Ravi?

Michael smiles, pushes on. "Ramona, this is one of those things that goes in the TV. Can you help?" Reluctantly, our whole group settles in front of the television.

Clarice starts screaming the moment the TV screen shows Michael and Beth standing behind a wedding cake. She jumps to her feet, and the screeches turn to splatters of words. "Oh my God . . . married? No . . . Beth . . . oh my God . . . ."

As our movie shows Michael putting a piece of wedding cake in my mouth, Clarice charges at me, grabs me up from my chair, and hugs me as both of us fall backward. We topple back in the chair, with Clarice sitting in my lap, gasping. I hope we haven't overdone it. My heart is pounding as Clarice's grip tightens around my midsection. An emergency room trip in the middle of our surprise would be distracting.

Clarice's eruption sets off a small tidal wave among the rest of our guests, save for Ravi who has calmly turned off the DVD as directed, and New Girlfriend, who up to this point has been wrapped around Lucas at the far end of the sofa. Ramona is dancing around her daddy as Jim pounds Michael on the back. Sunny is barking with what sounds like laughter and wagging his body from the neck down as Lucas tries to contain him. My view is somewhat obscured with Clarice in my lap, crying into my left ear as my right ear takes in the happy melee.

"Yes, everyone, Beth and I have a little something to tell you about our cruise."

Michael stills our crowd, his voice sweet, his hands raised, palms facing us, offering to share secrets if we all settle and listen.

"Ramona, should we call Mike's family so they can hear our story, too? I'll pay you back for the long distance."

"I think we can cover that, Pop, if your story is as good as it sounds like it will be."

Lucas pulls Sunny into a controlling hug. Ramona rounds up several phones, gives one to Michael and dials hers. The smells of pizza and savory soup drift to us as the room quiets. Clarice squirms into my chair beside me, the whole time squeezing my hand and whispering a barrage of questions, none of which I address. I pat her leg with my free hand and murmur, "I'll tell you everything tomorrow."

"Shouldn't you call Kate and Zoe, too?" she whispers in my ear.

"We called them this morning," I whisper back. Our conversation had been easy, flowing, filled with wishes of happiness. I had a perfect moment, talking to my daughter. Just as this moment, in the loving clutches of my dearest friend, is perfect. Painful, but perfect.

Phone lines open, voices hush, all eyes turn toward Michael, as my new husband begins to tell our story.

Book Two

Here are the two best prayers I know: "Help me, help
me, help me," and "Thank you, thank you, thank you."

—ANNE LAMOTT, *Traveling Mercies:*
Some Thoughts on Faith

Thank you for this day. Help me through it.
Thank you for this life. Help me live it.
Show us what we need. Help me help.

—MICHAEL BARTOLI

CHAPTER 1

✺

MARCH 2006

Michael

On Wednesday, I move into Beth's life. The first morning I jolt awake, my dream—something about a whale in a net—fades fast. Her bedside clock glares a bright red 6:09. The time feels wrong, but I know it's correct to the minute. After getting out of Beth's bed, I put on my robe and slippers in the dark, and creep down the stairs to make us a pot of coffee. As it brews, I wander through the chilly living room, looking for the thermostat to turn up the heat. It might be nice to just slide back to Beth, sleeping warm and still. Instead, I open the curtains and stare at the cement slab patio and evergreen hedge.

Endless ocean, sun-lit mornings, star-filled nights. Our eyes could see a thousand miles and further, the first week of our marriage. A three-hour flight on an airplane and an hour's ride in Ramona's car brought us back to where we started. My body misses the warm, salty air, my eyes need to see further than the thirty feet of Beth's backyard.

On Beth's desk the calendar is turned to a page with thirty-one empty squares. I carry it to the dining room table, place a pen beside it. We need to plan. By the time I finish my first cup of coffee, I've flipped through the calendar twice. January and February have lists and check marks, two or three or four every day all written in perfect penmanship. Beth's plans for getting us to a Caribbean Cruise. Then nothing. This new month mocks me. Beth would have another month full of lists and events and appointments if I hadn't barged in and erased her entire life.

"Do I smell coffee?" Her hair is flat on one side and curly on the other, she's wearing a red plaid sleeping shirt, she's barefooted. She's beautiful. And she looks so happy to see me. Or maybe it's the coffee.

I get up from the table and she slides right into my hug. She's warm from sleeping, her kiss tastes like mint. After living with Beth for a week, I know she brushes her teeth as soon as she gets out of bed. A new habit for her new husband? She glances at the calendar, pours herself a cup of coffee and sets it beside mine as I try to explain our need to plan, for now, for later and, well, for the rest of our life. I need to pay my fair share for electricity and water and cable TV. Will Beth get in trouble if I park in a guest spot permanently and is it OK to hang a few more shirts in the closet upstairs?

Beth laughs. She sets her cup aside, puts her hand on mine and picks up the pen. "How about we do this slow and easy? I'll take care of the details—you keep our life interesting. So far, that's working pretty well, don't you think?" She taps her pen on March. "So, what do you have in store for us?"

Beth lets me talk through my worries until they turn into plans, but she won't write them down. "Plans can change" she says. She won't flip the page to April, she won't look back at February. "I have half a mind to throw this calendar away," she says, but after a few more sips of coffee, her pen sets on the square that is today. Beth writes Coffee with Michael, makes a check mark beside it and chuckles. Both Clarice and Ramona want more details about our surprise wedding, so Beth writes down their names. By the end of today we'll get them caught up and checked off. Tomorrow's square gets filled up with unpacking and laundry. "Should we go to Des Plaines this weekend?" Beth asks.

"Sure," I say. After Emma heard my little speech on the telephone, she said she wanted us to show her our wedding movie in person. While we're in Des Plaines I can pick up a few things from my house, if I can figure out what I'll need to move from my old life into my new one.

The furnace comes on with a rumble, but Beth doesn't seem to notice. A puff of air warms my neck, the rest of me is still cold. Beth writes Des Plaines on Saturday and Sunday, then looks up at me.

"How does our life look so far?" she asks.

"Looks good," I say.

I watch Beth's pen linger over the rest of the squares, then write a **?** on Monday.

"Why a question mark?" I ask. "Aren't we driving back here after the weekend?"

"Who knows?" Beth says.

It's a puny plan but I feel better. I don't ask the hard question: *Where are we going to live?* I don't want to hear Beth answer *How about here?* I do say, "Maybe we could spend a little time at my house." I know I'd be warmer there than I am right now. "Maybe we could drive up to Green Bay if we have some extra time."

Beth pushes the calendar to the center of the table, sets the pen on top of it. "My darling," she says, "we have all the time we need."

Our calendar plan is working. This morning I carry one suitcase packed with my clean shirts and underwear, all neatly folded and tucked beside Beth's nightgowns and sweaters. Her black bag contains both our medicines and the new blood pressure machine in addition to crossword puzzle books and the *Our Wedding Cruise* movie. After a five-hour drive, we're standing by my old front door. I don't know what

I expect to find inside—memories of these rooms when they were flooded with the laughter and energy of my children. Remnants of a lifetime of happiness and love.

The key feels familiar in my hand as I open the front door and go in first. Clutching her pocketbook against her chest, Beth follows me. Fresh vacuum lines fan the carpet. Mike and Emma must have scurried over to spruce up as soon as we told them we were coming. The couch, the lamps, the hundreds of fancy collectible plates and figurines lined up on every horizontal surface—everything looks like a replica of my old life, cast in cement. Sterile, stiff, cold as stone. My house is no warmer than Beth's but at least I know how to turn on the furnace, so I crank it up to seventy-five.

I show Beth the three bedrooms with three perfectly made beds. Emma's doing, probably. In the last one I linger and turn to Beth. "This was our room up until a year or so before Evelyn went into the nursing home." I pause, remembering. "She thought a stranger, maybe a rapist, was trying to climb in bed with her. I started sleeping in Mike's bedroom."

Beth looks past me, to the bed. "I'm sorry," she says.

"Let's have a cup of tea," I say. "I imagine the coffee is stale."

In the kitchen Beth takes off her coat and hangs it over the back of a chair. She tells me her hair will be a mess if she takes off the little plaid cap. She puts her purse on the kitchen table Evelyn and I bought for our one-year anniversary. We'd always buy something for the house instead of each other. A weight lifts from my shoulders as I move from table to sink to stove. As the tea kettle heats, I open every cabinet, each drawer.

"This roasting pan was my Mom's," I tell Beth, pulling it from the back of the shelf. "She'd roast two chickens at a time in it, and on Thanksgiving she'd use it for our turkey. I'd sure like to take it back with us. Is that OK?"

"We'll make room for your momma's roasting pan," she says. "Bring back whatever you like."

When the tea kettle whistles, I set two steaming cups on the table and sit down across from Beth. "I wish I had time to make you a pie," I say, then realize I don't want to stay in this house long enough to bake anything. My eyes fill with tears. I can't talk for a few minutes as I try to span the distance between then and now. Sadness and joy wage a battle right here in my kitchen. Once I start talking I can't stop. "That sickness took Evelyn away from me, she got so small and mean. Trying to take care of her, trying to remember she was the woman I loved. It was hard." Beth eyes don't leave my face. "Her eyes were so full of hate when she looked at me, it almost made me hate her back." I scrub at my eyes with both hands, then wipe them on my pant legs. Beth folds her warm hands around mine. I stare at the little ring on her finger.

"Funny thing is," I say, "since I met you, I don't think about the bad times as much, and the good memories have started coming back. I remember I'd loved her. I remember how it feels being me."

Beth sits so still. Finally, she whispers, "Evelyn and I are both lucky to have you love us." She moves her hands from mine back to her teacup. The doubt in her eyes doesn't match her words, "This is a nice house, honey. If you want us to live here for a while, that will be fine with me."

"No, Libby has a friend in real estate. I'm going to call her and tell her to put this place on the market."

Not a speck of sunshine falls on my car as we drive up the interstate from Chicago to Green Bay. Outside it's winter-grey and thirty-five degrees, inside the car heater is cranked to balmy. North of Milwaukee, Beth peels off her coat. As I take the Green Bay, Downtown exit, she takes off her cap too, pulls down the visor to look in the mirror, and fluffs up

her curls. She sighs, pulls a lipstick out of her purse, puts on
a new layer of red and wipes some off with a Kleenex. I love
watching her. She sighs again and flips up the visor. Then
screams.

"Michael, watch out! We're going in the wrong direction."

I jerk the steering wheel to the right into an empty parking
spot. The tires slide on slush, then catch pavement as I stomp
on the brake. We bolt to a stop behind a parked car facing us
hood-to-hood, highlighting my error.

"I guess I don't know how to drive in this town anymore,"
I say after my heart stops pounding. "Seems like the whole
city's full of one-way streets. I'm sorry. Are you OK?"

"I'm fine. I wish I could help you, but I don't have a map."
She looks amused. She'd wanted to bring her atlas, but I told
her I knew where I was going.

With no cars on the horizon, I ease out of my wrong way
parking space, creep to the next cross street, and make a right
turn as Beth watches for police cars. I drive us around for a
while, still feeling like I'm going against the flow. I don't see
a familiar street or house or grocery store. Even the icy Fox
River looks different, contained by riprap rock instead of the
wild weedy banks I'd roamed when I was ten.

"We could ask someone for help, or have I married one
of those men who won't ask for directions?" Beth is not the
least upset.

"I'm not opposed to asking for help, I just don't know
what to ask," I say. "Can you tell me how to get to my grandparents' old house? I lived there sixty years ago. It was white
with green trim and there was a park a few blocks away."

"You're right, you're pretty sparse on specifics," Beth says.
"Let's regroup over lunch. I'm starving."

The side street is narrowed by dirty mounds of ice left
over from Green Bay's last major snow. We're in the grey
damp between storms. Gloom surrounds the bungalows lining both sides of the street, narrow shoveled paths lead to

every front door. If you don't clear your sidewalk, you don't get your mail.

"Did your grandparent's house look like these?"

"It probably did, but in my mind it was bigger and brighter. Full of family. These houses look empty."

"We probably need to get back to that busy street," Beth says. "I'll watch out for one-way signs."

I creep down another side street, this one sullener than the last. Midway down the block we pass a park with a few picnic tables and trash cans piled with dripping snow. A flash of recognition hits me, making me pleased and sad at the same time. "This might be my park."

Slowing the car to a stop, I scan a line of dreary houses. "My friend Larry lived on this street. His house had a big front porch and a swing, but we boys didn't spend much time playing at our houses. We'd meet here, to play army." I look at the sodden empty park. "All our dads were in the war."

The Green Bay I remember was a town of women and children and old men, grandpas like mine who were too old to be soldiers. All summer, my pals and I would fight invisible enemies since none of us wanted to play the role of the Germans or Japanese. We'd maneuver down the streets to the Fox River where we'd spot pretend U-boats. After bombing them, we'd travel back to our houses, victorious and hungry.

"Let's go get some lunch," I tell Beth as I pull away from the curb. I'd rather remember my park alive and green and full of boys wanting to be men. I was silly to think I'd drive right up to my grandparents' house and find my memories. I'd carried them with me all along.

The parking lot of the North Star Family Restaurant is well-plowed and packed with cars. Inside, we're seated in a booth bathed in neon. Our waitress gives us white mugs of coffee and offers us broasted chicken, the special, or anything except the brat platter. "We're out of brats," she says. "It was the weekend special, and the Packers had a home game."

The waitress asks us where we are from and if we have heard the latest weather reports as Beth scans the menu. "They say we might get another foot of snow tonight," she tells us.

"Our trip just keeps getting better," Beth says, not looking up.

Her pen hovers above her order pad. "Are you folks staying at our motel?"

"We just stopped for a bite to eat," I say. I still haven't looked at the menu, but Beth will have it memorized by now. "I used to live here when I was a boy."

Beth looks up and asks, "Do you really have twelve kinds of pie?"

"Yes, we do, and everything's homemade."

"We'll have six pieces of pie each, and you better book us a room for the night," Beth says.

We refine our order to vegetable soup and two pieces of pie, coconut cream for me, and Door County cherry for Beth. Our waitress says she'll have the motel hold a room and she'll set aside two more pieces of pie for our breakfast.

As our waitress walks away, Beth whispers, "Do you think it's too early for a second honeymoon?"

The smells of burgers and fried potatoes from the North Star's kitchen mix with the thick chilly air as we walk across the parking lot to the motel office, a small attempt at exercise. A woman who looks like she could be the sister of our waitress gives us a real room key instead of a plastic card. Our home tonight is Room 132.

By the time I drive the car to our door and haul our suitcase into the room, Beth has the lights on, her coat hung up, and the covers on our king-sized bed turned down. Desire, full and familiar, washes over me.

Unpacking is a ritual for Beth. As Beth sorts toothbrushes and lotions and pill containers into two piles on the bathroom counter, I strip to my underwear and hang my clothes by Beth's coat.

"Should we turn on The Weather Channel?" Beth asks.

"Let's just be surprised. What I want to do is huddle up in bed with my wife."

Breakfast at the North Star smells of bacon and hash browns but Beth is intent on pie. Will she think I'm a traitor if I order the Lumberjack Special? As we wait to place our order, Beth leafs through a Senior Living magazine she picked up in the hotel lobby. "I suppose we'll need to turn on The Weather Channel when we get back to our room," Beth says. "I wonder how far south our little emergency extends. We may have to rent one of these townhouses and hole up here for the winter."

In the early morning hours, I'd listened to the rumble of a snowplow waging battle against the snowstorm. Now, as I look out the restaurant window, I figure the snow might have won. Beth might be half serious about living in Green Bay, but I don't intend to shovel snow four months a year. I'm not even looking forward to cleaning off my car.

As soon as our waitress welcomes us, Beth inquires about out reserved desserts. "I was wondering who Beth and Michael were when I saw your names on those pieces of pie. Do you want them warmed a little?"

"I'll have mine to-go. This Lumberjack Breakfast sounds good," I say.

Sure enough, Beth sends me a disapproving glare. "My goal was to sample my way through all twelve of your pies, but I should probably order a proper breakfast too," Beth says. "And maybe a pie dessert?"

Our waitress puts her hand on Beth's shoulder. "There's plenty here for everyone. We'll get you whatever you need."

"I'm starting to realize I already have it," Beth tells her.

•

By mid-afternoon we make our Green Bay get-away. I had to make the call. Beth would have stayed at the North Star Family Restaurant as long as the kitchen kept churning out pies. The Interstate is plowed and salted, and traffic is moving at a nice clip. We make it through Milwaukee's rush hour without a hitch.

"Where would you like to spend the night?" I ask as we hit the Illinois border. "Mike and Libby would be happy to put us up again."

Beth sits quietly, her gloved hands folded on her lap. "If we don't stop, we can make Centerburg by bedtime. Let's keep driving." She doesn't reach in her purse for her cross-word puzzle book, she doesn't turn on my radio to search for a weather update. A semi blows past us, spraying the wind-shield with salty slush. Automatically, my hand turns on the wiper fluid. Luckily Mike checked the fluid levels and filled the reservoir with antifreeze before we left for Green Bay. I should have remembered to do it.

Beth watches the road as I drive. "If we're going to live a life of adventure," she says, "maybe we should get a cell phone."

After I drop Beth off at Clarice's house, I don't know where to go next so my car drives to Ramona's house. It's another day with no plans. The snow in her yard is zigzagged with paw prints and littered with yellow tennis balls. Just as I reach the front porch, the door flies open, and Sunny and Lucas explode out. Sunny storms past and picks up a tennis ball. He looks confused as Lucas grabs me in a quick hello embrace.

"I throw balls for him before I head to school," Lucas yells over his shoulder.

It's no calmer inside the house. A suit-clad Ravi is yelling down the hallway "Is it going to snow again tonight? Remember I have that re-org meeting" to Ramona who's standing in front of a TV blaring weather updates. The sounds of jazz pour from the kitchen radio. The house has a coffee and burned-toast aroma.

"Daddy, you're back." Ramona rushes at me.

"Michael, great to see you." Ravi slaps my back.

It's a nice welcome. I almost feel at home.

"I'll see you later, love," Ravi calls out. He goes out the door as Lucas and Sunny burst back in. Lucas grabs a book-bag and follows his dad out.

Ramona pours me a cup of coffee and joins me at the kitchen table. "Where's Beth?"

"She and Clarice are shopping for a cell phone." Sunny bounces over so I can rub his ears. "Can you imagine your dad having one of those contraptions?"

"Sure, why not? You're a man of the world."

My dog settles in a heap at my feet. "I sure do thank you for taking care of Sunny."

When I say his name, he raises his head and his tail thumps the floor.

"Daddy," Ramona folds her hands around her coffee cup. "I need to ask you for a huge favor."

Ramona never asks me for help. "Honey, I'd do anything for you. What do you need?"

"We need Sunny."

This time Sunny jumps up and saunters over to Ramona's chair. She smiles at him. I think he smiles back.

"Looks like you two have fallen for each other," I say.

"Sunny's a great dog. But I'm not asking for me," she says. "It's Lucas. I think it would break his heart if Sunny leaves us."

"Those two do seem to be pretty happy together," I say.

"He's happy plus he's awake and dressed and ready for school every morning and he comes home for lunch everyday so he can let Sunny out for a little while. Ravi and I used to plead with him to get up on time, let us know his plans for the day, just talk to us." Ramona pats Sunny's head.

"Sunny's the reason for the transformation," Ramona says as we watch him amble across the kitchen. "I see Lucas becoming an adult, just a little bit." Ramona sips her coffee. "I'll understand if you can't give him up. We can get Lucas another dog."

My Sunny, my special dog, is slurping water from his bowl. Some water goes in his mouth but a large amount of it splatters across the tile floor. He looks at me, water dripping from his chin. He doesn't know he's become a hero.

I pick up Beth after her shopping trip, drop her off at her condo and make it back to Ramona's house before Lucas gets home for lunch. Sunny hears my key in the lock and greets me when I walk in. He's kind enough not to look disappointed I'm not Lucas. A pitcher of Ravi's spicy tea is in the refrigerator, so I pour myself a glass and sit down at the kitchen table. Sunny sits by my leg, and I rub his head.

We both hear Lucas running up the sidewalk and Sunny charges to the front door barking. Lucas yells a hello to me over the quivering dog, grabs a leash from a peg on the wall. "I'll be right back," he says.

"You two take your time," I say.

All the energy in the house leaves with them. I smile and shake my head.

They're back just as I'm draining my glass. Ravi's tea is delicious, tasty with orange and cloves. I need to ask him how to make it.

Lucas flings open the refrigerator door. "Do you want a sandwich, Grandpa?" he yells over his shoulder.

A Grandpa's first instinct would be to say, *No, you sit down. You're a child. I'm old and wise. I'll make the sandwich for you.* But I stop before the "No" falls from my mouth.

"Sounds great," I say.

My lunch doesn't take long to prepare. Turkey slices on bread, presented to me on a paper towel. No mayonnaise, lettuce leaf or tomato. Lucas sits down to an identical lunch. I take a bite; it tastes like the love of a sixteen-year-old boy.

"Lucas, I wanted to talk to you without your folks being around," I start. "I need your help."

"Sure, Grandpa." He looks me square in the eye. I don't recall ever talking to my grandson, just the two of us face to face. If it weren't for Sunny, I wouldn't be doing it now.

"I appreciate you taking care of Sunny. He means a lot to me. He was with me through some real tough times."

Lucas's face falls. He thinks I've come to take Sunny back. I hurry into my next words.

"Beth and I got married so fast we haven't had a chance to plan anything. It's my fault but I don't regret it. I'm real happy and I think Beth is too."

Lucas doesn't falter in his attention, his eyes intent on my face, his sandwich untouched on the paper towel.

"I know you care about Sunny," I say. "I do too, but my life is an uproar right now. It's a wonderful uproar, like I said, but it's wrong for a dog. Sunny needs good, solid, steady care. He needs you." My grandson's eyes widen the tiniest bit. "So, what I'm asking is, will you take Sunny? I want to give him to you."

Lucas doesn't laugh or yell or hug me, like a child who just got a dog. He looks me in the eye, man to man, and says, "Yes, Sir, I'll take good care of him."

CHAPTER 2

✺

Beth

BETH'S CELL PHONE RULES

1. **The phone will be turned off unless Beth (or Michael, if he's so inclined) is making a call.** During my first three days of cell phone ownership Clarice called me seven times which I feel is excessive, perhaps even bordering on friendship-abuse. If someone (Clarice) needs to get in touch with me, she can leave a message and I'll call her back.

2. **Beth will learn how to retrieve messages.**

3. **Beth will never place a call from a standing position.** First, I'll sit down, get comfortable, perhaps sip a glass of iced tea.

4. **Beth will never place a call within earshot of a stranger.** Rules 3 and 4 preclude making phone calls from grocery store aisles, restaurants, and the checkout line at Walmart.

5. **Beth will call Clarice every day.** I had to add this rule so Clarice would stop crying after I told her Michael and I were definitely not going to live in Centerburg.

A hundred times a day I think *I need to tell Clarice about this when I call her tonight.* Like now, as Michael's car creeps down the main highway of my once cherished Panama City Beach, Florida. "Everything's changed here, Clarice." I'll tell her. "I hate it."

"Oh good," she'll say. "Come home."

Much to Michael's delight, I quickly ruled out Centerburg as the site for us to begin our new life together. "I think sixty-five years here was plenty," I told him. "I'm ready to explore someplace new." Since Michael had ruled out Des Plaines and Green Bay as potential locations to call home, I suggested driving south to kick off our exploration. "My folks would drive us to Panama City every Easter," I explained, "and my cousin Cheryl still lives there. Plus, there's a fairly good possibility we won't get caught in a snowstorm if we can make it out of Illinois." That was reason enough for Michael.

I try to spot a trace of familiarity as we creep along, Michael's hands clinched on the steering wheel, his eyes glued to the bumper of the pick-up truck three feet ahead of us. Our foreheads glisten with sweat. It's high-noon hot, here in the shadows of a cement canyon. No speck of beach is visible behind all the ten-story hotels and multi-story parking garages. My beautiful, cheap, tacky Panama City Beach has been ravaged by uncontrolled ambition and the ability to borrow way too much money. The developers have stolen the sun.

"Should we stop at one of these places and get a room?" Michael asks, hoping I'll say no.

"If we ever make it into town, we can look for a motel," I say. "There used to be one overlooking the bay."

Forty years ago, Beth darling, I remind myself.

At least Bea's Oyster Bar hasn't changed. Cousin Cheryl suggested Bea's for lunch when I called to say we were in town, then we talked for an hour before we hang up. Michael and I are sitting at one of the lopsided wooden tables when Cheryl throws open the door, scans the room, screams, and charges us. Michael barely has time to get to his feet before she has him in a hug.

Cheryl's mostly blond hair is tied in a knot with a few stray tendrils wisping down her neck. She's tall and tan and dressed in jeans, a sequined t-shirt, and turquoise sandals. Michael and I look like the tourists. "Bea, bring us three dozen steamed oysters and a gallon of tea," she yells into the kitchen. "We three have some catching up to do."

We've talked for fifteen minutes before we notice Michael does not seem to like oysters. "Honey, you know they're an aphrodisiac," Cheryl says. "But my second husband used to say that wasn't true. 'I ate twelve oysters last night,' he'd tell folks, 'but only eleven worked.' He was pretty, but he lied about most everything."

Cheryl slides Michael's platter of oysters to the center of the table and looks over her shoulder, "Bea darling, could you get this handsome man a pound of shrimp?"

We arrive mid-afternoon so we have the little dark room to ourselves except for a few regulars, most likely, silently drinking beer at the bar. I tell Cheryl about Kate's wedding and Michael tells her about ours. As he says the part about sunrise on the Bartoli deck, Cheryl gets tears in her eyes. "You two make me so happy," she says. "Lord, it's been too long."

"Beth says you have a granddaughter about the age of my grandson." Michael's looking much happier as he peels a shrimp.

Cheryl's shoulders droop. She rotates her iced tea glass one way, then the other. "Miranda is the love of my life," she says. "I'd do anything for her."

As we were talking on the phone earlier, Cheryl told me Miranda just found out she is pregnant, but she's strong-willed and smart and ready to face the road ahead. I told her Miranda sounds a lot like her grandma.

"Miranda lives with Cheryl," I tell Michael. "They're having a rough time right now."

"I'm sorry," Michael says. "I hope everything will work out all right." Michael is concerned. I knew he would be. "Are Miranda's folks around to help?" he asks.

Cheryl orders more tea, a basket of hush puppies. "Tammy was a wild child from the get-go," Cheryl shakes three drops of Texas Pete on her oyster, picks it up with her fork. "Wide-open, sweet as pie one minute, mean as a snake the next. I prayed she'd get better when she got grown."

"Tammy is Miranda's mother," I explain to Michael.

Cheryl pops the oyster in her mouth. "When she had Miranda I prayed harder, but she barely noticed she'd had a baby. She just dropped her off at my house and proceeded on with her life." Cheryl sets her fork on the empty plate. "Now I mostly pray Tammy just stays the hell away."

Cheryl tells us Tammy's latest poor decision is her current boyfriend whose list of indiscretions include drug possession, stolen properties, assorted frauds, and unsavory alliances. "He's so stupid he couldn't dump pee out of his boot if the directions were written on the sole," Cheryl says.

Tammy has an adventure addiction, Cheryl thinks. She made the diagnosis from watching *The Young and the Restless*. Her current boyfriend-addiction blew into town and started making promises to anyone who had five minutes to listen to him. Soon he was dealing with the police and creditors and worse, a network of dubious business partners who did not appreciate being out-conned. Tammy fell for him and his fast, fancy car.

"Until it was repossessed," Cheryl laughs. "They had to go on the run in Tammy's fifteen-year-old Buick. At least it's paid for."

Some man who's clearly a regular customer just like Cheryl, yells across the room, "How ya' been, gal?"

"Fine as frog hair," Cheryl yells back.

I know it's not true, so does Cheryl, and now so does Michael. But that's my cousin, facing every obstacle with good-natured fury, embracing both the positive and the impossible with passion and resolve. Had I not recently been told I'm perfect just the way I am, I'd want to be just like Cheryl.

I look at the local businessmen at the horseshoe bar. I turn back to Michael, now munching hush puppies. As Cheryl tells him about Miranda's pregnancy, I watch his heart break.

"Do you want me to talk to the boy, man-to-man?" Michael asks.

"No, he says the baby isn't his." Cheryl says. "On top of everything else, now his new girlfriend is calling Miranda to harass her."

Michael looks at me. He's thinking the same thing I am, *How can we help?*

"Is Miranda planning to stay here and raise the baby?" I ask. I think of Ramona, who would know just what to ask, what to suggest. Clarice would be sitting at this table fuming at the injustice, then correcting it. I picture this new Beth, the woman who knew what to say on her daughter's wedding day, who knew what to say to a man who wanted to love her.

When Cheryl says, "Miranda wants this baby and she'll be a great mom, but she deserves better than this hell hole," I know just what to say.

"We'll help you and Miranda get through this." My words sound confident, so I continue, adding ideas as they pop into my head. "Michael and I are just drifting for a while, looking for a place to settle," I say, taking pleasure in how non-Beth-like my words sound. "I have a condo in Centerburg I'm hoping not to use anymore. Maybe you should pack your bags and get out of this mess." Michael stops eating shrimp to listen. "You can live there as long as you need to. Tammy and her troubles won't know where to find you. You can take some good deep breaths and if it feels right, you two can start over in a new place.

Stillness settles over the table. Then Cheryl erupts, throws her arms to the heavens, and screams, "Yes, yes, thank you, thank you!" She jumps to her feet, jarring the table. The pitcher of sweet tea launches into the air and lands on Michael. Bea flies to his aid as Cheryl grabs me. Cheryl barely notices the havoc as I hug her and push her back into her chair.

"Are you sure you want to live in Centerburg?" Michael asks after she'd settled down.

"When we were kids, we'd spend summer vacations and Christmas in Centerburg." Cheryl is still a little winded. "My mom grew up there. Going to Centerburg was always a treat for us."

"I just can't imagine that," Michael says, wiping tea from his plaid shirt.

"I have an idea too, since you two lovebirds seem to be on the verge of being homeless," Cheryl says. "Stop by my house tomorrow and we'll talk."

The motel of my memory is still by the bay, only now it's a completely remodeled hotel with second floor balconies. Michael has rented us one of those rooms for three nights. I sit on our balcony, cell phone in hand, and watch Michael as he walks along the shoreline. Head down, hands clasped behind his back, too deep in thought to enjoy the morning sun.

I've prepared a little power point presentation for Clarice on the hotel notepad. Before I call, I try to add some details to my evolving ideas for Cheryl and Miranda's move to Centerburg. Michael waves at me and I wave back. He's a little doubtful of the plan but Clarice will be overjoyed. She answers my daily phone calls on the first ring, but this morning she is one ring late.

"What's wrong? Why are you calling now instead of this evening?"

"And good morning to you too," I say and begin my presentation. Clarice gasps and sighs, murmurs sympathy and acceptance. As I explain the Centerburg portion, I can sense her vibrating. If we were sitting face to face, she'd be kicking her feet and grabbing my hand, ready. I don't need to ask her to help. She's miles ahead, planning the perfect way to welcome Cheryl and Miranda into her life. I'm invigorated too, but a tinge jealous. When I hang up, I wonder if I've just handed Clarice a new and improved best friend.

After lunch, I direct Michael to Cheryl's house without looking at the directions she'd scribbled on a napkin. We park and Cheryl greets us, dragging a dripping water hose down her driveway.

"Good Lord, you gave me a shock! Your Buick looks just like Tammy's old car," she tells Michael. "I thought she'd limped home before we could make our get-away." She looks over her shoulder toward her backyard. "I was hoping I could get your surprise spruced up before you got here. Come on and take a look. You don't have to say yes."

Soap-filled water buckets, Wet Vac, assorted sponges and spray bottles and towels are scattered in a ring at the end of the driveway. In the center is a tiny silver trailer, squeaking clean and sparkling in the sunlight.

"She's yours if you want her," Cheryl says. "I know she's not a fair swap for a fully furnished condominium, but she could save you some hotel expenses as you two search for your perfect retirement love nest."

I stare at what looks like a traveling toaster. Michael edges a little closer. Cheryl pitches her end of the water hose in the general direction of her patio, picks up one of the towels and dries her hands. "This is Polly Jean the Airstream. She's all I got when I divorced Willard."

Cheryl turns to Michael. "My first husband. Lordy, we had us some good times with ol' Polly Jean. Come on, I'll give you a tour!"

We wedge ourselves in, facing a plaid curtained window over a plaid upholstered bench. The camper smells like the basement of my childhood home—musty with an undertone of laundry detergent. "There's storage under there," Cheryl points to the bench/table combo. "It makes into a bed, in case you have visitors." We rotate right to view the living room/bedroom and right again to face the kitchen. Under a counter there's a refrigerator big enough to store a leftover quart of soup, under a three-burner gas stove there's an oven big enough to bake a loaf of zucchini bread. Michael touches the stovetop with reverence.

"Back here's your bathroom." We take four steps to the rear of the trailer. Sink to the left, toilet to the right, big window in the center. "You step right in, close the door, and turn on the shower," Cheryl explains.

I guess one gets undressed in the kitchen.

I'm mentally preparing my *Thank you, but no thank you* speech as I watch Michael peek in the refrigerator and open each tiny drawer. He runs his hand down the length of the plaid bench, he stands on his tip toes to peek out the window. "How do you turn this table into a bed?" he asks. Cheryl pushes a lever and pulls down a mattress. Michael face beams. "Is it hard to drive one of these rigs?"

"A complete driving course is offered with the deal," Cheryl says.

"Beth, what do you think?" Michael is so excited. "Sounds like we have a new home."

CHAPTER 3

✳

Michael

We spend three days getting acquainted with Polly Jean the Airstream. The first day, Cheryl's mechanic friend puts a trailer hitch on my Buick, then Cheryl, Beth and I drive to an abandoned K-mart parking where I learn how to drive forward and backward and park. Beth learns how to drive forward, in case of an emergency. Cheryl's teaching technique is a combination of drill sergeant and high school basketball coach. At the end of our day-long training session, Cheryl makes me drive my Buick plus Polly Jean back to her driveway, then treats us to another supper at Bea's Oyster Bar.

Day two, Cheryl teaches me how to hitch and unhitch as Beth stands beside me and takes notes. "How about we try this without Cheryl's help?" Beth suggests just as I am thinking it's time to break for a long lunch. "I'll read the steps to you."

"Sounds like you married a retired fourth grade teacher," Cheryl says. "If you pass this test, I'll teach you plugging in and dumping out this afternoon."

At the end of my final driving lesson, Cheryl puts her

hands on her hips and declares, "Now you two are officially Old Farts. Michael, you'll need to put on a pair of Bermuda shorts and start wearing orthopedic sandals with brown socks." For graduation, Cheryl presents us with a brand-new copy of Directory of Campgrounds for the United States and a bumper sticker that reads: "If this rig's a rockin', don't come a knockin'." I'm pleased she doesn't insist we attach it to the trailer.

We drive south from Panama City to the tiny beach town of Port St. Joe which sets on a line separating Central and Eastern time zones. Losing an hour as we drive through the town feels wasteful and luxurious. The Gulf of Mexico is to our right, separated from view by the occasional line of two-story condos, most having a To Rent or For Sale sign out front. This morning was another whirlwind, first Cheryl's review of plugging in and dumping out lessons for Polly Jean, then Beth's tips and procedures for Cheryl's moving into Beth's life in Centerburg. Beth wrote out a whole page of instructions, then went over them item by item—change electric, cable, phone bills to Cheryl's name, cancel Beth's newspaper subscription, and most importantly, call Clarice or Ramona the moment you need anything. By the time we were finished with our morning's lessons, I had a scant forty-five minutes to plan a menu, shop, and stow groceries into any available nook and cranny of my new kitchen. As I set up my new kitchen, Beth moved our clothes from suitcases to camper and separated our merged toiletries into two drawers in the bathroom. "Can I have just one of your kitchen drawers?" she asked me. "Let's put our medicines here, so they'll be handy." After we finished moving into our traveling home, we took three minutes to rest on the daytime couch/nighttime bed. "Well, this might be fun," Beth said. "At least, it will be a new experience."

A sign tells us to turn right for St. Joseph Peninsula State

Park, our destination. "You'll probably have the whole place to yourselves," Cheryl told us. "And if you run into any problems, I'm just a phone call away."

"If I didn't have my heart set on driving out West, I'd say we should hunker down right here," I say as I roll down my window to catch the gulf breeze. With Polly Jean rolling along behind us, we look like a Vacations for Seniors commercial.

We pick campsite 100. We had our choice of empty lots, but 100 is closest to the restrooms and showers. Beth wants to forego the Airstream shower experience for another evening. She gets out of the car and waves her arms back and forth, per Cheryl's instructions, as I back into the camping spot. "Perfect!" she declares.

While I decouple and putter, Beth grabs one of the beach chairs Cheryl has thrown in the trunk of my car—a wedding present, she'd said. I watch her walk across the white sugar sands, plant the chair a few yards back from the water, take off her sandals and sink into a perfect peace. Watching her, I know all the turmoil of the last few days was worth it.

An hour later I yell "Soup's on" in the direction of Beth. She waves at me, folds up her chair and walks barefoot back to our home.

Our meal isn't really soup, it's supper in a skillet—shrimp and sausage and peppers in store-bought marinara. We have garlic bread to soak up the sauce instead of pasta—no room for a bubbling pot of water. On the counter is a container of bright red strawberries and store-bought pound cake. In the mini refrigerator, a can of whipped cream is wedged between lemons and butter and a carton of eggs. Tonight's dessert is strawberry shortcake, tomorrow's breakfast, French toast with strawberries.

Beth gasps, then kisses me before sliding into one of the

tableside benches. "Oh Michael, I could cry," she says. "This is wonderful." I light the candle, place two steaming plates of food and a basket of garlic bread on the table, wedge into the bench across from her and pour our wine.

Outside, close, there's a whoop of a siren. Then slamming doors, footsteps running on gravel. Flashes of cobalt blue through the little window over the sink. A bullhorn.

DONNIE ROSE, WE HAVE A WARRANT FOR YOUR ARREST. PRESENT YOURSELF.

I jump from the bench/storage bin, hitting my head on the curved ceiling. I grab the tottering bottle of wine. Louder, closer, we hear . . .

COME OUT WITH YOUR HANDS UP, DONNIE ROSE.

I rush to the door and open it as Beth screams, "No Michael, wait!"

"Hey, fellas. What's going on?" I shout toward two flashing police cars.

Two policemen crouch behind one car, the other car is blocking our driveway. I push Beth behind me and pull down the aluminum steps. A policeman stands and points a gun toward me. PUT YOUR HANDS IN THE AIR, the bullhorn blares.

I raise my hands and maneuver down the two steps. "You stop this right now!" Beth yells from the open doorway. Her voice is more ferocious than the bullhorn. "You have the wrong person, put that gun away!"

The officer's tone changes. "Put your hands in the air, Ma'am."

"I will not!" Beth says. "I told you, you have the wrong person."

The policemen seem to believe Beth and the scene calms as cops appear from the back of the trailer. "What's this all about?" I ask again as the six of us gather in an informal circle beside the campsite's picnic table.

"Do you have some identification?" the bullhorn officer asks.

"Sure, sure." I take my wallet out of my pocket, pull out my Driver's License and hand it over. As the officers study it, Beth collapses onto the picnic bench. She's silent but her face is angry.

"Is there anyone else in the camper?" the officer asks, handing the ID back to me. I guess my innocence is proven. "Do you mind if we have a look inside?"

"Sure, sure," I say.

It is decided four police officers will not fit in an Airstream so the other three return to the police cars as Officer Dolan, Beth and I make a quick tour, just to be sure a bad guy isn't lurking about, holding us against our will.

Officer Dolan walks four steps to the rear, peeks in the bathroom and walks back. "Sure smells good in here," he says looking at our plates of shrimp and sausages. "I'm sorry we interrupted your meal."

"I wish I'd made more," I say, "but we do have one more serving." Behind me, Beth groans.

Three officers drive away in one car and Officer Dolan— who likes to be called Greg—stays for supper.

By the time we begin our desserts, we know the whole story. Donnie Rose is, of course, the boyfriend of Tammy, Cheryl's daughter. The Panama City police received, and passed along, a tip that he and Tammy were back in town and making a second get-away in Tammy's old brown Buick pulling her mother's Airstream. As I reheated our meal, Beth called Cheryl to verify Polly Jean was a gift. I hope Officer Greg didn't overhear Cheryl's description of what she was going to do to her neighbor who she assumes called in the tip.

"We thought it was strange that two possibly armed-and-dangerous suspects were driving a beat-up Buick pulling an old Airstream like a couple of . . ." Greg stops and looks at Beth. "No offense, Ma'am."

"None taken," she says, glaring at him as he finishes his second helping of strawberry shortcake.

"So, are you folks going to winter here on the beach?" he asks.

"No, we're just practicing our camping skills." I pour the last of our sweet tea in Greg's empty glass. Even though he's off duty, he tells us he shouldn't drink wine while he's in uniform. Plus, wine's illegal in a State Park, but he's letting that slide. "Once I'm sure I can handle this rig, we were thinking of heading out West. We don't know where yet."

"You folks should check out Green Valley, Arizona," Greg says. "South of Tucson. My folks retired there." Greg drains the glass of tea. "You have to be over fifty-five to live there, but most everybody is way older than that. And the houses are affordable, not like those ritzy golf-course retirement places."

Greg doesn't seem to realize he's again implied we are old and cheap, but I'm sure Beth picked it up. It doesn't matter. Greg's suggestion sounds like a perfect plan.

Beth

After supper with Officer Greg, I grab my atlas, turn to Arizona and locate Green Valley, just where Officer Greg said it would be. I flip to Florida, scan the states in-between and check the major cities mileage chart. My research complete, I show Michael the route from where we are to where we'd like to be, trace the straight blue line with my finger. Interstate 10, eighteen hundred miles. "If we drive sixty miles an hour for six hours a day, we could be in Green Valley in five days," I tell Michael. "Do you want to attempt it?"

"Absolutely!" says Michael. "Let's give it a try."

We travel west, sunrises behind us, sunsets ahead. The road is wide, our route is well-marked, Michael drives with confidence as I sit beside him, enjoying each new mile. Bulletin boards promise us the tastiest lunch spots, our Directory of Campgrounds for the United States guides us to each new one-night home. If we falter in our travels, I have my atlas to guide us back to Interstate 10.

As we weave our way down the narrow lanes of each new campground, half a dozen established campers wave a welcome. Michael waves back to each one as I search for our assigned space. When we prepare Polly Jean for the evening, I remember the sequence while Michael performs the tasks Cheryl taught us. If we'd been married forty years, some arguing might intermingle with this nesting, but we are too new to each other to voice little irritations. *Always be kind to this dear man,* I warn myself as I watch him struggle to loosen a bolt or free a connection, then wipe his sweaty brow with his forearm and smile with success.

As soon as we get Polly Jean settled in for the evening, our fellow campers drift over to chat. License plates seem to be the campground ice breaker. "I see you're from Illinois. Where abouts?" Now Michael has a less awkward response. "I'm from around Chicago and my wife is from downstate," he says easily to each new visitor as I listen and smile and nod.

Tonight we plan to go for a seafood supper "just two miles up the road," as a billboard promised. I look out the kitchen window to see Michael at the center of the campground welcoming committee. I hope he doesn't forgo our dining plans and invite everyone for a something-else-in-a-skillet supper. While he visits, I should freshen up, but I still haven't attempted an in-camper shower and I don't want to venture out to the campground bathhouse for fear of being enveloped by Michael's group of new friends. Polly Jean the Airstream has become my safe hideaway.

I pour a glass of tea, curl up at the end of the couch and call Clarice. She's bubbling with updates. Ramona is at the ready with school and medical transition plans for

Miranda. Clarice has stocked my kitchen and put clean sheets on my beds. She calls Cheryl every day to check on their migration. In two more days, Clarice will welcome them to Centerburg.

As I listen, I watch Michael through the kitchen window. Waving his hands, pointing to the west, I know he's telling the story of us. His audience laughs, men adjust their ball caps, wave at the next trailer driving in for the night. Clarice says she'll take Cheryl to the Red Hat luncheon next week. A tiny pain stabs my stomach.

"Clarice, I miss you," I hear myself say.

"I know you do," she laughs, "but I did wonder if you'd ever tell me."

Michael is collecting scraps of paper with names and addresses of his new RV friends, assorted restaurants, Officer Greg. "Maybe we can send them Christmas cards," he suggests as he hunts for a place to stash them.

Each year, on December 26th, I buy a box of twelve Christmas cards for fifty percent off regular price. Each year, I have nine left after I send one to Cheryl, one to my brother and family in Denver, one to Kate with a check inside. I date the leftover cards and store them in the back of my bedroom closet. *Great*, I think, *I can finally use up all those extra cards*. Then I remember, my closet belongs to Cheryl now. Come December, we'll have to buy dozens of new cards, all at regular price.

Each evening as Michael socializes with new friends, I call Clarice to report on destinations and state of mind, and she gives me details of Cheryl and Miranda's move into my old life. Clearly, they are more successful at Centerburg living than I ever was.

It seems we've been driving through Texas for a month, but it's only been three days.

This afternoon, as Michael sets off toward a horseshoe court, I settle into dining room/ breakfast nook/office with an iced tea, cell phone, and atlas. I open the pages to where we are, flip to where we've been, turn to Arizona, Page 8. After I add the tiny red numbers along Interstate 10, I call Clarice.

"I probably won't call tomorrow," I tell her. "If I've calculated correctly, we'll make it all the way to Green Valley, but it will be late."

"I promise I won't worry any more than usual," she says. "But call me as soon as you can."

I smell coffee. I struggle awake, reach for the alarm clock on the floor by our bed—4:37. I'd set it for 6:30. I prop myself up on my elbow and scan the room. A flashlight shines on the coffee pot as Michael fills one of the two travel mugs on the counter. I can feel his excitement through the darkness.

Yesterday we bought gasoline, sandwich fixings and a gallon of sweet tea. Michael drove Polly Jean to the dump station and cleared the waste tank—our most unpleasant team task. He checked all the tires and fluid levels, squeegeed every window. The Buick is pointed toward Campground Exit, and a box of doughnuts sits on the dashboard.

To misquote John Denver, today we drive home to a place we've never been before.

It's smooth sailing until we reach the outskirts of El Paso, the only big city along our route. I'm on high alert, my finger tracing the miles on my atlas, my eyes flickering from road signs to page. Michael has been smiling for two hundred miles.

Michael keeps to the slow safety of the right lane as cars pass us on the left, going a good thirty miles an hour faster than we are. I spot the irritated glances as they speed pass, then cut in front to exit. Michael slows down a bit more each time this happens.

Slow and steady. "We just need to stay on Interstate 10," I tell Michael, to comfort myself. I smile at him, turn back to look at the highway just in time to read Exit Only, which Michael slowly does.

"No, don't turn here!" I scream, louder than I should.

Michael stomps on the break, looks at me with round-eyed bewilderment. Car horns blare all around us, drivers swerve, tires squeal. I wait for the crash of metal slamming metal, but it does not happen. "Don't stop, keep driving," I try to scream in a calmer tone as I search for our current wrong location on the atlas.

"OK, I see where we are. Just keep in this lane." My mouth is so dry my lips are sticking to my teeth. I sip a few swallows of cold coffee. "I see a way to get back to I-10."

"Should we just turn around?" Michael's voice is weak.

"No!" Too harsh. I breathe, sigh, explain. "We need to watch for Route 375. It looks like a little road over the mountains." Our first mountain! I try not to think of the brand new, rapidly approaching worry—do we have the skills and enough horsepower to drive over a mountain?

At Exit 29, we go East instead of West. I do not even mention the error as I rapidly plan our third route through El Paso. My heart pounds, my right foot pushes on a non-existent brake every time I see an Exit Only sign. Calmly, I suggest merging left. Never do we take a wrong turn toward Mexico. Only once, do we almost sideswipe a truck. We make a slow successful circle back to where we began.

"When do we get to the mountain road?" Michael asks. "This road looks familiar."

An hour later than anticipated, we leave El Paso behind us. A thousand drivers are not sad to see our departure.

Perhaps it's the tryptophan from turkey sandwiches for lunch and supper or my body's exhaustion after an hour of El Paso adrenaline, but by sunset every cell of my body wants to sleep. I turn to New Mexico, then to Arizona in my atlas. Michael's smile has returned, his hands are gentle and firm on the wheel. "I imagine it's real pretty in every direction," he says. "Too bad it's too dark to see anything."

My eyes gaze into blackness, my mind has no thoughts, my breathing slows. We have an easy drive west to Tucson, one turn south to Green Valley. I have a paper clip on a page of our campground directory—we have two, three, four options. "Turn south at Interstate 10," I murmur. "Wake me up if I fall asleep."

I dream of an orange moon rising over a purple mountain. Michael comes to me, rubs my arm, whispers, "We're here, honey. Let me get you to bed." I follow the glow of a flashlight, gravel crunches under my feet. Michael leads me to our bed, takes my shoes off, helps me undress. As I listen to coyotes singing, he slides in beside me.

Michael

I can hardly wait for Beth to get up. She'll not believe her eyes when she sees where I've brought us—a parking lot surrounded by five airstream campers, six counting Polly Jean. Scattered in front of the trailers are a dozen picnic tables, painted red and yellow and blue. Overhead are garlands of triangle flags in every color. An OPEN banner flaps from a little pole below a huge American flag. I bet she'll be as excited as I am. Maybe she'll tilt her head, give me that teasing smile and say, "Michael, have we decided to join a circus?" Then she'll laugh.

We got to Tucson about midnight. We'd have made it before dark, but I got us lost in El Paso. Beth was sleeping so pretty in the moonlight, her face turned toward me, her hands resting gently in her lap. I didn't want to wake her to ask if I should keep driving or take the road south, but I saw a Green Valley sign and for once, took the right exit. When I spotted a little RV park by the side of the interstate, I decided to stop for the night. There was no office sign anywhere, so I just pulled into an empty space and got us both to bed.

Beth's going to have to get in line to laugh at me this morning. My new friend Hector has been laughing at me since sunup. "I was wondering why I have six food trucks here," he'd told me when I tried to pay him. "Last night when I left, I had only five."

"So that sign over there doesn't mean RV Park, I'm guessing." I laughed too. The sign sits in the middle of a rocky flower garden. In swirling blue letters, the words *La Cocina de Milagros*. The Kitchen of Miracles, Hector told me. His wife thought up the name years ago, when this group of five Airstream food trucks was just a dream.

"*Mi amigo,*" Hector says. "Would you like another coffee?"

After talking to Hector for two hours, I know we are *amigos*. As soon as he saw me step out of the Airstream this morning, Hector waved. We've been talking ever since, sitting at a blue picnic table. Hector has hung up a menu, wiped off all twelve tables, made a vat of coffee which we're now busy emptying, one cup at a time. I'm itching to peek inside his Airstream to see how Hector's turned it from a camper into a kitchen. All I see is that the serving window is cut through the wall where the little kitchen table sits in our trailer.

Hector jumps up as a little blue Ford drives into the lot. A tiny woman gets out and walks toward the food truck, her arms loaded with supplies.

"My sister Maria," he says before he goes to help her. "Now that she's here I'll have it easy for the rest of the morning."

An orderly flow of customers comes and goes. Smells of roasting meat and coffee drift over. Maria takes orders and passes breakfasts through the serving window. Hector watches and sits across from me, telling me about his wife, gone now for ten years. Hector's wrinkled brown face is beaming, his black eyes are laughing. He's about my size, a little shorter, a little stockier. His hair is curly, grey mixed with black. He might be about my age, but I suspect he's younger. I tell him about Evelyn. I tell him about Beth, our heart attacks, meeting up as we were healing. Pick-ups rumble into the parking lot, and I tell Hector about the last six months, an entire new lifetime. "Hector, you're an A-1 listener," I say.

"You have a fine story," says Hector. "I'm proud to hear it."

I look back to see if there's any sign of Beth. After she gets up, I'm thinking we'll eat breakfast right here at this blue table.

I tell Hector I'd be too old to run a place like this, even if I had a sister helping me. I wonder if he has family other than Maria, how he managed after his wife died. How long did it take him to be happy again?

Hector looks at the mountains to the south. "Like most love affairs, mine began with my eyes. We were both at a party. I watched her laughing as she danced, and I could tell she was more in love with the music than the boy she was dancing with." Hector's face changes to the face of a young man as he tells me about his Teresa dancing, her black hair swirling. "It's been a while since I've told these stories," he says.

The sun is hot on my face. The air dry and still, the only sounds are the Interstate traffic and Hector's low, rich voice. Hector and Teresa were married a year after that day he saw her dancing. Teresa's momma knew a family from Hector's hometown in Mexico, a letter was written, an answer came back.

"I passed," Hector says. "Every day I lived with her was a blessing from God." He turns his wide-open face to me. "When He took her back, I hated Him with all that was left in my heart," he confesses. "I hated Him until my heart was empty."

Hector's sigh is deep. "As I watched our children and grandchildren, as I watched my sister make the same foods our grandmother used to make, love replaced the hate." He pats his chest. "Now my heart is full again."

"Meeting Beth did that for me," I tell him.

"Life goes on, does it not, *mi amigo?*" he laughs. Again, Hector looks at the mountains, then nods toward the desert behind the food trucks. "I see so many people walking across that sand," he says. "Some are hungry and thirsty. Some are lost and have no money. God shows them the path." His eyes search me as he speaks.

"I suspect God has brought you here too," Hector says.

"Oh no, nothing so grand," I tell him. "That policeman I told you about just happened to mention his folks liked it here."

Hector looks past me and gets up from the table. "Good morning, Señora Beth," he says.

Sure enough, Beth is laughing. She extends a hand and Hector encloses it with his.

"I'm pleased to meet you," Beth says. "It appears you're very kind to squatters."

Hector leaves and returns with another steaming cup of coffee. I thought she'd be full of questions, but she just stares at the mountains, the sun full on her face.

"The Santa Ritas," Hector sets the coffee in front of her and follows her gaze. "Named for the saint of impossible causes."

"Which we are," Beth says to the mountains.

When a person from Illinois sees mountains for the first time, they get quiet. They wonder how can this be? They wonder what took me so long to get here. They wonder how can I ever go back to a state where land is used for growing crops and holding roads and supporting cities instead of reaching up to God?

I wish I was clever enough at words so I could call Ramona and tell her how pretty a scene it is. All I can do is sit here, tears running down my cheeks.

Hector gives Beth the name and number of Desert Song RV Park. He says we're welcome to stay right here if we want, "Although I'm afraid you'd tire of people knocking on your window to order lunch."

I take out my hankie and wipe my face. Then we head out for Desert Song.

Desert Song is the fanciest place we've camped in yet, and it's pricey. Beth said in Centerburg we could rent an apartment and have enough left over for a car payment for what it costs to stay here for a month. I'm hoping she won't suggest traveling on. I'm tired of driving and I want to stay put long enough to buy some real groceries.

Each morning I dress in the dark and drag one of Cheryl's folding chairs behind a utility shed where the view to the south is just desert and mountains. Every morning the sunrise is different. I never much cared for being alone, but I don't feel the least bit lonesome. I feel like the whole world is waking up and saying Good Morning, Michael.

Once the sun comes up, it grabs back all the color from the sky. By the time I carry my chair back, the rest of Desert Song is waking up. Doors on trailers bang open and shut, car engines crank, and vacationing dogs start barking. Every once in a while, I get a whiff of bacon frying. In addition to a swimming pool and tennis courts and exercise classes, the park sets out a complimentary continental breakfast in the recreation center. The food isn't much, but Beth says we might as well eat breakfast there, since it's included in the rent, and she figures the walk there and back is good exercise. She's starting to fret about our health.

"I feel great," I tell her every time she asks me if I'm tired or thirsty.

"Good, let's just keep it that way," she says as she takes my blood pressure, then hands me a glass of water.

At least we're settled enough to unhook my car. Every day we drive over to Hector's place for lunch. On the way, Beth will say something like "Let's try the *pupusas* today when we get to *La Cocina de Milagros.*" She says the words so pretty.

By lunchtime, Hector usually has a chance to sit down with us as we eat. He tells us he owns all five Airstreams and the land they're sitting on. "I rent them to folks who want to start a business to make a better life," he tells us. "We're a family."

Hector's burritos are top notch, the best food here. Hector calls them traveling burros, crock pots full of slow roasted beef and pintos. By the time Maria has her first batch of tortillas ready, Hector's fixings are ready to stuff inside.

"Hector, you are a fine chef," I tell him.

"Yes, I know," he says.

Each afternoon we stop to pick up groceries and drive back to Desert Song. Tonight, we're having Salisbury steak over instant rice. I bought a bag of salad greens, but we had to buy bottled dressing since I don't have vinegar and garlic and spices to make my everyday Italian. The groceries cost thirty dollars. Beth gasped as I pulled my credit card out of my wallet.

I start flouring the steaks as Beth settles in at the kitchen table to call Clarice.

"Mike left you a message. Listen to this," she says as she shoves the phone at me.

"Pop, you need to take it easy with your credit card. Call me when you get a chance."

We call him back. "Am I out of money, son?" I ask. Beth's eyes get huge.

"Not yet, but right now you have more money going out than coming in." Mike's real voice is calmer than his cell phone message. "I know being on vacation is expensive but I'm afraid you'll be in a jam if you max-out your credit card." Then he talks about interest rates and cash flow, and well, here's the deal. I don't understand half the words Mike is saying. I've never paid a bill. Evelyn handled all our finances, taxes and banking and investing. Every week she'd put fifty dollars in my wallet. When she couldn't handle money anymore, Mike took over.

To make me feel better, Mike changes the subject to a play at Emma's school. After he hangs up, I tell Beth, "I guess I got myself into some trouble."

Beth looks scared. I try to remember all the words Mike said to me. As I talk, her neck gets red and she starts biting her lower lip, like she's trying to keep her words from flying out. I tell her I need to start handling my money instead of imposing on Mike.

"Michael, I'm so relieved," she says. "I've been wanting to bring up the subject of our finances, but I didn't want to be pushy." She gets up and hugs me. "I'm so glad Mike called."

I'm not sure she should be loving me right now. We've got big problems. "Do you know how to fix a max-out on a credit card?" I ask. "I'm not sure what that means."

"It means you've been paying for everything instead of letting me help." Beth's sounding almost joyful. "We're going to sit down and go over our finances, see what money we have coming in, and then we'll figure out a budget."

"You know how to do all that?" I ask.

"I've been doing it all my life." Beth sits back down, pushes the cell phone aside and grabs the pen and notebook she keeps handy on the kitchen table. She turns to a clean page. "We'll call Mike and have him collect all your financial information." I see her write Checkbook, Bank Statements, Bills-Credit cards? House? Health Insurance and Medical Bills? She stops, chews on the end of her pen. "Tomorrow we need to buy a post office box so we can get our mail delivered to Green Valley." Beth stares at the paper.

"We'll both need to fill out change of address forms." She writes that down too.

Beth is so deep into her new plan she doesn't seem to notice all the trouble I've dumped on her. "I'm sorry," I say. "This is so much work for you."

Beth looks up at me like she forgot I was standing two feet away. Her face is even happier. "We do want to settle in here, don't we?" she says. "Are we ready to start looking for a home?"

CHAPTER 4

⁂

Beth

I'm not the type of person who gasps when confronted with the extraordinary, especially in the presence of a real estate agent. I strive to maintain a neutral stare and offer only non-committal responses as Sandy, one of the dozens of realtors in Green Valley, shows us her wares. Michael, in contrast, has been audibly delighted by every single house she's paraded us through, *oohing* and *aahing* over granite kitchen counters and beehive fireplaces and whirlpool baths. But as I walk into the bathroom and see this lovely, unexpected sight, I gasp.

My involuntary vocalization is apparently loud enough for Michael and Sandy to hear from the townhouse kitchen, and they rush in.

"Are you OK?" Michael's gasping a bit himself.

"Oh, I'm fine, honey," I say. "I was just taken aback by how pretty this is."

Setting in the center of a cobalt blue tiled counter is a work of art posing as an ordinary bathroom sink. Every inch of the porcelain surface is covered with flowers and leaves and swoops and swirls of vibrant yellow and red, turquoise and green. Scallops of blue and white race around the border of the bowl. The mirror above is framed in bright yellow tile. I look at my face. I see lust staring back at me. I want to own this sink. It's easily the most beautiful household fixture I have ever seen.

"Yes, isn't this bathroom fun?" says Sandy. "This sink is Talavera, Spanish folk art. They're handmade in Mexico. And you'll notice the flowered tile around the mirror is also hand painted. This townhouse has lovely upgrades."

At the word *upgrade*, I regain my composure. This townhouse is one of the few dwellings we may be able to afford. Upgrades could slide the price into six-digits. I haven't been able to successfully convey our price range to Sandy since Michael insists on saying "It won't cost anything to take a look" every time she offers to show us a listing.

"Let's have a look at the master bedroom," says Sandy. "And then I'd like to show you two more houses, a single family that's just come on the market and a town home in a new retirement community south of Green Valley."

No, I've found our home, I want to say.

"Sure, it won't cost anything to have a look," Michael says.

Michael is ready to buy any house Sandy shows us, as long as it has a front door, a kitchen and a bedroom. I sit in the back seat of Sandy's Lexus and listen to them chat as we drive away from every showing. *Wonderful house, prime location, new listing—won't be on the market for long.* Michael listens attentively to each comment, answers every question with enthusiasm. My darling husband has not a shred of cynicism. My brain is urging me toward panic over potential financial ruination. What am I doing in a car with a realtor, driving past billboards bragging of "Homes Starting in the $200s." We can't afford half that amount. Maybe we can't afford any amount. We don't even have a joint checking account. Michael owns a seventy-year-old bungalow with a For Sale sign on the front lawn, and I own a condo occupied by a pregnant teenager and her grandmother. Does Michael have CD's or investment portfolios? Liens and second mortgages? We have two retirement checks to cover the bills arriving each month to a post office box in a town where we don't live.

I was doing so well. Drifting, loving, accepting, abandoning. Everything Michael and I needed we had. All our decisions were tiny—what to eat for lunch, where to stop for the night to sleep. We've found amazing sights, delicious tastes. Our days are filled with lazy wandering and our nights, well I think both Michael and I are pleased to be sharing the little bed in Cheryl's Airstream trailer. House hunting involves all the niggling mind-tasks I thought I might abandon: self-doubt, dread, the paralyzing fear of the imperfect choice. The illusive lure of something better, just a few miles down the road. A name on a bottom line, promising unending monetary commitment. As Old Beth and New Beth engage in silent battle between control and acceptance, I realize I'm rooting for New Beth.

"I was so afraid Beth wouldn't marry me," Michael is telling Sandy, as we barrel down the Interstate.

Stop fretting, my heart tells my brain. *Let's sit back and enjoy the ride.*

Michael's beaming as he returns to my table at the Green Valley Public Library. Instead of hunting for a good read, he's in search of new friends. "That guy at the Information Desk is a real interesting fella," says Michael. "He's from Michigan. He says no one in Green Valley is really from here. This town is younger than any of us."

"Well, that makes me feel fairly ancient," I say. "Sit down for a minute and let me show you these figures. I'm just not sure we can buy a house yet."

The papers of our combined financial history are arranged in orderly piles across the library table. Mike's packet of mail was the first delivery to our new post office box—banking statements, credit card invoices, check books, receipts of paid bills, copies of last year's tax forms and the listing agreement on Michael's house. A financial forensic jackpot. Next to arrive was the box sent from Cheryl, per my request—every paper from my desk drawers, my entire financial life.

"I thought you liked that townhouse with the pretty bathroom," Michael says, pulling out a library chair and sitting by my side. "What's in these papers that say we can't afford that little house?"

"I do like it but I'm not sure we can buy it." How do I explain my mixed emotions to Michael when I can't sort them out myself?

Michael's eyes glaze over as I summarize my financial findings. Total combined assets—not great, not bad. Liquid assets, non-existent. But what about down payments and mortgages, loans and interest rates, the burden of long-term financial obligations? "It's been a long time since I've had to worry about debt," I explain firmly, "and I don't want to live like that ever again." Michael sinks in his chair, his shoulders droop. I try to soften my message. "Honey, we don't have the money right now. Unless you have a pile of cash hidden somewhere?"

Michael is not cheered by my joke. "No, no, I don't think so," he says, shaking his head, clasping his hands into a fist. "It's my fault. Evelyn saved and saved. We had plenty, enough to send Ramona to college, enough to give Mike the restaurant." A pause, remembering. "Those five years in the nursing home, it cost a lot of money, thousands a month. Mike just said 'Don't worry about it' when I'd ask him. But I imagine my money is mostly gone."

Michael looks at the papers I've spread across the table. They document his disappointments and guilt. I've turned his joy to sadness with my cold, no-nonsense approach to our dreams. I need to remember we don't view life the same way. Michael expects positive outcomes. I've been trying to do the same, haven't I? But I'm still a little leery of optimism. I know there's a hidden price.

Michael's new friend from the Information Desk walks

past and nods. I watch him tidy the little sitting area, four tan and grey upholstered chairs facing each other, shoved into a square. The Green Valley Public Library occupies one end of a sparsely-used strip mall, but a poster by the front door promises a new Library and Recreation Center, opening next year.

"Honey, I'm sorry," I say. "We'll find a wonderful place to live. I just think we need to slow down, maybe rent a little apartment. Or just stay in Polly Jean, if we can find a cheaper RV park."

"I don't want a halfway life with you, Beth. I want to get us settled." His fist pounds the closest stack of papers. "We've worked hard, both of us, for our whole lives. I want to buy you that little townhouse. You just said you liked it, didn't you?"

I put my hand over his. "Yes, it does seem perfect for us," I say.

I don't tell Michael I've fallen in love with that tiny stucco home. It's plain and tidy, the end apartment in a row of similar, sensible units. It's original Green Valley, a senior housing project, row after row of parallel buildings, some faced with brick, others stucco. All landscaped in desert plants with names I long to learn. When I close my eyes, I see us living in the house with the Talavera sink, Michael stirring a pot of savory Mexican stew as I sit in a teak patio chair, sipping iced tea, or maybe even a glass of wine—an elegant daily celebration. Every evening I'll call Clarice and watch the mountains color with the setting sun. We'll sleep soundly and safe in our own real bed, my back against Michael's chest, his hand on my stomach. And every morning Michael will rise early to sit on our porch, ready to begin another day, just as perfect as the one before.

But we don't have the money for perfect right now.

"If you think it's best, I'll tell Sandy we've decided to hold off on buying a house," Michael pulls the words out.

"I think that's the wise decision," I say.

•

I tumble into logical resolve as we drive back to our rented space at Desert Song. In the kitchen/dining room/living room, Michael and I bump into each other, as I gather my glass of iced tea and cell phone, while Michael slices tomatoes and red onions for our sandwich supper. We excuse ourselves with polite sadness.

Sandy's sunny message awaits me when I turn on my phone. She's organized tomorrow's house search.

"Do you want me to call her back?" I ask.

"No, I better tell her myself," says Michael.

I hand him the phone.

"Hello Sandy. It's Michael. Well first, I want to tell you how much Beth and I appreciate the time you've spent showing us around."

Michael listens. "I'm sure you picked out more nice places for us to see, but no, we better not look at any other houses."

I can hear Sandy's encouraging buzz. I've spent enough time with her to know what she's saying, even though I can't make out any words.

"Well, the thing is," Michael says during a lull in Sandy's sales hum, "we love that townhouse with the pretty sink. We'd like to buy it."

I freeze and stare at Michael. He looks puzzled as he listens to Sandy's overjoyed response, now lifting to crescendo. *Sandy wait!* I want to scream, *Michael forgot to say "BUT . . . We'd like to buy it BUT . . . ."* I rush to grab the phone and explain, but before I can correct the huge mistake, Michael says, "Sure, I suppose it won't hurt to ask them," and hangs up.

"I think Sandy's going to tell the owners we want to buy their house," says Michael.

"Oh Michael," I hear myself moan. I can think of no other words. I need to call Sandy fast, before she makes the next phone call, but I can't move. All I can do is moan, "Oh Michael, what have you done?"

Michael loves me. And he wants to fetch me the moon and the stars. He wants to gather up my heart's desires and present them to me on a golden platter. So of course, when I moan in desperation, he hears a cry of heartfelt delight.

And perhaps my Michael hears me correctly.

We are Under Contract. I made a lowball offer, knowing it wouldn't be accepted. It was. We signed a provisional contact, hoping no bank will be foolish enough to loan us money; we have just enough wiggle room to prevent my total emotional breakdown. Every day, I try to explain our situation to Michael. "We need to talk to a loan agent and no bank here will even cash our checks. We'll have to negotiate with strangers. I don't know the current interest rates. Do we ask for a 30-year fixed mortgage? Michael, we won't have this house paid for until we're a hundred."

Everyday Michael says, "Oh, I'm sure everything will work out." Every day, we drive past *our house* on the way to errands or lunch. As Michael pulls out the skillet to make our supper, he tells me about the feasts he'll prepare *when I have a real kitchen*. When he bangs his head on the ceiling as he gets out of bed, he swears softly.

My phone calls to Clarice have taken an ugly turn. If Michael is in the camper, I go outside. If he leaves Polly Jean for any reason, I grab the opportunity to place a private call. In the freedom of our friendship, I voice my irritations. The sentences "I don't know what I was thinking" and "Michael has no clue" and "Never before in my life have I felt so out of control" dominate my diatribes.

Clarice is delighted.

"Honey, you've finally learned the words to The Hymn of the Married Woman," she says. "I was getting a little annoyed with how wonderful your life had become in comparison to mine."

This afternoon my agitation focuses on my prized lifetime

collection of Certificates of Deposit. "I suppose I could cash out my CD's, but I'd have to take a penalty. Plus, I can't do that over the phone. We'd have to drive back to Centerburg. It would take weeks. Maybe I should just call the realtor and tell her we can't find financing."

"Did you even talk to any lenders?" Clarice asks.

"No, I just can't bring myself to do that. And that's another thing. Michael thinks we can just walk into a bank and some dapper loan agent will run over to us with two cups of coffee and a check for ninety thousand dollars. Michael doesn't understand. It's all up to me."

"Oh honey, you're smart and you love that house. I'm sure it will all work out."

Over the next week, Michael and I receive an amazing collection of new cell phone messages. Apparently the Centerburg rumor mill is up and running. We listen to each one, over and over. We hear them so differently.

"Daddy, Ravi, and I had a discussion last night and we'd like to loan you the down payment for the house you and Beth have found. Call us back."

"Pop, Libby, and I have been talking and we're in a good position to loan you some money for that new house. Call us back."

"Beth honey, listen here. Miranda and I have cozied into your condo like two ticks in a hound dog's ear. We love it. I'm going to start paying you rent as soon as I can get my money flowing in the right direction."

"Momma." *Momma* feels like a long-distance embrace. "Zoe and I would like to offer you and Michael an advance to assist you in purchasing the property you're considering. Call us and we'll arrange the particulars."

I trace the messages to my afternoon rants to Clarice— Clarice to Cheryl to Miranda to her new best friend Lucas to his mom Ramona to her brother Mike, then back to Michael and me. Kate's message was not Clarice's fault.

After I'd told her about our house hunting misadventures during last Sunday's phone call, she said, "Mom, I can't believe you're trusting me enough to discuss your worries. Thank you."

"Honey, I wish I'd been more open about my feelings years ago," I told her.

"So now we can call Sandy and buy our house," says Michael.

"Absolutely not," I say. "We are not going to accept loans from everyone we know. They were all very kind to offer, but we are not that desperate. I imagine everyone thinks we've gone crazy, running across the country, and now trying to buy a house we can't afford. I think we may have gone crazy too. I'd borrow money from a bank before I'd accept money from family and friends."

So, one by one, Michael and I respond to every well-meaning offering. We try to convey our appreciation as we decline the generosity. At least I do. Michael just says, "Beth doesn't think borrowing is a good idea." And then he says, rather half-heartedly it seems, "And I suppose she's right."

We've left the dubious comfort of Polly Jean the Airstream's living room/dining room/kitchen to bask, or more accurately, bake in the al fresco dining at La Cocina de Milagros. The mingled smells of bubbling chilies and beans, roasting beef and pork, hang in the air. Breathing is a hot and spicy effort.

"I believe I could sip these smoothies all day long, if they weren't so expensive," I tell Michael. The only cool place on my body is my tongue. Michael is munching a burrito from Hector's, which he will share with me eventually. When I complain about our calorie-laden lunch, Michael says he could cook us healthier foods if he had a refrigerator to store them and a stove with more than two burners.

"*Mis amigos,* I've missed you for the last few days." Hector's pale-yellow shirt is short-sleeved and crisp from ironing, his head is bare. No hat, no sunglasses. I visualize his bachelor life, a row of shirts, fresh from the cleaners, in his closet. Not a speck of sunscreen in his medicine cabinet, only orange juice in his refrigerator. He shakes my hand as he always does and claps Michael on the shoulder. "I hear you have found a new home."

"We've found one that would meet our needs," I say, "but we've decided to put our house hunting on hold for a while."

"We don't have enough money and Beth won't let us borrow any." Michael's statement sounds too brisk, too simplistic. He's been irritated for days.

Hector is the perfect person to explain my fiscal policy, sitting here in the middle of his business empire, calm and in charge.

"Hector, you're a businessman. You know how complicated borrowing can become. Michael and I are too old to barter away our retirement security for a mortgage, and I just can't accept the charity of our families." I feel a flush spread across my neck as Hector gives me his full attention. "I know our families and friends mean well, but Michael and I are getting along just fine."

Hector is drinking coffee in spite of the midday heat. He holds his cup with both hands and gazes at the Santa Ritas. When he turns back to me, his smile is accepting, his eyes sad.

"When I look south," he says, "I think of my family, and I'm filled with sweet memories. When my sister Maria looks south, she's filled with sorrow. Beth, I don't think Maria would mind if I told you her story."

"When Maria came here from Silao, she was recently widowed, and she brought her son Alex who was eight. She was desperate, I was desperate also, to get her here. As I tried to arrange the necessary papers, contact the correct people,

Maria pulled together all her money and fled for safety. She and her son arrived illegally.

"My nephew was smart in school and was a good worker like his momma, but he was stubborn, like his uncle. By the time he was eighteen, he had the money to buy a car. 'Be cautious,' I'd tell him. 'You're an adult now. You don't have papers. Everything you have can be gone in an instant.'"

"Couldn't Maria and Alex apply for those papers?" Michael asks.

"You and Beth have arrived here in a very complicated time. Maria is not wealthy or powerful. People like Maria are not granted visas, and without a visa, one cannot apply for citizenship."

"It doesn't seem fair," says Michael.

"It's not fair, but it is the way it is." says Hector.

He continues. "This is the ugly part. Alex was caught speeding in his car. He was found to have no proof of citizenship, no green card. He was arrested and then deported, back to his 'homeland'. Now he's home in a foreign land." Hector takes a deep breath. "He's been away for two years. We hear of his attempts to get back. He almost made it last year, but the Border Patrol found him just after he had crossed, and they had to send him back."

"I'm so sorry," I say.

"I'm not telling you this story to complain about injustice," says Hector. "I'm saying from where I sit, I see what a wonderful gift it is to be allowed to help one's family."

La Cocina de Milagros buzzes with lunchtime, groups of friends linger at colorful tables, working folks carry bags of food back to their cars, trucks storm away. I wonder how many times a day Maria looks up from her work to scan the desert, longing for a glimpse of her son.

I look at my sad Michael. "Money is only paper, Beth," says Hector, the businessman. "It has no value other than what we give it. It sounds like your family has attached love to this gift of money. Love is given back when you accept their gifts. We hear it's more blessed to give than to receive, but I think it's more sacred to receive. And much harder."

"Everybody was real disappointed when we told them we wouldn't take their money." Michael looks at the half-eaten burrito.

"I can imagine." Hector picks up my empty glass. "Beth, would you like another smoothie? My gift."

I have spent my lifetime refining my attributes. My most polished strength is responsibility, in all its proud forms— practicality, self-discipline, attention to detail. Hector's words crush my rock-hard reasoning, hammering it to dust. It doesn't hurt a bit. Dust is lighter than stone and it doesn't have to be carried. It's blown away with the desert wind. Hector and Michael laugh over the gift of a six-dollar smoothie, thinking I will never accept it.

"Yes, Hector," I say. "I'd like another Tropical Smoothie. Large, please. And I'd like it in a To Go cup. Michael and I need to get back to the RV park and make some phone calls."

Michael can hardly drive, he's so excited. He takes the second Desert Song speed bump much too fast, and my cost-ly smoothie almost pops out of my grip. We bolt to a stop in front of Polly Jean, gravel flying. As soon as we settle at our kitchen table, I turn on my cell phone. A message from Mike is waiting for us.

"Pop. You've just had an offer on your house. It'll be a cash deal. I'm thinking you'll want to accept it. Call me back."

And so, forsaking pride and accepting happenstance, Michael and I are home.

CHAPTER 5

✺

Michael

We swap a check for a key, drive to our new house, unlock the front door and walk into our new life. When we buy the house, we buy everything in it—furniture, dishes, curtains, a little TV with a DVD movie player. Sometimes Beth and I rent a movie, microwave some popcorn and crawl into bed to watch it. And the best part, sometimes one thing leads to another, and we don't finish the movie.

I want to write a thank you letter to the couple who sold us the house, telling them how much we love it, but Beth says giving them eighty-five thousand dollars is thank you enough. Beth's cautious with our money. After we exchange the check I got for selling my old house to buy this new one, we have money left over. I tell Beth I'll buy her whatever she wants, a new car or some diamond earrings, but she wants one of those savings CD's. I'm proud to buy her one.

"Where's Beth?" Hector asks me. I'm sitting by myself at the blue picnic table, drinking coffee and watching folks line up for lunch. Hector's food truck gets the bulk of the business, but the Sonora hot dog place is doing OK too. I'm worried the smoothie stand might not make it. As Beth says, it's way too expensive.

"I dropped her off at the library," I tell Hector. "She said she needed a change of scenery."

Hector sits down on the other side of the table. "A little

time apart will help the romance," he laughs. "In a few hours, she'll realize she's missing you."

We watch the lines of customers. I know Hector's calculating his food inventory and his profits. "I better get back to work," he says, "but first, there's something I'd like to discuss with you."

Hector says he's had this idea ever since we got to be friends and now seems a good time to say it out loud. "Do you want a new job?" he asks me. "You're here most days anyway, you know the restaurant business and you could earn a little extra spending money—very little!" He laughs.

I am going to have a new boss. His name is Hector.

Hector's idea is working great. I'm a part-time, minimum wage employee. Three mornings a week, fifteen minutes after sunrise, I drive to *La Cocina de Milagros* in time to help Hector set up for the day. Beth gets shed of me for three days a week so she's talking about buying a computer and taking a class to learn how to run it. Hector says next year he'll try to convince me to open for him so he can walk in the mountains a few mornings a week. It won't take much to convince me. And if I can learn to make tortillas and salsa, Maria can take off work every Sunday morning and go to her church.

The first time I chop the tomatoes, peppers, onions and cilantro, Maria stands beside me, offering soft instructions as I mix the vegetables, spices, and lime juice in her special bowl. "It's good, Michael," she says when she tastes it. "It tastes like my grandmother's." Her words go straight to my heart.

Now my eyes can measure the flour, shortening and water for the tortillas. My hands know the feel of the dough when it's properly kneaded. My fingers know how to pinch off enough dough to roll into a perfect twelve-inch circle, to brown the tortillas and place them into a stack to warm until they're needed.

Hector tells me the weather can affect how busy we'll be. He explains tourists come on weekends and workmen come Monday through Friday. Then he tells me one of our most important jobs is to watch for the walkers. "After a while, you'll know," Hector says. Men, dust-covered and smelling of fear, approach from the south, eyes darting. Hector can spot them from half a mile away. Hector teaches me what to put in the paper bags he carries to them—two burritos, two bottles of water, one twenty-dollar bill.

Our life takes on a new rhythm. For a few hours a week we drift apart to view different sights, hear others' voices. We have stories to share when we return to each other. Some days I drop her off at the library, pick her up after my work is finished. She tells me about the progress on the new library, she's bubbling with the information she's found in the books she brings home each week. As we walk around our neighborhood before sunset, she tells me the name of every cactus.

"Hector is talking to the ladies who run the smoothie shop," I tell Beth. "He thinks if they share a truck with the burger guys, they can save on rent and make more money." I report how many walkers pass by each day. Some days we see none, sometimes we might spot four or five solitary walkers in the distance. As it is with the folks who drive into our parking lot, weather and hunger influence their arrival. Seeing the walkers makes Maria sad, I tell Beth, but watching Hector stroll across the desert to hand them a brown paper bag makes me happy.

"Just be careful," Beth tells me. "You know it's against the law to assist folks who cross the border illegally."

"That's a mean, stupid law," I say.

"Yes, it is," says Beth.

One day flows into the next. Amid this amazing procession is our first wedding anniversary.

Somebody has tied balloons to every shrub, somebody's

hung a banner of paper flowers from Hector's truck to the flagpole. *La Cocina de Milagros* is jam-packed with people, laughing and yelling and trying every taste offered from the food trucks sparkling in the afternoon sun. A good portion of these folks are our party guests.

Beth and Clarice planned it all during a hundred phone calls. At our house, a van arrived with Clarice and Cheryl, Miranda, and baby Kaitlyn, fresh from a Centerburg to Green Valley road trip. Clarice's husband Jim stayed home, refusing any involvement with a van-full of women and a new baby. Soon after, a plane from Chicago landed, bringing Mike and Libby and Emma. Another, from St. Louis, held Ravi, Ramona, and Lucas.

Lucas was a reluctant flyer, his mom informed us. He'd tried to convince her to let him drive cross-country with the women, helping with driving in case of emergency. Ramona said no. He told her he could bring Sunny with him in the van, so Sunny and I could visit. Ramona said no. He suggested he and Miranda could do homework together in the van, since they'd be missing a week of school. Ramona said no. Ramona told me Lucas and Miranda are just very good friends, but after watching them together for a day, I know Lucas is deep in love.

Our surprise guests are Kate and Zoe. An hour after the Centerburg van arrived at our house, they were knocking on our front door. Beth cried, then all of us cried.

At our favorite blue table, Beth and I sit side-by-side, trying to take it in. Picnic tables have been shoved into a sloppy triangle in an effort to corral our herd. In the center is a cluster of Hector's personal lawn chairs, three occupied by our teenagers, all focused on Kaitlyn as she holds court from her shaded stroller, a purple sunbonnet on her head. Is she hot, hungry, sleepy, or just simply adored? She reaches a tiny hand to touch her momma's cheek. Miranda kisses each finger.

Lucas watches them.

"Hector, darling, these burritos are making me fall in love with you," Cheryl yells over her shoulder. "You play your cards right, I might even let you marry me. This wedding anniversary's putting me in a romantic mood and there's nothing sexier than a man who knows how to cook, right Beth?"

Libby and Ramona are deep in conversation, each grasping a sweating bottle of sweet Mexican soda pop. At Ramona's side, Ravi watches the teenagers as they watch Kaitlyn.

Beth dips a french fry in guacamole, a touch of US/Mexican fusion from the Burger Bus and Smoothie Bar. She leans against me, gives me the first bite.

Hector pulls his folding lawn chair up to our picnic table, plants himself beside Cheryl. "So you think this old grandpa is sexy?" he asks. Cheryl stops talking mid-sentence and turns bright red. "I'm sorry, my dear." Hector puts a hand on Cheryl's shoulder. "I didn't mean to embarrass you."

Cheryl recovers. "Don't you apologize. I'm intrigued to have met my match."

Suggestions are floated for this afternoon—hotel swimming pools and naps. Ravi, three teens and a baby are ready to leave. Activities for tomorrow are discussed—golfing or the Desert Museum. Ravi and Kate are the first votes for golf.

"Michael and I want to treat everyone to smoothies for dessert," Beth announces to our crowd. Hector laughs.

"Momma, wait." Kate speaks to Hector in Spanish. They disappear into his food truck and emerge carrying a two-tiered wedding cake topped with three lighted sparklers. On top, a tiny bride and groom stand by a cactus. Kate's face is sparkling brighter than the cake. Everyone cheers and claps until the sparklers burn out.

Kate makes a speech. "Tradition dictates the eating of leftover wedding cake on a couple's first anniversary, but since that first cake has already been shared, Zoe and I want to celebrate your happiness with this cake."

Unlike Beth's embarrassment at our cruise ship wedding reception, now Beth laughs as I feed her the first bite of cake.

"You play golf, you speak Spanish," Beth says to Kate as everyone begins to eat our second wedding cake. "My daughter is full of surprises."

"Momma, we are sitting in the Sonora desert eating burritos to celebrate your first wedding anniversary. Don't speak to me of surprises."

As I sit beside my bride, I close my eyes and try to grasp the wonder of this moment, this string of moments, that have brought us all here. I can't grasp it, so I just let this moment pass into the next.

Beth

My anniversary present to Michael—a huge lasagna pan— sets on the kitchen counter, full of bubbling cheesy spicy goodness. When I gave it to him at our party, he announced he'd make lasagna for all our guests tonight, their last evening in Green Valley. As soon as all our visitors are squeezed into our townhouse, Michael pulls the garlic bread out of the oven, gives the saladz a toss and surveys the jam-packed scene for Kate. She told him to hold off serving dinner because we get one last surprise. "And don't buy any wine," she'd said, which sounded like a big hint.

"Kate honey," he yells. "Soup's on."

We scrunch together near our dining room buffet. In the center is a pile of red, blue and green towels. On top is a yellow washcloth folded up to look like a bow.

"I'd like to offer a toast to the anniversary couple," Mike says, "but don't we need some wine? Beth, come unwrap your present."

"Those towels are from Cheryl and me," Clarice yells from the center of the group. "We didn't buy beige!"

"Beige is the only color that won't work in my bathroom," I laugh. "Thank you." I pick up the whole pile of towels, hand them to Michael and gasp. Sitting at the center of our buffet is a wine rack made of wrought iron and tiles painted just like our bathroom sink. All twelve compartments hold a bottle of wine.

"Talavera! Where did you ever find this?"

"We had to take valuable time away from our golfing and visit a few wineries," Ravi says.

I stare at our perfect anniversary present as a line forms toward the kitchen. "How many bottles should I open, Pop?" Mike yells.

Michael surveys the room. "Two," he says.

Ramona gathers glasses and passes them to Ravi who has put himself in charge of wine distribution. When all the adults have a glass of wine, Mike raises his glass to us, "To you Beth, for bringing love and happiness to my father, and to you both, for sharing that love with all of us. *Salute!*" We all raise our glasses. I wish I were close enough to Michael to toast him with a kiss, but he's wedged against the kitchen wall. Our eyes meet, he winks, raises his glass to me and takes the first sip of our anniversary wine.

Ravi taps the rim of his glass with Cheryl's "The sommelier at the vineyard believes this wine will cellar well for decades," he says.

"Well then, I've got an idea," Cheryl says. "How's about we all come back here every year and open up a bottle?"

On our second anniversary, only Cheryl returns to Green Valley to share a bottle of wine with us. She called around the first of February. "Beth, I'm declaring Grandma Closed for Vacation. I'll be there in three weeks," she told me.

Cheryl has a game plan. She'll drive my car here and fly home, Clarice is going to babysit for Kaitlyn while Miranda is in school. Once Cheryl rests up here for a week, she's going back to Centerburg and looking for a house. Kaitlyn is walking now, and soon she'll be running; she needs her own bedroom and a yard full of grass. We can discuss putting my condo on the market, Cheryl says, and she can orchestrate the sale. My condo won't fetch much money—maybe a fourth of what Michael made from selling his house in Des Plaines, but with Cheryl's help, this might be a good time to convert real estate into a little CD.

The reasons for Cheryl's trip are good and logical, but I suspect the real reason for her visit to Green Valley is Hector. She is uncharacteristically silent about him. He hasn't said much about her either, other than a neutral "Cheryl is a fine woman. She fights for her family." But Hector seemed to know she was coming before I did, and Cheryl casually mentioned, "If Michael and his boss aren't too busy, maybe the four of us can go out for supper."

We glide south down the Interstate in Hector's lemon-yellow Cadillac. Sitting shoulder to shoulder in the huge backseat, Michael and I watch the romantic comedy playing out in front of us. Hector is wearing a suit and tie, Cheryl's blouse is a silky tropical print. Her fingers fiddle with her hair, tucking errant stands into the French twist. On her arm is a collection of thin silver bracelets. Clarice's? After she's arranged herself, she begins punching buttons on the dashboard. Angry talk radio, oldies rock, current rock, twangy western, a local Mexican station. As the car is fills with the rich music, Hector sings along.

"Those words are so pretty," Michael says to me. "I wish I could learn to speak Spanish."

As Cheryl looks at the desert landscape rolling past her window, Hector turns to watch her, then focuses back to the road ahead. I don't have to see his face to know he's smiling.

"Riding in this big ol' Caddy makes me feel like a movie

star." Cheryl turns to me, "Beth, don't I look a little bit like Lauren Bacall? Hector, you could pass for Humphrey Bogart."

"Thank you, but I'm perfectly happy being Hector this evening," he says.

On the horizon, a life size wooden steer stands on the roof of a restaurant. Hector drives toward it, pulls into a crowded parking lot. He opens the car door for Cheryl and extends his hand to help her out. Michael does the same for me. A double date. I do believe this is my first.

The steakhouse is dark and cool. A painting of a barely clothed lady hangs over the long wooden bar, an empty stage rests by a back wall, and over the sound system, Willie sings, "But you were always on my mind. You were always on my mind."

"Sit wherever you want," a waitress yells. We choose a round corner booth, Cheryl and I at the center with our dates beside us. Our pseudo-Lauren Bacall fidgets over the collection of steak sauces until our waitress brings the menus, then starts to read.

"Beth, liver and onions!" Cheryl taps my menu. "Grandma used to make it for us. Your brothers hated it, but we thought it was a gourmet treat. Remember?"

"Sure I do," I say.

"How's Charley?" Cheryl asks.

"My brother in Denver," I explain to Hector and Michael. "Fine I guess," I tell her. I feel a fading away, a sadness. "We were never close . . . my brothers were older." A feeble sentence.

"Hector, do you have brothers and sisters other than Maria?" Cheryl asks.

"No, only Maria," Hector recalls a baby sister in Silao crying as her big brother left home to travel north. Michael tells us about his father returning home from a war and a ten-year-old boy soon had two sisters, too young to bother with.

Platters arrive, two with steaks, two with liver and onions. The conversation lulls as we eat.

"I have an idea." Hector says as our table is cleared. "Why don't I close early tomorrow and the four of us can take a hike in the mountains. I'll bring a picnic."

Michael and I look at each other. Nothing about this idea sounds like Hector, especially the part about an early close. Everything about this plan sounds like a fellow who would like to spend a little more time with a special lady. Michael knows just what to say.

"Tell you what," he says. "How about I help out Maria tomorrow. Then you won't have to close early. Besides, I'm not sure Beth and I are up to a mountain hike."

Hector is very pleased with Michael's alternate plan. He turns to Cheryl and says, "My dear, how about a picnic tomorrow?"

I only miss three things about Centerburg—visiting with Clarice face to face instead of on the phone, the Dairy Queen, and Doctor Sam. Having a car of my own was the fourth thing I was missing, but I can check that off the list since Cheryl drove my Chevy back to me last week.

I drive my car to our next doctor's visit. Our appointments are back-to-back with the same doctor, a handsome young man who spends most of the exam time scrolling through his computer, asking the same questions we've answered on the form given to us in the waiting room. I chose this clinic because it's right across the parking lot from our new library.

The waiting room is almost empty. Michael barely has time to complete the insurance and health questionnaire before a nurse calls his name. "I'll meet you at the library when I'm finished with my appointment," I remind him as he follows her through the door to the exam rooms.

In fifteen minutes, I'm escorted to an exam room. A few

minutes later, my doctor knocks on the door, comes in, smiles, and plants himself in front of his computer. "The results from your last blood tests look good," he says, scrolling down the screen. "We'll wait until your next appointment to check them again. How are you feeling?"

After I tell him "Fine" he reads a few questions from his computer screen: Have I ever smoked? Have I fallen in the last three months? Do I feel safe in my home? He records my answers, looks up and says, "Let's take a listen to your heart."

Apparently, my heart is just fine. He shakes my hand, tells me he'll renew my prescriptions and see me in six months. My handsome new doctor doesn't nag me about my weight or inquire about my exercise regime or diet. He accepts all my answers without a sneer or a comment. He doesn't say "Tell me about your new life. So much has changed" or ask, "Is there anything I can do to make sure you and Michael are happy and healthy for the rest of your years together?" After my easy ten-minute appointment, I don't even feel like I've been to see a doctor.

I miss Doctor Sam.

As I walk across the parking lot to the library, I decide if our new doctor isn't going to nag us about our health and wellbeing, I might as well do it myself.

Our new library is decorated with Arizona in mind—mountain mauves and sunset corals, Navajo weavings hung on a sky-blue wall. It smells of fresh paint and carpet. I spot Michael sitting at a grouping of chairs in front of a huge window. He's so intent upon reading the brochure in his hands, he doesn't see me walk up.

"How was your appointment?" I ask.

"Great," he says. "I didn't even have to get undressed. Look what I found at the information desk." Michael hands me a glossy brochure entitled Spring Classes for Adult Education. The cover shows an immaculately dressed senior woman sitting at a computer as a dignified gentlemen towers over her. I could be that woman, except for the expensive clothes and perfect hair.

"There's a class to teach Spanish. Do you think I could learn it?" Michael's eyes are wide open with wonder.

"Of course you could," I tell him. I sit down and read through the courses: Looking at the Night Sky. Oil Painting Desert Landscapes. Conversational Spanish. Everything You've Wanted to Know About Computers (But Were Afraid to Ask). I take a hopeful breath and read on. For fifty dollars, a retired PhD from the University of Wisconsin will spend every Monday morning giving me tips on how to buy a laptop, set it up and use it to communicate with the rest of the world, as well as organize all my financial records. I imagine myself with flow charts of budgets, checking account updates, credit card invoices, CD balances including interest accrued daily. I could request library books online! Everything will be available at the touch of a button. Ah, but which button to touch? Soon I'll know.

"Michael, do you want to go to college together?" I ask, teasing.

"Sure," he says. "You'll be the prettiest, smartest coed there."

Our evening menu tonight is a nod toward healthier options—scrambled eggs with salsa and tortillas, all made by my husband. I've begun my Beth and Michael's Healthy Lifestyle Plan. After supper we might take a walk.

"Look what I forgot!" Michael has a bottle of wine in one hand and two wine glasses in the other. We are having supper on our patio, sitting in our two new teak chairs.

"We should have shared a bottle of our anniversary wine with Cheryl and Hector last week," I say. "I entirely forgot too! Although, I don't think a bottle of wine would have made their week any happier than it was."

I watch Michael open the bottle. "Has Hector mentioned Cheryl since she left?" I ask.

"No, not a word," says Michael. "Did Cheryl say anything about Hector to you?"

"No, she just said she hoped we'd invite her back next year," I say. "My, my! This may be serious."

Michael kisses me on the cheek, hands me a glass of wine and says, "To us, and to Hector and Cheryl. Lovebirds, old and new."

CHAPTER 6

＊

Michael

I'm smack dab in the middle of a traffic jam in Sedona, a detour on our route to the Grand Canyon. My wife of soon-to-be three years is sitting in the passenger seat, her atlas open, trying to navigate me through the mess. Cheryl and Clarice are in the back seat, fussing at each other. Attached to my bumper is Polly Jean, the Airstream. We're a wild, wacky family on vacation.

Beth's been planning our anniversary trip for months, ever since she got herself a new computer. She looked up hotels and places to eat and campgrounds at the Grand Canyon, then called everybody to ask them to come with us. Cheryl and Clarice said yes. They are going to stay at the fancy hotel on the rim of the Grand Canyon, but Beth and I are camping, on account of "cheaper." When she found out Cheryl and Clarice were going to drive with us, Beth found the prettiest roads and places to see along the way. She sent them stacks of papers, piles of brochures, all the information she found in her computer. I suppose Sedona would be real nice if I could park this rig someplace and get out to look at it.

The reason for the detour is Cheryl.

"Cheryl, this is your fault," Clarice declares as I watch the stoplight cycle from red to green to red without any forward movement in traffic. About an hour ago, Cheryl yelled from the back seat, "Can we stop at Sedona? I need to get my aura read."

After two more stoplight cycles it's our turn to move through the intersection. Clarice is fuming. "Explain to me why you need to get your aura analyzed?"

I hear papers shuffling in the back seat. Cheryl reads aloud. *"Knowledge of your aura helps you to align your path and channel Universal positive energy to move yourself forward in your life pursuits."* Cheryl rattles more papers. "Look at the pictures of these folks' auras. They got colored lights shooting out of them in all directions."

"Beth, you should have screened these brochures before you sent them to Cheryl," says Clarice. "I've finally managed to get her life situated and now she's veering off again."

Beth ignores the backseat commotion in her job of getting us through Sedona. I creep forward as she reads off the street names. Clarice is looking for restaurants and Cheryl is looking for aura-reading stores. Everybody's yelling "There's one" and "Look at that" and "I think we've passed it" as my foot pops back and forth from the ignition to the brake. Even if I find a space, I'll never be able to park a car hauling an Airstream trailer.

"Maybe I should just let you girls out and circle around for a few hours," I say.

"No way, Michael," Cheryl yells. "I'm afraid you won't come back to get us. Beth honey, we need a Walmart parking lot."

My foot hits the brake again for stopped traffic and a horn blares behind us. In my side mirror, a huge black truck looms. The honking continues.

Cheryl flings open her door and storms out into the traffic jam. In a minute the honking stops and she's back in the car.

"Go another mile and turn left," she says. "That truck driver says there's some motels where we can park and walk to a great burger place. And he said he's sorry."

"How'd you have enough time to yell at him, make up,

and get travel recommendations?" asks Clarice.

"I'm an efficient communicator," says Cheryl.

It takes less time to eat our cowboy cheeseburgers than it did to drive, park, and walk to the Sedona Cowboy Grill. As soon as we pay our bill, Cheryl gets antsy for her aura reading. "Come on Beth, you don't want to sit here all by yourself, do you?"

"That's exactly what I want to do," Beth says as she takes her crossword puzzle out of her purse. Since all-by-myself doesn't seem to include me, I get up with Clarice and Cheryl and give Beth a quick good-by kiss.

"You two make me want to slap Jim," says Clarice. "I can't remember if he even kissed me good-by when I left Centerburg and I'm going to be gone a week."

"You might want to pay a little extra for a romantic evaluation, honey," Cheryl says as she flings her purse over her shoulder. "I'm going to get me one."

I follow the ladies to Cosima's Cosmic Plateau, which is housed in a corner of a strip mall built between red rock formations. The outside is aqua with sparkly silver stars around the window frame. Tinkling music is playing and the whole place smells like smoky perfume. In the corner is a little sitting area with a sagging red couch and a rocking chair. In the rocking chair is a thin blonde woman in a purple dress. She has her head in her hands and she's crying so hard she doesn't even hear us walk in.

"We're sorry to bother you," I say. "We'll just be going, unless there's anything we can do to help."

"Oh, I've had a little bad news." She pulls her hair back from her face and attempts a smile. "A good cry is so cleansing, isn't it? Come in, come in. How can I help you?"

"We were looking for a Cosima," Cheryl mumbles. "We just needed a little information on auras." She doesn't sound nearly as enthusiastic as she was when she was reading the brochure.

"I'm Cosima." The woman wipes at her eyes with a tissue. "I'd love to analyze your auras. You'll find it's an amazing experience. So helpful. So powerful." She blows her nose and tells us about energy fields and her special camera. "I can give you a personal interpretation, for a bit more, or I could give you a group rate, if you're interested."

When Cosima tells us the full-service group rate, Clarice gasps and Cheryl says, "Well, thank you anyway, but I think we'll take a pass for now. I sure hope you get to feeling better."

"Thank you for stopping in," says Cosima. "Yes, I'm feeling much better."

Then she sits back down in her chair and returns to crying her eyes out.

An hour later, Cheryl, Clarice, and I are sitting in a line on the sagging couch and our new friend Trudy—Cosima's real name—is sitting in front of us, rocking in her chair, showing us our aura photographs, giving us her personal interpretation. Cheryl's paid for it all. We got a special rock bottom rate since Trudy wants to talk to us as much as Cheryl wants to talk to her.

Trudy's chair has a little creak as she rocks back and forth. I sink into the crushed velvet couch and listen to Trudy talk about the greens and yellows of Clarice, confident and creative, hard-working and dynamic. Unconditional love. Cheryl is red, red, red. Passionate and sensual, generous, quick to anger. Sounds like Trudy has hit the nail on the head. Trudy turns to me. "Michael, your aura shines with purples and whites, the colors of peace and wisdom." She picks up my aura paper and reads, *"Auras of white indicate a spirit open and receptive to the Divine, one that can merge with All-That-Is."*

"Everybody has real pretty colors, don't they?" I say to Trudy. "Thank you for telling us about them."

Trudy leans toward me and touches my hand. "I knew you were special the moment you walked into my shop."

Her eyes are mostly dry now. She's lived her whole life around Sedona, Trudy tells us. It was magic, the prettiest place in the whole world, but lately it's changed. People with a lot more money than Trudy have come for the Sedona magic, and she can't afford her hometown anymore. Twenty minutes before we walked in, Trudy had a visit from the sheriff. "I should have gone into law enforcement," she told us. "There's plenty of work around here issuing eviction notices." She has one week to vacate her shop; she lost her house last year. Trudy's hand brushes away the remnants of a tear, then she gathers her hair in a rope over her shoulder. I watch her fingers weave it into a long, blond braid as she talks.

She'll have to hunt up some waitress work, maybe hire on to housekeeping at a local resort. She still won't have enough money for rent.

"Maybe you could move in with a friend for a while?" Clarice suggests.

I'm forty years old," Trudy groans. "I don't want to be sleeping on a futon in someone's family room."

"You know Trudy," I say. "I have an idea, but I need to talk to my wife first."

Beth's exactly where we left her—corner patio table, iced tea by one hand, pen in the other, crossword puzzle in her lap. She looks so peaceful.

"So, tell me about your auras."

"It was fun," Clarice slides into a chair. "Two of us are very special."

Cheryl takes the bait. "It's true, all my picture had was red. I was upset over all the honking and I ate too much and then we walk in and find the person who's going to organize my life journey crying her eyes out."

"Cheryl has aura-envy." Clarice waves for a waitress. "Beth, your husband has an A+ aura. Michael, show her your picture."

Our waitress comes over, trying to look happy at the prospect of us occupying her table for a few more hours. "Can we have four drinks To Go," I ask her, reaching for my wallet. "Beth, I want you to meet our new friend Trudy."

Trudy's couch won't hold the four of us so I stand and lay out my idea as fast as I can. As Trudy weeps and hugs us and blows her nose and cries some more, Beth, Clarice, and Cheryl refine my idea into a workable plan. Beth says a loan isn't needed. We can just give Polly Jean the Airstream to Trudy. As Clarice points out, it will take Trudy a few days to find a parking place. When Cheryl asks her about trailer hitches, it turns out Trudy has a dozen friends with pickup trucks so it shouldn't be too difficult to figure things out. Trudy cries some more before we hug and say good-bye, promising to return in a few days.

It turns out Clarice, Cheryl, Beth, and I are pretty good at helping folks with their life journey, even if we don't have an aura camera.

After two nights at the Grand Canyon, the four of us return to Sedona to deliver Polly Jean to her new home, a piece of land sitting square between sunrise and sunset. Clarice, Beth and I sit in folding chairs to watch Cheryl introduce Polly Jean to Trudy. Beth reaches over and grabs my hand.

By mid-afternoon, my Buick is floating back toward the Grand Canyon without the strain of a ton and a half of Airstream camper. Since we are homeless for the rest of our trip, Clarice suggested getting Housekeeping to put a couple of cots in their room. I figured Beth would jump at the plan, but she surprised me. Tonight, after we celebrate our third anniversary dining at a table overlooking the Grand Canyon at sunset, Beth and I will sleep in our own room at the El Tovar. It will be the most romantic place we've ever slept.

CHAPTER 7

Beth

Tonight we dine at our little red patio table. We are trav-el-weary after an extended holiday trip to Illinois, in need of the solitude winter brings. As I do nothing except languish in the moment, Michael is in the kitchen, putter-ing and happy. A simple supper will mark our anniversa-ry—a bowl of soup, a piece of pie, a glass of special wine. Michael has uncorked the bottle and placed two glasses beside it.

As I sit in my teak chair, my eyes trace the peaks of the Santa Ritas. I could draw them from memory. On the other side of our patio wall, a white-winged dove sings to me from the branch of the palo verde. The first time I heard the call I thought it was an owl, so I ran to grab my binoculars and bird book. Now I know his song is *hoooo*, not *hoot*! My next Adult Education course just might be Birds of the Sonora Desert now that I've completed my computer classes and we've both finished Conversational Spanish. After two class-es, Michael begged me to take Spanish with him. "I can't remember the words," he said. "You're so smart and we can do the homework together."

Mi esposo brings me a glass of wine and sits beside me. Before we have a chance to toast, our neighbor walks by. Michael stiffens.

"*Buenas noches, Senior. Me gusta su camisa azul.*" My voice is casual and friendly. Our neighbor waves half-heartedly, not looking up.

"What did you say to him?" Michael asks.

"I told him I liked his blue shirt," I say. "Too bad he doesn't understand Spanish."

I taunt our neighbor because he wounded my husband. It happened two, three years ago. I was up early, Michael was leaving for work. I heard voices through our bathroom window as I was washing my face. A gravely drawl, growing louder with each sentence, then Michael's pleading voice, soft and sad. I stood by the open window and listened.

It started with an introduction, probably a handshake.

"You're an early riser. Where you headed? Don't tell me you're going to work," a man said.

"As a matter of fact, I am." Michael's proud voice. "I work part time at La Cocina de Milagros over by the Interstate."

"The hell you do. You don't look like a damn wetback! Squatter trailers crawling with illegals and drug dealers, somebody should burn that place down."

My face burned as I heard Michael. "It's not like that. Hector's a US citizen. He owns the land. Hector's the finest man I've ever met."

"Listen neighbor." The voice growled. "You're new here. You better be careful or some taco jockey's gonna knock you in the head and dump your body in the desert."

By the time I got to Michael he was standing alone in the parking lot, trembling.

We watch our neighbor round the corner toward his house and disappear. "I just don't get that guy," Michael says every time he sees him.

"Don't worry about him, honey. He's just a small, mean man," I say, as I say every time. "People who are different scare him."

"Everybody in the world is different," Michael says.

Oh, my heart, you are so full. Michael is wearing the lavender Hawaiian shirt Cheryl sent him for his birthday, a gag gift she thought he'd never wear. He loves it. He sees me watching him and raises his glass to mine.

"*Te amo, mi amigo.*" His words are slow.

Our glasses tap, I chuckle.

"Did I say it wrong?" he asks.

"You said it fine. I love you too, my friend," I tell him.

After one sip of wine, the phone rings.

"I had a feeling we wouldn't be celebrating alone," I say. Ramona's name is on caller ID.

Had she called thirty seconds earlier, she could have heard Michael's toast in Spanish, I tell her. As we talk, Michael travels back and forth carrying steaming bowls of soup, a platter of garlic bread. He pauses to pick up his wine glass, lifts it toward the phone in my hand. Again, he says, "*Te amo, mi amigo.*"

"I believe that toast was for you," I tell her. "Do you want to talk to your father?"

As Michael listens to Ramona, I eat. The soup is delicious, the garlic bread even better. Finally, he says, "Lucas is a fine young man. Everything will work out."

When Michael gets off the phone, he says, "Lucas asked Miranda to marry him. By the way, Ramona says happy anniversary."

As Michael clears the table and tidies the kitchen, I call Clarice who, of course, knows the entire story, via Cheryl. Lucas gave Miranda a little ruby engagement ring on Valentine's Day. He is proud, Miranda is happy, Kaitlyn is ecstatic. Ramona and Ravi are in an uproar—what about college, medical school, any type of gainful employment? Miranda is nineteen, Lucas is twenty! The ages sound like a disease, a diagnosis of impending doom. "It's so much easier to fall in love at sixty-five," I tell Clarice.

After we hang up, Michael brings two glasses of iced tea to our teak chairs. "Fill me in," he says.

In the glow of the full moon, I watch a grandpa's face change from concern to amusement to pride. Apparently, Lucas and Miranda feel more comfortable talking with Cheryl than with Ramona or Ravi, who have two decades of hopes and dreams invested in their son, as parents do. Ravi's dream of a Dr. Lucas has never been Lucas's dream, but the Patel family still may have an upcoming doctor. Miranda has her sights on medical school and has applied to every university in St. Louis. She and Lucas are hell bent to make it happen. Lucas has a plan of his own, not well received by his father but instantaneously embraced by Grandpa Michael. After two years of training at a culinary arts school in St. Louis, Lucas will become Chef Bartoli.

"I didn't even know Lucas liked to cook." Michael is aglow. "Their plans sound pricey. I sure wish we could help."

Dreams come true; I know that now. Even dreams no one dares to voice. "Honey," I tell my husband. "You help everyone with every breath you take. That's just who you are."

Michael is silent. He's used to my teasing, not my testimonies of adoration. It takes him a few seconds before he holds out a hand for me. "How's about I make us some popcorn and we can watch a movie in bed?" His seduction sentence.

"There's nothing I'd like better," I say.

A month or so after their engagement is announced, I get an email from Lucas.

Grandma Beth,
Can you tell me how to arrange a wedding on a cruise ship?

I want to take Miranda and Kaitlyn on a short Caribbean cruise next year for Valentine's Day and surprise Miranda with a wedding like you and Grandpa had. Would this be terribly expensive?

•

"Looks like Ramona's dream of a long engagement for Lucas and Miranda might not be working out," I say after I print the email and hand it to Michael.

I get Michael's approval before I send my reply:

Lucas,
I would gladly assist you with your plans—you are a very romantic young man—but first you and Miranda may want to consider discussing this lovely event with your families.

A wedding and reception aboard ship is very costly, I believe, but I have some ideas on how to cut expenses.

As Michael reminds me, if one's intentions are good, everything else falls right into place. Lucas, with just a little assistance from everyone he knows, will wed Miranda today, February 14th. If Lucas and Miranda had waited another few weeks, Michael and I could have celebrated our fifth anniversary aboard a Disney cruise ship, surrounded by family and friends.

Unlike at our wedding, Michael and I get to observe the chaos unfolding deckside, as opposed to being at its center. Dressed in a pink princess gown, Kaitlyn races from one costumed Disney character to the next with Grandma Cheryl in hot pursuit. Clarice is trying to corral them both as Ramona yells a countdown of minutes until we must board the boat that will ferry us to shore. Ravi, Kate and Zoe form a line, ready to respond to any of Ramona's orders. Thirty feet away, the bride and groom stand hand in hand at the ship's rail, their backs to the commotion as they gaze ahead, toward Nassau. In addition to our wedding party, several hundred other passengers have plans to spend the afternoon in the city. "Stay together!" Ramona begins to yell as she realizes the next hurdle will be to arrive ashore with an intact wedding party. Clarice takes up the frantic shouts. A thoughtful Minnie Mouse rushes to Kaitlyn with a pink helium balloon and ties it to her wrist. "Follow the balloon, y'all," Cheryl yells, grabbing Kaitlyn's hand.

•

Brother Carlos sees us before we see him. He walks to us and our group calms. "Thank you for including me in this day." He puts his hand on my shoulder, then shakes Michael's hand.

"Are you a preacher?"

Brother Carlos drops to one knee to address Kaitlyn face-to-face. "No, I've never learned how to preach," he says, "but I do know how to marry people. Is it going to be all right with you if I marry Lucas and you mother?"

"Yes sir, my momma loves Lucas. So do I."

"Well then, let's all drive to a pretty beach," Brother Carlos says to Kaitlyn, "and there, since it is your wish, we'll marry Lucas and your momma."

Michael

As Brother Carlos drives us back to the dock, I feel the tug of time. How can a wedding be over in the time it takes to wash a car or buy the week's groceries? As I watch Brother Carlos walk away, I want to yell, plead with him. "Wait, please, help me slow down this day."

Everybody else is ready to do the next thing. Kaitlyn wants to go swimming on the ship. Miranda suggests a pool-side wedding reception, hot dogs, and water slides. Ravi tells everyone not to eat too much, he's made reservations for supper at the ship's fancy restaurant. Clarice and Cheryl think napping would be a good plan.

Kate and Zoe hold back, Nassau has a lovely park, places to explore. I look at Beth.

"Honey, you look as tired as I feel," she says to me, "and I know you're hungry. Don't you want to go back to the ship?"

I look at the cruise ship where I've already been, then toward a town I've yet to visit. "I think I'll stay here with

Kate and Zoe," I say. "Maybe I'll try some of the Nassau food."

Zoe tells me Bay Street is a few blocks up to my right, Kate tells me I can use my US money to buy anything I want. They want to go for a walk in a park, do some shopping. "Let's meet back here in two hours," Zoe says. "Have fun exploring."

Hawkers yell about fishing boats, snorkeling trips, and cheap rides to the casino. When I say no thank you, the venders move closer and talk louder. I walk fast, trying to find a calm, quiet spot in this city where I can be me, not a tourist from a cruise ship.

In front of the first restaurant I come across, the crowd is so dense I can't read the placard of Daily Specials. Deep inside music blares. I walk on, turn down a side street. Two ladies walk toward me, dressed like they work in one of the pink stucco banks. "Good morning," I say. "Could you recommend a nice place to eat?"

The tall lady is friendly. She tells me the fish fry. I can walk or take the Number 10 jitney. She says a jitney is a bus. "A bargain, you can ride all day for a dollar and a half." They smile. "Welcome to Nassau."

After fifteen minutes, I've left the tourists behind. By the time I find the fish fry, I'm hot and tired. Instead of one building, the fish fry's a whole mass of restaurants. I spy a dozen picnic tables, each one painted a different color. It looks like Hector had a hand in the decorating. I go inside the first building and plop down at a table. At the next table, three guys are eating plates of fried something. By the time a waitress comes over, I'm too hungry to read the menu she hands to me.

"What are those fellas eating?" I ask.

"*Cracked conch 'n Kalik*," she says.

"I'll have that," I say.

My waitress hands me a bottle of beer, leaves again. I glance at the next table. All three men have beers, I guess I've ordered one too. It's cold and crisp. After another sip, my body cools and relaxes. By the time my food arrives, the bottle is empty.

"Another Kalik?" my waitress asks.

"Yes ma'am," I say, "and tell me what I have here. I've never eaten Nassau food before. By the way, I'm Michael."

A smile softens her square brown face. "I'm Sally."

My meal is peas and rice and conch, she says. "Conch, like those," pointing to a line of seashells on the windowsill. She smiles as I tell her about Lucas's wedding, nods and agrees when I say time goes too fast. A laugh bursts up from her stomach when I ask if she knows Brother Carlos. "Everyone here knows Brother Carlos," she says.

Brother Carlos lives everywhere. He raises money for Sally's church, but he's not a member. He just shows up when people need him. Sally says I better eat my meal while it's hot, and she'll bring me another Kalik, if I want one. They're brewed right here in Nassau. She'll bring me fresh fritters to sample. She'd bring me the Nassau specialty, raw conch and lime juice, but they just ran out. "We're making more. Come back and try it later. It's sexy. Bring your wife," she laughs.

The conch chews back at my tongue as I eat it. The crust is crispy and greasy and blazing hot from the fat fryer. I see the men at the next table sprinkle their plates with red sauce, so I do the same. Hot on hot. While I sip another ice-cold beer I decide if I like my meal. Before I can make up my mind, my plate is empty.

I pay Sally and promise her I'll see her soon. As I walk from darkness to sunshine a sadness hits me. Men are playing checkers at a table under a tree. I'll never meet them. Musicians are gathering at a stage at the end of the parking lot. I'll never hear them play. I can't bear the thought of never tasting the special sexy raw conch.

Stay here? Travel on? Watch Kaitlyn soar down a water slide? My feet walk on before my brain has a plan. On the sidewalk nobody's rushing, I don't either. My feet stop when I get to a little clump of people. A bus shutters to a stop, the little clump of folks forms a line and starts to board. I board it too.

"Can I sightsee awhile from this bus, or does it take me back toward the cruise ships?" I ask the man boarding in front of me.

"Both," he says.

I pull a dollar fifty from my pocket. The bus lurches on as I fall into an empty seat halfway back. My body's glad I've found a place to sit down and my brain's glad I don't have to make any decisions. I'll just go where this bus takes me.

Travelers flow off and on the Number 10 jitney. Mommas herd their children up and down the aisles, workers talk in a soothing stream. I settle into the stiff seat and rest my head against the vibrating window. My eyes close to the sight of hotels and restaurants and beaches rolling by. A woman laughs, rich and thick as molasses. All sounds merge into one. I'm just a part of the whole as I sway with the motion of the Number 10.

I wake in a fog, time and place just beyond my grasp. The ocean's moved to the opposite side of the bus, the sun's disappeared from the cloudless sky. I ask the fellow sitting next to me if he knows where my fish fry place is. He chuckles. "Two more stops. Did you have a nice nap?"

I trudge across the parking lot to Sally's place. Brother Carlos is sitting atop a red picnic table. When he sees me he waves, picks up a cell phone, and puts it to his ear.

"What a surprise." I shake his hand and sit down by his side.

He looks at me, calm and serious. "I'm happy to see you again, Michael."

Brother Carlos hurries into an explanation of what

happens when a person doesn't make it back to a cruise ship on time. Families get frantic but the ship has to leave without the person. Cruise ships have schedules and a need for timely departures, you know. As I listen, I start to get scared. "What are you trying to tell me?" I ask.

Brother Carlos puts his hand on my shoulder. "As the saying goes Michael, you've missed the boat."

My brain seizes up. I must look funny because Brother Carlos says, "Everything is fine."

Fine means this: Beth, my Beth, has been frantic for hours. She's stationed herself at the ship's Communication Officer's desk awaiting news about her husband. Kate and Zoe have been frantic even longer, ever since I didn't show up to reboard with them. They contacted the ship, found Brother Carlos, searched with him until the ship's departure warning horns began blaring. After Brother Carlos assured them he'd find me and return me to my family, Kate and Zoe had to reboard the ship.

Fine means this: Brother Carlos called the harbormaster who will call the ship. Soon, Beth will know I'm found. Brother Carlos has a friend who owns a yoga retreat where we will spend the night. Tomorrow another one of his friends will take me to Disney Island on his fishing boat, and I will be reunited with my family.

Fine means this: It's wonderful Brother Carlos has so many friends. It's wonderful I'm one of them.

"Michael, praise the Lord. You're back." Sally rushes to me. I stand up and she throws her arms around me. I start to cry.

"Oh, honey honey honey, there there baby, you're all right now, honey honey honey."

Sally brings me a huge glass of cold water with limes and a tiny bowl of freshly made sweet, sexy conch since she knew I wanted to try it. She brings me a big bowl of okra stew, so I can get my energy back. She sits beside me, as Brother Carlos and I tell her the adventures of Michael in Nassau.

The conch is spicy-hot from peppers and cool from limes.
The stew tastes like love in a bowl, I eat it all. At the end of
the parking lot a streetlight brightens the deep blue sky. The
musicians I'd longed to hear are playing. "What time is it?" I
ask Brother Carlos.

He looks at his cell phone, seven forty-five.

I look at my watch: 4:45. "I guess I forgot to reset my
watch," I say. Sally comes with a pitcher of water, more
glasses, a bowl of limes. The three of us sit at the red table
and listen to the musicians. "How did you find me anyway?"
I ask Brother Carlos.

"Zoe said you were hungry, and Sally has the best food on
the island. I figured you'd find her."

But what if I hadn't? What if I'd walked another direction, stopped at the first restaurant I saw, got on the wrong
bus? What if Sally didn't remember me? "No need to dwell
there," Brother Carlos tells me. "Isn't this a lovely night?"

At the end of the parking lot, a new singer takes the stage.
Her music is pretty but I'm too far away to hear the words.
"Sally says you always show up when people need you," I
say.

Brother Carlos squeezes a lime into his glass of water.
"Perhaps it's my need that brings me, I don't know." His
words are as far away as the singer's. "Do you ever feel guided by something, a tug toward where you need to be?"

"Seems like I'm mostly guided by my stomach," I say.

Brother Carlos chuckles, puts his hand on my shoulder.
"You're a kind and humble man." He picks up his cellphone.
"Let's make sure my friend Carol has a room for us. We may
get there in time for her evening yoga class."

"Can I call Beth on your phone?" I ask Brother Carlos. "I
sure would like to say good night."

Sally hears me ask. "Lord, Honey, you been scaring that
woman to death all day long," she says. "Now she knows
you're all right, her worry's going to change into mad as a
hornet. Just go on over to that yoga place and get some rest."

•

Carol's place has little cabins scattered around a huge gazebo where all the yoga people gather. The sea is only yards away. The sky is black. Carol's voice is strong and certain. I watch Brother Carlos on the mat in front of mine and try to do what he does. I breathe in the warm salty air, then breathe it out.

Relax your shoulders, let go of the burdens that are not yours to carry. Bring to mind your greatest fear, your fondest dream. Release them both, into the Universe. You have no need of them.

Every word she says is a word my heart needs to hear.

Mind, body, spirit, totally at peace. Truly, all is well, and everything is happening just as it should, in Divine Order.

Tears trickle down my cheeks. I don't wipe them away.

Silently, Brother Carlos and I and a dozen other folks walk from the gazebo back to our cabins. "Carol's words were beautiful, some of the best words I've ever heard," I whisper. "I sure hope I can remember them."

When we reach our cabin, Brother Carlos opens the unlocked door. "Don't hang onto the words too tightly," he says. "Your soul will remember."

The room has two twin beds, a desk and a chair, pegs on a wall. I have no pajamas or toothbrush. All I have to do is get undressed, hang my shirt on a peg, and go to bed.

"Thank you for all the help today," I say into the darkness. "Life goes by so fast, and I'd hate to miss out on any of it. Soon it will all be just memories, and those might slip away too." I think of a wedding on a sunny beach, another wedding on a balcony at sunrise.

"Michael, you don't need to hold onto life too tightly either," says Brother Carlos. "Relax your grip. Then life can hold you."

Before I fall asleep, I try to remember the words of Carol and Brother Carlos, but the only thing I can remember is *it's okay to forget.*

CHAPTER 8

Beth

I give Michael the too red, too sweet cherry, then dip my spoon down through whipped cream, hot fudge, ice cream. I want a precise blend for my first bite. He pops the cherry in his mouth. Every day he wears the straw hat Hector bought for him even though it's a bit too tight. Now it sits beside him in our booth. Before we leave, I'll remind him to take it. He won't put it on his head until we're outside because his momma taught him manners.

"Let's go to Mexico," he says. "Maybe we can find Maria's son, visit for a while, see if he's safe. Maybe Hector can draw us a map. Maria could come with us." His face is innocent, sad, yearning.

Too quickly I say, "Oh Michael, you know we can't do that!"

He looks at the dessert. "I figured you'd say no."

Most days Michael comes home from work grinning, a treat in his hand. A new smoothie flavor, two Sonora hot dogs. *Try this,* he'll say as he hands me a cupcake from a new food truck vender. He'll tell me about the sunrise I missed. *A beauty!* How three walkers made it that day. *I saw them before Hector did,* he'll say, his voice so proud. "Maria was singing as she made the salsa."

Other days Michael tells me Maria was crying. Her fingers trembled as she rolled the tortillas. Michael soaks up the sadness of those days, faster than he sips in the sweetness of a new smoothie flavor. When he comes home, he sits in the teak chair all evening, gazing south.

My sundae is gone, his almost. I try again. "Where else would you like to go for our anniversary?"

"I don't care," he says. "You decide."

After two months of research, I make the decision for both of us: we'll go on a bus tour that promises to show us in two weeks everything we've missed here in the last six years.

"Why can't we drive," Michael asks.

"Your car would never make it and you won't drive my new car," I tell him. "I don't want to do all the driving by myself."

"OK, but why don't we ask Hector and Maria to come with us?" he asks.

"Honey, they have to work," I explain. "Don't you think it will be fun, just the two of us?"

"It's fun staying home with you," he says.

The only way I can convince Michael to go is to promise a side trip to Sedona to visit Trudy and Polly Jean.

Polly Jean the Airstream is now Polly Jean the Food Truck. She has a service window in her side; under it there is a counter lined with baskets of cookies and muffins. Her customers stand in the shade of a turquoise awning as they wait to get their sandwiches and soup. Above her counter, Trudy has painted a desert scene with red rocks on one side and a flowering cactus on the other. In the middle, *POLLY JEAN* is painted in swirling turquoise and orange.

"I tried to change her name, but she wouldn't let me," says Trudy.

"Let's buy some lunch," Michael takes out his wallet. "I need to sample your cooking."

"You'll not buy a single thing here." Trudy takes Michael's

hands in hers. "Everything I have is yours." She and Michael stare at each other, tears in their eyes.

As our bus drives out of Flagstaff, our tour guide Ellen stands with microphone in hand and welcomes Michael, me, and fifty other passengers. Astonishing sights await us, she promises. We'll see layers of earth dating back to the beginning of time—thousands, millions, billions of years ago. We'll learn how canyons and arches and deserts were formed. In the parks, speakers will tell us the history of the people who live here—the Navajo, the Mormons.

"And now I will tell you the rules of our bus," Ellen laughs. "Rule number one is to get up on time each morning so you don't miss the bus." Everyone groans.

"I'm going to keep my eye on you," I tell Michael and put my hand on his.

He laughs. "I do have a history of getting left behind, don't I?" He wraps his fingers around mine and we settle into our bus seats, as comfortable as a La-Z-Boy recliner. We hold hands and look out the window.

"We're going to see some amazing sights on this trip." I say. "I'm excited. I hope you're going to enjoy it too." Michael looks at me for a few seconds, his sweet face lit with sunlight.

"You're the most beautiful sight I'll see on this trip," he says. "If I don't see another pretty thing, I'll be fine."

"Our first stop is Tuba City," Ellen says into her microphone. She explains we are in the Navajo Nation and we need to be mindful of their laws. No alcohol, no hiking without a Navajo guide. "Now we're in Daylight Saving Time, adjust your watches if any of you still use one." A few folks chuckle. I look at my watch, so does Michael.

The bus driver turns off the highway and maneuvers into a huge parking lot. After he parks, Ellen looks at her watch. "It's eleven o'clock. Everyone needs to be back here before twelve-thirty. This is your first test, don't disappoint me," she says.

Tuba City is all worn out from the thousands of tourists who stop here every day to go to the restroom, eat a sandwich, then travel on. Since the line to buy an Indian taco is so long, I suggest an ice cream lunch which is fine with Michael. We make it back to the bus fifteen minutes early.

Ellen introduces us to our first speaker Harold who stands at the front of the bus and solemnly and precisely begins to tell the story of his people, the Navajo. As the bus eases through the maze of other tour buses in the parking lot, Michael listens intently as we learn about the Navajo Code Talkers of World War II.

"Our ancient name is Dine." Harold tells the Creation story, sprinkled with Navajo words sounding sharp and clipped, pebbles falling on a tin roof. We hear of four clouds above four corners of a newly forming world, First Man, First Woman, Angry Coyote, a flood. Watching Michael listen to Harold makes me glad I insisted on this trip. Together, we'll again explore sights we're never seen before.

Michael claps for Harold when he finishes the story. Harold looks at him, nods his head and the rest of the bus starts clapping. When the applause ends, I take Michael's hand and hold it as we look out the windows, enjoying Harold's land. Ellen sees a coyote, out the left windows, ten o'clock. "There, there, there," I point out the window. "Do you see it?" Michael says no.

Again, Harold stands, faces us. His words are painful, this story is real.

"Now our name is Navajo. This name reminds us of our pride and of our sorrow." Harold's talk winds us through places of overwhelming injustice, scenes of unbelievable cruelty. Canyon de Chelly. Soldier's horses grazing beside Navajo sheep. Raids and broken treaties.

Thundering horses, the blood of slaughtered sheep and

warriors. Starvation, relocation, desperation. The Long Walk back home.

No one claps when Harold finishes this story. The bus is still, the only sounds are the pulse of the wheels speeding down pavement, the rhythm of the turn signal as our driver changes lanes to pass a pick-up truck. Harold turns his back to us and sits down in the seat opposite Ellen. Michael sits beside me, stricken.

"I'm sorry, I'm so sorry" he says, turning the sorrow of the Navajo Nation into his own.

Ellen tells us to go straight to our balconies as soon as we get to our rooms. When we get to our balcony, I understand why. The sky is orange, the rocks and the land, darker orange. Blood orange. Fire orange. Michael and I stand shoulder to shoulder and watch until the colors change to pinks, purples, finally the deep blue of evening.

"How could they have done that horrible thing?" Michael says.

"Who?" I ask.

"The Army," he says. "That walk."

A sunset over Monument Valley cannot ease the horrors my husband has heard today. I take his face in my hands, kiss him, try to think of a few words to lessen the pain. There are none.

We gaze at the rock formations below the indigo sky. "They're named The Mittens," I tell Michael, holding up my hands, palms facing me. Fingers together, I wiggle my thumbs. "Get it?" He doesn't smile.

"Honey, we're both tired," I sigh. "Let's get ready for bed." Michael stares at the night sky as I organize the room for our two-night stay—toothbrushes and toiletries on the bathroom counter, medicines beside the coffee pot on a bureau. I pull the nightshirt from my suitcase as I chuckle at the memory of the black peignoir Clarice thrust upon me seven years ago. As I unzip Michael's suitcase, a sickening stench hits my nostrils. I throw open his suitcase and scream.

"Michael!"

Michael

I rush to her, look where she is looking. My suitcase, open, underwear and t-shirts wallowing in a soggy red pool. A fruity smell, wafting up.

"Don't touch anything . . . it's glass . . . it's broken," I stammer.

Beth fires questions at my back as I maneuver the suitcase into the bathroom, push the shower curtain aside, and set the whole mess down in the sparkling white tub.

"I'm thinking that used to be a bottle of our anniversary wine," Beth says, looking at the leaking pile of clothes.

"I wanted it to be a surprise," I say.

"Well, it is," Beth says.

She reminds me alcohol is illegal here, I'll probably go to jail. She says it like a joke. I shouldn't help her fix this, we'll need to call Ellen. I'll be wearing pink underwear for the rest of the trip. Another joke.

In fifteen minutes, Ellen is at our door with plastic bags and gloves and paper towels. I tell her our anniversary wine stories and I'm sorry and I'll pay a fine and let me help, please, I feel so bad. The ladies tell me to relax on the balcony, they'll take care of everything. I sit in the empty darkness, getting smaller and sadder and dumber by the second, as sounds of gasping and laughing drift out to me. "Michael, all the glass smashed in the plastic bag," Beth yells to me. "I don't think we'll have to get you sutured up every evening after wearing glass shards in your britches all day long." One last joke. I still don't laugh.

By the time Ellen and Beth run back and forth from the

hotel laundry a few times, I have a neat pile of clean pink underwear and a stack of slacks and shirts and black socks. My suitcase is deemed salvageable after the purple blotch is blotted with a pile of paper towels and lined with a garbage bag.

"I'm sorry to be so much trouble," I say.

Both women murmur that everything's fine and go back to chatting like they're best friends at a tea party.

Finally, Ellen leaves. I watch Beth lay out our clothes for tomorrow, brush her teeth, and change into her nightshirt. All the while she's acting like nothing's happened, like she hasn't noticed she's married to the most stupid man in the world.

"Are you mad at me?" I ask.

"Of course not, Michael." She hugs me, then goes on and on about Ellen, who's smart and funny and wonderful, a retired high school counselor, they have so much in common. She and her husband own the bus. He's the driver. (Not like you Michael, Beth doesn't say, you can't even drive our new car.) Now they have a touring business, just imagine! Ellen organizes everything—hotels and meals and speakers in all the parks. So full of energy, Ellen is so much fun. Sounds like Beth had the best evening ever, washing her husband's underwear and socks with a new friend.

Beth is sparkling. She hasn't sounded so happy in months, the months she's spent alone with her husband. I add jealous to my list of feelings for today.

Beth

Michael sits in the bus seat by the window this morning, quietly staring as the view turns from spectacular to ordinary. As each mile passes he seems to sink lower into the blue leather cushions. He's asked me a dozen times if I'm mad at him.

"I could never be mad at the most wonderful husband in the world," I answer every time. My superlatives don't cheer him.

Ellen stops at our seats to talk every time she walks up and down the aisle. We chat about teaching, compare the retirement benefits between Arizona and Illinois. She asks Michael about his restaurant in Chicago, his children, his grandchildren. He answers politely, without a shred of enthusiasm or pride.

We have lunch in a sad little town that was settled by Mormon pioneers. Solid stone houses lining square streets. On the outskirts are trailers and falling down shacks. The Navajos and Mormons co-exist now by law. We get out of the bus to take pictures of two rock pillars in a parking lot next to a gift shop. "This is a sacred site, The Navajo Twins," Ellen tells us.

"Michael, the Navajo twins are from the creation story," I say. "One was named Monster Slayer. I don't remember the other's name."

Ellen hears me. "Born of Water is the brother," she says. "You get an A for remembering, Beth."

"How come you know that?" Michael asks me.

"Harold told us yesterday," I say.

"Who?" says Michael.

Michael naps on the way to Moab as I look out the window toward every new sight Ellen announces on her microphone. As the wonder of this strange landscape starts to overpower me, I take Michael's hand. He wakes enough to close his fingers around mine and murmur "I love you" before he falls back asleep.

Our bus stops at a plateau overlooking a canyon. We sit on stone benches and listen to a park ranger put to voice my emotions. "This place is too large to see, too amazing to understand," she says as she begins to play the music of a symphony from her cell phone. "Just feel, just listen."

When the music is over, I look at Michael. His blue eyes are sparkling. When we get back on the bus I say, "Wasn't that wonderful?"

"Yes," Michael says. "It was nice. Are we going home tomorrow?"

"No, tomorrow is Bryce Canyon," I answer.

Every morning, every evening before we go to bed, I take our blood pressure. At home I only check it two times a week, per our doctor's suggestion. Here, we are askew. Michael is tired, grumpy, totally un-Michael. His time is shifting between too short and too long, his mornings come too early. I've put him in this situation. Each new day is an adventure for me and a burden for my husband. I'm guilt-ridden one moment, overjoyed the next. Again, this evening, our blood pressure readings are just fine, and yet, we are out of sync.

At Bryce Canyon I buy a poster showing all the layers of the earth under Utah. Michael and I look at it as everyone else from the bus takes pictures. "See this blue layer. It's called chinle. Uranium can be found there. We learned about that yesterday," I tell Michael. I sound like an excited fourth grade teacher. Michael is an unenthusiastic student.

We sit on benches listening to another park ranger. The land before us doesn't seem real, a valley full of tall red statues. Hoodoos—made by Coyote who turned people to stone. Hoodoos were sacred to the Paiutes, our ranger tells us. When the Mormons came, the Paiutes were displaced. By my side, Michael stiffens. We both know the next words may be hard to hear but the ranger slides past the why's and how's of *displaced* and tells us Mr. Bryce bought this land to harvest timber and raise cattle.

"Why would they name this place for him instead of the people who loved it?" Michael asks.

"Politics," I whisper to him.

At the next National Park, Michael wants to stay in our room instead of going to the evening lecture. "My stomach is full of steak and potatoes and my body is craving a bed," he says.

Ellen has organized the park ranger's lecture especially for our group. I don't want to miss it and I don't want to leave Michael alone in our room, so Michael and I sit together at the back of a warm, wooden hall filled with folding chairs. The late arrivals swarm and whisper *excuse me, sorry,* until the room settles to listen to a tiny, uniformed girl who looks too young to be a park ranger. She stands beside a movie screen Michael can't see due to the bushy-haired gentleman in front of him. He says he doesn't care.

The lecture is about the peoples of this area. As the slide show flashes at the front of the room, showing the bright and dark of her story, I glance at Michael whose eyes are closed. We learn about the people, thousands of years ago— moving, staying, living their lives. Hundreds of years came the Mormons, persecuted, stoic, hard-working, devout. Turning deserts to orchards. Building roads through cliffs. Zion, a Jerusalem. The ranger's tone changes as she tells of a Mountain Meadow a hundred miles away, a hundred fifty-five years ago . . .

I feel Michael jerk awake although his eyes remain closed. I know he's hearing the sweet voice at the front of the room say the unbearable words. A wagon train of one hundred, twenty. Men, women, children. Settlers dressed as Paiutes, faces painted. Massacre. A softer sentence . . . Seventeen children spared, taken to be raised by the families of the men who slaughtered their parents.

Now I'm the one to say *I'm sorry* over and over and over again, as we walk through the darkness to our lodge bedroom.

Michael

I'm sweating, my heart is pounding, Beth sleeps soundly at my side. I remember it all, as soon as I wake up. Instead of a tour bus, a school bus. Instead of Ellen, Beth. She stands, chalk in hand, in front of a blackboard. "Who can spell uranium?" she asks. "Michael, do you remember?" If I can't remember, she'll hate me. I look out the window. The bus changes into a train. There is no driver. Out the window, a line of people walking. Babies in their mothers' arms. A coyote walks with them, upright, wearing a black suit. One by one, he turns the people to stone. The train changes into a wagon train. No, I know what will happen next. Beth, run! I run so fast I become a horse. The horse running next to me is Beth. Her eye looks into mine, white rimmed with fear. My heart is exploding.

I lie in the tiny bed in the small dark room, trying to breathe. Just a dream, just a dream. Beth is sleeping at my side, giving me more safety than I give her. I need to get away before she smells my fear. Slowly, softly, I get up and pull on my clothes. I don't shave or shower. The heavy wood door opens and closes without a creak and I'm standing in pine-scented darkness.

Other people are awake and walking and I join the flow. We go to the coffee shop. Beth has put two twenties in my wallet, I have money for my coffee. I walk with the congregation into the cathedral. Last night it was the noisy main hall. Instead of pews, rows of comfortable chairs facing a wall of windows. Instead of a wooden cross, the Grand Canyon at sunrise.

I sit in a chair, alone and off-kilter. My coffee is too hot to drink. I hold it in both hands and try to put some distance between myself and my dream.

"Michael, you're up early." I hear the woman's voice behind me. Beth? No, Ellen. I feel my face fall. Ellen sees I'm disappointed.

"I won't disturb you," she says and starts to turn away.

"No, wait," I say. I stand up, offer her my chair but she sits in one opposite me.

We watch people file into the room, look out the windows, take a picture. The hush of sunrise is gone, families call to each other, move furniture, pile backpacks on the floor. The room smells like coffee and bug spray and anticipation. "How many more days before this trip is over?" I ask. She looks hurt. I tell her I'm sorry.

"No, you're right," Ellen says. "Sometimes I plan too much." She sips her coffee and looks toward the windows. "I want everything to be perfect for everyone. To be honest, I'm looking forward to getting home too. I just want to relax with my husband." Ellen sounds like she's happy to talk to me, she sounds like she's my friend.

"It feels so sad here." My words slide out. I try to sip my coffee, but my hands are trembling. I sit my paper cup on the table between us. "I had a crazy dream. You know, sometimes they stick with you for a while."

Ellen leans toward me. She doesn't say anything, but I can feel her asking.

"It's as pretty here as where we live, Beth and me. Maybe prettier." I pause. "How can such awful things happen in such a pretty place?"

Ellen nods and smiles. "Michael, tell me your dream."

I say every part. Screaming and hating. Folks hurting other folks. Over and over and over again. Hundreds and thousands and millions of years, hundreds and thousands and millions of people. Then I tell her about Hector and Maria and Maria's son and our walkers. Folks still hurting other folks. "Ellen, why, why, why?"

"The persecuted persecute," she says. "The fearful hate."

Her words are soft and kind, her brown eyes sad. I gave her my sadness. Again, I tell her I'm sorry.

In the corner of the room is a bronze statue of a little burro. Ellen and I watch as children run to it and rub its nose. A little girl squeals "Brighty!" and throws her arms around the burro's neck. A boy who must be her big brother joins her, her momma says stand still, her daddy aims a camera. Ellen goes to them, takes the camera, the whole family gathers for the picture.

"You're a kind lady," I tell her when she comes back.

The statute is a memorial, Ellen says, to a little guy who roamed the trails of the Grand Canyon for decades. He carried water to folks who needed it, helped build a bridge, met Teddy Roosevelt, had a book written about him. "All his life, he brought joy to everyone he met," Ellen says, "and he still does."

"That's the best story I've heard in days," I say.

CHAPTER 9

٭

Michael

In the desert folks are thirsty. I bring them water.

I gave myself this new job after Beth and I got back from the long, sad trip. *Michael,* I said, *you have the time, and this work needs to get done. So how about it?* Now every morning I'm happy.

This job I gave myself lines up fine with the new job Hector gave me. "I'd sure appreciate it if you'd run by the store each morning and pick up supplies," he said. "I'll write out a list."

Every morning I go to Walmart and push the cart up and down the aisles looking for paper cups and napkins and water, always a case or two of bottled water. The nice stock boy helps me find the hard stuff like those huge boxes of lunch bags. And for the job I gave myself, I put six gallons of water in the cart. At the checkout counter, I use Hector's credit card to pay for his supplies, then take ten dollars out of my wallet to pay for my water.

"You must be real thirsty, Michael," the checkout lady says.

"I've got some real thirsty friends," I tell her. I don't say much more. The job I gave myself is a secret.

This morning I drive the same roads I drove yesterday, the same roads I drove last week, last month. Feels like I've trained for this job my whole life. I drive south, down the

Interstate, the sun just over our mountains. South, past the steak house with the statue of the steer. South, past the town where they sell the pretty sinks like the one in our bathroom. South, past the Border Patrol station on the north bound side of the road. This morning no bus is parked there. This morning no walkers are getting a ride back to the place where life is so hard. I'm happy I don't have to see that bus this morning. I watch for the signs and turn left, toward the sun.

When I first started this job, I'd turn right, toward the turmoil. A whole river of people flowing across the parched earth, meeting an army of other people. Thousands of feet scrambling toward *Better*. Thousands of throats screaming *Go Home*. To the right of the Interstate the problems are heart breaking and no one wants to fix them, seems like, so I turn left toward my small, easy job.

They report on the main ruckus most every night on the TV—night runs and road stops, a trail of empty water bottles and back packs and plastic bags soiling the pretty land. Old pickup trucks packed tight with people, speeding toward North. The TV shows folks crying and yelling and dying. And dead. When Beth sees me watching the turmoil, she turns off the TV. I heard of a man and a woman who take food and clothes to the folks in jail waiting to be sent back to Mexico. I asked Beth if we could do that too, but she said no.

I don't want to think Beth doesn't care. I want to think she's afraid for me. She doesn't want me to be sad or hurt or in danger. "Michael honey," she'd probably say, "you are too old to get involved in this situation. There's nothing you can do to change anything. The problem is huge and you're just one man. One old man."

So, this is the way I explain my new job to Beth: I don't tell her.

When I see the sign I've been looking for, I turn on my blinker and exit toward the left. There's not so much hubbub to the left of the Interstate, no speeding trucks loaded down with too many desperate people, no lines of cars waiting to be checked by the Border Patrol. I drive past sights of every-day life—rundown stores where the same people buy the same things every morning, a few fancy houses, more than a few ranches, where living is hard for both man and beast. This road leads to the next, which leads to the next.

I drive a dozen more miles until I spot my little path run-ning down to a clump of cottonwood trees. A walker would know cottonwood means creek bed, seems like. I know it from watching John Wayne. I pull my car off the road, care-ful not to drive over a cactus. I don't want a flat tire out here, a hundred miles from home. I keep an Arizona map on the front seat, folded to where I am now. I circled a town up the road. If I get stopped by the Border Patrol, I plan to lie. "I'm trying to get to Patagonia," I'll say. "I had to make a pit stop," and I'll nod my head toward the cottonwoods. "Am I on the right road?" I'll ask. The Border Patrol will think I'm just an old guy who doesn't know where he is. Some days, they'd be right.

It's 228 steps to where I place two gallons of water, here at my first stop. I count as I walk, breathing in and out, the smell of creosote and hot earth heavy in my nostrils. Each step sends up a little puff of dust. My socks turn rusty brown. I imagine I'm a walker, tired and hopeful and thirsty. I imag-ine how happy I'd be when I spot these two jugs of water. By the time I count to 228 my heart is peaceful and my soul is free.

My lips smile when I don't see the two gallons of water I set down here yesterday. I hear the winds whisper *muchos gracias. You're welcome,* I whisper back. I count 228 steps as I walk to the car. Maybe the walker who took the water was Maria's son. Maybe tomorrow I'll meet him when I stop to help Hector set up. "Michael, it's a miracle," Hector will say. "*A milagros.*"

I'm a mile down the road before I remember I forgot the special honk. I can't seem to get that part of my job to stick in my head. I have to drive another mile before I find a good place to turn around. The cottonwoods look shorter when I spot them from the opposite direction. I stop my car on the road and honk my signal. Three fast honks, three slow honks, three fast honks. SOS, Save Our Ship. I remember it from when I was a kid, playing war with my buddies in Green Bay. SOS, we'd tap out with a rock on a metal pole. We thought we were real smart knowing the Navy code. I don't imagine anyone knows the code anymore, but a walker might hear a special honk, find some water, and tell a friend, "There's an old guy who drives around in the desert every morning. He'll bring you some water. Listen for him."

I didn't have my wits about me when the fire started, but Maria came running as soon as she saw the smoke. She grabbed the thing that puts out fires and sprayed stuff all over the range and the grill and the wall. I sure hope I didn't start that fire. I don't think I did. Like Hector said, "These things happen. No one was hurt. I can buy a new grill and paint the wall. Don't worry, *mi amigo.*" Maria had only been gone a little while before the fire started. She's a modest lady and when she and I work alone, she goes over to the food truck where the ladies make cupcakes to use the restroom instead of using the toilet at Hector's. We had to close down Hector's place for a week to do the repairs. The insurance man said grease fire, maybe. Or maybe a towel dropped on the hot grill. Or a whole batch of tortillas burned up because no one was watching them. Or maybe all three. Someone left a mess on the yellow picnic table so I went out to clean it up. The smoke was horrible. Maria was coughing after she put out the fire, but she was OK by the time Hector got there.

I call my second stop The Roadrunner in honor of the little guy who led me here. When I was setting up my routes, a roadrunner darted in front of my car, and I had to slam on my brakes to keep from squashing him. I watched him run south down a two-tire-track dirt road. *Well Michael, maybe he's trying to tell you something,* I thought so I parked my car and started hiking after him. I never spotted him again, but the dirt road sloped down to a dry creek bed, then rose up and ran out of sight. Maybe running all the way to Mexico. I liked what I saw in that dry creek bed: a couple of plastic bags and an empty water bottle. *OK Michael,* I told myself, *this is water drop two.*

The Roadrunner is the hardest of my three stops, I have to concentrate to find it. At first, I'd tied my handkerchief to a creosote bush growing on the side of the dirt road, but it blew off so I put an empty pop bottle from Hector's over one of the branches. Some days I can spot it, some days I don't. Today I do. Another hard part is remembering to drink some water from the bottle in my cup holder before I start my hike. I won't have to remember to drink water when I get back to the car. Then I'm thirsty.

I park my car a few feet past my bush, gulp some water, and check the code I wrote out on the top of my map. Walking with a gallon jug in each hand and counting 417 steps is no simple task. After I grab the water from my trunk and check to be sure my keys are in my pocket, I start my hike *properly hydrated*, as Beth would say. My brain counts each step. I breathe in and out. The sky is searing blue, not a cloud of moisture filters the sunlight. The only moisture on this desert path is in the jugs I carry. They get heavier as I count higher. Gravity pulls at my arms. My legs and shoulders ache.

Sunny's got bad hips, Ramona says, but the Vet has him on some newfangled dog food with arthritis medicine cooked into it. She says it helps. Sunny was well loved by Lucas after he was well loved by me. Now he's well loved by Ramona. Sunny's an old dog now with arthritis instead of a young pup racing after a tennis ball. I wonder if he feels time sliding by. I forget to count as I remember Sunny. Happens most days on my Roadrunner hike. Looking back, my car is out of sight, looking forward, the trail dips into the creek bed. I didn't overshoot by daydreaming and walk all the way to Mexico. Tomorrow I'll keep my mind on 417. Remember, remember, remember.

Setting in the dust of the creek bed are the two gallons of yesterday's water. Nobody found them. Sadness rushes over me. Doubts and fears prick at my brain. Should I put the water somewhere else? Is this place too far, too close, too east or west? Did someone die last night, because the water was in the wrong place? I sit down on a rock. Unfound water is the worst part of my job. A tired brain welcomes ugly thoughts about wasted time, wasted money, wasted life. I stare at the two unfound jugs of water and forgive them. *You were here if you were needed,* I tell them. *You did all you could do.*

Looking up, my eyes spot movement in the swelter of the desert landscape. A coyote, a walker of another sort. Beth and I heard a story about a coyote on the sad trip. This coyote zigzags with purpose across the desert looking for his next meal. I'm scared for my roadrunner, but a hundred days, or there about, separate him from this coyote. Besides, I don't need to take up sides between a hungry coyote and a pretty little bird. *We all do what we have to do,* I say to the coyote, forgiving him. Hoping the water I leave today will be found tomorrow, I say my words to the desert and the cloudless sky.

> *Help me help*
> *And when I'm tired and lost*
> *Guide my feet, then help me help*
> *And the walkers*
> *When they are tired and lost*
> *Guide their feet so*
> *You can help me help.*

Figuring out what to do with unfound water is another

tough part of my job. Leaving only the fresh water feels like the right thing to do. I drink a few swallows of the old water and set the new in the same place before I lug the warm water back to my car. The hike back is just as hard as the hike to the creek bed since I'm still carrying two full jugs of water, minus a few gulps. I count 417 steps. I breathe in and out. I imagine I'm a little burro on a canyon path, I imagine I'm a machine with a steel rod running from my tired shoulders to my aching wrists. When I get back to my creosote bush, my numb fingers manage to twist off the two bottle caps. *Thank you for helping me find my way,* I say as I pour two jugs of unfound water at the base of the bush. It feels like the right thing to do.

The last water drop is easy, 103 steps to an abandoned lean-to, the open side facing east toward a hundred miles of high desert and purple mountain ridges. I can see the backside of the lean-to from the road so I don't need to count my steps, but I do it anyway, enjoying the rhythm of my brain and legs and heart and breath. At step 103, I look inside toward the crumbling back wall and see no water. Most days my water is gone. The lean-to is my most successful site. I set the water against the back wall like I do every morning. The shade will keep the water cool and hidden until it's needed.

I wish I could meet the walkers some days, like we do at Hector's. You'd think we would run into each other now and then. I can't offer anybody a ride or a place to stay on account of laws, but I'd like to talk a little bit. Then again, I never learned much Spanish. It's best I just say welcome with two gallons of water. I walk back to my car and remember to honk my code. Three fast, three slow, three fast. Welcome, good luck, safe travels.

Today's work is over. My route back home ends my big loop, this last part circling north, then west over the mountains. I only have to make three turns, the roads are paved,

I hardly ever get lost. Come winter, it might snow. I'll take a day off. Beth and I will have a snow day, like we did that time in Green Bay, making love and eating homemade pies while the snow piled up outside our motel room. Sweet, sweet times. I think I'll stop by Hector's food trucks on the way home and buy one of those fancy cupcakes for Beth.

Each morning is a circle. Beth's arms around me, her sleepy words as I slide away from her, *Is it that time already? Tell Hector and Maria hello.* The grocery cart travels up and down and around, empty to full to empty again. Hector's handshake, Maria's wave. The cottonwoods. The roadrunner. The lean-to. The sun circles overhead as I circle below. My car drives from where I want to be, to where I need to be, to where I love to be. Beth is sitting at her computer, her back to me, when I bring her the cupcake.

I sneak up to her and kiss her neck. She jumps and laughs. "I was sitting here missing you and now here you are," she says as she turns around. "And what is this?"

"I guess it's lunch," I say, "unless you have something else planned."

Beth sticks her finger in the swirl of pink icing and touches it to my lips. Her finger is strawberry sweet. "Well, yes, I just might have something else planned," she says.

"Your heart sounds great," the new doctor says, "and you've lost seven pounds. Whatever you're doing, keep it up."

"I plan to," I say.

Then the questions start. Do I sleep well, wake up in the middle of the night, pee too much or too little? Am I sad, depressed? Suicidal! Dumb questions—What month is it? Who is our president? Each answer makes me sadder, madder. Beth's put him up to this.

It's air-conditioning cold. I sit in my underwear and socks as Beth sits in the corner, wearing a nice warm sweater. She's pretending to read a magazine, but I know she's listening.

The new doctor wants to see me in six months and tells us, mostly Beth—the meds seem fine for now.

On the way to her car, Beth asks me if I want to go to the new pizza place for supper. "No," I tell her. "I want to go home."

Beth gets up too early, why? "Clarice and Cheryl are coming, remember?" she says. She sighs when I say I don't. Instead of going to my job, she wants me to go to the airport with her. She sighs when I say I won't.

"Are you mad at me?" I ask.

Beth isn't mad, it's just something, something, something. Beth has two sentences. "Michael, remember, remember, remember" and "Michael, something, something, something."

Beth never asks me if I'm mad at her but if she did, sometimes I'd say yes.

"Beth, where did you put my lasagna pan?"

She didn't put it anyplace, she says. She hasn't seen it for a year and besides, I'm not supposed to make lasagna tonight, I'm supposed to go out to supper with her and Clarice and Cheryl. Remember, remember, remember?

The best friend says they want me to go exploring with them, but the cousin says she wants some of my famous lasagna. Beth rolls her eyes at all of us. She finds the lasagna pan right where it's always been. She piles the kitchen table with jars of sauce and boxes of noodles, cheese, more cheese, eggs, butter, flour, spices, sausage, too many things, bowls and spoons and knives. "Do I need all this?" I ask, so she finds Michael's Cookbook that Lucas made me for a Christmas present. Lasagna is on page one.

On their way out the door I hear Beth whisper, "I wonder what the kitchen will look like when we get back."

•

I watch women in another kitchen in another house in another time. Sheets of pasta cover a round wooden table. A huge pot sits on a white stove.

"Michael, you can help us," says my mother. "Come here and we'll show you."

My grandma cuts the lasagna into noodles with her special knife. I stand by the stove and stir and stir. The meat sizzles. My mother adds olive oil and garlic, tomatoes and spices, mushrooms and peppers. We gossip about the neighbor, her husband overseas. She's too chummy with her new boarder, my grandmother thinks. "Momma, big ears," my mother whispers and looks at me. "Put some nutmeg in the white sauce, Michael. Now put more cheese on top." Some of the sauce goes in jars, some of the noodles are stored for next time. Layer upon layer go in the pan. My mother ladles, my grandmother smooths just so. The lasagna is in the oven, and we clean the kitchen. "Now you know how to cook," says my mother. My grandma hugs me before I run off to play.

Hector and Maria come for supper, too. We six squeeze around the kitchen table. "If there's not enough room, I'll sit on Hector's lap," Beth's cousin says. I think she's Hector's girlfriend.

I serve Maria first. We stare at the circle of red cheesy ooze on her plate. Something's wrong.

"Honey, I think you forgot the pasta," says Beth, so softly, so sadly.

"I thought Grandma put it in the pan," I say.

Silent faces stare at me. Endless moments.

"I get confused sometimes," my soul says to Beth.

"I know. It's OK," Beth's soul says back to mine.

Beth's best friend says I've invented no-carb lasagna, but Beth's cousin wants some pasta with her sauce. I help Hector get a pot of water boiling and Beth pours a box of macaroni in it. "Look, Beth's cooking!" I say. Everyone is so happy to laugh.

•

It's snowing in the mountains. The big metal gate is drawn and padlocked. ROAD CLOSED. The sign is blunt, no nonsense. I back up, spin my tires, inch around until my car is pointing back to where I was before. Everything looks new. I'm lost.

The Border Patrol man finds me and calls Beth. He says she doesn't sound mad, she'll meet us at the station in about an hour. "Follow me in your car," he says. "We'll have a cup of coffee while we're waiting."

Beth brings Hector. The Border Patrol man gives everyone coffee. We are wasting Hector's time; I can drive myself home. I say it over and over, but everybody acts like I'm invisible.

"What were you doing driving around in the desert?" Her questions start as soon as I get in her car. "Where were you going? Why, why, why?"

"I guess I turned left instead of right," is all I have to say to make her stop asking and start crying.

When she stops crying, she says, "Michael, I'm going to buy you a cell phone for our anniversary, so this never happens again."

The snow is gone. The cactus is blooming. "Let's go for a ride up to Tucson to the Desert Museum," Beth says. "We can have lunch at the fancy restaurant."

She looks so happy I don't say no, I want to stay home. I say yes, let's go.

"When is Ramona coming?" I ask Beth.
"In two weeks," says Beth.
"Why is Ramona coming?" I ask Beth.
"To help us celebrate our anniversary," Beth says.

"When is Ramona coming," I ask Beth.
"Next week," says Beth.

"Why is Ramona coming?" I ask Beth.
"To help us celebrate our anniversary," Beth says.

"When is Ramona coming?" I ask Beth.
"Tomorrow," Beth says.
"Why is Ramona coming?" I ask Beth.
"To help us," Beth says.

We eat our supper on the patio. Ramona thinks burritos and cupcakes and wine are a perfect anniversary meal. I tell her I planned the menu.

When Beth finishes her cupcake, I pick up the bottle of wine. "There's enough left for two glasses," I say. "Beth, another?"

Beth says no, there's only enough wine for a glass, looks like to her, let Ramona have it. I move Ramona's glass next to mine and pour two perfect servings, emptying the bottle. "Never doubt my eye for wine," I say and Ramona bursts out laughing.

"To my daddy and his bride," she says as she lifts her glass.

The damn phone Beth gave me for an anniversary present starts ringing at the Walmart checkout, just as I hand the cashier Hector's credit card.

"Aren't you going to answer that?" she asks.

"I wasn't planning on it," I say. *I don't know how to answer it and I don't plan to learn,* I don't say.

When the phone rings while I'm at Hector's, he always starts laughing at me. "One of the women in your life wants to tell you they love you, *mi amigo,*" he says. "If I were you, I'd want to hear those sweet words." Then he'll take the phone from my pocket and show me how to answer the call I don't want in the first place. "This is Michael Bartoli's secretary," he'll say. "May I help you?"

Sometimes it's Ramona, sometimes it's Mike or Emma,

most of the time it's Beth, wondering when I'll be home. Sometimes I remember how to answer the damn phone. "I'm here. I'll be home later" is all I have to say to make Beth happy.

I pluck two empty pop bottles from Hector's recycle bin. Yesterday, a surprise at the Roadrunner—a new Mexican pop bottle hanging beside my old one on the creosote bush by the side of the road. The plant is growing strong and sturdy with the help of unfound water. Nothing is wasted. My walkers and I will make a bottle bush, to guide us all.

Another month, another week, another day. The desert is burning hot. With lead feet, we walk toward where we need to go. I walk south, arms weary with the weight. I stop and sip our warm water, walk on. They walk north. Soon they'll stop, sip our warm water, walk on. Our brains are too tired for plans. We carry only one thought, survive.

At the lean-to I see a horrible sight. Yesterday's water bottles, slashed and empty. A rusty butcher knife, plunged into the muddy dirt beside them. I feel the searing cold of fear grab my heart, shoot down my spine. I drop the new water jugs I carry. My mouth turns to dust, my feet hold me tight to the earth even though my brain screams run. Again, my heart cries *Why, why, why?* Again, Ellen's soft answer. *The fearful hate.* I open my eyes to stare at the message on the muddy floor of the lean-to: Go Away and Never Come Back.

"There is no comfort here," I whisper as I pick up the full jugs of water. "I'll carry you to another place." I walk 103 steps back to my car, get in, crank the engine. A careful U-turn, a mile of paved road. When I see a pile of rocks in the distance, my heart tells me to stop. I park my car, gather the water in my arms and begin. I'm a thirsty walker, I'm Michael, together our souls will help me place the water. Around a clump of scrub, over a hill, down to a wash. I set the jugs of water at the base of a lone boulder, sitting proud and strong under the noonday sun. In the boulder's shade, I sit beside the jugs of water and look south. The desert wind knows all the words of my prayer, my brain remembers only *Help me help.*

I count my steps back. At 198 my car is still not in sight. I look behind me. The boulder is gone. I turn slowly, my eyes searching the entire landscape. Nothing is familiar. I'm an old man in a new world. The earth is hot and I'm so tired. And thirsty. 198 steps away, two jugs of fresh water sit in the shade of a boulder. I don't know the way back to water. I don't know the way forward to home. And the blinding sun, straight overhead, offers me no clues.

I sit alone in the middle of this blazing place, missing the strength and shade of my boulder. If I live, the boulder will be my new water spot. I close my eyes to the sun. I'll rest for just a moment. Maybe later on, I'll survive.

My dream takes me to winter, to Green Bay, to snow. Cold still whiteness. A morning miracle, this snowstorm. I can't get into it fast enough. Precious moments wasted wrestling into hooded coat, boots, mittens. Wait, you'll freeze, let me wrap the scratchy scarf around your neck. Ignoring my mother's pleas, I rush out the door. A ten-year-old boy is never too cold or too hot.

My buddies and I meet in our park, divide into teams, attack with snowball weaponry. We win and lose and call for rematches. My grandmother appears in her huge black coat, holding a yellow bowl. "Before you ruin all the snow, fill this up and I'll make you snow ice cream."

Down the hill, over by the river, comes the sound. *Tap tap tap.* "Hey you guys, shut up. Listen." *Tap tap tap.* Our secret code. We're off toward the sound in search of make-believe ships to save.

I open my eyes. Two thousand miles, seven decades, race into now. My dream lingers. The snow cools me in the desert, my mouth wants the icy sweetness of snow ice cream. *Tap tap tap.* I bolt to my feet. I only need to listen and follow.

At the top of the hill, I hear my sound, see the flash of black and white as the woodpecker darts from brush to cactus, busy at the task of living. The land is open, the air is clear. My eyes and ears and feet follow the woodpecker's lead, taking me where I need to be.

The body is lying under a shadeless scrub. I don't call out to him, most of my strength is gone. One step, then another, I walk toward the man I've been waiting to meet. The man I've always known.

The man is younger than I am. His hair is black instead of grey, thick instead of thinning. His t-shirt bears the grime of days of travel. I took mine fresh from the drawer this morning after I got up and showered and kissed my wife, still asleep and safe in our bed. It's wet with the sweat of a few hours of work under the Arizona sun. His eyes are closed, his heart is still instead of pounding with fear.

I kneel beside him. "I had water, but I lost it. I'm so sorry," I say. I touch his shoulder. His body is warm. His eyelids quiver, his eyes flicker open, look toward the sky. His cracking lips begin to move, but his words are too soft for me to hear, even in the stillness of the desert.

"I'm Michael," I say as I lean close to his ear. "We've got ourselves in a pickle, haven't we?"

His lips move again. I struggle to understand his words.

"I'm sorry. I tried to learn Spanish, but I couldn't do it. Beth learned it. She's my wife."

I don't ask him what his name is or where he's from or how long he's been walking. None of that matters anyway.

"You know," I say. "You should have picked yourself a better person to find you. I don't know which direction to walk to get us help, even if I had the energy to do it."

The walker doesn't whisper more Spanish words to me, but I feel like I should keep on talking, in case his ears aren't too tired to hear a friendly voice.

"I hope you get the chance to get old," I say. "I wouldn't trade my last few years for anything. But the thing about getting old is this: it's sneaky. Age comes and goes. Some days I'm a hundred and some days I'm ten. Mostly, I'm just Michael."

The walker opens his eyes and looks right at me. I could be wrong, but I think he smiles. His lips move and he whispers *Michael*, but I could be wrong about that too.

"I wish we'd picked a spot with a little more shade," I say, "or maybe a couple of rocks to lean up against." I slide around so I can put my back against the puny trunk of the scrub. It's barely strong enough to hold me up. "If you want, you can rest your head against my leg," I say but the walker has closed his eyes again. I breathe the desert air and look at the sky.

"I imagine Grandma's got that snow ice cream ready," I say, and I close my eyes to see the cold, still whiteness.

As I taste the first bite, the telephone in my pocket starts ringing. This time, I remember how to answer it.

CHAPTER 10

❋

Beth

Ramona, call me when you get this message. Your father is in the hospital. He's had . . . there's been . . . we don't know what happened. The Border Patrol found him in the desert. There was another man, he didn't make it. The doctor is cautiously optimistic, so . . . I'm sorry, honey, for this call. Maybe I'll know more soon.

My voice falters and jerks, trying to find the path between panic and hope. My finger trembles as it pushes End Call. I'm so glad Ramona didn't answer. Maybe I'll have an hour before she calls back. In an hour, maybe Beth-in-crisis will morph into a Beth who can handle life when everything changes in an instant.

I suppose I should be praying. Or maybe it doesn't matter, maybe every breath is a prayer.

Hector is here. He came as soon as I called him. That call was easy. *Help us* was all I had to say.

Michael is no longer in Emergency. The doctors have triaged and tested and diagnosed. Now Michael is in Intensive Care. His eyes are closed, his body is still and monitored. The numbers on the bedside machines indicate stability, we are told. Soon Michael will move to a regular hospital room.

I find paper and a pen in my purse and write the numbers for Ramona. She'll want to know. Then I try to write down all the sentences the doctor said to us. Writing the sentences now is easier than hearing them hours ago.

> Hyponatremia. Encephalopathy. Electrolyte Imbalance. Brain Edema. Low sodium. Norms: 135-145, Michael: 122. Dangerously low. Treatment: increase electrolyte levels slowly, very slowly, to prevent permanent neurological damage.

I reread my notes. I should underline permanent neurological damage, but I don't. Will these words wound Ramona more than my horrible phone message or will the facts ease her into this new direction we're going to need to travel? I don't want to go down this road yet. I'm not ready. I loved where we were. Again, I whisper, *Help us.*

Hector and I sit side by side, facing Michael's bed as nurses come and go. We are out of questions to ask them, they have given us all the answers they have. Over and over Hector and I ask each other the unanswerable question—what has happened to bring us here? Finally, Hector takes my hand and says, "Beth, we may never know. It is what it is."

I do not voice all my newly forming fears: Are the drops of electrolyte finding their way to Michael's swollen brain cells? Is he healing slowly, slowly? In a dozen more moments, will he be creeping back to me or sliding away? In an hour, what will I say to his daughter? In a day, will he open his eyes and know he's seeing his wife who loves him? Will he talk to me in Michael's voice, without confusion? In a week, in a month, in a year, will everything I love be gone?

Help us, I pray, looking at these two dear men.

Why am I so comfortable here in our bed, all by myself? I should be too tired to sleep. My brain should be churning with multiplying worries. Black fears should be arising from under my blankets, waiting to attack me as I dream. Michael sleeps in a bed twenty miles away, under the watch of Hector and his night nurse. It's their shift.

Last night I stayed in the fluorescent-lit, too cold hospital room. Michael's nurse snared me a roast beef supper from the rack of patient's trays, a leftover from someone released early. I ate every bite, even the jello. I chewed a piece of gum before bedtime, instead of brushing my teeth. Shifts changed and Michael's night nurse handed me a pillow and a blanket before turning her attention to Michael, safely fenced in cold metal in the high sterile bed.

As I made my nest in the corner chair, I heard her say, "Well, Mr. Bartoli, how do you feel?"

I'm your nurse. You're in the hospital."

"You need to call my wife and tell her I'm here. She'll be worried about me."

"She's right here," his nurse said.

I bolted from chair to bed. I touched his cheek. He looked right at me. "Please call my wife. I need to go home. There's no one there to take care of her," the man who looked like Michael said to me.

I managed to say, "Don't worry. I'll call her. Everything is fine. You just go back to sleep."

Our nurse eased me back into my chair with murmurs of this can happen and medication side-effects and too early to know and not even twenty-four hours yet. Rest and wait and rest and wait.

I returned to the ugly turquoise chair. I punched the pillow until it softened the corners and creases of leatherette—a good upholstery option, easy to wipe clean after a wife spends her night spilling coffee and tears. I watched Michael sleep, my head propped high enough to see the numbers on the oxygen and blood pressure and heart rate monitors. Sights and smells and sounds that should terrify and repulse turned ordinary and comforting. The flurry of activity from the nurses' station after a button was pushed for alarm or pain, the lingering whiffs of disinfectant mop water and roast beef grounded me throughout the night. Stiff backed nurses became best friends. I craved their quick visits. In the first twenty-four hours, Room 606 became my entire world.

I smile as I lie alone in our bed, twenty miles away from Michael. My body relaxes with thoughts of stable and cautious optimism. Before I drift to sleep, I say the next prayer. *Thank you.*

Ramona asks if she should come and I answer no. We're both relieved.

"Is Daddy awake? Can I talk to him?"

I was hoping she wouldn't ask. I'm feeling protective of Ramona, of Michael, of me. This morning as Hector was leaving, Michael grabbed his arm and raged, "Help him. Don't go to the lean-to, they've ruined it. Look for the boulder, there's water there you can take it to him he's so thirsty. Hurry."

We called our nurse, she calmed Michael, then Hector. Again, the murmurs of just a dream, too soon, let the medicines work. Rest and wait and rest and wait.

I look at my husband, Ramona's father, as he sleeps. I'm not afraid when Michael is sleeping. "He's not awake right now, honey. Do you want me to call you back when he wakes up?"

"No, I'll call tomorrow," says Ramona. We're both relieved.

Michael is home. We sit in our same chairs, eat the same foods, watch the same sunsets. We say the same sentences, over and over and over.

"How long was I there, at that place?"

"A week."

"I don't remember a thing. Does Hector know?"

"Yes, he was there with us. We took turns staying with you."

"That was nice, thank you. Well, I better get to work."

Michael's work conversation is peppered with delusions of seeing knives in the mud, carrying water to roadrunners. Everyone is so thirsty, he says over and over and over. My stomach cramps every time our talks veer this way. I try gentle reason, deflection, concern mixed with firmness. My tone is getting better, I get a lot of practice. I lie. "Hector will take water to the roadrunners," I say. "Yes, he knows how. He'll do a perfect job." My lies are easy, guilt-free. My lies calm Michael's delusions and my anxiety.

"Michael, don't go to work today, stay here with me. We'll have a wonderful time. I miss you," I say, no longer lying.

Michael goes to bed early, gets up late. I adjust my sleep patterns to chisel out free time. Seven a.m. On sentry duty, I place myself in the lounge chair sitting halfway between our bedroom and the front door, just in case Michael decides it's a workday. I escape, reading books about red-haired heroines adored by sexy, rich men. I decode crossword puzzles and Sudoku, feeling smart and competent for a few minutes at the end of each puzzle, a little energy charge for the next few hours of uncertainty. I calm myself with lists of groceries, errands for the day. Sometimes I write down all my fears, then stare at the list until worries become just words on a piece of paper.

I finish the last page of the last romance novel and plop it on top of the pile of library books. It's left me irritated and resentful. Per usual, the heroic couple overcomes societies' pressures and their personal fears and egos to merge blissfully and forever, their perfect future implied and hazy.

Today we'll return library books after a bite of lunch. I dread the outing. Michael will order whatever I'm having, then tell me it doesn't taste good. At the library I'll try to find him a comfy chair and this month's copy of *Bon Appétit* or *Arizona Highways* so I can browse for fifteen minutes. Since our favorite librarian is summering in Seattle, his assistant is filling in at the information desk. She has taken it upon herself to chat with Michael in a condescending tone as she throws me pitying, conspiratorial glances. To avoid any additional interaction, I use the self-checkout computer. One would think a librarian in a retirement community would have more insight with patrons showing a touch of mental decline.

I'm introspective enough to name my mood depression. Clarice will be proud of my self-reflection. I'll call her this evening, after Michael has gone to bed. I'll vent, then laugh. She'll laugh, then comfort.

I pour myself another cup of coffee, check on Michael. He's curled around my pillow, sleeping so soundly. My heart swells, my throat tightens. I go into my office, turn on my computer, veer my chair toward the bedroom hallway. I've been avoiding this next project.

"Beth, we'll need to make some tough decisions," Ramona says at the end of every phone call. "This is new to you; I've been through this before." Our darling Ramona, we're not fighting the same demons, but we'll go into this battle together. Into Google Search I type: assisted living, Green Valley, AZ.

The screen lists a dozen entries. To the right, a map with a dozen markers. Maybe this will be easy, maybe we have choices. I start clicking and scrolling and deleting. I learn new phrases: aging in place, continuum of services, memory care, on-site nursing. Vague suggestions of looming hardships. Photos show handsome couples frolicking in idyllic landscapes—a Harlequin Romance for the elderly. Spacious meeting rooms are filled with folks laughing and toasting their good fortune to live in these charming places. I dig deep into websites to find Plans and Pricing. These healthy, vibrant couples may reside in this senior paradise for five thousand dollars a month, the price goes up as one's health declines. Eight, nine, ten thousand dollars a month is the cost of aging.

I search more websites, looking for hopeful words, affordable prices. Hacienda Oros is a senior apartment complex offering continental breakfast. I find a price—$1095 per month. This looks to be the same living arrangement Michael and I enjoy now for zero dollars a month, except for the platter of donuts and bagels.

I click and scan and delete, searching for hopeful words, affordable prices. A ten-resident home in the desert, a picture of two young women in nursing scrubs. A picnic every year. A van with a wheelchair platform. "The staff treats residents with respect and kindness." The statement sickens me. Why would I not assume these standards of conduct? What past atrocities made the web developer feel it necessary to state "We're nice to the people who give us thousands of dollars a month, all of their life savings, to live here." But I paraphrase. Michael will never leave my side to become a resident at a facility that lists compassion as a bonus selling point. "We are in this together, my love," I whisper to the dark hallway as I delete.

My coffee is cold, my stomach is empty and aching. If we lived at Hacienda Oro, I'd be having hot coffee and donuts right now. My brain numbs. Without the chore of thinking, I return to Google and type: assisted living, Centerburg, IL.

Parkside Manor's web site is straight forward, designed on the cheap. No mountain ranges in the photo galleries, no hidden pricing levels, just a picture of the front lobby, another of residents in the dining room, several of whom I recognize. I read *Affordable.* Instead of clicking Contact Us, I call Clarice who is thrilled to continue my research. Four hours later she calls back, bubbling with complete information and instructions.

"Clarice, thank you but I'm just weighing our options," I tell her. "I have no intention of moving back to Centerburg." Even as I say the words, I know our next step.

I spend most of my free time worrying about finances. Sometimes I run the numbers in my head, sometimes I write them down. I have columns of debits and credits in the margins of my Sudoku books, on scraps of paper scattered over every horizontal surface in our house. Michael's social security plus my teacher pension plus the meager interest from my CD's minus monthly rent at Parkside Manor minus Medigap health insurance minus car upkeep and gasoline and toilet paper and, oh my, I get so weary of thinking sometimes. Usually, the Money In matches the Money Out, but I don't let the numbers calm me. What if I need to buy another car in my lifetime? What if we want to travel again? There are what-ifs I can barely allow myself to think, let alone price. One evening Hector calls. He's been doing some thinking himself, he tells me. The local real estate market is depressed, but vacation rental prices are soaring. "Don't even think about selling your townhouse," he says. "It's income. It will cover the cost of an apartment in Centerburg." Hector will be able to find renters, he thinks. "Beth, let me handle this investment for you." After he hangs up, I cry for an hour.

Mid-January is the best time to be in Green Valley. Hector is here for the day, visiting with Michael as I pack. Packing is easy, easier than explaining. Michael walks to each empty closet, peeks in every cardboard box. "Why?" he asks over and over and over. The why is too huge for Michael to grasp, too painful for me to put into words. I try to be consistent in my vague answers. "We're going to need more help as we get older" and "It's cheaper to find help in Centerburg" and "I've found us a lovely apartment."

Hector has taken to deflecting the blame to Ramona when Michael directs the questions to him. "Ramona misses you. She'll be able to see you every day instead of twice a year. This is a good plan, Michael. Do it for your daughter."

Hector and I decide we won't need to rent a U-Haul. I pack only clothing, linens, the coffee pot and toaster. A few pots and pans, in case Michael decides to cook a supper sometime. "A continental breakfast and evening meal are included," the web site said. "Weekly housekeeping provided." I don't pack the vacuum cleaner.

Cheryl is flying in this evening. Since she's moved to St. Louis with Miranda and Lucas after all the Centerburg real estate was sold, her flight will be easy, and Hector's sadness over our move will be sweetened with her appearance. We'll pack our life into two cars, Michael's and mine. Two back seats and two trunks should hold all our earthly possessions. On Monday, we'll begin our three-day cross-country drive, Cheryl and I in my car, followed by Hector and Michael in the old Buick.

"He'll be more comfortable in his own car," Hector told me. "We'll talk. We'll enjoy this trip together."

As Michael and Hector sit on the patio in the teak chairs we'll leave here, I carry two plates, two bowls, two coffee cups into the bathroom and wrap them in the red and yellow, blue and green towels Clarice and Cheryl gave us to match my Talavera sink. As I pack the towel-cushioned dinnerware into the cardboard box, all the colors fade from my bathroom. I sit down on the stool, put my face in my hands and weep.

Michael hears me. He walks into the bathroom, wraps me in his arms and holds me until I stop crying. He doesn't say a word until Hector asks what's wrong. "Beth loves that pretty sink," Michael says. "It breaks her heart to leave. She doesn't want to move—she's doing it because she loves me."

Clarice is ablaze with decorating fever. She has used my Talavera wine rack as her inspiration piece, she informed me on one of our pre-arrival phone calls. She'll decorate our new apartment in the colors of Tuscany. "Talavera is Mexican, not Italian," I pointed out, but she was not to be deterred. She gathered furniture and lamps and knickknacks from family and friends throughout southern Illinois to make our apartment her most recent showpiece. Two weeks before our arrival, she wrenched our key away from the Parkside Manor administrator (and a Red Hat devotee) and began staging our apartment. As we four weary travelers limp into the parking lot on a grey Friday afternoon in late January, Clarice is dancing and waving and yelling at the front entrance. My teetering world comes into balance.

No words are needed, our hug is fierce and quick. Clarice bites her lip, grabs my hand, and pulls me into my new life. Michael, Hector, and Cheryl follow. The front lobby is large and welcoming, decorated in burgundy and forest green. "They haven't changed a thing in this lobby in twenty years," Clarice snorts. To the left is the dining room, to the right, a hallway. We walk to 124.

Our apartment is cute. It screams *Clarice has been here for two weeks*. A red couch, a bright rug atop the bland carpet. A navy-blue recliner, an afghan draped over it, just so. On a side table, a yellow and green runner. "I thought you could put your wine rack here," Clarice says.

"Isn't that table from Ramona's family room?" I ask. I have no idea how many people have been shaken down to furnish our new life.

Boxes and suitcases are carried in. Jim arrives with pizza. Clarice pulls iced tea from the refrigerator, sets the table with new placemats and napkins, in the colors of Tuscany of course.

"Beth, I have an idea," she says halfway through our meal. "Let's have your anniversary party right here, in the dining room!" Cheryl joins in and the plan for the imaginary celebration escalates. Light appetizers and cake and coffee. A little open house to show off the apartment. Family and old friends and the new friends we've yet to meet. Jim rolls his eyes, Michael and Hector calmly eat pizza, Clarice is breathless. "What do you think?"

"No, absolutely not," I say.

Today is the party. Since I'm being characteristically stubborn and anti-social (Clarice's phrase but I concur) Clarice has detoured around me and enlisted husbands Jim and Michael to assist her with our anniversary festivities. In the Parkside Manor dining room, tables are shoved, chairs are placed, tablecloths and napkins are arranged. Michael rides with Jim to pick up platters of Subway sandwiches and veggie platters from the IGA.

"You do intend to come out of your apartment when your guests arrive, don't you?" Clarice asks me. "Or at least unlock your door for the open house?"

Cheryl, Lucas, and Kaitlyn show up an hour early. "Miranda couldn't come. She has hospital rounds," says Cheryl, "and we'll have to leave by four so Lucas can get back to the restaurant."

"Don't tell me, tell Clarice," I say. "I'm not sure she's approving any early dismissals."

The dining room fills with guests. I recognize a few faces, recall fewer names, but Clarice stands close by to clue me. Michael greets everyone, his blue eyes sparkling. A squadron of Red Hat women arrive wearing their civilian clothing. Cheryl and Clarice rush to them, screaming with delight, upping the energy level of the room. One by one, the ladies are pulled to us for proper introduction. "How do you know my Beth?" Michael asks each one. "I'm so happy to meet you." He charms my old nemesis Shirley Eubanks, who I've not thought about in years. As I watch them talk, I wonder why I was so intimated by this chatty, nondescript woman. "This is a fine town" Michael says to the mayor. "We love your cooking," he says to my former student who still owns the Dairy Queen.

"Shouldn't we put the candles on the cake?" Michael whispers as he pulls me aside.

"No honey, I don't think we need candles," I say.

"Well, I'll thank everyone for coming, then we can sing."

As Clarice whips by to check on the coffee urn, I grab her, and we stand arm in arm as my husband addresses the crowd.

"We'd like to thank you all for coming to this special event. I've known some of you for a good long time, haven't I, Ramona?" Ramona beams at her father. "And Beth is sure enjoying seeing her old friends, aren't you?"

"Yes, I surely am," I say.

Michael continues his speech. "It's good to tell each other we care and to celebrate the important times with the folks we love." Then he puts his arm around Clarice, pulls her to him and leads our guests in singing Happy Birthday to You.

"Of course he thought Clarice was throwing herself a birthday party. It looks more like her party than yours," Ramona says as we watch Cheryl and Clarice and Michael serve the anniversary/birthday cake. Michael scans the room looking for guests who need more coffee, another sandwich. Ramona's eyes follow him as he carries plates of cake to the mayor and his wife. "Pop sure loves a party." Her smile is huge, full of pride.

"Your father is quite a guy, I'm pretty happy I married him," I say.

Ramona sighs, closes her eyes, opens them to look at me. "I know this is so hard, but thank you for bringing him back to me."

CHAPTER 11

❈

Beth

"H ow are you doing, Beth?"
It's not Clarice asking the question, nor is it Ramona or Cheryl. They know from the tone of my voice or the time it takes me to answer the phone. But when I'm at Walgreen's, comparing prices of ibuprofen, and the old neighbor whose father knew my father asks the question I know she'll ask, I answer with words she knows I'll say: "We have good days and bad days. We're taking it one day at a time." Trite, banal, surface-skimming sentences intended to snap the conversation shut. A vague and efficient interchange.

She nods and smiles in sympathy. "Call anytime," she says. "It's so good to run into you. We'd heard you moved back."

Centerburg. I've migrated back to my homeland. I'm a member of the herd gathered for safety at the edge of the river. We touch noses, smell each other's scent, share the information carried in the winds. If I'm in danger, the herd moves closer to my trembling body. We are one as we sleep, feed, mate, bear and raise our young. Birth and death are familiar and accepted. Back in the homeland, in the pain relief aisle of Walgreen's, I find unexpected comfort.

"Yes, it's good to see you again," I say to the old neighbor whose father knew my father.

A Good Day

I wake to the smell of coffee. Michael is up before me and has organized Folgers and filters and water to brew us a pot. I read the *Sentinel*, delivered to our apartment door, as Michael watches *The Weather Channel*. We sip our in-house coffee and wait until seven-thirty, when we go to the dining room for breakfast. Michael teases his favorite waitress who serves him a piece of pecan Danish because she thinks it is his favorite. He prefers cherry but he acts delighted.

A Bad Day

It's raining. Michael wants to go to Wendy's for lunch, again. I suggest we have a turkey sandwich, made by me in our kitchenette. Or maybe a BLT, since Clarice brought us a big garden tomato yesterday. "No, I want to go to Wendy's," Michael says. "You never want to take me anywhere."

"That's not true." I know I shouldn't say it. "We've gone to Wendy's three times this week. It's raining."

"No, it isn't," says Michael. "You just don't want me to have any fun. You want me to be in prison here."

I cry. Michael wonders why I'm so sad. We go to Wendy's for lunch.

A Good Day

"It's Ramona's birthday," Michael says as soon as he wakes. "Did you remember?"

Cheryl, Lucas, Miranda, and Kaitlyn are coming for supper at Ravi and Ramona's house. Michael and I are supposed to arrive early, to reheat the lasagna in Ramona's oven. Yesterday morning Michael said, "I want to make a lasagna for her party." I thought No but I said Yes. After locating Michael's Cookbook, our treasured gift from Lucas, we made a list and bought the ingredients at the IGA. Yesterday afternoon Michael stood at the stove and sautéed and stirred as I sat at the kitchen table and read the recipe to him, step by step. "I think I'll remember the pasta this time," Michael laughed.

I watched him place the layers in the pan I gave him years ago, the pan I thought he'd never use again. His hands spooned the meat sauce over the pasta, as his eyes, focused and wise, guided them. So intent on his task was he, he didn't notice my tears. "Now bake at 350 degrees for one hour, until the cheese melts and the sauce is hot and bubbling," I read with blurred vision.

As the lasagna baked, Michael and I sat at the kitchen table, drinking coffee and leafing through Michael's Cookbook, remembering the when and where and who of past meals. "This is wonderful," Michael said. "Thank you."

A Bad Day

Betty Lou, the social director, knocks on our door fifteen minutes after we return from breakfast. Apparently, she overheard our argument as we were leaving the dining room.

"The Reminiscing Group meets in an hour," she says, "How about joining us, Michael? We talk about all sorts of things."

I have a check-up with Doctor Sam this morning. Being under his care again is such a comfort for me but apparently Michael doesn't share my feelings today. He doesn't want to go with me, he doesn't want to stay here. No, no, no, he doesn't want to go anywhere but home, and no, no, no, this is NOT HOME.

Betty Lou is calm. "Your new friends will be there, everyone talks about old times, today we'll talk about jobs, you can tell us about your restaurant." Her pitch is practiced, encouraging.

"Oh, I don't work there anymore," Michael says.

"Betty Lou knows that," I say, "It's reminiscing!" I look at the kitchen clock.

"Are you going?" Michael asks me.

I feel my control drain away. "No! I have to go to see Doctor Sam."

"Are you sick?"

Betty Lou puts a hand on my shoulder as she talks to Michael. "Why don't you help me set up for our meeting, Michael?" she says. "Then Beth can get ready to go."

"Well, okay," Michael says.

As I'm leaving Doctor Sam's office, my cell phone rings. It's Betty Lou.

"Everything is fine, Beth, but I wanted you to know Michael is a little upset." Thirty minutes ago, Doctor Sam said my heart sounded wonderful, perfect. Now it's pounding in my chest as I close my eyes and picture the scene described by Betty Lou—Michael sitting in his car in the parking lot, staff members pleading with him to come back inside. Betty Lou finding the right words so he'd hand her his keys. "He's not going anywhere, I'm sitting in the car with him. Don't rush back. Take your time. We'll just do some reminiscing right here."

I charge back to Doctor Sam and leave armed with a new prescription for agitation medication. Perhaps Michael will share some with me. I attempt to breathe and drive at the same time, as I aim my car in the direction of Parkside Manor. Half of my brain is screaming *drive faster*—the other half pleads with me to turn around and flee to anywhere else.

I park up close to Michael's old Buick at the far end of the parking lot. Betty Lou waves at me from the passenger seat. "Hi Beth," she says so calmly I could hug her. She gets out, leaves the door open for me, and hands me Michael's keys.

"Michael was telling me about the mountains and the desert and how much he liked working there."

"Michael, why are you in the car?" I ask, leaning in through the open passenger door.

Michael stares straight ahead, hands clamped on the wheel. "I need to get to work. They're counting on me."

I try to match Betty Lou's tone. "Honey, Hector's doing that job now. Your job is taking care of me."

I see Michael's eyes inch back from his beloved Green Valley to look at the person talking to him. I feel his brain struggling to remember the cross-country trip that stole him away from there and placed him in a parking lot in Centerburg.

"Why don't you take me out for lunch," I hear myself say. "Let's take my car."

"Well, OK," Michael says, returning to me. "I bet you'd like to go to the Dairy Queen instead of Wendy's."

The next day the facility administrator pulls me aside on our way back from breakfast and whispers, "Beth, if you need to talk, let me know. We may need to make some tough decisions. Not now, but soon. And you probably need to hide Michael's car keys."

The tough decision is only steps away, on the other side of the dining room, down a windowed hallway, through a locked door. At Parkside Manor, it's not called Memory Care. Here it's called the Alzheimer's Unit.

We have good days and bad days, Michael and I. We can take it one day at a time, as long as that day doesn't take us to the other side of the dining room, down a windowed hallway, through a locked door.

"Remember Michael, you have a doctor's appointment this afternoon." "You just asked me that, remember?" "Remember to brush your teeth." "Remember to put on clean socks." *Remember* . . . I never need to say the word to him again. Do I really think I'm being helpful, throwing that dagger of a word at him, at the beginning or ending of every sentence? "Where did you put your glasses, do you remember?"

On good days, he'll dive into the mud in his brain, slosh around looking for the memory. He'll swim through the muck, grab the memory, pull it to the surface and hand it to me. A gift for the wife he adores.

On bad days, the word shuts him down. He looks at me with the eyes of a confused stranger, new to this place we find ourselves. He'll repeat my questions, saying the words perfectly. The words don't make the trip to his brain, they just bounce against his eardrums and his voice tosses them back at me.

"He can't remember what his brain hasn't stored," Ramona says, from the distance of daughter.

Beth, I tell myself, for Michael and for you, remember to never say remember.

The day is typical for southern Illinois in late November— gray sky bearing no hint of the time of day, damp chill holding no promise of clearing or threat of real precipitation. Thanksgiving is too jubilant a word for southern Illinois.

Somehow Michael and I pack ourselves into my car along with one suitcase, two pillows, our pills, a Google map, and directions from Centerburg to Mike's house in Des Plaines.

A month ago, the phone calls began. "How about Dad and Beth driving up to Des Plaines for Thanksgiving? And Emma's Birthday? She's flying in from Minneapolis for a few days," Mike asked Ramona to ask me to ask Michael.

"He'll have to ask his father himself," I tell Ramona to tell Mike. "If I ask him he'll say no."

Mike called Michael three times. Michael said No twice, but last week, one week before Thanksgiving, Michael said, "Well, OK."

One hundred times, Michael has asked, "How long will it take? Why are we going? Where will we sleep?" One hundred times, I've answered, "No, not Green Valley, Des

Plaines. Thanksgiving with Mike and Libby and Emma. Just two days." Two long, long, long days.

After four hours of driving, I turn onto the Tri-State Tollway. The weather is more purposeful in Chicago. Cool becomes cold. Damp becomes snow. Michael's eyes change from listless to interested. "Look, it's snowing. Are we in Chicago? Do you want me to drive?"

A month of ill-conceived phone calls and planning and pleading and explaining and re-arranging tumbles away with Michael's excitement. I look from him to the fresh snowflakes, melting too quickly on the hood of my car.

"I'm OK with driving. How about you tell me when the next toll is due," I say.

The table is set for twelve.

"Pop, you remember Libby's folks and her sister and family?" Mike says, reciting a litany of names. Michael walks from person to person, he is happy to meet everyone.

Mike puts his hand on the shoulder of a handsome young man standing next to Emma. "And this is Emma's boyfriend, Matt."

"I've heard so much about you, Mr. Bartoli." Matt shakes Michael's hand.

"Is this your wife? Michael asks.

The gathering falls silent, just for a few long seconds.

"Pop, this is Emma, your granddaughter," Mike says too slowly, too loudly.

"Why Emma, I haven't seen you since you were a little girl," says Michael. "Is this your husband?"

Emma's pretty face freezes, just for a few long seconds. "No Grandpa, this is my boyfriend Matt."

"Pleased to meet you," Michael says as he shakes Matt's hand a second time.

Our feast proceeds efficiently. We do not join hands around the table and take turns voicing our expressions of thankfulness. Was the omission previously discussed or a last-minute adjustment? We pass the platters around the table, volley light conversation, compliment the food between bites. Michael eats with total concentration, using his spoon to scoop green beans and gravy and dressing against his biscuit for easy pick-up. The turkey is mounded at the side of his plate, untouched. If we were eating alone, I'd cut it up for him.

Plates are cleared. Pumpkin pie is presented.

"This is Evelyn's favorite. Can I take a piece to her?" Michael says.

The silence lasts longer this time.

"Dad, Mom's dead. Remember?" Mike says. If Ramona were here, she'd kick her brother under the table.

Thoughts of Evelyn seem to fill the dining room. I share none of these memories, but I've inherited the sadness—an unfair burden it seems, at this moment. For Michael, and for his family, I push aside my resentment long enough to deflect the conversation. "Michael, you never told me Evelyn liked pumpkin pie," I say. "Did you make it, Libby?"

"No, a kind baker at the Jewell Food Store made it for us," says Libby.

We laugh too loudly at the small joke. Michael returns his concentration to his plate, gathering spoonfuls of pie, each taste reminding him of Evelyn.

For Christmas, Hector wants us to come to Green Valley. "Stay at my house. Let me pay for your airfare."

"Thank you but no," I tell him.

Lucas calls. "I'm the executive chef now. Could you bring Grandpa for Christmas Eve? I'll reserve my best table."

"Thank you but no," I tell him.

Kate calls. "It's our anniversary. We've bought a new flat with a proper guestroom instead of a sun porch. Can you come?"

"No, my darling. Not now. Maybe sometime but not now. Thank you but no," I tell her.

I don't tell Michael about any of the phone calls. Lies of omission.

In the lobby of Parkside Manor, a Christmas tree is decorated in burgundy to match the two couches. We pass it every day without comment. Our Christmas presents for each other, new winter coats. I love mine, Michael refuses to wear his. Ramona gave him a bright red sweater which he wears instead. "No, I want the pretty one," he says every time I try to hand him his new coat. He never complains about being cold. On Christmas Day, we feast on turkey and ham in the dining room instead of traveling across town to the large hubbub at Ramona's or Clarice's, a much-discussed decision. Deviations, however well-meaning, cause confusion for Michael and a dull pain in the stomach for me.

I've always preferred January to December, this year is no exception. Our life settles back to routine. We walk through the treeless lobby for breakfast, spend the rest of the morning discussing what we'll have for lunch. Ramona arrives at our apartment every Saturday to spend the afternoon with her precious pop, doing all the things she believes he wants to do—going to a movie, taking a walk, eating lunch at her house so Michael can visit with Sunny. She says I must use this time for myself, a break, a reward. I usually go to see Clarice. When I'm with her I want to be with Michael. When I'm home with Michael, I long to be with Clarice.

In February, Clarice decides I need an extra special birthday celebration, just the two of us. "We'll have dinner at the Country Club," she says. "Ramona can stay with Michael. I'll call her and arrange everything. You won't need to do a thing."

Michael doesn't want the sandwich I make us for Saturday

lunch. He doesn't understand why I put on my good suit instead of pajamas after my shower.

"Where are we going now?" he asks.

"I'm going out with Clarice and Ramona is coming to see you," I say every fifteen minutes until Ramona knocks on our door at four o'clock. I grab my purse and bolt. By the time I walk through the lobby to the parking lot, I'm ready to turn around and go back. Instead, I walk to Clarice's car and she drives me off to celebrate my making it through another year of my life.

Michael is asleep in his chair when I return. Ramona is reading my *Good Housekeeping*. She looks exhausted but her voice strives for perky.

"Did you have a nice evening?" she asks.

"Yes, the food was delicious. I had surf and turf." I also strive for perky. "How about you?"

"We had a nice visit," Ramona says. "We talked about Mom and old times. He sounded like my old Dad."

Ramona leaves. I get ready for bed. Michael wakes up just as I settle into my chair and pick up my Sudoku book.

"Where did she go?" he asks.

"Ramona went home. You were sleeping," I say.

"I've got to go home too. She needs me." Michael struggles out of his chair. "Where's my keys? I have to hurry."

I place myself between Michael and the door.

"Honey, everything's fine. Let's go to bed. You'll feel better in the morning," I say.

"No, I won't. Get out of my way," he screams. "I have to find Evelyn."

Michael glares at me, the woman standing between him and his wife. He's spent all afternoon and evening talking about her, his first love, the mother of his children. Now he's fighting to save her as I struggle to save him. We three are engaged in this battle that will see no victors. Evelyn is here, in our life, in our marriage. I resent her memory and her name. I resent having to feel resentment.

Michael and I stand facing each other, glaring, bodies rigid. Silent rage drains us both. Michael can't pull up the words he needs, I block all I want to say. I lead Michael back to his chair, then slump into mine.

"You're a nice lady," he says. "I'm sorry."

"It's OK, Michael," I say.

"Can I ask you for something? Can you please help me find Evelyn? She needs me."

I snap.

"Michael, look at me. Say my name." I scream at him. I stand up, tower over him. I beat my chest with my fist. "I'm your wife. Say my name."

Michael's eyes struggle to focus. "You sound like you're mad at me," he says.

I fall back into my chair, saying nothing. His look is so confused as he turns and shuffles off to bed. I don't follow him. I don't care if he can't find his pajama bottoms. I don't care if he doesn't brush his teeth. He can sleep alone and dream of Evelyn.

I place my numb body in Michael's chair, my back to our bedroom. Instead of crying I call Clarice. She answers after one ring.

"What's wrong, honey?" she says.

It spills out . . . I don't know if I can take this much longer right now he doesn't remember I'm his wife he'll spend tomorrow trying to find Evelyn or pleading to go back to Green Valley or maybe he'll come back to me but he's drifting further and further away and I'm so scared I think it's time but I can't call to arrange it and it could be years like this neither one of us can manage it and the money, Clarice, the Alzheimer's Unit costs eight thousand dollars a month I don't have the money to keep him safe I've saved all my life we don't have enough money to be old it will cost everything we have so he can sit on one side of a locked door and I can sit on the other side I can't do this.

I hear the sobbing. It's not me. Michael is standing in our bedroom doorway, wearing his baggy blue plaid boxer shorts and the flannel shirt he's had on all day. His face is wet with tears.

"I'm sad too," he says.

"Clarice, I have to go. I'll call you tomorrow." I put the phone on the coffee table and go to him. "Honey, let's find your pajamas," I say as I unbutton his shirt. "Then we'll go to bed. We're so tired. We both need some sleep."

CHAPTER 12

＊

Michael

I'm not doing any good here in this dark little town. Beth is crying. She cries with her eyes when she talks to me. She cries with her voice when she talks to the telephone. I traveled a thousand miles to make her smile. I'll travel a thousand more to make her smile again.

She sleeps as I gather my treasures. There are just a few to put in the IGA paper bag. The others I carry in my heart. Two keys—one silver, one gold—lay at the bottom of Beth's purse. I take the silver one.

My hands remember where to put the key to make my old Buick ready to go. My finger remembers the button to push to turn cold to warm. My foot remembers the pedals, my hands remember the endless circle of the steering wheel. My eyes don't remember, they just look ahead.

A small highway to a big highway. A straight easy road from today to tomorrow.

My right eye catches today's first sunlight. My right cheek feels its warmth. My belly sings to the sunrise, full and empty at the same time. I'm happy.

I drive for a minute, an hour, a day, a lifetime. I remember without thinking, without joy or pain. Memories rise from my belly. I hold them in my heart, then let them drift to the place where nothing is all there is.

St. Paul's United Church of Christ. I park under the old maple tree. She's survived longer than a man's lifetime. The planning committee still hasn't found enough votes to have her cut down.

"Hello, my darling old girl," I say to her. "I'm glad to see you."

"Hello, Michael," she says. "I'm glad to see you too."

I grab my treasures and head out. It's a short walk to Mike's Chicago Dogs. I open the door and the smell of mustard greets me. I'm so hungry.

"Is Mike here?" I ask the man at Order Here.

"No, he had some kind of family problem. He's not coming in today."

"Oh, I'm sorry. I bet you're kind of shorthanded," I say. "Give me two Chicagos, all the way. And a cup of coffee, if you have some made. A Coke, if you don't. Take your time. I'm in no hurry."

Beth makes sure I always have a twenty-dollar bill in my wallet. I give it to the man. He gives me back some bills and some change. I put it all in the tip jar. The Chicago Dogs go into my brown paper bag. Another treasure.

I carry everything back to my maple tree. The only warm part of my body is my hand folding the coffee. I set the warmth down on the car hood and put my hand in my pocket to search for the silver key.

"Do you know where your keys are, Michael? Remember, remember, remember," I hear Beth say.

The hood of my car purrs and pulses under the cup of coffee. Through the window of the locked door, I spy my key, hanging still and proud in the ignition.

"Well, don't that beat all," I say to my tree. I carry my lunch over to her and hunker down, my old back nestled against her old trunk. The Chicago Dog tastes the same as it did when my Pop taught me how to make them, the same as it did when I taught Mike. As I taste the taste I've known all my life, the last of the gasoline flows from gas tank to engine and my Buick vibrates and mutters, then falls still.

"You don't suppose Pastor Terry would have left a church door unlocked?" I ask my tree.

"Go see, try them all. If you can't get in, come back. You can say your prayers to me," says the tree.

The side door by the pastor's study is open. Inside smells of old leather hymnals and last Sunday's carnations, furniture polish and discount sanitizers from the urinal in the men's restroom off to the right. I walk straight ahead and turn left into the sanctuary.

There's no comfort, seeing this place again. There's no comfort for my old back as it rests against the wood of the rear pew. The air in the church is stale and cool, the thermometer set at weekday minimal. I'm not here for comfort, I'm here to state my case. Death, life, death. This is the third time I've voiced my desires. I won't call it praying. I'm not that noble and I'm not asking permission from a God I cannot see. I'm just asking for a little help.

I finish the last bite of the second Chicago Dog. I sip the last of the stone-cold coffee. I walk back down the hallway to the men's restroom, throw away the wrapping paper and empty cup, pee, wash my hands, pick up my treasures, and head out for my journey north.

The stop for the commuter train to the Loop is hearing distance away. I walk toward the commotion of folks traveling to work, back to their lives, to supper, to their kids doing homework at the kitchen table, to wives coming late to bed, to bellies pressed against bellies, warm all night. To folks getting up and traveling again the next day.

When the next train pulls into the station, only a dozen of us board. I rumble toward the city until the conductor puts me out at the Park Ridge Station since I put all the money in the tip jar.

"Which way is Green Bay?" I ask the security cop.

"Move along," he tells me.

"Yes, I will," I say. "Thank you."

I set my eyes to north and walk along the highway's edge, slower than the traffic flying past me, faster than not traveling at all.

The black truck has orange flames burning down its sides. It roars past me, slows down fast, and pulls off the highway, half a block in front of me. The tall leather-covered driver unfolds himself from the seat and ambles toward me like a cowboy without a horse, a rider without a Harley.

"Ya' need a ride?" he yells.

"I sure do," I yell back. "I'm trying to get to Green Bay. My name's Michael."

"Michael, Hacksaw." We shake hands. "Green Bay, sure. I was driving to Sheboygan, but I can run you up to Green Bay. You live there?"

"I used to. My family's there. I'm going for a reunion."

My voice says it like a truth.

A man can tell another man the story of his whole life in the time it takes to drive from Chicago to Green Bay. I finish up as Hacksaw drives across the bridge into the city.

"Do you want to call your family? Let them know you're here?" Hacksaw asks.

"No, no, they're expecting me. If you wouldn't mind, you can just drop me off at the house. It's just a few blocks up ahead. I'd like to pay for part of the gasoline."

As Hacksaw says, "No, my pleasure," I remember I have no money.

The whole world looks familiar. My neighborhood is snow. White mounds cover shrubs and parked cars. Tunnels lead to porches . . . Safe paths into the warm heart of family.

"You can let me out right here," I say. "This is my home."

"Listen Michael, you call me if you need a ride back. You

call me if you need me." He pulls a business card out of his wallet and hands it to me. I put it in my pocket.

"Much obliged," I say. Silently, my heart tells him his kindness has returned me to the place I've been seeking, the place to which I've always traveled.

"Enjoy your visit," Hacksaw says.

"Yes," I say. "I have."

I'm home.

Tired old eyes relax at the sight.

Tired old ears rejoice as the sound of footsteps drown out the noise of Hacksaw's truck, retreating into the cold blue night.

A tired old brain understands. Everything is fine. It's all simple and huge and right.

A tired old heart, ravaged by too much love and too much sorrow, warms at the knowledge. It will never hurt again.

I'm home.

I turn around to face my family.

"So, I did find the right house," I say. "It had me worried some, it's been a while."

Warm round woman bodies greet me. Mothers of mothers. Eyes, full of love, look me up and down. Soft mouths smile. Strong arms surround me. Fathers of fathers hold me close, then release me so everyone else can get a chance to welcome me home.

"Where's this reunion shindig going to be held?" I ask. "I had no idea everyone would be able to come."

"We thought we'd celebrate over by the park. Wasn't that your favorite spot when you were a little guy? It's just a little walk and we've got everything set up. Come on, Michael. You've never seen anything like it."

My feet barely touch the ground as my loved ones lead me to our feast. A pretty woman joins me, her steps matching mine.

"Michael Jr. and Ramona, they're well and happy, aren't they? I know their poppa's proud of them. And I'm glad you found Beth," Evelyn says. "She needed you."

"I needed her too," I say. "Sometimes my needs got too large for her."

"Well, that happens. We know that, don't we?" She winks at me.

"You and Beth lived in a warm place, didn't you? Warmer than here, that's for sure!"

"Green Valley." I still love to say the word. "We love it, Beth and me. But it's a hard place for some people. A lot of folks are thirsty."

"That's the truth, *mi amigo*," says the walker from the desert.

He rushes to me, shakes my hand. Our arms wrap around each other. His heart beats proud and strong against my chest.

"I can't believe it," I say. "I've been wanting to talk to you for such a long time. What brings you here?"

"I heard you were heading this way and I had to come see you. I've brought someone who wants to meet you. Momma, this is Michael. *El ultimo hombre amable en la Tierra.*"

The last kind man on Earth . . . I understand the words. I know the words to say back.

"*Yo quiero haber ayudado mas.*" I'm sorry, I wanted to help more.

My friend understands. "Your Spanish, it's improved! Did you ever find that water you misplaced?" He laughs.

The ground is white, whiter than the full moon lighting our path. My family and friends surround me. The love of hundreds, thousands, warms the Green Bay night. I smell oregano and cinnamon. Roasted peppers and chestnuts and garlics. The smells of my childhood, my parents' childhoods. Every shape, every color. Cheeses-creamy white and golden, in rounds and squares, their rinds stamped with the towns of their origins. Oranges, lemons, tomatoes. Eggplants and artichokes. Olives, shining black and green and purple. Every treasure of the earth, every food I've ever tasted. Tureens of soup. Platters of grain rich pasta covered with the sauce of my family's kitchens. Cakes flavored with apples and figs, almonds and bittersweet chocolate. Breads shaped by strong hands. Even on this cold night, the centers of the loaves are warm and tender.

"In all my life, I've never stood before a table like this," I say. We all sit down to feast.

I open my paper bag. "I've brought wine, a special bottle. We've been saving it, Beth and I, for this very evening. Let me open it. There's enough for everyone."

We eat the food. We drink the wine. With every sip, toasts float like prayers to the heavens.

When our bottle is nearly empty, I replace the cork. The last glass is for Beth.

CHAPTER 13

Beth

I sleep late today, the day Michael dies. When I finally wake up—refreshed, anger gone, and confidence restored—I feel ready to tackle the next eighteen hours.

A rested brain can recognize an emergency situation in two minutes. Michael isn't in bed, in the bathroom, in the Parkside Manor dining room, in any lounge or hallway or closet or outside garden or bench. In five minutes the staff of an entire residential facility can ready themselves for another search. Just one phone call can round-robin to fifty, then a hundred. I call Clarice, it was all I needed to do. Then I sit in Michael's chair for the rest of the day.

The police dog's name is Champ. Champ trots from Michael's bed to the bathroom to my purse, out the door and straight to the empty parking place where Michael's car had been. The official search Champ begins fans out to every patrol car in Centerburg, to every Highway Patrol vehicle in the state. Silver Alert signs are turned on across all Illinois Interstate Highways. A plea and a description of Michael's old Buick and license plate number stretch from Centerburg to Green Valley. *If you see Michael, please help. Tell him we want him to come back.*

Clarice brings me coffee, some Danish. She installs herself between me and the telephone, between me and the people knocking on our door to request an audience with Mrs. Bartoli. Some folks make it past Clarice's screening:

"Here's Ramona."

"This is Detective Copple."

"Beth, Mike's here. He drove down from Des Plaines."

When Cheryl and Lucas drive over from St. Louis, Clarice stations them in the lobby of Parkside Manor to run the information center, fetch supplies, and entertain my supporters.

Clarice guards me as I shower. She sends Lucas out for chili dogs and chocolate malts. Later she tells me Mike is driving back to Des Plaines. The police have found Michael's car.

Clarice does not think the Parkside Manor dinner menu options are proper comfort, so she quickly trains Cheryl in Beth-sitting and sets out for Kentucky Fried Chicken. She returns in an hour with a bucket of chicken and side fixings, her pajamas, and toothbrush. "I'm staying here until they find him," she announces.

I'm not sure why the officer from the Green Bay Police Department calls Mike instead of me. Some details don't matter, others have come to mean everything.

Mike drives to Green Bay. As he arranges all that is necessary for Michael to legally switch from alive to deceased, Clarice watches over me and feeds me fried chicken and Klondike Bars. I move from Michael's chair to our bed, back to Michael's chair. Clarice keeps a telephone log for me, a list of people who stop by, another list of folks who bring casseroles and pies.

"Don't these people realize I'm in an independent living facility? Meals are included in the rent," I tell her.

"Honey, be nice," she says. "I'm not going to be able to hold these folks off forever. You'll need to decide if you want to make a run for it or stay here and let people comfort you."

"Let's have a piece of that coconut cream pie," I say, "then we can drive over to Ramona's and pull together a Memorial Service. But I have to hug you first."

Clarice holds me and lets me cry. She cries along with me, as friends do. We eat some pie, and then she walks me back to my life.

"Beth, I don't know what to do with Dad's ashes."

I sigh into the phone. I hope Mike doesn't hear me.

"You and Ramona should decide but I think he should be with your mother. He was so worried about her, at the end."

"Thank you," Mike says. "And there's the car and a box of stuff from the Green Bay police . . . clothes and a bottle of wine."

"Wine?"

"Yes, it looks like the kind Ravi bought you guys years back."

"Sell the car and send me Michael's things," I say.

Beth and Michael

I'm all alone when I open the Fed Ex box. "Well, Michael, let's see what's in here."

A flannel shirt, shoes and socks, his slacks and wallet and a belt. Why is it old men can forget to put on underwear but never forget their belts? An IGA paper bag enclosed in bubble wrap. Inside, a nearly empty bottle of our anniversary wine, with the cork replaced. Without pouring it into a glass, I know it would be a perfect 4 oz. serving.

The last glass is for you, I hear Michael whisper in my ear.

I find Hacksaw's business card in the pocket of Michael's shirt.

Call him, Michael whispers. *He's our friend.*

"You don't know me but I'm the wife of Michael Bartoli," I say to the man who answers the phone.

"Is this Beth? Is Michael OK?" Hacksaw says.

I've told almost everyone who needed to know. I've

accepted their sympathy and tried to muster the strength to send sympathy back when I hear my words wounding, when I hear their voices change from disbelief to dismay. I've called the official numbers to delete Michael Bartoli from government computers and banking systems and health care bureaucracies. It's easy to say a happy lie to a stranger whose telephone number I found in a pocket.

"Yes, he's fine," I say. "He wanted me to call you."

"I guess my ol' buddy Michael made it back from his reunion then. Did his family drive him back or did you drive up to get him? The weather was wicked. He couldn't have picked a worse day for car problems."

"His son brought him back," I say.

"Mike? The one who owns the hot dog place?" Hacksaw asks.

For the next thirty minutes, Hacksaw tells me how my husband had spent his last day. Again, I hear the story of Michael's life, this time in Hacksaw's voice. Our surprise wedding on a cruise ship, our cross-country trip in an Airstream trailer, our search for the perfect retirement home and our joy in finding it in Green Valley. Hacksaw knows about Hector and his nephew. Hacksaw fills in the missing piece of puzzle—carrying jugs of water into the desert for the illegals, *the folks who are so thirsty*.

"He told me he almost died," Hacksaw says. "Talking to Michael kinda made me want to give up my bachelor life and find me a Beth. That ol' boy sure does love you. He said he couldn't wait to get back to you."

"Well, he's back now," I say. "Thank you."

In the movie *The Life of Beth*, the scene would be of me, taking a crystal goblet from the cabinet, uncorking the nearly empty bottle that had traveled from Arizona to Southern Illinois to Wisconsin and back to Southern Illinois, and pouring a perfect ruby red glass of wine. A tear would run down my cheek. I'd smile and sip and muse about the gift Michael had given me. A message pure and elegant. Music would play, perhaps *Moon River*, and the set lights would dim.

Instead, I uncork the bottle, pour the contents in the kitchen sink, and rinse the remnants away. I know Michael well enough to know he would have shared sips from that bottle with any person he'd met on his last adventure. I am sentimental enough to put it back in our wine rack, next to the remaining bottle of anniversary wine.

> Cause of death: Hypothermia, exacerbated by acute alcohol consumption. Underlying conditions: Dementia, cardiovascular disease.

By the time I read of the implied tragedy on his death certificate, I know it wasn't a tragedy. Michael's last day was full of life and joy.

A week after Michael's death, Maria's son walks north, across the desert, into his mother's arms. Hector calls me moments after their reunion, weeping and laughing. "We know he didn't cross the desert alone, don't we Beth," Hector manages to say through his tears. Through my tears, I manage to say, "Yes, we know."

I plan to never eat at Wendy's again. *Not even a small vanilla Frosty?* Michael whispers. "Well, maybe that," I say.

Sometimes my brain thinks I've never left Centerburg. I've proceeded from teaching to not, from heart attack to healed, from my old condo to Parkside Manor. And then my heart remembers Michael until my every cell is singing. Loving is a very healthy state for a human body.

I don't know exactly how this death thing works but I'm amazed to report I do not miss Michael. After his little jaunt to Green Bay, he's returned to me. He resides to my right, just a few inches behind me, and whispers in my ear in the most endearing manner. His sense of humor has improved.

I do not tell this to anyone.

Hector calls me every Monday morning as he sits at the blue table at *La Cocina de Milagros*. Sometimes we talk about Michael, sometimes he just tells me what he's doing at the moment—watching the sunrise or enjoying the sight of Maria teaching her son to make the tortillas and salsa. "My nephew is filling in for *mi amigo* Michael," Hector says, his voice breaking a bit with the words. "Now I have some free time again."

Every Monday after he calls me, Hector calls Cheryl. Sometimes he chats with Lucas for a few moments, swapping cooking tips or stories of Michael. Clarice is totally frustrated by Cheryl's reticence about their relationship. I contend her silence says more than her words.

In November, my mood turns as gray and forlorn as the weather in Centerburg. "Beth, come back to Green Valley for Christmas," Hector says on his Monday morning phone call. "Cheryl is coming so you two could fly together. I want you to meet my nephew, we'll make it a huge celebration. Oh Beth, Maria longs to see you again. Please come—we miss you."

"Hector, that sounds lovely. Let me think about it for a few days," I say.

"Mom, come to London for Christmas. Stay a week, stay a month. We could have a little holiday in Spain. Zoe and I will buy your airfare. Please come, we miss you."

"Let me talk to Hector and Cheryl," I say. "We were in the midst of making plans."

Cheryl calls. "Listen girl, I'm fine with going to Green Valley by myself. You go spend the holidays with Kate and Zoe. You haven't been able to visit them for years."

•

Zoe and I spend our first few hours together weeping, laughing, then weeping again. Kate comforts us both. "He was the kindest man I've ever met," Zoe says. We three attempt to make a lasagna for Christmas day but after dismal results, settle for turkey sandwiches. Zoe says she thinks she hears Michael chuckling.

"Yes, you do!" I tell her.

In mid-January, Clarice picks me up at the St. Louis Airport Arrivals when I return from London.

"Cheryl has gone crazy," she says instead of asking me about my trip. "She's going to leave us and move to Green Valley."

Clarice is extremely annoyed by my glee.

Cheryl called Clarice on Christmas Day to announce, "I'm planning on shacking up with this ol' Mexican boy out here, name of Hector." On New Year's Day, both Hector and Cheryl called to announce they were getting married, pending everyone's approval.

"Let's tell Hector no," Clarice says as she drives across the Poplar Street Bridge into Illinois. "No, darling, we'll tell them Yes, Yes, Yes!" I say.

In mid-February, a caravan of three cars heads out from Centerburg to Green Valley, Arizona.

Hector is in the lead, driving solo in Cheryl's new red Ford Mustang, a wedding present to herself. I follow Hector in my car with Cheryl as navigator, although about one hour west of St. Louis, I start to doubt her abilities.

"Are we still in Missouri?" she asks.

"You shouldn't be asking me," I tell her. "It's the navigator's job to know. Look in the atlas."

"I'll call Hector, he'll know," she says. "There's a GPS in my car."

I know our two cars will roll into Green Valley just fine,

but I'm a little worried about the car behind us. I look in the rear-view mirror. Jim and Clarice are still following, a safe six-car lengths away, but Jim could turn around and drive back to Centerburg at any time. Of course, he'd have to listen to Clarice shrieking the whole trip back.

After Hector and Cheryl's big announcement, I slowly, cautiously, gently said, "Clarice, honey, I'm going to move back to Green Valley too."

She was quiet for several seconds, followed by a week of crying and fuming and pleading. After Cheryl hatched the idea of Jim and Clarice also coming to winter in Arizona, Clarice turned her energies toward Jim, but it took Hector and Cheryl to convince him.

"You'll be able to play golf every day," Hector told him. "Do you really want to spend another cold winter in Centerburg? I can find you a place to rent for a few months."

"Clarice is going to be miserable without us," Cheryl added, "and you're the one who's going to be spending everyday with her while she's wishing she were in Arizona."

"I hadn't thought about that," Jim said. "Good point."

Hector found them a condo to rent in the building across the parking lot from mine. He told my renters I would be moving back at the end of their one-year lease. "Beth, I think the condo next to yours will be going on the market in May," Hector told me.

They'll buy it, Michael whispered. *Jim and Clarice will be your new neighbors.*

I repacked the same things I packed to move to Parkside Manor, minus one empty wine bottle. Clarice redistributed all the furniture she had acquired on my behalf, but she insisted I take all the new Tuscany accent pieces. "And I wish you could take this red couch," she said. "You know it's prettier than the one you have. Oh well, I'll just have to help you spruce up your place once we get there."

•

I get up early on my first morning back. I pull on my robe, walk through every room, look out every window. After our supper last night at *La Cocina de Milagros*, I unpacked every suitcase and box. Except the hard one, it still sits on the kitchen table. Inside is a lone bottle of anniversary wine, carefully wrapped in the towels that match the colors in my Talavera sink.

Our anniversary is in four days. Clarice and Cheryl haven't mentioned it. They're waiting for my cue, they'll follow my lead. I don't think I'll be able to open the wine to share with my friends, I can't bear the thought of placing it in the empty wine rack. Maybe I'll open it and pour the wine down the sink, like I did with the last bottle. Oh, I dread this.

Just open the box, Beth, Michael whispers. *Everything is OK.*

A sweet fruity smell greets me as I cut open the cardboard flaps. I peek inside, lift the top towel. Yellows and blues, greens and reds are swimming in a burgundy pool, a familiar sight. Diamonds of shattered glass lie at the center of the box.

I gasp. How could it have broken? I packed it so well!

You know I have a history of breaking wine bottles. Remember, remember, remember. I hear Michael's laughter across the mysterious gossamer separating us, so much thinner than a locked door. *Throw it all away. Buy new towels in the colors of your pretty sink. Fill your life with color. Happy Anniversary, Beth.*

I'm laughing and crying as I call Clarice.

"Honey, can you come over right now? I need to show you something," I say. "And bring your purse. We need to go shopping."

ACKNOWLEDGMENTS

This book, of course, is a work of fiction, but its inspiration and spirit was born of a lifetime of friendships. To my friends, OLD! and newish, my love and appreciation for enriching my life beyond measure.

Suzanne Kingsbury, my writing coach, mentor, sweet friend. You drifted into my life before the first word was written and you've nurtured me and my words ever since.

Dede Cummings, my Publisher. You were my first and constant choice. Thank you for your wisdom, support and grace.

Maria Tane, my Editor. You are the Gold at the end of my pale and weary rainbow.

ABOUT THE AUTHOR

Sueann Pugh was born and raised in a small town in southern Illinois and attended Illinois State University, graduating with a degree in Special Education. She taught children with Learning Disabilities for Milwaukee Public Schools and has worked with special needs children and adults throughout her lifetime. In addition to traveling, painting and practicing Yoga and Tai Chi, writing has become a beloved senior endeavor. She lives in Raleigh, North Carolina, where she works part-time, plays part-time, and embraces senior living full-time with her husband, Mark.